"Lora Leigh delivers on all counts."
—*Romance Reviews Today*

Praise for Lora Leigh's Novels of the Breeds

MERCURY'S WAR

"Erotic and suspenseful . . . Readers will laugh, readers will blush and readers will cry."
—*Romance Junkies*

"With two great twists, fans of the Breed saga will relish [Mercury's War]."
—*Midwest Book Review*

"Intriguingly powerful with plenty of action to keep the pages turning. I am completely addicted! A great read!"
—*Fresh Fiction*

DAWN'S AWAKENING

"Leigh consistently does an excellent job building characters and weaving intricate plot threads through her stories. Her latest offering in the Breeds series is no exception."
—*Romantic Times* (4½ stars, Top Pick)

"Held me captivated."
—*Romance Junkies*

"Heart-wrenching."
—*Fallen Angel Reviews*

"Erotic, fast-paced, funny and hard-hitting, this series delivers maximum entertainment to the reader."
—*Fresh Fiction*

TANNER'S SCHEME

"The incredible Leigh pushes the traditional envelope with her scorching sex scenes by including voyeurism, intrigue and passion ignite! . . . Scorcher!"
—*Romantic Times* (4½ stars)

"Sinfully sensual . . . [This series] is well worth checking out."
—*Fresh Fiction*

HARMONY'S WAY

"Leigh's engrossing alternate reality combines spicy sensuality, romantic passion and deadly danger. Hot stuff indeed."
—*Romantic Times*

"I stand in awe of Ms. Leigh's ability to bring to life these wonderful characters as they slowly weave their way into my mind and heart. When it comes to this genre, Lora Leigh is the queen."
—*Romance Junkies*

MEGAN'S MARK

"A riveting tale full of love, intrigue and every woman's fantasy, *Megan's Mark* is a wonderful contribution to Lora Leigh's Breeds series . . . As always, Lora Leigh delivers on all counts; *Megan's Mark* will certainly not disappoint her many fans!"
—*Romance Reviews Today*

"Hot, hot, hot—the sex and the setting . . . You can practically see the steam rising off the pages."
—*Fresh Fiction*

"This entertaining romantic science fiction suspense will remind the audience of *Kitty and the Midnight Hour* by Carrie Vaughn and MaryJanice Davidson's *Derik's Bane* as this futuristic world filled with 'Breeds' seems 'normal.' . . . [A] delightful thriller."
—*The Best Reviews*

"The dialogue is quick, the action is fast and the sex is oh so hot . . . Don't miss out on this one."
—*A Romance Review*

"Leigh's action-packed Breeds series makes a refreshing change . . . Rapid-fire plot development and sex steamy enough to peel wallpaper."
—*Monsters and Critics*

"An exceedingly sexy and sizzling new series to enjoy. Hot sex, snappy dialogue and kick-butt action add up to outstanding entertainment."
—*Romantic Times*

STYX'S STORM

LORA LEIGH

BERKLEY SENSATION, NEW YORK

THE BERKLEY PUBLISHING GROUP
Published by the Penguin Group
Penguin Group (USA) Inc.
375 Hudson Street, New York, New York 10014, USA
Penguin Group (Canada), 90 Eglinton Avenue East, Suite 700, Toronto, Ontario M4P 2Y3, Canada
(a division of Pearson Penguin Canada Inc.)
Penguin Books Ltd., 80 Strand, London WC2R 0RL, England
Penguin Group Ireland, 25 St. Stephen's Green, Dublin 2, Ireland (a division of Penguin Books Ltd.)
Penguin Group (Australia), 250 Camberwell Road, Camberwell, Victoria 3124, Australia
(a division of Pearson Australia Group Pty. Ltd.)
Penguin Books India Pvt. Ltd., 11 Community Centre, Panchsheel Park, New Delhi—110 017, India
Penguin Group (NZ), 67 Apollo Drive, Rosedale, North Shore 0632, New Zealand
(a division of Pearson New Zealand Ltd.)
Penguin Books (South Africa) (Pty.) Ltd., 24 Sturdee Avenue, Rosebank, Johannesburg 2196,
South Africa

Penguin Books Ltd., Registered Offices: 80 Strand, London WC2R 0RL, England

This is a work of fiction. Names, characters, places, and incidents either are the product of the author's imagination or are used fictitiously, and any resemblance to actual persons, living or dead, business establishments, events, or locales is entirely coincidental. The publisher does not have any control over and does not assume any responsibility for author or third-party websites or their content.

STYX'S STORM

A Berkley Sensation Book / published by arrangement with the author

PRINTING HISTORY
Berkley Sensation mass-market edition / October 2010

Copyright © 2010 by Christina Simmons.
Cover art by S. Miroque.
Cover design by Rita Frangie.

ISBN: 978-0-425-23739-7

BERKLEY® SENSATION
Berkley Sensation Books are published by The Berkley Publishing Group,
a division of Penguin Group (USA) Inc.,
375 Hudson Street, New York, New York 10014.
BERKLEY® SENSATION and the "B" design are trademarks of Penguin Group (USA) Inc.

PRINTED IN THE UNITED STATES OF AMERICA

10 9 8 7 6 5 4 3 2 1

This book is for you!

The men and women, lost and lonely, searching and wary, uncertain and ill prepared for what the heart can lead them into.

Sometimes, love is right around the corner. It's the road not taken that has suddenly intersected with that congested road of life you're traveling, bringing you to a harsh and sudden stop.

It's a look. It's a smile that warms you to the depths of your soul, steals your breath, and pulls you aside as that moment in time screams to a halt and leaves you struggling to adjust.

It's the love you didn't expect.

It's the love you didn't ask for, hadn't thought about, and you realize it's the love that heals the wounds in your soul.

It's the love that will reveal the person you are, and the life, though never perfect, that you never knew you dreamed of.

Call it destiny, call it fate.

Or call it a gift from God.

Whichever, it's the dream and the everlasting hope for the future.

From Storme Montague's journal, age 14

They're Breeds. Dad says man created them, but only God could give them a soul. At the moment, the world, as well as the scientists that created them, are debating if they have souls. I once believed no creature on Earth could live without a soul, without the blessing of God at the very least, but the majority of the Council scientists believe otherwise.

And still, I'm torn.

Dad and my brother, James, are scientists working here in the Andes Mountains, in the Council compound known only as Omega. It's one of the few remaining functioning Breed labs because Breed rescues have destroyed the others.

Dad and James feel the rescues will be attempted here soon. They seem so confident of it, and even act as though they look forward to it. And I can't understand why.

I see the Breeds. They are perfect specimens, so beautiful and strong, like the lions, tigers and wolves whose DNA they were created from. But it doesn't matter how you dress up an animal, does it? Isn't it still an animal?

When they howl in rage, rip at each other with teeth and claws, and fight for the food the soldiers bring to them each day, they are animals, not humans.

And yet, I look in their eyes when I accompany Father to the training facilities or labs, and in them, I swear I see such desperation and such rage. It's the rage that truly terrifies me.

They speak. They never laugh. They flash sharp canines, and strain at the chains that bind them, and I feel their rage. But I also see the animal inside them. It shines in their eyes, turning them nearly red, glowing with such strength that I know if they were free, they would first seek to kill the men and women who created them.

My father, my brother, even myself. Anger suffuses their expressions when I look at them, as though they cannot bear to be seen, or to see another outside the bars of their cages.

The tension is growing here at Omega. Breeds, soldiers, scientists and lab technicians seem to be holding their breath as they fight to keep the secrecy of this lab intact. To hide the few Breeds held, not for their fighting capabilities, but for some special project Father and James have referred to as an affront to humanity.

How could humanity be offended more than it has been with the Breeds? I've asked my father this, and in his eyes I've seen such disappointment, such a sense of sorrow that my chest clenches in pain.

I just want it to be over. I just want to leave here with Father and James, and I just want to be free.

I can feel the end nearing. We all can. Especially Father and James, who are working such long hours, well into the night, to destroy and to hide whatever they've been working on secretly. I wish they would hurry. I wish we could escape ourselves, just slip out and never return.

Father says, "Once the Council has its grip on you, they ensure you can never be free." And I see in his eyes as well as my brother's that feeling that they too are no more than captives here in this hidden compound.

I won't let them get a grip on me. I won't be like the Breeds, I won't be like the scientists. One day, I swear, I will be free.

✦ P R O L O G U E ✦

GENETIC EXPERIMENTATIONS LAB OMEGA
SCIENTIFIC HOUSING COMPOUND
ANDES MOUNTAINS

The lights were off, the electricity having sputtered out, leaving them to navigate with only the dim emergency lights to see by. Outside, flares of light from the explosions that rocked the labs illuminated the windows. Gunfire and screams echoed, coming closer, filling Storme with a fear so agonizing it shuddered through her body.

"Storme, you have to hide. Don't let anyone find you, do you understand me? No one can find you." Her father helped her slide into the narrow crevice between the walls in the back of her closet.

She stared up at him in terror, aware of her brother working behind him to erase information contained in the computers and on the discs filed along the wall.

"Take this." He grabbed her hand.

The antique sapphire ring her mother had once worn was shoved onto her finger. He had showed her the secrets of the ring days before. The hidden compartment beneath the hollowed out stone and the data chip he had placed here. He had warned her, so many times he had warned her, that if anything happened to him, then she would become the protector of the information contained on that chip.

"Daddy, come with me." Storme could feel panic tightening her chest as the sounds of gunfire, screams and animal rage grew closer to the living area of the genetics research laboratory where her father had worked her entire life.

"No, we can't go with you, baby." Tears filled his tired brown eyes, grief creased his face. "Your brother and I will be fine. Get to the safe house; we'll meet you there after we're certain we've done what has to be done here."

No, they wouldn't meet her. She would never see them again, and she knew it. She watched her brother for long, panicked seconds. She couldn't see his beloved face. The creases that were forming on his forehead and next to his lips. He rarely laughed, though he smiled at her often.

She was only fourteen. She didn't want to face the dark alone. She was frightened of the dark.

"No, don't make me go by myself, Daddy." Sobs were fighting to escape her lips as the tears began to fall.

She stared back at him, seeing the fear and worry in his eyes, the mussed gray hair, the grief he was trying so hard to hide from her. And the courage. She didn't have his courage.

She wasn't strong like her father and her brother were. They faced every day the savage human-animals they had created and trained in the compound behind the houses. They lived with the monsters that Storme had only glimpsed from a distance as they trained. Monsters that could rend flesh with their teeth, that could tear limbs from bodies with only their bare hands. The monsters that howled at night with a savagery, with a horror that haunted Storme's nightmares.

"Storme, be strong for me." He shoved a backpack into her hands before pulling back. "Remember the promises you made me. You swore you would do this, Storme."

Her fists clenched as the panel slammed closed, leaving her in the darkness with the terrifying black void stretching out below her.

She had promised. She had sworn to protect herself and

the secrets he had been amassing over the years. Secrets that were to go to one person. A person with no name. A person he had promised would find her, protect her. A mysterious someone who would know what to say, and what to do, to gain her trust.

The information the ring held was all that would save her, all that would save so many innocent people, he had insisted. And he had entrusted her with it.

She tried to step down the narrow steps that led to the tunnel beyond. She did. But as she took the first step, she heard an enraged, savage snarl as an explosion rocked the house.

She almost screamed. Struggling to keep her balance, she pressed her hands tight against the wall and fought to keep from falling down the stairs.

Fear held her motionless, her eyes wide as she stared through the crack in the wall into the bedroom and watched her father as he stared toward the doorway in fear.

"We have to get out of here." His voice wavered as James moved in closer to him, protectively. "The Breeds will come after those of us who created them first."

Storme saw the realization in both her brother's and her father's faces, and she knew that the horror she had always feared was upon them.

"But not those of you who helped them." The voice was guttural, angry.

Storme swallowed tightly at the sound as her fists clenched in the effort to stay in place, to keep from trying to protect her father as well.

She had promised she would run and hide. That she wouldn't endanger herself.

"Where is the girl?"

The girl? Her?

"I sent her away yesterday," her father replied, his voice shaking.

"Because you knew what was coming?"

Her father shook his head. "How could I have known?"

"You thought you were so careful." The voice was filled with fury. "You aided our destruction, JR. You'll pay for betraying us by aiding the Breed sympathizers in this fucking rescue."

"I aided nothing," her father, JR, James Robert, denied.

A harsh laughed filled the room.

"We'll find the girl. No doubt you sent what I need with her. Or did you? Give me that research, JR, and I'll let her live."

"What are you talking about?" Fear was thick, heavy, surrounding her father, her brother, even as Storme felt it stealing her breath.

"I want that data chip."

"What data chip?" Even Storme could hear the nervousness, the lie, in her father's voice.

An animalistic, harsh snarl filled the room as shadows moved. As though there were many, not just one. Dark, brutal shadows, glowing eyes advanced.

Storme stared at the aberration. The merciless eyes, the face that seemed too young, and yet too cruel. And she memorized it. Memorized the creature that she knew would kill what was left of her family.

Her brother jumped in front of their father, to save him, Storme knew. That was James, so protective, so loving. As the Coyote latched onto her brother's fragile shoulders, Storme covered her mouth with her hand to hold back her screams and watched in horror.

Dear, beloved James. He played word games with her, made her laugh, and as she watched in horror one of those horrible monsters grabbed him, bent his head, and tore James's throat out.

Blood sprayed as another explosion outside lit the room with brutal light, displaying the scene in harsh detail.

Bile rose in her throat as it tilted its head back, the face, so like a human's, covered in blood as its lips opened and a howl echoed around her.

They could smell fear. They could smell her. Her father had warned her of that. He had made her swear to protect herself and the secrets he had risked his life to steal.

If she stayed, she was dead. Her brother was already dead, and she knew her father wouldn't survive.

Because of the Breeds. Because of the human animals these scientists had created, trained, and were now turning loose on the world. Breeds, like the one now tasting her brother's blood.

She backed down the stairs. The darkness enfolded her, wrapped around her. She could hear her father screaming, denying that his daughter was there. She was gone. He had sent her to stay with relatives.

He swore he had no information. He stole nothing. His daughter had nothing. He was screaming in pain and fury.

They would know better. They would have smelled her presence in the house if they had passed by it. They were that good. But here, deep beneath the earth, cocooned as though in a grave, she was safe.

The smell of her father's and brother's blood above, the smell of smoke, fear and death would hide her for a little while. And once she was through the tunnel and into the small town beyond where the tunnel exited, she would have a chance to run.

She was alone.

She could feel it.

A strange sense of disassociation filled her, washed over her and stopped the tears. Fear choked her, made it hard to breathe, but her mind felt mercifully numb.

As she felt her way through the drainage tunnel her father had dug into years before, Storme knew he must have foreseen the chance that he and her brother could be caught doing whatever it was they had been doing.

She had known for years that they were frightened of the people they worked for. That they couldn't leave. That only Storme had the ability to travel back and forth from school in America to this small community her family lived within.

The place her mother had died just after Storme's birth.

Had those who had killed her brother killed her mother as well?

This place, these Breeds—because of them, because of her father's loyalty to them, everything she had held dear had been destroyed. They had destroyed everything that was love and security to her.

She shouldn't be alone. Her father and her brother should have come with her. They should have saved themselves and damned the information they were so desperate to destroy.

Information that her father swore would destroy so many innocent Breeds. Were any of those creatures truly innocent?

As she made her way through the damp, muddy tunnel, the sight of her brother's death flashed before her eyes, over and over. The memory of the Coyote's head bending—canines curved and wicked, flashing in the light of the explosions outside and tearing into his throat—sliced through her mind.

There was nothing that could numb that memory. Nothing that could erase it or the nightmare vision that insisted on invading her soul at the thought that her father was suffering the same fate.

Breeds. Killers. Animals. They were monsters. Evil, wicked monsters that man had created, that man was now losing control of, just as her father had warned them they would lose control. The Breeds were turning on their creators, escaping, killing, turning the world into a place of conflict where their very humanity was in question. There was no redemption for the Breeds; they had no mercy, no compassion, just as the other scientists had always warned her father. A Breed was a Breed. A Coyote was still a Breed, and a Coyote had just destroyed her world.

They were without souls.

And now Storme was without family.

As she reached the metal ladder below the drainage gate just outside the small Chilean town, Storme forced herself to find the energy to climb to it and push it open.

The serene calm she had seen in the town during short visits didn't exist now. People were pouring out of their homes, standing and watching the display of light and explosions on the mountain above their homes.

Storme slipped silently along the edge of the crowd, her

gaze locked on the mountain. Howls echoed from above, enraged and filled with fury as gunfire and explosions continued to rip through the night.

Moving quickly, hurriedly, she began to run through the shadows to the house outside of town. The one her father had promised he would meet her at.

He wouldn't be there. It wouldn't matter how long she waited, he would never be there. Only death would find her there if she waited, and she had promised her father she wouldn't allow death to find her.

As she reached the house, she didn't wait around. Racing into the small attached garage, she threw the canvas from the old, rusted pickup that sat there.

It looked like shit, but she knew it would run. It was strong and fast; the tinkering her brother had done with the motor had ensured that whoever drove it would have the best chance possible of escape.

The passports were still in the glove box, the small box of cash was still hidden in the back of the seat. Birth certificates, records needed to hide their identities if all escaped together—everything was still there.

Carefully, she pulled her father's and brother's papers from the glove box, pushed them into the backpack, then shoved the key in the ignition.

She knew how to drive. She knew how to shoot the powerful gun strapped to the door, and she knew how to fight. She was only fourteen, but her father and brother had been planning this for years.

They had taught her how to survive in case the worst that could happen, happened. As though they had known, despite their assurances to her, that they wouldn't be with her.

As she accelerated from the garage, lights off, nothing but dust moving in her wake, she was aware of the heli-jets lifting off from the mountain.

Breeds or scientists, she didn't know which. Whoever it was, they were no friends of hers. She had no friends, she had no family, there was no one to protect her until whoever her father had been working with found her.

If he found her. And when he did, he damned well better be sure he had proof of who he was, because Storme knew in her soul that she could never trust anyone after this.

Everyone was the enemy.

TᴇN YᴇᴀʀS Lᴀᴛᴇʀ
HᴀᴠᴇN, Wᴏʟꜰ/Cᴏʏᴏᴛᴇ Bʀᴇᴇᴅ Cᴏᴍᴘᴏᴜɴᴅ

Jonas strode into the small meeting room, paused and stared at the scientists and the Enforcer staring back at him. Dr. Jeffrey Amburg was a human genome advanced design scientist. He had been involved in more than twenty-five years of Council-backed Breed genetic research. He'd created Breeds, his experiments had killed Breeds, and he was here, in Haven, for the first time. It was the first time in two years that he had been allowed out of the specially secured rooms he had been confined to after Jonas had captured him in Buffalo Gap, Virginia.

Dr. Nikki Armani, Wolf Breed genome specialist and physician, was also human. She too had worked for many years with the Council. The difference was, Nikki had conspired from day one to find freedom for the Breeds she had cared for when they returned from missions wounded and nearly dead. Or when the experiments conducted on them had weakened them to the point of death.

Dr. Elyiana Morrey was the exception here. She was a Breed. A Lion Breed created to treat her own kind. Training had begun with her from conception, introducing her in vitro to the complicated process of manufacturing and repairing the often complicated Breed physiology. She was both physician as well as scientist, and her breakthroughs in the mysterious mating heat afflicting the Breeds had given them the additional time needed to continue hiding the phenomenon from the world in general.

Navarro Blaine was one of the higher ranking under-cover Enforcers. A Wolf Breed with specialization in several forms of martial arts, the man was more of a shadow than even the shadow he cast.

This meeting, outside of Jonas's normally preferred base of Sanctuary, home of the Feline Breeds, was the first meeting to bring all three scientists together, along with Dr. Elizabeth Ambrose Vanderale, the ninety-some-year-old mate to the first Leo, Leo Vanderale.

Elizabeth stood at Jonas's side, sleekly tailored in a gray silk skirt and matching blouse, looking barely old enough to be the mother of the self-proclaimed thirty-year-old Dane Vanderale.

It was a damned good thing the Vanderales had adapted and learned how to make themselves appear older before appearing in public; otherwise, Leo and Elizabeth both would have been given away by their acknowledged son's widely known age.

"Ladies and gentlemen." Jonas nodded as he and his mother, Elizabeth, moved to the conference table. "I hear we may have a problem."

As usual, Jeffrey Amburg sat back silently. If Jonas wanted information from him while in the presence of the Breed scientists, then he would have to force it from him. The scientist was aware of the hierarchy of the labs now, and he was at the bottom of the food chain.

"Jonas, this meeting was uncalled for," Ely was the first to speak. "I have things to do at Sanctuary, as does Dr. Vanderale. This subject does not require such an in-depth meeting."

Nikki Armani narrowed her gaze on Ely. It was no secret that the doctors rarely saw eye to eye, which wasn't surprising. It seemed that Feline and canine physiology could be as different as night and day once one began probing into the more intricate aspects of DNA and genetic sequencing.

"The Enforcers being used for this little mission Sanctuary has dreamed up to capture and gain the trust of this woman, are Wolf Breeds outside of the cooperative units detailed in Sanctuary," Nikki reminded her. "Excuse me, Dr. Morrey, but when Haven has requested the assistance of Feline Breeds, they do make the trip to Sanctuary without voicing such protests or showing any irritation they may harbor."

Jonas sat back and looked to Ely. She was his favorite. Like a little sister, Jonas watched out for Ely where he could, especially since his own mating.

Ely had been through hell in the past year, and the consequences of others' actions had nearly destroyed her mind. But in this, there was no protection. She had opened her mouth, and she would now have to defend her stance.

"Dr. Armani, this matter would have been taken care of much more easily at Sanctuary for the simple fact that all the scientific research, with the exception of your personal files, reside there."

"And are accessible by Haven, in their entirety, last I heard," Nikki argued. "Or is there some reason we don't have files that you do indeed possess?"

Ely's lips thinned. "The files in question are Feline Breed, rather than Wolf, but in many cases, we've been able to cross-reference and find answers for the wolves' medical problems as well, as you very well know. I had no doubt our files wouldn't have the answers to whatever is in question now."

"In this situation, I doubt that's possible," Nikki stated as she turned to Jonas. "I'm aware you have the files on the Montague girl, Storme. As you're aware, her father and brother were based with the Omega lab. That lab was primarily occupied by Wolf Breeds. The pack leader, Navarro," she glanced to the silent Breed, "managed to access and acquire the majority of the files before the scientists could destroy them. We believe the information we've found may shed some light on the anomalies showing up in the blood work on Jonas's adopted daughter, Amber, as well as Phillip Brandenmore's."

Jonas stilled. Tension ratcheted up in the room. Brandenmore was believed dead by the world at large. He wasn't dead. He was confined as he had once confined Breeds, while Jonas searched to find the answers to whatever the bastard had injected his adopted infant child, Amber, with, as well as himself.

Brandenmore was in his seventies, but the physiological tests done on him since his capture showed a man perhaps a decade younger. And whatever had caused that was still working on him. Repairing internal organs, regenerating cells, and destroying his mind.

"Navarro?" Jonas questioned him roughly. "What have you found?"

Navarro leaned forward slowly. "We've been working on a particular file taken from the compound home of Drs. James Robert and James Montague, father and son, who were based at the Omega lab. Those files have several references to a project known as Omega. A reference I believe you found in Brandenmore's personal files." Jonas nodded sharply before Navarro continued. "The information we've uncovered suggests Project Omega dealt with experimentations on two Breeds believed to be in the grip of a syndrome known then as 'mating fever.' There were certain attributes to the syndrome, though, that the scientists focused on, rather than the syndrome itself. One of them was the decrease in cellular and physical aging; another, and I believe Brandenmore must have gained information on this, was whether or not cellular or genetic alterations could be produced using the unknown hormones generated in the mating couple."

Jonas felt the implications of the project as his body began to tighten in rage. Brandenmore was doing as the Bureau of Breed Affairs and the Breed alphas feared. He was trying to create a vaccine or virus that would alter human genetics, using research on Breed mates that had been confined in the labs.

"I thought the Bureau as well as Sanctuary had all files pertaining to those labs. I've seen nothing known as Project Omega," Jonas growled.

"All files that our alpha, Wolfe Gunnar, had possession of, Sanctuary and the Bureau of Breed Affairs have copies of," Dr. Armani amended. "There are several encrypted files from those labs that Navarro and I have been working on that Wolfe hadn't been made aware of, simply because we had no idea what they were."

Navarro wasn't just, as Nikki stated, an elite Enforcer, he was also one of Haven's best code breakers.

Fuck, he didn't need this, Jonas thought, the Breed society in general didn't need this. This could create an outcry against the Breeds that even mating heat wouldn't cause. The ability to "infect" the population and change the most basic makeup of their creation, could begin a quick spiral down to the extermination of Breeds.

Montague was assumed to have wiped all information regarding Project Omega from all Council files. For ten years, Jonas had believed the scientist had been successful, despite the fact that there were rumors the daughter knew something, or had been given information by her father or brother.

If she had that information, then she would have traded it years ago for her own safety, to either the Council Coyotes or the Bureau of Breed Affairs. She wouldn't have run and fought for ten years to hide the very information that would assure her safety.

He turned to Navarro once again. "You were pack leader there. What were the parameters of Project Omega?"

How much did Haven know about a project that should have been destroyed before it ever began? A project Jonas had never truly believed had gone far enough to have attained any answers, let alone live trials.

"The parameters I am uncertain of," Navarro answered, his pronunciation precise and with just the lightest Asian flavor of an accent, compliments of the team of scientists that ran that particular branch of operations in the Omega labs. "I know that the mating fever phenomenon they were studying in another sector of the labs was what we now call mating heat. It was believed to be somehow related to the feral fever. There were several Breeds confined there, but they escaped during the rescues and I have not heard of them revealing themselves since. The search I conducted turned up no rumors of their whereabouts or information concerning them. For all intents and purposes they are most likely dead. Without them, or the rumored data chip that the daughter knows the location of, then there are no true answers concerning the success of their investigation into whether or not such an aging or Breed creation vaccine could be made. I personally do believe they are dead."

Yeah. Right. Jonas knew better than to believe such a thing until he actually saw the bodies himself.

"The files you've unlocked, what was in them?" There were some experiments whose results Jonas prayed were never revealed. Project Omega was one he'd once felt that way about, until now.

"Most of the information was destroyed, and we were unable to retrieve all but a few vague references to the project," Navarro admitted. "I've been unable to retrieve anything of any worth other than the notation that the doctors involved were the Montagues and that there was a suspicion among the scientists that JR, as James Robert Montague was often called, had managed to hide the contents of the destroyed files rather than losing the results forever. This could be why the Council has chased the girl for so many years; they suspect she has that information as well or they could be aware that the Drs. Montague had actually succeeded in some way."

No doubt. Montague, like most scientists with the Council, would risk his life, as well as his children, to protect his project. It made no sense to Jonas. There wasn't a single Breed he would risk to save the contents of such files or experiments, which could so change the course of humanity that, in his eyes, humanity would be irretrievably destroyed.

"We have to have the Montague girl, Jonas." Nikki leaned forward imperatively, her dark gaze intent. "I've asked the other scientists here so they can help me to go over the parts of the files we have retrieved in the hopes that they'll understand some of the formulas . . ."

"Retrieving the girl won't be so easy," Navarro stated. "I know the Bureau has been trailing her for years now because of the rumor that she carried vital information. What you didn't know was that I was working with the Montagues while in those labs. JR, the father, told me that if he managed to get any information out, then it would be with Storme. I was to find her immediately after the rescues, if you hadn't already done so." He nodded to Jonas.

Jonas shook his head. "She wasn't at the safe house. She and the vehicle we provided for escape were gone. The GPS tracker we had installed on it had been deactivated."

Navarro nodded. "She's terrified of Breeds, and she hates them for the loyalty her father had to them. For the fact that he and her brother died to protect that information. In her mind her father and her brother chose the Breeds over her."

"And forgiveness doesn't come easily," Jonas sighed. "And we can no longer allow her the convenience of coming to us on her own. Find her, and have her brought in."

Navarro nodded, his lips parting to say more when Jeffrey Amburg came abruptly to his feet.

"Destroy the formulas, and destroy the files. I'm finished here." Amburg's gaze was icy as he stared at those around the table. "Destroy the files and the girl immediately. If the information she's rumored to be carrying ever falls into Council hands, then it has the power to not just destroy the Breeds, but also the world." He turned to Jonas, the icy blue of his eyes like shards of pale glass now. "Project Omega is something you never want to resurrect, not for any reason."

Jonas stared back at the scientist. "What is it, Amburg?"

For a second, pure, raw fear flashed in the scientist's eyes. "You don't want to know, Jonas. And trust me, you sure as hell don't want the Council possessing it. Above all other threats against the Breeds, Project Omega could be the most dangerous."

And here Jonas had believed he was beginning a new phase of his life with a measure of peace.

A mated wife, a babe he called his own, and for the past six weeks, life had been, if not peaceful, at least without any major catastrophes.

"What was the project, Amburg?" Even Ely was taking notice now.

Amburg shook his head, his gaze imploring as he stared back at Jonas. "I won't be a part of this. I wouldn't be a part of it then, and I won't be a part of it now. And there's no threat the Breeds could use against me to force it. I'm ready to return to Sanctuary now."

He left the room.

Jonas stared after him thoughtfully, knowing the reasons Amburg cooperated so well with the Breeds. Besides the fact that he lived for Breed research in whatever form he could do it, Jonas also held his granddaughter, Isabella Ross. She was free. She lived, worked, laughed and enjoyed friends, but at all times there was a Breed close by. A Breed who, Jonas had assured Amburg, was more than willing to kill the only human he loved.

Amburg was willing to risk Isabella's life to keep the secret of Project Omega. And the hell of it was, at any other time, Jonas wouldn't have blamed him.

Turning back to Navarro, Jonas hardened his compassion for Amburg, the Montague girl and anyone else who dared get in the way of protecting the child he called his own.

"What do you need?"

Navarro sighed with a grimace. "Her mate would be nice. Because honestly Jonas, short of undying love on her part, I doubt anything but her father's resurrection would convince her to tell us where that data chip is located."

Jonas tilted his head thoughtfully before turning to Dr. Armani. "Did the Breeds confiscate the blood samples being held in the Omega lab?"

Nikki nodded slowly.

"Were there samples of the girl's blood?"

Realization lit the doctor's eyes. "There were. Several vials actually. The scientists there were very thorough."

Rising to his feet, Jonas gave a sharp nod. "Start testing your Enforcers first. Let me know the possibilities and get it done quickly."

"I can help." Ely came to her feet, the compassion, the generosity that he feared absent now; something else sparking in her gaze. "If we're going to do this, let's get it done quickly, before the Council can get a jump on us."

The two scientists met at the head of the table, turned in unison and headed for the exit.

It would begin here.

Jonas turned back to Navarro. "Is she your mate?"

Navarro shook his head. "If she were, she wouldn't be running."

Jonas gave a sharp nod. "Let's find out who the lucky mate is then. And let's bring her in."

"If she has a mate." Navarro didn't rise. "What happens, Jonas, if she has no mate?"

It was a question he hadn't considered. It was one he wouldn't entertain unless he had no choice.

Because no mate meant no hope of resolving this without death. And that was a resolution Jonas refused to entertain.

The bar was hopping, music pounding, drinks flowing smoothly and customers packing the bar area and dance floor. It was one of those country hole-in-the-walls that attracted both criminal elements as well as the upper class and everything in between. It was one of those places Storme could slide into, and her scent became masked by the dozens of sweating, lusty, alcohol-infused bodies that filled it.

It was one of the few ways to hide from paranormal senses and extrasensory capabilities. It was one of the few places Storme had a hope of resting before she had to run again.

And God knew, she was tired. Exhaustion was beginning to swamp her, desperation was clawing at her back, and fear was a companion she hadn't separated from in far too long.

She wanted to rest.

Was there a saying about no rest for the wicked? There was. She must have been wicked in a former life though, because this life had just been spent running.

"Whiskey shot and a beer," she said wearily as the waitress came to the table.

Pulling a few of the precious bills from her pocket, she slid the money to the waitress when she returned.

She tossed back the whiskey, then chased the burn with the icy bitterness of the beer and blew out a slow, deep breath before looking around.

The band was actually pretty good here, the lead singers sultry when they needed to be, hard and filled with desperation when the song called for it.

The smell of cigarette smoke, booze, sweat and lust was so strong it didn't take Breed senses to detect it, Storme Montague decided as she sat in the corner of the room and watched the customers milling through the large area. A human with any sense of smell could detect it.

Moving to the corner of the booth, she hunched into the shadows and watched the crowd, knowing that even here there was danger. She had glimpsed it as she rushed inside and skirted the edge of the room to get as far away from it as possible.

From where she sat she could see the Breeds in the far corner as the crowds shifted and moved between them. There were four, and she knew all of them. Not personally, of course, but Storme knew a lot of Breeds; she'd made it her business to learn who they were, especially when she caught them trailing her.

Navarro Blaine, and this one, she knew well from Omega. He was a Wolf Breed with Asian heritage. He was tall, dusky skinned with the exotic slant of eyes and high, flat cheekbones. Black, brown and a hint of gray filled his hair, though the gray wasn't from age, it was from the gray Wolf genetics he carried. He was dressed a bit more sophisticated than the three he was with. Black silk slacks, leather shoes and a white silk shirt matched with an expensive black leather jacket.

That hair was long, falling nearly to the middle of his back as his black eyes, narrowed and intense, surveyed the room.

This Breed she knew, unfortunately. He had been in Omega while she had been there with her father. If she wasn't mistaken, he had been one of her father's favorite creations. Several times she had heard her brother refer to Navarro with worry and fondness, and several times her father had actually stated that he could have considered the Breed a son.

Her father had a daughter, but this Breed had concerned him far more than his daughter's safety had, and for that, Storme had once hated him with a passion.

Lawe Justice and Rule Breaker were Lion Breeds. Both men were extremely handsome, as all Breeds were, and rumored to be full brothers, perhaps even twins. Shoulder-length black hair was pulled to the napes of both men's necks, while powerful bodies were attired in jeans, boots, T-shirts and denim jackets.

It was the fourth one that seemed the odd Breed out. He sat back casually in his chair, one hand lying on the table, his fingers tapping to the music as he glanced at the dance floor and the women that sauntered by the table to draw the men's attention.

Blue eyes. Ocean blue. She could see those eyes each time she caught a glimpse of his face through the crowd. Long red hair flowed past his shoulders, coarse rather than soft, tied back at his nape as the others' was, though it had the appearance of having been tamed only under protest.

Squared, strong features drew instant female attention, as did the exotic eyes that appeared to be lined with the faintest edge of kohl. High cheekbones, well-molded male lips, broad shoulders, a strong chest and impressive biceps. He was larger and broader than the other men, and looked exactly like what he had been created to be. A Scots warrior. He would have looked at home in a kilt with a sword strapped to his waist.

Leather pants, heavy boots, a white long-sleeved shirt and leather riding jacket were the perfect covering for him. They made him look harder, broader, more dangerous.

He was Styx Mackenzie, the one Breed she was seriously growing tired of playing games with. He had been on her ass for more than a year now, off and on, determined to track her down and force her to listen to the proposition the Breed community had for her.

She already knew the details. Protection in exchange for information.

She wanted to laugh at the thought. As though a Breed could ever protect her. They would be more inclined to tear her throat out if she displeased one of them.

A flash of memory, buried so deep that she rarely let herself remember it, had her eyes closing briefly as she fought it back.

Her brother's death. The Breed ripping out his throat, the sounds of James's last gurgled breath and her father's cry of fear and pain.

They should have gone with her. They should have escaped as well rather than staying behind to destroy the last of the files they had on whatever secret project they had been involved in. That information had been more important than their lives. More important than her life, because her father entrusted her with the care of it, despite the fact that he should have realized that the Council would know exactly who he had given it to.

The Council scientists knew, and the Breeds knew, and she had been running from both for the past ten years.

She was tired of running, but there was a part of her that still refused to give up the information she had.

Glancing down at her hands, she watched as she twisted her mother's antique ring on her finger. The wedding band her father had given her mother had been in the Montague family for generations upon generations. The diamonds, sapphires and emeralds were family jewels, the blues and greens family colors. And Storme was now the last of the Montague line. There were no sons left to carry on the name, and there would be no daughters left to wear the ring.

The ring had been intended for James's wife, a wife he had never had because the danger of the job he had undertaken with his father had been too great.

Creating Breeds.

She glared across the room at the four Breeds. Monsters. Animals. She hated every damned one of them. As far as she was concerned, there was no crime greater than that of creating such farcical replications of humans and trying to convince the world they deserved to move freely among them.

Hatred swirled inside her for the loss of her father, her brother, the loss of her childhood and the dreams she had had of freedom. Dreams that had never come to fruition because each time she thought she had found peace, Breeds had managed to find her.

It didn't matter if they were the few Breeds still aligned with the Council or those who proclaimed to desire nothing but peace and freedom. They were all killers. They all wanted her for a reason, for the information they thought she had.

As she glared across the room, his head turned. Blue eyes, radiating amusement and warmth, met hers and locked. For the space of no more than a second, Storme felt mesmerized, locked in a circle of hatred, anger, laughter and hunger.

She had rarely looked into a Breed's eyes. They were too intuitive, their senses too sharp to hide from if they managed to look into your eyes. But this time, for that second as the crowd parted, his gaze held her.

Then, like an erratic school of fish, dancing bodies separated them, flowed between them, breaking the contact but leaving Storme assured that she was hidden no longer.

She came out of the booth instantly, moving along the edge of the crowd at a near run as she headed to the restrooms at the back of the bar.

She would hide there a few minutes then see about slipping out the back entrance of the bar.

She had to get out of there. She had rushed inside to hide, only to find the four bastards that had obviously been tailing her. She had thought, this close to Haven, the Wolf Breed sanctuary, that maybe she could rest for a few days, stay hidden, and figure out what to do next.

They were getting too close. Her hotel room had been ransacked the night before; the only reason she hadn't been there was that she had slipped out for fast food and walked to a nearby restaurant rather than driving. Her car had been parked in the parking lot of the hotel, and in addition to the belongings in her room being destroyed, the car had been broken into also.

There was no escape there. Until she acquired another vehicle, she was fucked. If she didn't get the damned Breeds off her ass, then she was fucked anyway.

As she rushed through the crowd, several couples parted at once; a path was created, then suddenly blocked as she slammed against a hard, wide chest.

Her gaze jerked up, locked. Her lips parted in shock, a shudder racing through her as warm hands gripped her shoulders lightly and canines flashed in a smile.

"Weel now, I was goin' for a drink, but I could be convinced to settle for a wee dance," he laughed.

She noticed it then. The music as it moved into a slow, dark strain of desperate love and passion unquenched.

Her hands pressed to his chest as his moved to her hips and he pulled her easily the rest of the way to the dance floor she had been moving by.

She'd taken a scent neutralizer earlier, one of the precious last few she possessed. She prayed it worked.

She was too shocked to fight. In all her life she had never found herself this close to a Breed, in a situation so shockingly dangerous that it could destroy her world in an instant.

"Do ye need the ladies' room so desperately that a dance will interfere?" he asked as she continued to stare up at him. "Ye look as though the hounds of hell chase ye, lass. I can wait a moment or two if I must."

He didn't know who she was? Didn't know her scent?

She shook her head. "I didn't expect to see Breeds here." The lightness of the response was desperate, and she was certain it fell far short of the casual comment she'd intended.

"Don't be frightened, please." Sincerity suddenly marked his expression as they moved slowly to the music, more because he was leading than from her own conscious thought.

"My friends and myself are just takin' a break from a wee bit of business is all."

"Business?" She swallowed tightly. "This close to Haven, that's not unusual, I guess."

He chuckled at that, and she was shocked at the husky warmth of the sound.

"It should be unusual. Alas, I find myself at the end of this particular job though, and I'm lookin' forward to the downtime."

"A job? I thought Breeds were taken care of by the government?" She knew they were. The bastards didn't have to do anything. The only jobs they seemed to have were those of tracking down scientists and murdering them.

He grimaced at her comment as she felt his fingertips stroke down the back of her jacket, as though caressing her spine. "Lass, no mon or government takes care of me. I've a mind to pay my own way."

"What sort of work do you do then?" Keeping conversation going was imperative. Keeping her mind away from the fact that she was in a Breed's arms would be the only way to stay sane.

"I've been aiding a friend in a small investigation the past year or so." He shrugged as though it didn't matter. "Too little information and too many false leads have brought me home though. Finally."

He sounded tired, not as tired as she knew she was, but at least weary of whatever game he had been playing with her.

"Your friend didn't have all the information you needed then?" She didn't have to pretend interest.

"Too little information and too little cash," he chuckled. "Perhaps when he can pay my fee, we'll be talkin' again."

Too little information. Too little pay. Navarro might know what she looked like, but it seemed she had stayed far enough ahead of them that the other Breed hadn't been able to point her out to his friend.

She never took pictures. The driver's license she carried was under an assumed name, just as the credit cards she carried were.

"You're going back to Haven then?" she asked, wishing he would hurry and go. Wishing he had left before he managed to run into her.

"Only if ye make me, lass. I could spend the night in much more interesting pursuits than those to be found at Haven if you're willing."

Styx Mackenzie was a flirt, a true Breed man-whore, she had often thought. He wasn't as newsworthy as other Breeds, but he had a following of female groupies who congregated on the Internet, and who posted every sighting of him possible. Whose home he was seen entering, what time the next morning he left. His current lovers, past lovers and possible potential lovers.

He made no secret of his approval of their posts each time he joined them online, and despite his attempts to remain camera shy, he was caught often in both video as well as photo.

He was becoming the poster guy for the flirtatious, unthreatening Breed. Which never failed to shock her, because the potential for killing was there in his eyes.

Wasn't it?

"No answer? Is that a stern and forbiddin' no then?" That smile flashed, and those blue eyes filled with warmth and a latent lust that had her thighs tensing.

God, she was wet!

She felt the sharp inhalation of surprise that she couldn't hide. She aroused. That easily, that quickly. As though her body was suddenly refusing to cooperate with her mind in hating every Breed she met.

She couldn't hate and want at the same time, could she?

"I don't like Breeds," she whispered.

She couldn't lie to him. She wanted to. She wanted to play the game, she wanted to tease and lure him until she escaped his clutches as easily as she had other Breeds.

He almost paused. A frown touched his brow, touched those incredible blue eyes.

"I'm a mon, lass, not just a Breed. It's a wee like sayin'

ye dislike all Chinese, ye dislike all Italians or all people in general, wouldn't ye think?"

His voice was gentle, almost understanding.

His hand stroked up her back, his fingers pressed against her spine, and she found herself wishing she was stupid enough to sink into him.

"Perhaps I just dislike all Breeds," she stated. And she was lying, because she knew a part of her hated all Breeds.

"I'll tell ye what." That smile was back. "Try me on, lass, see if ye dislike all Breeds, or just dislike all Breeds but me."

Try him on.

The thought of it was enough to cause her juices to gather and saturate the folds of her sex.

"No." She stepped back, the temptation, the sudden aching need that wrapped around her, had the power to send her heart racing with what she knew had to be fear.

It was fear. It couldn't be anything else.

"Lass . . ."

"I have to go. Friends." She looked around as though she were actually with someone else. "I'm sorry. I have to go."

She left him on the dance floor, assuring herself it wasn't a mistake. That there was no way she could have felt the warmth, the security that she had imagined she felt in his arms.

Entering the crowd, she brushed against the bodies, fought to diffuse her scent and headed straight for the back door, and for safety.

A quick check behind her had her sighing in relief as she pushed through the back entrance into the dimly lit back alley behind the bar.

Aldon, Colorado, had grown over the past ten years, after the Wolf Breeds had been granted the nearly three hundred thousand acres of land the government had once set aside as a wildlife preservation area. The grant had given the Wolf Breeds the land in reparation for the American government's part in their creation and torture for so many decades.

Storme didn't advocate torturing any creature, but she didn't advocate allowing them to run wild outside confined areas either, or so she had always stated. Then she imagined Styx Mackenzie in those labs, that smile, the warmth and humor in his gaze replaced by rage and violent hunger, and it made her feel sick.

Wishing she had the weapon she usually carried beneath her jacket, Storme closed the door behind her and began moving quickly for the end of the alley.

Head down, she pulled her cap from beneath her jacket and yanked the bill down to shade her face, praying the small amount of scent neutralizer she'd applied to her body and the smells from the crowd in the bar had hid her scent enough to assure Styx Mackenzie remained off her ass for a while longer.

She was running out of the formula used to hide from the Breeds, which she tried to keep on hand for emergencies. The spray-on camouflage had saved her life more than once in the past years, but lately she'd been forced to rely on it more and more. It was almost as though it wasn't even working.

"Well it's about time."

Storme drew up short, her head jerking up at the malicious tone as a dark figure stepped from the shadowed indent of a closed doorway at the edge of the building.

Coyote.

Stepping back, she stared into the cruel dark eyes as the Coyote Breed was joined by a partner from the building on the other side of the alley.

She knew this Coyote. He'd been chasing her for the past four months. He seemed to be a bit more tenacious than most, or else just more scared of whoever controlled him. It did surprise her that he'd brought company though. He normally worked alone.

"Two against one. You boys like to hedge your bets, now, don't you, Farce? So, are you Council or Haven Breeds?"

They had been doing that for a while, sending teams out rather than a lone Breed to capture her. Farce, a Breed with no last name that she knew of, had shed more than his fair share of blood over the past six months as he followed her.

But the Breeds chasing her for the past ten years were known for that.

"Does it matter who sent us?" the first Breed asked, his tone rasping, rough with a cruel edge of intent.

Hell, she would have thought she could have figured out who his handlers were by now, but Farce was a bit more mysterious than most Breeds. There were no records of him, period, in the Breed or Council databases she had managed to hack. Even her sources within the Council didn't seem to know who he was or who he worked for. Not that she trusted those sources, but it was the best she had to work with.

"Well, a girl likes to know the origins of the Breed courting her," she said mockingly. "It does make all the difference."

Between life and death in some cases.

She hadn't managed to truly upset Haven's Breeds yet. Of course, she hadn't been forced to kill one either. The Council bitches on the other hand were another story.

She slid her hand beneath her jacket, fingers curling over the butt of the precise, illegal laser blaster she carried there.

"Come on, bitch, let's not get into a firefight here," Farce suggested, though his tone was anything but conciliatory as he noticed the movement. "I don't think our bosses would like it near as much if we brought you in dead."

Which still didn't tell her which faction had sent them.

"Ten years, and you still haven't given up." She shook her head in disbelief. "What will it take to make you understand that whatever you want, I simply don't have it."

"You have something," the other Breed growled. "Or you'd already be dead."

That she didn't doubt in the slightest. Neither the Council nor the Bureau of Breed Affairs were known for their patience in acquiring whatever they wanted.

Storme shuddered. She recognized that voice now. As he came farther from the shadows, she recognized the Breed as well.

Dog. Just Dog—she'd never heard if he had chosen a

last name as other Breeds had after their rescues, or if he was one of those Coyotes that continued the Council tradition of no last names for their pets.

Dog was no longer a Council pet though, according to him. He was a freelancer. A freelancer that could strike fear into the hearts of Breeds as well as humans.

He ranked up there with Cavalier, Brim Stone, and the rarely mentioned Loki, a known assassin rumored to hunt rescued Breeds.

"Well, I guess we're just going to have to quarrel over this." She could feel the panic beginning to edge inside her now, the fear she had fought since the night her father and brother were killed.

She gripped the hilt of the only weapon left to her, a small sheathed dagger she had pushed into her right front pocket, beneath her jacket, as her gaze moved quickly behind the Coyotes. She didn't want the Coyotes to hurt innocent bystanders if they wandered by, but she wasn't letting them take her. She didn't dare. At least, not alive.

Life meant a lot to her, and freedom, as dangerous as it could be at times, was still a hell of a lot better than what was waiting for her in either Breed or Council control.

They both wanted something from her. The same thing. Information they believed she held. Information her father had given her before he was killed.

She had sworn she would only give it to the person her father had promised would come for it. It was the only task he had ever trusted her with, the only vow he had asked her to make. He and her brother had died for her safety; she wouldn't betray them.

But she was so tired.

She was tired of having to fight to live, so tired of running, of never being warm, never being safe.

Farce stepped closer.

"Please, let's not play this game," she whispered. "Tonight, one of us will end up dead, Farce. That's not what I want."

A hard, sardonic chuckle rasped from his throat as Storme felt resignation begin to fill her.

"The only weapon you have, bitch, is a blade," he sneered. "What do you think you're going to prick with that?"

She felt the weariness, the acceptance. If they came too close, she would prick herself. She would kill herself before allowing this Breed to take her.

"Hell, lads, what ye doin' cornerin' a pretty lass like this in the dark?" Mocking, smooth and sexy, the Scots brogue had the Coyotes facing her stilling, even as Storme restrained the curse rising to her lips.

How had he managed to find her so quickly?

Storme turned, careful to keep both the Coyotes and the newcomer coming from behind her in the corner of her eye, and watched as Styx Mackenzie moved from the back entrance of the bar into the alley.

"Well isn't this my lucky night?" she drawled.

"I was rather thinkin' the same thing, lass," he chuckled. "See now, wouldn't ye have done better to have continued the dance we were havin' inside?"

Her brows lifted. "I was definitely doing much better."

He chuckled patiently at the admission, and the sound, deep and filled with warmth, had her stomach clenching.

The weapon he carried loosely in the crook of his arm was big, heavy and lethal. The fully automatic laser rifle would put holes in a Breed that would leave nothing left to identify, let alone survive.

She let her gaze flick to it slowly before returning to the blue, amused gaze. "Hell of a weapon," she drawled. "Where were you hiding it?"

"The jacket at the table." He grinned as he shrugged his shoulders to indicate the leather jacket he hadn't been wearing on the dance floor. "I never leave home or a bar without it."

She almost laughed. She wanted to. The small spurt of amusement was out of place, and definitely out of character for her.

"You're making a mistake, Wolf," Farce growled, but she heard the defeat in his voice.

"Lad, anytime I'm rescuin' a pretty little thing from

your clutches, then my time's not bein' wasted." Smooth as aged whiskey, rough, filled with determination, that brogue seemed to caress the senses despite the fact that there was nothing about Breeds that she considered being the least bit caressable.

"Run along now, puppies, and I'll pretend to be the nice Breed everyone thinks I am and let you live for another day."

Storme searched for a way to escape, and came to the conclusion that she was stuck between a rock and a hard place, in the most literal sense.

"This isn't over." Farce directed his comment to her as she watched Dog slowly disappear into the shadows as though he had never been there.

Storme kept her mouth shut. The Wolf Breed standing so imposing and determined to her right seemed to have the bluff on the bastard to her left.

That meant the Coyotes were Council controlled. She knew Styx was a part of the Wolf Breed community, Haven. Since he appeared less than friendly with but certainly familiar with Farce, it answered the question of who the Coyote's handlers were.

Farce snarled back at her, his canines gleaming in the dim light before he too slowly eased back and disappeared around the side of the building.

Running was an option now.

"Lass, they're just waitin' until you try to run," Styx warned her as he lowered the weapon before moving to the lethal black motorcycle she had only now realized was parked in the shadows. "I can give ye a ride wherever you're goin' if you like. I didn't rescue your pretty self just to see them jump you again later. They don't like losing a play pretty when they pick one out."

She stared at him in confusion. This Breed had been tracking her for nearly as long as Farce had been, yet he acted as though he didn't know her, just as he had acted inside.

She almost smiled.

"Ye know, the scent of your fear is being overshadowed

by the vaguest scent of pure devilry." His smile flashed in the darkness. "Come on now, I've work to be doing tonight as ye've already turned me down. Rejection tends to depress me, ye know. I'd hate tae be left in tears afore the night is over."

She rolled her eyes in exasperation. The man didn't seem to have a serious bone in his body or a lick of bloody sense. Which was more or less what she had already decided over the years as she followed him online.

"You never did tell me exactly what that work is." She didn't budge as he watched her expectantly.

He grunted at that. "Chasin' shadows if you be askin' me. I've been on the same assignment for a year now, and I've had enough of shadows." He sighed as though truly fed up with chasing her.

"You're a Breed. I thought Breeds enjoyed chasing things?" She posed the question while making certain she did nothing to deliberately deceive him. She was very well aware that Breeds could clearly scent emotions, deceit and lies.

"Aye, I'm a Breed. As for chasin' shadows, I've always preferred more entertainin' prey and lass's that don' run near so fast." He laughed back at her as he pushed the weapon into a compartment at the side of the cycle's base before turning back to her. "Come now, don't leave me to worry about ye for the rest of the night. I'd like to head to my bed for a wee bit of a nap sometime before dawn."

"Lost a woman, did you?" She stepped closer. It was possible that he didn't know what she looked like now, that the neutralizer she wore had hidden her scent enough that he had no idea who she was. That and the temporary hair color, the colored contact lenses. She could get lucky.

She couldn't imagine he would get this close to her and not jump her if he knew who she was, if he knew she was the shadow he was chasing.

"Let's say, there's a lass that enjoys playing hide-and-seek," he chuckled as he reached back and scratched at his neck with the air of a man that found that confusing. "Some women enjoy games, I've found."

"And you don't?"

"Only if it involves chocolate and sweet heated flesh," he drawled with a quick, charming grin before straddling the motorcycle and turning back to her.

Patting the seat behind her, he watched her expectantly.

"And I'm supposed to trust you?" she asked.

"Beats the alternative, lass." He glanced back at the entrance to the alley. "You can ride out of here with me safe and sound or take your chances with Farce and his buddy."

"They didn't seem like the type to take home to mother," she commented as she took another step toward him.

"Hell, are any of us?" he chuckled. "Come on, sweets, pony up and let's ride."

He had no idea who she was. Storme moved closer to the cycle, watching him warily as she felt a strange tingle of anticipation running through her.

"So you're searching for your shadow tonight then?" she asked, as she did as he'd suggested and mounted the bike behind him.

"Perhaps." He shrugged. "I'm the new Breed here tonight, you might say. When I couldn't find the lost little waif on my own, they sent in reinforcements."

He didn't sound as though it bothered him.

"I thought Breeds could scent their prey a mile away," she commented as the powerful motor began to throb beneath them.

"Here, lass." He handed her a helmet.

Pulling it on, she found that the headgear was equipped with communications, evident by the short mic that rested close to her lips.

Following suit, he pulled on a larger, full-faced helmet he had taken from the handlebars and strapped it on.

"You'd have to get a scent of your prey to track it first," he told her as he slid the powerful machine into gear and moved toward the entrance. "Hold on, we're gonna blast out just in case."

Just in case Farce and Dog were still waiting at the entrance.

He shot out of the exit as Storme gripped his waist and leaned in close to maintain her seat. The exit was exhilarating, filled with the throb of the cycle beneath her, the heat of the Breed in front of her, and the danger that could be waiting just outside the alley.

But it seemed Farce and Dog had slunk back into whatever slum they were hiding in. They weren't waiting outside the exit, though she was sure they were watching from nearby, just to be certain Styx hadn't left her alone.

"Where're you stayin', lass?" he asked through the comm link.

"The Lincoln Arms," she answered. It seemed she would be renting another hotel room for the night.

"You'll be easily found there if Farce and his buddy decide tonight's the night for havin' fun," he told her. "Ye'll need to check out and find another hotel."

"Suggestions?"

He was silent for several moments. "Hell, get a room at my hotel for the night. I'm not leavin' till mornin', and knowin' Farce, he'll definitely be lookin' for ye tonight."

What an interesting invitation.

Could she be wrong? Was he simply more deceptive than most Breeds?

"I thought you were chasing shadows tonight."

He chuckled again. "Join me for dinner and I'll let my friends continue the chase while I enjoy your fair company for an hour or so. It's not as though I've picked up the scent of her yet. I'll be of little use to them."

She had been successful. In the months this Breed had been tracking her, she was aware that he had never really gotten that close. He was always several steps behind her, there but not really a threat.

Maybe the neutralizer combined with her attempts to stay on the move had managed to put enough distance between them that she could remain hidden for just a little longer.

"So how 'bout that offer of dinner?" he asked. "The hotel I'm at has excellent room service."

She could rest. Maybe he would even be nice and get the room.

"The Lincoln was the cheapest accommodations I could find," she said regretfully. "I can't afford anything more expensive."

"Never fear, I've a suite. I know how to share."

She just bet he did.

"What about your friends?"

"They're not invited," he growled good-naturedly. "Let's say I know who to share with, and some treasures are like fine chocolate, and meant to be enjoyed without company."

So his friends wouldn't be there.

"Are there strings attached?" She had no intention of becoming his playmate, or his chocolate for the night.

"Only if you want them," he promised her. "Come on, lass, I'm the knight in scuffed and dented armor tonight, remember? Besides, some things a man doesn't force, if ye know what I mean."

She knew a bit about this Breed and that seemed to be a philosophy he lived by. Of all the Breeds that had been sent for her, Styx was the one known more for his playfulness toward women than his mercilessness, or bloodthirsty abilities.

At the moment, he was the safer bet. No doubt Farce and his buddy would track her to the Lincoln before the night was over. They had tracked her to the last hotel she'd taken; she'd lost the security of her vehicle, her clothing and several weapons.

She was hungry, tired and wanted just a chance to rest for a few hours. A nice meal would be a hell of a bonus.

Styx Mackenzie was still a Breed though. He killed, as they all did, and it was rumored he killed with a smile. But the only hits she knew of him making were against Council soldiers, Breeds or scientists.

She wasn't naive enough to think she knew all there was to know about him, or that this Breed wasn't as deceptive, bloodthirsty and capable of damned near anything any other Breed was. The simple truth was that he was her only chance of escaping a fate worse than him tonight.

Of course, could there be any fate worse than a Breed?

"Here we go, sweets." The motorcycle roared into the entrance of the most exclusive hotel in the sprawling city.

"You're a Breed, why not stay at Haven? It's not far from here," she asked as she dismounted and pulled the helmet from her head.

"Lass, I told ye, I'm supposed to be workin'. If I were at Haven, then my boss would realize I'm more intent on the pretty lass some Coyote Breeds were harassing than the one I'm tae be lookin' for." He winked with a quick grin as he pulled the wicked black helmet from his own head then secured both pieces of headgear to the side of the motorcycle before tossing the valet the keys. "Did you know we were followed?"

He placed his hand against the small of her back, forcing her forward rather than allowing her to turn and glance behind her as she would have done. As self-preservation urged her to do.

"They followed then?" The weariness was dragging at her.

The Coyote Breeds chasing her had stayed hard on her ass for weeks, giving her very little time to sleep, and no opportunities to find the odd jobs that had sustained that pesky desire she'd acquired for food.

"They followed, but we'll take care of it," he promised as he guided her through the elegant lobby to the elevators on the other side. "It would be interesting to hear how ye managed to acquire their attention though."

The edge of amusement in his voice assured her that he wasn't really suspicious . . . maybe.

"Same ole, same ole." She shrugged, thankful that certain Coyote Breeds had the same reputation that a member of a criminal family might acquire. "All you have to do is be in the wrong place at the wrong time."

"That's fairly accurate." There was a hint of a growl

in his voice now, and less of that Scottish brogue that she realized had managed to calm her some small amount.

That surprised her. Breeds had a tendency to make her incredibly nervous, and she never allowed herself this close to one. She wasn't nervous with Styx though. Perhaps she was just too damned tired to care anymore.

"Here we are." The elevator came to a smooth stop on the top floor, the doors opening soundlessly to the secured eleventh floor. "I've a suite here. You can have a lovely meal with me; the chef in the kitchen is damned near a genius with food, and let's not discuss his abilities with chocolate." There was an edge of love in his voice.

That was right. This was the Breed known to love his chocolate. She'd heard rumors, jokes and had even eavesdropped on a conversation between two other women several nights before regarding his penchant for women and chocolate together.

He was known to kill with an easy smile and a complete lack of mercy, then turn around and devour chocolate as though it were the nectar of the gods.

"Here we go." He opened the door to the suite and escorted her in as though he were no more than a good Samaritan, eager to please and score brownie points to heaven.

The suite was elegant; soft cream carpeting, caramel leather furniture grouped in a seating area in front of a large screen television. To the side, an eight-place conference/dining table sat, and through double doors she glimpsed a king-sized bed that looked airy and comfortable.

"There's another room through here." Styx opened a second set of doors to reveal another bed, which looked just as comfortable.

God, she would have given her eyeteeth to curl beneath the snowy white comforter and just sleep until she couldn't sleep another wink.

"Dinner menu is on the table," he told her as he strode to a wet bar behind the table. "What would ye like to drink, lass?"

Something strong enough to make her forget he was a

Breed. That was what she wanted. Something that would loosen the knot of nerves in her stomach and allow her to relax long enough to enjoy a few hours without the threat of Breeds hunting her.

Styx had no idea who she was. As far as he was concerned she was just another woman he wouldn't mind fucking. The fact that he obviously had an ulterior motive for helping her should have pissed her off rather than intriguing her. Maybe she was just too damned tired to care?

Moving to the menu, she stared down at it for long moments, mouth watering, fighting to make a choice.

"Why don't I just order a sampler of the chef's favorite fare?" he suggested when she didn't answer.

"That sounds perfect." Clearing her throat, she looked around the opulent room once again. "Haven takes care of its Breeds while on a mission."

He chuckled at that. "Ah, lass, if only I could convince them to be so kind. No, the suite was in exchange for a fine hand of poker I played. The owner lost, I won. Unfortunately, he was a bit short on cash at the table, and I don't take IOUs. So we made a bit of an exchange."

"Must have been a hell of a hand," she commented.

"Lady luck was smilin' on me. Now, about that drink?"

It was possible she had had too much to drink. She'd definitely had too much to eat.

Storme stared at the remains of the sampler platters spread across the table and took another sip of what had to be the best wine she had ever tasted.

Styx sat across from her, watching her with a hint of a smile on his lips as he sipped at another whiskey. He'd been watching her for a while as she enjoyed the food, those ocean blue eyes filled with warmth.

No, that couldn't be warmth, unless he knew how to fake it. Of course, he probably did know how to fake it. She had no doubt that if he did, then the Council had taught it to him.

"Are ye ready yet to tell me your name, lass?" he questioned, that wicked, smooth voice rasping just a bit with a hint of animalistic pleasure.

He was enjoying himself. They'd talked through the meal. Talked about a variety of topics, yet never once had he asked her again why the Coyotes were chasing her, and until now, he hadn't seemed to care what her name was.

"Perhaps I prefer to remain a mystery." Yes, she had definitely had a little too much wine, but she took another sip anyway and let the soft, heated glow radiating inside her, grow. It had to be the alcohol that had her flirting as she seemed prone to do tonight.

"Ah, lass, I have a feelin' you'll always be a mystery," he chuckled as he rose to his feet and moved to her. "Come then, I'll show you to your room and let you sleep for a while. Ye look ready to pass out in your chair."

"I'm not drunk." She frowned up at him.

"Now, was I sayin' ye were drunk?" A red brow arched slowly. "I was merely commentin' on the exhaustion marking your pretty face. You're a bit pale, and definitely not at your best. Seducing a lass is always more pleasurable when she's not fallin' asleep on a mon."

"You can't seduce me." No Breed could seduce her, she wouldn't allow it. And she didn't dare allow a human male to talk her into bed. She had no desire to see another friend die.

"Can't I no'?" Lifting the wineglass from her suddenly weakened hand, he set it on the table and drew her to her feet.

She felt lazy. The exhaustion of before had eased a bit with the food. She was tired of course, but sleep wouldn't come for a while, especially considering the fact a Breed was in the suite with her.

"No, you can't seduce me." She finally shook her head. "I don't do Breeds."

To which he laughed. "Pretend I'm a mon then," he suggested. "A nice, unthreatening male eager only to satisfy your every whim and desire."

Her lips quirked. He was amusing at least.

"No one would mistake you for a normal, unthreatening man of any species."

He stepped closer. Storme stared up at him, feeling a sense of vulnerability she didn't want to feel. He wasn't a man, he was the epitome of everything she had hated for ten years.

"Lass, I'd never hurt you," he promised, his voice so deep, so gentle, his hand reaching out, so close to touching her before Storme flinched back and gave a hard shake of her head.

Life must have really become hell in the past months, she thought. So hellish she had nearly stood there and allowed him to touch her.

His gaze narrowed. "Take your shower, woman."

It was a command.

Storme stared back at him, teeth clenching as she felt her emotions rising, felt rising to the fore the anger that always simmered in the back of her mind.

"It's time for me to go." No Coyote could be as dangerous to her as this Breed could become.

The sense of self-preservation began to ratchet up inside her, tensing, tightening through her body as she swung on her heel and meant to march straight to the door.

"And ye think I risked life and limb to protect that pretty ass of yours so you can flaunt yourself right out that door and into their clutches?"

Before she could evade him, and she was damned good at evading Breeds, he gripped her arm, dragging her around until he could pull her against his chest.

Her hands flattened in instinct on the hard, broad contours. She swore she could feel the heat of his flesh pouring through the material of the shirt he wore. Heat, and something else. The beat of his heart, pounding faster than it should, as though being close to her affected him, as though touching her excited him.

Her heart was racing in fear. At least, that was the excuse she was sticking to. Of course, fear had never made her clit swell before, nor had it caused her pussy to throb, her juices to gather. Her nipples were hard. Her lips were sensitive, and she realized in a flash of insight that she wanted him to kiss her.

She had never been this close to a Breed, at least not in this situation. In the ten years she had been running, she had been shot at and had shot back, had hit and been hit by Breeds. But never had she been held by one.

Her fingers curled against his shirt, a distant part of her amazed at the feel of the flesh beneath the clothing. Her hips were held close to his thighs, the length of his cock pressing against her lower stomach, beneath the material of his leather riding pants.

There was heat there as well. Full, thick heat, a subtle pulse and throb of lust.

She knew too much about Breed physiology, she thought with panicked nerves. Too much about the length and width of the male Wolf Breed's cock, the hard tone of his muscles, the impossible strength of his body.

Outside this room, certain hell awaited her, and she knew it. Inside this room, in his arms, possibly in his bed, there would be exquisite pleasure. A pleasure unlike anything any woman who hadn't been with a Breed could imagine.

They were trained in the labs to pleasure a woman, and they acquired that training for a variety of reasons, most of them to deceive, to infiltrate, to gain trust and to steal information.

"Where's the fear of earlier, lass?" The crooning whisper eased over her senses as his lips lowered to her ear, his tongue stroking against it with an insidious stroke of enticement.

Her lashes fluttered. It felt good. It felt too good. For a second, a flash of guilt rushed through her, only to be followed by the alluring sensation of his lips moving along her jaw, his tongue giving gentle, brief little licks as his lips caressed her.

She fought to pull up the memory of the Breed tearing at her brother's throat, but the image wouldn't come to mind. It couldn't slip past the warmth sizzling through her body.

"Don't do this to me," she whispered, praying he would pull back, that he would take his touch away.

"Donna do what, little love?" His lips brushed against

hers. "Donna give ye pleasure? But, lass, there's no need greater at this moment than to hear your cries of pleasure."

And her need for pleasure intense enough to cry out, for it was beginning to burn inside her.

"Please," she whispered again. "Let me go."

A low, wicked chuckle vibrated against the side of her lips. "If ye want to be free, ye've only to move away."

But he was holding her. His hands, big and strong, were smoothing down her back, over the rise of her buttocks and back again.

Stroking. He was stroking her, pulling her close as those big hands returned to her buttocks and lifted.

Her back met the wall behind them as his thigh slid between hers, tucked against the core of her and rubbed against her with a smooth, seductive stroke.

Sensation raced from her clit to her nipples. Pure, unadulterated pleasure. It was heated, soothing, exciting. A mix of sensations she'd never had time to experience until now.

"You're not movin', lass." His lips feathered over hers.

No, she wasn't moving, she couldn't move.

"Such a lovely wee mystery." The brogue intoxicated her, held her mesmerized with the pure, male seduction it contained as she felt his fingers at the buttons of her blouse.

God, she was letting him touch her. Her brother had been killed by a Coyote whose life he had saved more than once when the Coyote had returned from a mission gone bad. Her father had created him.

Wolves and Coyotes had been her father and brother's specialties. Their genetic genius had created Breeds other scientists had been in awe of. Breeds that had turned on their creators.

And one of those Breeds was touching her. Not one they had created, but one created just as they had created others.

She looked down, watching as the fingers of one hand loosened the buttons of her plain black blouse. The material parted slowly, the edges easing apart to reveal her unbound breasts.

Storme stared down at the flushed, swollen mounds of

her breasts. Her nipples, normally a soft pink, relaxed and uninteresting, were now hard, pointed and much darker.

"Lord love a Wolf." The soft breath of sound had her gaze jerking up to his expression.

He looked rapt, staring at her breasts as his hands slowly cupped the hard mounds, feeling them, holding them in his palms as though they were in need of his support.

The feel of the calloused flesh rasping against the silken curves had her nipples throbbing. They were tight and hard, painfully sensitive and aching for touch.

He wasn't gentle. He wasn't rough. His fingers caressed, molded and experienced the feel of the hardened flesh as Storme felt her knees weaken from the sensations tightening. God, she just needed him to touch harder, firmer.

No, she needed more. She wanted, needed his lips on her. She wanted them covering the tight peaks, suckling on them, drawing them into his mouth and driving her insane with the pleasure.

"Styx," she whispered his name, just to feel it on her lips, to feel a part of him on her lips.

She wanted to taste him as desperately as she wanted to be tasted. She wanted to give and to take. She ached for an intimacy she had never dared to even consider before tonight.

How dangerous was this? So dangerous she knew she might never recover from this night if it continued in this way.

She was going to have to stop this, very soon.

But she didn't want to stop it. She could feel the conflict rising inside her, beginning to tear at her. Fear and need, memories and past hatreds, a decade of running, hiding, fighting for just a few moments to find peace, to find warmth. In ten years she hadn't found it, until a Wolf pulled her into his arms.

Until the enemy touched her.

"Sweet mystery," he whispered. "Tell me, if I suck these pretty nipples, will you be a good lass and tell me your name?"

She didn't dare. God no. She couldn't handle the thought of having him realize who she was, of having the lover, the protector, turn into the jailor.

Storme shook her head.

"I'll be making a name for you then, love, because sucking those nipples is something I cannot resist," he warned her as his lips brushed against hers and his thumbs stroked over her nipples. "I'll not suck your pretty nipples without a name to lay to one who possesses such a perfect bounty though."

She was going to melt right there in his arms. Was it really fair that a creature such as this should exist? That he could tempt and seduce where only hatred should exist?

"My little mystery. My sweet, tempting little Sugar."

He found his name for her at the same time he found her lips.

Storme felt the moan trapped in her throat as the most incredible lash of sensations began to rush through her. His lips, impossibly knowing, heated, hungry, flowed over hers as his tongue licked against the seam of her mouth.

She swore she tasted the chocolate he had relished at dinner. That and perhaps a hint of cinnamon. A hint of heat.

Her lips parted.

She couldn't help but open to him, to allow his tongue to lick at hers, his lips to slant over hers, as his thigh pressed tighter, harder against the mound of her pussy.

She was incredibly wet. The feel of moisture collecting between her thighs added to the sensitivity of her suddenly swollen clit as she felt her arms lifting, her hands gripping his strong neck.

She wanted his kiss, and she shouldn't. She should fear the feel of his longer canines as he nipped at her lips then returned for a deeper, hotter kiss.

His lips moved over hers, creating a fire she couldn't control as she felt the need tightening in her belly and clenching in her pussy.

Storme felt her senses dissolving, her fear evaporating. And they shouldn't be.

She promised herself she would figure it out later. As

her head tipped back against the wall and she allowed his lips to skim down her neck to the rise of her breasts, she consoled herself with the promise that as soon as she could draw a breath, then she would make sense of it.

For now, she simply wanted to be a woman. And she had never felt so much a woman as she did now.

She didn't have to worry about Coyotes killing this man when it was over. She didn't have to worry about being disturbed, about being in danger. There wasn't a chance Farce and his friend would dare to make such an attempt.

"Oh yes." The words tore from her lips as his tongue suddenly stroked over a nipple, dissolving her thoughts.

Her gaze jerked down once again, watching, lips parted as he stared up at her with those ocean blue eyes, parted his own lips and sucked the tight, hard tip of her nipple inside with exquisitely slow motion. Damp male lips parting. His tongue curling over the hard tip before it disappeared inside his mouth and cold flames engulfed it.

Immediately, blazing sensation seared the tender bud before streaking hot and luscious straight to her clit. There, it tightened the muscles of her vagina and sent a surge of moisture to lubricate the sensitive folds of her pussy as the muscles there clenched and tightened in need.

She was wet and hot. Her body was sensitized, sinking, melting, and suddenly, nothing mattered but this man and the feel of his lips surrounding her nipple, suckling at it with firm, strong draws of his mouth, as his hands slid to her ass again to move her against his thigh. The pleasure was exquisite. It tore through her senses and rasped over her nerve endings like a wave of electric sensation.

Her stomach clenched, tightened. The overwhelming feeling was like a fire tearing through her pussy.

Fighting him wasn't an option, unless it meant fighting to keep him in place. Her fingers pushed into his hair, dislodging the leather that held it at his nape. The coarse warmth of the strands flowed over her hands and was the perfect counterpoint to the rasp of his tongue over her nipple.

It was just a bit rough. Just a bit rougher than it should

have been, just rough enough to send lashes of surprising ecstasy straight to her clit.

"There, Sugar." His lips lifted and smoothed over one nipple before kissing their way to the other, as the hands on her ass moved her against his thigh, rubbing against it with wicked, sensual mastery.

He was seducing her and she couldn't fight it. The insidious warmth began to burn its way through her system, igniting a flame she couldn't fight, couldn't deny.

Why him? Why this Breed when there was nothing she hated worse than she hated Breeds? Why did the warmth of him, the need and the aching desperation inside her coalesce to destroy years of hard-won control?

Because she was tired.

Because she needed just a few hours of warmth, of safety. Just a few hours to be a woman, even if she had to pretend he wasn't a Breed, but a man she could hold on to when the night was over.

Guilt would flay her when morning came. When her senses were working once again, then she would remember the horrors she had seen over the years.

But Styx hadn't been there.

"Ahh, Sugar, lass," he growled against her nipple as she stared down at him, his expression so sensual, so completely absorbed in giving her pleasure that it held her entranced.

She wasn't a virgin. She wasn't completely innocent, but never had a man stared at her with such naked hunger and complete absorbing need.

"Sweet as candy. As the finest, sweetest dark chocolate." A wicked smile, a flash of those sharp canines, and she should have come to her senses. Instead, her head fell back against the wall as he raked the blunt tips down her neck and one hand moved to her waist.

"Bad idea," she breathed out roughly as the snap and zipper of her jeans loosened.

"Ah, lass, the best idea I'm sure I've had in ages," he assured her with a groan as she fought herself onto her feet, only to find her jeans sliding down her hips. "I can smell your pussy, Sugar, sweet and hot and near to intoxicating me."

And that brogue was sliding over her senses with the same narcotic effect, just as his fingers slid farther inside her jeans to cup the bare, slick curves of her pussy.

Storme went to her toes, a keening moan leaving her lips as she felt a sensual explosion of pure heat whipping through her body.

The pad of his palm lay just over her swollen clit, sensitizing it further, holding her still in his grip as she stared up at him, terrified of the pleasure rising inside her now.

"We don't want to do this." She was going to hate both of them come morning.

"Sugar, we want to do this more than we want tae breathe."

She was in his arms, cradled against his chest, feeling more feminine, weaker, more sensual than she had ever felt in her life as he turned and carried her to the bedroom and the large bed waiting in the center of it.

As her back met the incredibly soft comforter, she felt her boots being pulled from her feet and, a second later, her jeans sliding from her legs.

Her panties were no barrier, and the sound of her blouse tearing was only a distant thought as he rose over her, his lips covering hers with a growl of pure pleasure.

His tongue pressed inside her lips, taking them as his fingers slid between her thighs and parted the swollen, slick folds of her sex.

Her hips arched. Agonizing pleasure ripped through her vagina, clenching it tight around the wicked finger that slid slowly inside. And stroked. Caressed without thrusting, rubbing against nerve endings so sensitive she cried out in brutal need.

Clenching her hands in the heavy strands of hair that fell over his face, Storme held him to her, desperate for more of the mindless, incredible pleasure building between her thighs.

She could feel the need whipping through her, that aching, intense lust, as it only grew between them.

This one night.

Tonight she would be a woman with a man she knew couldn't suffer for it when morning came. Coyotes wouldn't kill this man, and if the Breeds from Haven or Sanctuary learned of this night, then there was nothing he could say, no way he could know where she'd gone once she slipped from his arms.

"Yes!" The word tore from her lips as he pressed another finger inside her, opening her, stretching her as her hips writhed against him, driving him deeper.

"There, love," he groaned, his fingers driving inside her as his lips nipped at her neck, licked and sent flames coursing through her bloodstream. "You're so tight. So sweet you make a mon forget his control."

"Good, you stripped mine." Arching, neck tilting as his lips moved to lick at the area where it curved into her shoulder, Storme gave herself to the night, and the touch of this man.

He was a man. She refused to think of the extra genetics he held. God, she just wanted one night, one night of pleasure rather than fear. She just wanted to be warm for a little while before she had to run again.

As he nipped at her shoulder, her hands moved to his shirt, pulling, tugging until buttons tore and slipped free, allowing her to push the material over his shoulders.

She wanted to feel him against her. All that hard, hot flesh, muscles rippling, the strength of him honed and sculpted for pleasure or for pain.

Tonight, she would have pleasure. He didn't know who she was. He had no idea the gift he was giving her, the sheer warmth she had ached so desperately for.

"Sugar, you taste like heaven," he groaned as he shed his shirt, his fingers slipping from inside her as he rose to his knees to discard the material.

Storme rose to meet him, sitting up in the bed, her hands going to the leather of his pants and tugging at the heavy buttons that held the material tight along the length of his cock.

She knew Breed physiology. She knew the length and breadth of a male Wolf Breed's shaft. She'd seen it, as a young girl in the labs. Like animals, the Breeds hadn't been allowed clothing in the labs.

As she released him, she realized that she hadn't understood or considered the sensual aspects of that endowment then. As the heavy, thick flesh speared out from his body, she felt her pussy heat further, felt her juices flow between her thighs.

"Sugar, not yet." His fingers curled over her wrist as she lifted her gaze to him.

"Tonight's my night," she whispered back to him, feeling that determination as she allowed her fingers to grip the heated, iron-hard shaft.

Heated, throbbing and so hard. Her thumb smoothed over the tip of the head, easing away the light dampness that had gathered there.

"I shouldn't want this." Her throat tightened in sudden fear, the realization spearing through her that she might never forget this night.

"Why shouldn't you want this?" His fingers lifted to smooth back her hair as it fell over her cheek. "Why should ye not have all the pleasure I can give, love? And I know pleasure as you can never imagine."

Of course he did. Breeds were trained not just in giving pain, but also in giving pleasure.

"And what pleasure can I give you?" Compared to Styx, Storme knew she was as innocent as a virgin.

Her hand stroked down the length of his cock, feeling it jerk in her grip as his expression tightened and pleasure flashed in those bright blue eyes.

"Lass, you'll destroy me with pleasure at this rate," he assured her, his voice deeper, rougher as sensual enticement gleamed in his eyes.

The knowledge of seeing her effect on him did something to her. He wasn't lying, he couldn't be lying. She could see the truth of it in his eyes. She was giving him pleasure; he wanted her, ached as she ached, needed as she needed.

Moving forward, her tongue licked over the wide head, tasting man and heat, feeling it intoxicate her as her lips parted and sucked him inside.

This wasn't her, she assured herself as she felt the last restraint loosen inside her. This was the woman she might have been, the woman that perhaps she could have been if she hadn't spent the past ten years fighting to survive, to hide from the horrors chasing her.

This was the woman she had dreamed of being. In Styx's arms she had no fears of being disturbed, no fears of being surprised as the pleasure rose inside her.

Beneath one hand his abs tightened, spasming tightly as her mouth worked over the flared crest of his cock and sucked at it hungrily.

She could have sworn he pulsed in her mouth, a small ejaculation as the taste of spice filled her senses. She hadn't expected that. Hadn't expected that rich, male taste to infuse her, to drive her hunger higher.

Her fingers curled over the shaft, feeling it flex and throb as she stroked, sucked, relished each taste of him.

The feel of his hands threading through her hair, his fingers clenching in the strands as a hard growl left his throat, sent pure pleasure sizzling through her body. His fingers kneaded her scalp, his hips thrust forward, and Storme was certain she would explode from the sheer excitement of feeling his pleasure as she gave it.

It made her own pleasure rise higher, made her hotter, wetter, more desperate to feel him inside her.

A ragged cry pulled at her throat as he pulled back, forcing her to release him as he jumped from the bed. He shed his clothing quickly. Boots, pants, they dropped to the floor, leaving him gloriously naked as he came back to her, pushing her to the bed as he hovered over her.

His thighs spread hers, his fingers tested her readiness once again before Storme felt the heavy press as the wide head of his cock parted the folds of her pussy.

Instantly, hunger flooded through her. She thought she had wanted, that she had ached before. It was nothing compared to the need assailing her now. The muscles of her vagina flexed and shuddered as he began parting her. Slow and easy, he began working the heavy flesh inside, stretching and burning her as Storme felt a wash of dizzying euphoria begin to overtake her.

It was pleasure and pain. A burning, exquisite ecstasy that began to rise and build inside her with each inch that penetrated her.

Storme felt the width of the crest pushing inside her, the throb of it, a spurt of heat and then a blinding wildfire of pure pleasure racing through her.

Arching, she tried to drive him further as she felt her pussy clenching, milking the head of his cock as her juices flowed around it.

It was incredible. Blinding, delicious heat unlike anything she could have imagined as she gasped and stared up at him in dazed wonder.

"Styx," she whispered his name on a sob. "Oh God. What are you doing to me?"

"Loving you, lass." His voice was so deep, so filled with tenderness that for a moment, fear almost overwhelmed the sensations.

"What are you doing to me?" she asked again. Was this normal? She had never known anything like this, never felt anything like it.

Her thighs opened wider, knees bending, legs lifting until they cradled his hips, opening herself further to him as her hands smoothed down his biceps and back again. The muscles were tight beneath her touch, sweat sheening his face as she stared up at him.

"Giving you pleasure, Sugar," he crooned as he smoothed dampened strands of her hair back from her cheek. "Just pleasure, love."

"I was cold," she whispered, wondering where the hell those words had come from and why they were escaping her lips now.

His gaze flared. "Are ye cold now, lass?" His voice was strained as she felt his cock move deeper, felt it throbbing tight and hard as her pussy strained to accommodate him then relaxed marginally as another deep, heated pulse of semen ejaculated inside her.

A sob tore from her throat as the pleasure built, as the need for more began to throb inside her. It was like fingers of flames burning across the sensitive flesh.

"I'm not cold now." She could feel the whimper in her voice, feel too many emotions, too many fears threatening to flood her as with one final thrust he buried deep inside her.

"Styx." A sob jerked from her. "Don't let me think."

It was there, the threat of reality returning to steal this moment from her as the fear threatened to return.

These sensations were too unusual, too hot and striking too deep inside her pussy.

"No thinking allowed, Sugar. Sweet, sweet little lass. No thinking allowed in my arms."

And he wasn't lying.

Tucking her closer against him, he began to move again, thrusting strong and deep, as though each impalement was an exercise in restraint and control. His hips shifted, moved, worked his cock inside her, filled her and opened her until he was moving with harder, stronger strokes.

Storme wrapped her legs around his hips, her head pressing back into the bed, her nails digging into his flesh as the first cry tore from her.

He was fucking into her as though the hunger had the same hold on him that it had on her. As though he shared the pleasure-pain sensations and they were imprisoning him, locking inside him as they were inside her.

Each stroke pushed her higher, dug deeper inside her until she was crying out his name, her hips writhing beneath him as the need for release began to torment her, to claw at her womb and shudder through her pussy.

Each thrust raked his pelvis against her clit, stroking that little bud closer to release as she cried out his name and fought to find an anchor while ecstasy began to overwhelm her.

It was a hopeless battle. There was no anchor, no way to hold herself to the earth as her orgasm began to overtake her. Each hard thrust stroked her higher, driving deep as he fucked her faster, harder, a growl tearing from his throat and igniting that last flame that struck the fuel of rapture.

Storme felt herself explode. She felt that first strike of agonizing sensation before it overtook her and threw her so high, so hard, into a maelstrom of pure heat that she lost all concept of right and wrong, reality and fantasy.

She felt him above her, thrusting, heard him groaning, and a second later the heat of his release as it burned through her pussy and pushed her higher.

The sensations felt never ending, spearing through her, exploding in her clit, her pussy, across her nerves, and finally hitting her brain with a surge of the pure fiery waves of pleasure.

A hard, desperate throb in his shaft echoed through her flesh, as though his cock were pulsing, threatening to swell harder, wider insider her. The pleasure of that additional pulse against the sensitive walls of her pussy became almost overwhelming.

It was a good thing breathing was natural, because anything that took thought was impossible. Anything but riding the waves of rapture wasn't happening.

And when it was over, she collapsed beneath him, snuggled against his heat, and let another need have her.

Exhaustion.

Satiation.

Warmth.

She just wanted to sleep in his arms now.

"Ahh, lass," he whispered as his lips touched her shoulder, his voice filled with regret. "My sweet Storme. If only the world were different . . ."

CHAPTER 3

She was caught.

Storme sat in the sitting room glaring at Styx as Breeds filled the room. The contents of her duffel bag were spread out on the table, every item in it thoroughly examined by the Breeds that had arrived after she dressed.

Styx stood to the side of the room, his arms crossed over his chest as he watched her with an inquisitive expression. As though he were trying to figure out a particular problem.

Lips thinned, anger burning inside her, she stared back at him.

He had played her. Him, Navarro, Rule, Lawe, and Jonas Wyatt.

She turned her gaze to Wyatt.

She'd never seen him dressed as he was now, all in black, weapons strapped to his thigh, his eerie silver eyes so hard, so cold they were deadly. Of all the Breeds Storme had fought to avoid over the years, the director of the Bureau of Breed Affairs was almost at the top of her list. He was damned scary.

Perhaps Styx was scarier though. He'd managed to get

beneath her defenses, to play the perfect game without once arousing her suspicions. And she could be a damned suspicious person.

Hands clasped tight in her lap, she tried to think, to force her brain past the exhaustion and fear to find a way to escape. There had to be a way to escape; she had always found one before.

Admittedly, she hadn't allowed herself to be in this position before though. In the ten years she had been running, since she was a young, tender, fourteen, never had she allowed herself to be surrounded by Breeds.

Now here she was, no weapons, no way out, and she was surrounded.

"I want the data chip."

She flinched at the sound of Wyatt's voice. It was razor sharp, cutting, and merciless.

"People in hell want ice water too," she sneered back at him. "You're going to get about as lucky as they are in your wants."

"You don't want to fuck with me over this, Ms. Montague." The latent violence in his tone had the hairs at the back of her neck rising.

"I'll tell you what I've told you for the past ten years, I don't have your data chip."

Two factions chased her. The Bureau Breeds and the Council Breeds, and to look at them, it was impossible to tell which was which.

Jonas contacted her often through the old email account of her father's that she checked regularly. It was always the same. When she was ready to give him what he wanted, then he could protect her.

Her answer was always the same. She didn't have what he wanted.

It seemed he was tired of playing nice.

"Ms. Montague, the time for lies is over." The growl in his voice was frankly terrifying.

As he stepped toward her, Styx moved as well. His action surprised her. It appeared as if he was placing himself in line to protect her against what might well be the most powerful Breed in the world at the moment.

Jonas's gaze flashed to the Wolf Breed. "She's not yours," he bit out, his tone icy.

"Doesn't matter," Styx growled back. "I pulled her in, I'm responsible for her."

A mocking smile curled her lips. He had fooled her once; she wouldn't allow him to fool her again. No doubt this fake protection was no more than another game to draw her in.

Jonas glanced back at her. "She doesn't appear to want your protection, Styx."

Storme sat up straighter. "By all means, Styx, protect me." Mocking and sweet, Storme kept her tone even, hoping to hide the fear rising inside her.

His gaze flashed back to her, irate and glittering with a warning.

"She knows what she has, Styx," Jonas growled back as he stared back at Storme. "She knows, and she's holding on to it for a reason."

Because she had sworn she would hold on to it. Because it was the only thing her father had ever asked her to do. To protect that information.

"I'm not holding anything . . ."

"Breeds can smell a fucking lie," Jonas snarled back. "And you, Ms. Montague, are lying. Tell me what the fuck you want for it and we can conclude this piece of business before the night is over."

She had always known she couldn't lie to their faces. She was too aware of what she was holding, too aware of the fact that their sense of smell would betray her.

There was no doubt Jonas Wyatt was enraged at this moment as well. It was there in every controlled inch of his body, in the glitter of his silver eyes.

"Storme, this has gone beyond whatever you believe you're protecting that information for," Styx stated quietly. "We can protect you, but we have to have the data chip."

"So you fucked me for it?" she sneered with a harsh

laugh. "Tell me, Styx, are you one of those Breeds that were trained to be gigolos for the Council?"

His gaze narrowed, and for just a second she could have sworn she saw a flash of confusion mix with the anger that ignited in his gaze.

"Are you one of those humans that believes we're nothing but animals that don't deserve to live?" Jonas accused her, the rabid fury in his voice at odds with the cool control she knew he was famous for.

She didn't flinch, she didn't cower back in her chair, but God she wanted to. She did flinch though as Styx jumped between her and Jonas, a fierce Wolf's snarl vibrating from his throat.

"Back off, Jonas!"

Navarro moved slowly into position to jump between the two Breeds if necessary.

The other Breeds moved behind Jonas, as though flanking him, protecting him.

"I want that chip, Styx," Jonas snapped. "The implications of this have gone beyond one woman's life. Don't doubt for a second I won't do whatever it takes to force what I want from her."

"Jonas, enough."

All eyes turned to the woman who had stepped into the room.

Rachel Broen. "Hell, all we need now are the Breed alphas and a few Council members to complete this little meeting," Storme stated, forcing the mockery in her voice as Rachel stepped forward.

Jonas's assistant and new wife looked concerned as she moved to her husband's side. What Storme saw then had her chest clenching in some emotion she didn't understand.

Jealousy perhaps? Envy? Storme knew whatever it was had regret flaying her and a hunger rising inside her that she couldn't control. An emotional, overriding hunger she didn't understand and refused to look too deeply into.

For a second, the icy fury in Jonas's eyes was replaced

by worry, pain, and a split second of agony that was gone just as quickly as it had come.

His wife walked to him slowly, her gaze focusing on Storme, her navy blue eyes heavy with concern.

"You shouldn't be here, Rachel," he grated, though his hand settled at the small of her back with the utmost gentleness as she neared him.

Rachel Broen was human. There had been several articles in major newspapers about the marriage of the Bureau director and his assistant. The woman had a child if Storme remembered correctly, an infant. There were rumors in the underground anti-Breed networks that Phillip Brandenmore, a silent partner with the Council, had found a way to use this woman's child to get something he wanted.

What Brandenmore had wanted no one seemed to know, but Storme knew what Brandenmore had been doing. He had been trying to replicate a project from the Omega labs and had actually believed the girl would want to see her father's work resurrected.

"It seems that perhaps I should have been here earlier," Rachel said softly. "What are you doing, Jonas, trying to terrify this young woman and fight with one of your best Enforcers?"

There was an edge of chastisement in his wife's voice now, one that had Jonas staring back at Storme with a promise of retaliation.

Yeah, retaliation. She could see who wore the pants in this family, and it sure as hell wasn't Jonas Wyatt. Though the thought was mocking, Storme was still fascinated with it. Rachel wasn't more dominant; it was more that Jonas seemed to be that attuned to his wife, perhaps that much in love?

Could a Breed love? Didn't one have to have a soul to love?

"Ms. Montague." Rachel stepped around her husband, then the hulking form of Styx. "I'm afraid you're going to have to come to Sanctuary . . ."

"Haven." Styx moved between them again as Jonas stepped closer to his wife.

"Sanctuary would be better, Styx," Jonas stated harshly. "We can sneak her easily into the underground cells . . ."

"The hell you will. She goes to Haven," Styx stated again. "She goes with me."

"She's not yours, Styx," Jonas stated again.

At this point, enough was enough. "I'm not a bone between an oversized cat and dog," she informed them all bitterly. "Why don't I just settle this little argument myself? I'll just be going on my merry way if you all don't mind."

She rose from the chair, until Styx turned so suddenly she came to a hard stop. Hands braced on the arms of the chair to hold herself up, she stared up at him in surprise.

His expression wasn't furious, but rather so dominant and intense she sat back down in her chair slowly. A primal sense of self-preservation seemed to kick in. It wasn't the same warning sense that kicked in when she knew she was dealing with a dangerous animal. It was different.

"Maybe I'll just wait a minute," she stated calmly.

"Maybe you'll get ready to take another ride," he stated, his voice harsh. "We're going to Haven."

"She's needed at Sanctuary, Styx," Jonas argued again. "We have to have that data chip."

"Then it seems you'll be coming to Haven for a while," Styx stated.

The brogue was gone. There was no accent, no tonal shifts.

Jonas's jaw clenched as Rachel turned back to him. "We'll go to Haven, Jonas."

"Like hell," Jonas growled. "Rachel, this isn't the plan."

"Then it appears the plan is changing," Styx informed him coolly before turning to the other Breeds. "Get her stuff together. I'll be transporting her to Haven. Navarro, get the Range Raider ready to roll and have one of the wolves outside pick up my cycle."

"My, aren't we the dominant Breed here." Crossing one knee over the other, Storme smiled back at Styx mockingly. "Why bother, Styx? You performed well. You captured the dangerous little girl, you can run back home now, little Wolf. I don't care to take a trip to Sanctuary. I hear the Felines can be very sociable when they want to be."

Sanctuary had its vulnerabilities, ones she was aware of and knew hadn't been detected by the Breeds. A vulnerability such as a hidden exit built into those underground cells. An exit she knew Brandenmore was slowly being maneuvered close to by a Council Breed spy in Sanctuary.

Styx's lip lifted in a silent snarl as a flash of blue fire lit his gaze.

"Ms. Montague, antagonizing Styx isn't the route I would take," Rachel advised her softly. "This situation will become difficult enough for you . . ."

"She isn't his," Storme heard Jonas mutter.

"What is it with this 'his' crap? Sorry, guys, last I heard this was a free country and I'm not a Breed. I pretty much belong to myself. Right?" She was fighting back the fear.

Anger and mockery were always her defenses against that fear, but this time it wasn't working as it usually did. There was something about the look, the wary caution in the Breeds as well as Rachel's eyes, that warned her that this situation could become even more serious than she imagined.

"It doesn't matter what he means, and freedom, Sugar, is an illusion. You haven't been free a day in your life and you're not going to be free until this is over." Styx watched her with cool purpose as he spoke, determination echoing in his voice.

Her freedom was an illusion?

She stared at the Breeds, at Rachel. "So what am I, Mr. Wyatt, another of your little pets like Dr. Amburg and Phillip Bradenmore? Do you think there aren't those who are aware of the fact that you're holding them?"

Jonas's eyes narrowed.

"It doesn't matter what anyone is aware of," Styx snapped. "It doesn't change the fact that you're coming back to Haven with me until we have this little problem resolved."

"You call this a problem?" Storme laughed in disbelief. "We've far surpassed the problem stage here. You are not kidnapping me."

Styx's brows lifted. "I believe that's exactly what we're doing, Storme. Kidnapping you. You let yourself be caught, and that tells me all I need to know about the fact that you can no longer protect yourself. I've been chasing that pretty ass of yours for more than two years, did you truly think I didn't know everything there was to know about you, right down to your very unique scent?"

She could feel herself shaking, feel the shuddering realization of what he was saying striking to the very heart of her.

She had known Styx Mackenzie was chasing her several months, perhaps a year, before, but she hadn't realized it had been for two years. Someone was always chasing her, always right behind her, waiting to pounce, but she'd always known who they were before, whether they were Breeds or Council soldiers—until Styx.

And still, she had played right into his hands, just as he said. For the first time in ten years, she hadn't protected herself as she should have.

"Ms. Montague, you have information that is imperative to the Breeds," Rachel stated then, compassion and determination in equal measure filling her gaze. "Information that could possibly save my child. Trust me, Jonas isn't going to allow you to escape, and neither will anyone at Haven until they have that data chip. There is no other option but to relinquish it."

"I don't have it," she lied again. She would always lie.

She had no idea what was on that chip. She had never been able to break the encryption on it, no matter how hard she tried. What she did know was that whoever was supposed to collect it had never found her.

She couldn't fail her father. He and her brother had died to protect whatever was on the chip. They had died to save her, so she could protect it.

And she had lived a life of hell ever since.

"And once again, I'm calling her a liar," Jonas's voice was deeper now as he broke into her thoughts, the latent edge of danger in it causing the hairs to rise at the back of her neck.

"The Range Raider's ready, Styx," Navarro stated as the

tension began to grow ever higher in the room. "Haven's Enforcers are waiting outside the hotel ready to escort you and Ms. Montague as well as the director and his wife back to Haven."

Navarro. Storme focused on him. She remembered him well, the pack leader of the Wolf Breeds in the Omega labs.

"You just couldn't stop until you tracked me down, could you, Navarro?" she stated quietly.

"Hello, Storme." There was no warmth in his voice, though she would have never expected any. She knew him, she had seen him, she had feared him. "As the director said, you've been given every opportunity to resolve this yourself."

"Let's go." Styx's fingers curled around her arm to pull her from the chair before the ready retort could pass her lips.

"Styx, this is a mistake," Jonas advised him as Storme was forced to her feet. "Don't make the same mistake Mercury did when he was younger. You can't try to claim what isn't yours."

She stared back at Styx, a vague suspicion pricking at her mind. They couldn't be talking about that damned mating fever the Council had been warning the pure blood societies was true, could they? Surely not. There were symptoms of that. She didn't have symptoms, did she?

"This has nothing to do with one of your Lion Enforcers, Jonas," Styx stated, his voice harsh as he tugged Storme behind him. "This has to do with Storme and me, no one else."

"Nothing has anything to do with us," she promised him as she turned to stare over her shoulder at Jonas and Rachel. "Hey, I'm all for Sanctuary. Haven just doesn't sound like my kind of place, ya know?"

Besides, if the mating heat crap was true, she wanted to be as far away as possible from this particular Breed. He already seemed to have found some hidden entrance to emotions she had no idea she could feel. She sure as hell didn't want to risk an even bigger vulnerability.

Besides, there was more information to be had on Sanctuary, security wise. Where Haven was concerned, there was supposedly no weaknesses in their security, no way to escape the almost clandestine atmosphere of the Wolf Breed mountain.

Adding to the security were the Coyote Breeds that inhabited the sharp rise that led into the mountain. Caves were said to be carved into the mountain there, allowing the Coyotes a view that assured constant surveillance of each entrance into the main compound, as well as the compound itself.

Once, Coyotes, all Coyotes, had been the enemy of both Wolf and Feline Breeds. Now certain factions of Coyotes were banding together and joining the side that seemed to be winning in the battle between Breeds and Council supporters.

"Come on." Styx pulled her after him, gently but firmly. The hold on her wrist assured her that she wasn't going to get away easily.

There would be a chance though, she assured herself frantically. There was always a chance, right?

"Go ahead and try to escape," she heard Jonas mutter just behind her. "I dare you."

Fear shook her then, listening to Jonas. On second thought, she didn't dare let herself be forced under his control. Styx would be the far better choice. For the moment. She hoped.

Stepping up, she gripped his arm with her spare hand before casting a wary glance over her shoulder to Jonas's cold, hard-eyed gaze.

There was death in those eyes. The latent fury gleaming beneath silver ice was frankly terrifying.

Perhaps there wouldn't be a chance to escape, yet.

"This is a mistake," she warned Styx as he pressed her into the elevator. "I will escape, Styx."

She couldn't forget how easily he had tricked her, how easily he had played her. She had given herself to him for a few moments of warmth and peace, and now she was truly paying for it.

"You can try." Still no brogue, no warmth. "That's all I can promise you, Storme, is that you can try."

◆　◆　◆

What the hell was going on? Styx kept his expression clear, his temper calm, and that wasn't easy to do. He could feel the animal raging inside, clawing, snarling in fury.

Something wasn't right. The glands at the side of his tongue were irritated, swollen, but only the most minute quantity of the hormone had slipped free. As his release had torn through his cock earlier, he had felt the mating knot pulse in the middle of it, throbbing, the flesh trying to swell outward as his semen jetted inside her. Yet it had never fully emerged.

Beneath his flesh he could feel a low-level hum of electric sensation that he couldn't shake, that he couldn't eradicate.

As though she were almost his mate.

What the fuck was up with that? There was no such thing as an almost mate, was there?

As the service elevator they took came to a stop on the main floor and the doors opened, the Wolf Breed Enforcers waiting outside surrounded them and escorted them to the waiting vehicles.

He could smell Storme's wariness now, her mounting fear. As each second passed with the realization that there was no escape, her desperation was beginning to grow.

Exiting the rear of the hotel, he pushed her quickly into the back of the vehicle before climbing in beside her and hemming her in as Navarro slid in on the opposite side.

There was no escape. No way he could allow it. Jonas was wrong. She did belong to him; it was just that something seemed to be stopping it. He had to find out what that "something" was before he went crazy.

Jonas stood back and helped his mate into the wide seat in front of Styx and Storme. Rachel watched Storme compassionately yet firmly as Jonas slid in beside her.

There was no compassion inside Jonas though. This woman possibly held the answer to the hormone that had been injected into the infant Jonas had claimed as his own, Rachel's child.

Amber was a well-loved, well-protected babe within

Sanctuary now, but months before Brandenmore had managed to outthink Jonas and take Amber as a hostage in exchange for her mother's agreement to steal certain documents from the Bureau.

Jonas had been waiting for Brandenmore's next move when Rachel had shown up, hysterical, bruised, beaten, and terrified that her daughter was being held by one of Jonas's enemies.

While in Brandenmore's less than tender care, Amber had been injected with what at first was thought to be a sedative. Now Jonas was certain there had been something more, despite the Breed scientists' inability to track any problems.

Jonas wasn't paranoid. If he said Brandenmore had somehow managed to inject Amber with something that was as of yet untraceable, then Styx believed him. He was a hard-edged, icy, controlled, dangerous bastard, but nothing in this world mattered to him as much as his mate and child did.

Once, the Breeds had been Jonas's full focus; now that focus had narrowed to two frail human females who held the heart of the silver-eyed bogeyman of the Breeds in the palms of their hands.

Since his mating, Jonas had become more dangerous, more determined to ensure their safety and security. At the moment, learning the truth of Project Omega, Jonas was certain, was all that could save his child.

Beside him, Styx felt a shudder, barely restrained, as it moved up Storme's spine.

She was moving past the anger now, and fear was turning to terror. He could feel it, scent it, just as Jonas could.

"Ms. Montague, no harm is going to befall you." The words seemed pushed between Jonas's gritted teeth, as though he hated admitting she had nothing to fear. "But you will not know freedom, or even your perception of freedom, again, until I have what I want."

Rather than stilling her fear, it only seemed to agitate it.

Rachel laid her hand on her mate's tense arm.

"Let her be, Jonas," she said softly, regretfully. "As you said before, she's spent ten years being terrorized by Coyotes and the few remaining Feline and Wolf Breeds that the Council controls. She won't overcome that hurdle overnight."

"Try never," Storme sneered as that fear began to fill the air of the vehicle. "I saw how compassionate and merciful Breeds were the night my father and brother died."

"Your father and brother had every chance at safety for months before those rescues, with or without their fucking secrets," Jonas snapped. "I extended to them the offer of rescue for your father as well as his son and daughter, and he refused. He was unable to walk away from the research that meant so much more to both of them than you did."

She flinched. For a moment, the scent of her confusion was so strong he knew it must be strangling her.

"Enough, Jonas," Styx warned him again. " Give her a chance to see she's safe."

"And if we don't have the time for that?" Jonas questioned him with icy disdain. "Excuse me for not having your exacting patience, Wolf."

"You're forgiven." It was Storme who bit out the words as she glared back at the Bureau director. "And there is no convincing me to give you something that isn't mine to give."

She wasn't lying. Oh, she had that data chip, but she truly believed it wasn't hers to give, that something prevented her from using it to secure her safety.

"Eventually, you will," Jonas assured her. "If for no other reason than to escape the pure fucking insanity that often resides in Haven. You would have been smarter to demand a bit more forcefully to be taken to Sanctuary, rather than entering the Wolf Breed lunacy."

Her head turned sharply, as though in surprise, as she stared back at Styx. Obviously she hadn't heard that Haven could actually be enjoyable.

"We just have more fun," Styx assured her as he shot Jonas a fulminating look. "Felines seem to have a more restrained concept of entertainment than wolves have."

Jonas grunted at that, as Rachel sighed heavily.

Jonas's mate was growing used to this argument, Styx was certain.

"I think you're all missing vital mental genetics myself," Storme stated, as though there wasn't a latent quiver in her voice. "But then, you've proven that over and over in the past years as you tracked me."

"As we protected you." Jonas leaned forward then, the danger that hummed through his system placing the animal inside Styx on instant alert. "Do not be in doubt, Ms. Montague, had we known the importance of the information you carried, then I would have been sure to capture you years ago rather than believing you would come to your senses and accept our protection over the Council's certain torture."

"Well weren't you wrong." Storme was almost nose to nose with Jonas before Styx gripped her shoulder and pushed her back against the leather seat.

"Enough," Styx ordered both of them as Rachel merely shook her head in resignation. "She's not ready to believe you, Jonas."

"She'll never be ready." She tried to jerk out of his grip as she glared back at him and spoke of herself in the third person with mocking emphasis. "And she won't make the same mistake again where you're concerned."

He smiled back at her, knowing there would be no comfort in the curve of his lips or the flash of the canines at the side of his mouth.

Oh, she would indeed return to his bed very soon. He had no idea what the hell was holding back the mating heat, the biological bonding of a Breed and his or her mate, but something was definitely blocking it.

She was his woman, the one woman he had thought he never wanted to meet until Dr. Armani had come to him with the results of the mating tests she had done with the blood the Council had taken while Storme was in the labs. He hadn't truly known possessiveness, though, until he held her in his arms and realized there was something holding back the natural progression of claiming her.

He wouldn't allow it for long. Whatever the problem was, he could feel the clawing fury of the animalistic genetics that lurked just below the surface of the human male whose appearance he had.

His gaze slid back to Storme as he felt her breathing deepen, roughen. She was terrified, and that knowledge had his fingers curling as he fought to keep from clenching them in fury.

His woman was fighting to hold on to her control because of fear of him, of Breeds. She didn't trust him to protect her, to hold the danger at bay whether she gave up her secrets or not.

There wasn't a force on Earth that could convince him to give her over to danger simply because she did not obey Jonas's dictates. Nothing short of death would change his determination to protect her.

"Don't do this," she suddenly whispered, turning back to him, her gaze imploring as the vehicle made the turn out of town and headed along the back country road to the mountainous compound of Haven. "Let me go, Styx."

"Give us what we want, and we'll let you go, Storme," Jonas answered for him, likely sensing that at the moment Styx couldn't possibly force that lie past his lips.

She shook her head. "I can't."

But she could. And she would lie about it until hell froze over, or until the Council scientists or soldiers forced the information from her, Styx thought wearily.

Whatever had happened the night her father and brother died had forever altered any trust Styx might have had a chance at inspiring where the Breeds were concerned in Storme's eyes.

She had been raised among them, but she hadn't seen the horror of their lives, she had instead seen the horrors of what they could be, Navarro had once told him. She was brought into the labs and allowed only into training areas, or the cells where the most violent of the Breeds were kept for research and experimentation.

During the rescue of that lab, it was suspected that Coyote Breeds had killed JR and James Montague, possibly as Storme watched from some hidden point. Jonas was certain she must have seen it, based on the terror his Enforcers had scented on her each time they or Council Coyotes became close.

Styx would have to fight that fear to get to the bottom of the reasons why the mating heat seemed to be blocked between them. This was a problem he hadn't thought of. Hell, as far as he knew, this had never happened before. Never had a mate not been mated, yet his wasn't.

He hadn't wanted a mate. He hadn't been ready for one until he'd realized he could claim her.

Now he was determined, no matter what it took, no matter the lies he had to tell, that she would be his mate.

Leaning back, forcing himself to allow her a few fragile inches of space, he gave her what he knew was a convincing, charming grin.

"Lass," he said, forcing the brogue back into his voice. "Such stubbornness is endearing and, I must say, sexy as hell."

She stared back at him in disbelief as Jonas and Rachel narrowed their gazes on him.

"Sexy?" Confusion filled her voice.

"Aye, sexy as hell," he promised her. "I verra much look forward to seducing those secrets from you. Verra verra much."

Her eyes widened, and the terror rose and ebbed several times before he caught the faintest hint of feminine heat flavoring her scent.

He wouldn't let her forget the pleasure he had given her. He wouldn't let her forget the safety she found in his arms, nor would he allow her to resist the hunger he knew lay between them. A hunger that raged just beneath the surface and threatened to burn out of control if mating heat ever took its grip on them.

She would be his, or he would give up his chocolate for life.

Unfortunately, he feared that if his mate had her way, he might be giving up his chocolate.

As the Range Raider pulled into the receiving entrance

of Haven, they pulled to a stop several feet from the light utility vehicles used within the main grounds.

Gripping Storme's arm, Styx helped her from the Raider and steered her firmly toward the lighter security vehicles. It was then his wee little mate did something he had to admit he hadn't expected, though he should have. They were at the entrance to Haven, the gates swinging open, Breeds guarding them, the flicker of lights beyond drawing his gaze. Behind them was the freedom Storme felt was her only salvation.

A salvation she wasn't yet ready to see for the illusion it was.

With a graceful twist and arc, she broke the hold he had on her arm, pulled his weapon from its holster and had it trained on his face.

Breeds moved into position silently, the click of weapons suddenly the only sound in the night as he gazed into the desperate, fear-ridden gaze glittering within her paper white face.

He looked from her to the weapon, before shaking his head in regret. "Good night, lass."

In the next breath, she crumpled in his arms, the weapon falling to the ground as he caught her. Lifting the slight burden into his arms, he gazed into the trees beyond.

He didn't see the shadowed Breeds there, he didn't see the tranquilizer that pierced the back of her neck. He had the proof they were there though, in the now sleeping form of the young woman he held in his arms, and the knowledge that she would risk certain death to escape him.

It was a hell of a position to find himself in.

• C H A P T E R 4 •

Styx stood just inside the bedroom door while Dr. Nikki Armani, the fierce, often irritable Wolf Breed expert geneticist and physician completed her examination of the young woman, as the sun began to rise over the cabin he owned within the Wolf Breed community.

He, a Wolf Breed, created to kill and to die painfully, owned a cabin. His name was on the deed. He, who hadn't been created to have even a name that he could lay claim to, claimed this cabin, a vehicle, a bank account and clothing.

And here he stood, watching as a woman slept in a bed he had never brought another woman to, and he found that the possessiveness he had once thought he felt about that bed was noticeably absent.

Styx had detected the low-grade infection from the weeks-old wound on her ankle as he held her in the hotel bed. He'd noticed the scratches on her arms and shoulders, the bruises on her ribs. The proof that the past weeks of running had taken a toll on her health.

She hadn't been eating well, she hadn't slept enough. She was on the point of exhaustion, and if he hadn't taken her when he had, then there would have been no way she could have continued to outrun the Coyotes the Genetics Council had sent for her.

"I wish I could kill every fucking Council member, soldier and scientist that was a part of this," Nikki cursed as she cleaned a particularly nasty scratch on Storme's hip. "Bastards. She's run herself to exhaustion."

"How's she doin', Doc?" he finally asked when the doctor gently tucked a quilt around her shoulders.

"She'll sleep for a while longer." Nikki tossed back the riot of heavy black braids that fell from her head to her shoulders as she rose and turned to him. "I've taken the blood and saliva samples, but until she's conscious I refuse to take the vaginal swabs I need to figure out what the hell is going on with the mating." She cast him a confused look. "I've never heard of a mating as you've described, Styx. I'm not comfortable even guessing the problem here."

Solemn dark brown eyes gleamed within the café au lait creaminess of her flesh as she gave a heavy sigh and began collecting the vials of samples and storing them in the heavy-duty medical case she carried with her. The medical case held samples of his own—enough blood, saliva swabs and vials of semen to create a little Styx army, he thought mockingly.

Lord love a Wolf, he'd known this woman was trouble the minute Jonas had given him the assignment to track her. When Nikki had called him back to Haven to inform him of the results of the mating tests she'd done on the girl, she had only confirmed it.

"Is there any way to fix this, Doc?" he asked on a heavy sigh, as he restrained the urge to shift the heavy erection beneath the jeans he'd changed into.

He was so damned hard his cock throbbed in near agony.

Nikki propped her hands on her hips and gazed back down at Storme for long seconds.

"I don't know, Styx," she finally sighed. "Until I do some tests and consult with the other scientists working on this, I hesitate to even guess."

Styx grimaced. "I think I'd rather face a pit of rattlers, Doc, than suffer this much longer."

It was a well-known fact within Haven that Styx hated snakes. Viperous, poisonous bastards, the mountain seemed overrun with them at times.

Styx could think of far better ways to torture himself than with an arousal that refused to relent. Though he couldn't blame it all on the mating heat. Truth be told, he'd stayed hard for the wee lass since the day he'd first caught sight of her.

With all that black hair flowing around her, those wary green eyes searching the shadows where he hid and the weariness in her too somber expression had tugged at him. He'd wanted to hold her even then. To protect her, to ease the pain he could sense just beneath the surface. Hell, what sin was he paying for, he wondered, that had nature playing this little joke at his expense? Hadn't he been a good Wolf? He'd always strived to excel, whether in killing or in loving. Yet still his mate didn't carry his mark, and the Wolf inside him was snarling in impatience.

He'd give his rather impressive canines for that brand to be in place as it should be now. For her silken flesh to be flushed in arousal, the heat of the mating making her wet and eager for his possession.

Storme Montague was his mate. She was his. The one and only woman who completed that part of him that he hadn't known hungered for such a thing.

He hadn't imagined how important it could become until he had tasted her kiss, felt her touch, and found his release in the tight, sweet grip of her silky pussy.

"I can smell your impatience and I'm not even a Breed," Nikki said, accusing him lightly. "I'll tell you what I've told the others. I've never seen mating heat react the same on any two couples. It's an anomaly, Styx. Nature is refining as she goes, and we're just going to have to deal with it. You're mating heat just may be particularly complicated, likely because of your odd genetics." She grimaced.

Complicated didn't come close, he thought with an edge of anger.

"Last I heard, lass, I was a red Wolf mixed with some fine Scots blood. Do you know something aboot my genetics the good scientists neglected to mention?"

Nikki rolled her eyes. "Of course, learning that those genetics come from one of history's greatest warriors shouldn't concern us, should it?"

He winked back at her. "One of history's greatest lovers as well, I've heard."

She snorted at that. "Watch it, Red, or I'll see if I can't mess up those fine genetics for you."

He winked flirtatiously. "You can play with my genetics any day, Doc. When are ye wantin' to start?"

At the moment, he'd much rather tease, flirt, or face those snakes than face the complications of the hard-on throbbing in his jeans.

She shook her head before her eyes did a quick, mocking roll.

"Styx, keep it up and I'm going to begin to suspect there's more human DNA in your mix than Wolf." She chided him with a tired smile before indicating the medical case, a gesture that told the assistant who accompanied her to collect everything so they could head out.

"Ah, Nikki my love," he sighed. "Such insults to my fair self. Have ye ever known a human that could compare to my rather rare talents?" He shot her a quick grin as he stepped back from the doorway to allow her to pass him.

His talents were indeed rare. His father's genetics mixed with those of the historic Robert the Bruce had created a true Scots warrior, but it had been a fine friend of his father's who had trained him in a nearly extinct, deadly form of martial arts.

His martial training had been secretive, and conducted under the good Dr. Mackenzie's eagle eye. After all, Styx and several of his litter mates had been created using the sperm and DNA of Mackenzie's dead son, and he considered them all part of his blood. So much so that he had risked death himself several times to ensure not just their safety but also their well-being.

"Chocolate-eating Breeds are a dime a dozen, Red," she quipped as she paused in the large open living area and grinned back at him. "Or do you possess talents outside of breaking into the alpha's cabins to steal their mates' chocolate?"

She damned well knew he did. Styx laughed at the apparent insult though, knowing the good doctor meant more jest than harm.

She knew the truth of his training, just as she knew he had been trained to gain information, no matter the method used to unlock the secrets.

Seduction was but one of the games he knew to attain what he wanted. There were other ways, other calculations, other routes to twist a woman's emotions and desires until a Breed gained what he had been sent for.

"That they are, love," he agreed with her. "But, ones such as I are so rare as to be all but nonexistent."

"And they need to stay nonexistent," she reminded him. "Watch yourself with her, Styx. Unlike many of your playmates, she just may know more than any of us are comfortable with. Or much less than Jonas could hope. She's dangerous to us either way, and I'm afraid the reason the mating isn't fully present could be the fact that you suspect she can't be trusted."

Styx shook his head. That wasn't the problem and he knew it.

"I believe it's because of her." He nodded to his slumbering mate. "Perhaps the heat, the animalistic qualities of it are more than she can handle at present, Doc. She's terrified."

"She wants to be terrified." Nikki shrugged. "She knows not all Breeds are like those who killed her family, Styx. But for whatever reason she can't let go of that disc. Perhaps she uses the fear to rationalize that. A lot of our female Breeds still have that problem where socializing is concerned. They can't let go of the enforced training that punished them for it."

There were many of them, males as well as female Breeds, who had problems rising above that conditioning.

Laughter, socializing, emotion had been heavily punishable offenses in the labs.

"She could be dangerous to us, Styx," Nikki warned him. "Be careful. You've claimed her. If she betrays Haven, then her punishment could be yours as well."

That was the law, technically. Though Styx knew that if his mate betrayed Haven in a manner that meant she was sentenced to die, then he would die himself trying to protect her.

She was worth the risk, he told himself. The hint of a smile he'd caught on her face the night before, the scent of gentle laughter she'd tried to hide. It was all worth it.

"But if life were lived without dangers, what adventures would we then find?" he asked Nikki as he tilted his head and stared back at her seriously. "I'll take the adventures any day, as well as the risks."

"No doubt you would." Nikki shook her head, the tiny braids swinging past her shoulders as she chided him gently. "You're too wild, Styx. Much too wild. You should discuss that with your grandfather."

His grandfather. His creator. What-the-fuck-ever, Styx thought with a hint of cynicism. His grandfather was the man who had dreamed of bringing back the dead, only to learn the value of allowing the dead to rest in peace.

"Call me if you need me." Nikki lifted her hand as her assistant opened the door and stepped from the cabin. "I'll send some vitamins and more antibiotics once I get to the office. Now let her rest. No sexual hijinks until she's stronger."

Styx grunted at the order before moving with Nikki through the cabin to the front door.

Closing the door behind her, he didn't bother to lock it just yet. It was something he rarely did, preferring instead to face the challenge that if Haven did possess spies, as Sanctuary did, they would take the dare to enter his home.

Life could be lived to the fullest or he could hide and worry himself bald about the security he felt Breeds would never know. Styx preferred to live, and he was going to have to teach his mate to do the same.

Leaning against the door frame as he stared at the

fragile form beneath the quilts that covered his bed, watching her, he wondered, not for the first time, how he had managed to end up in a situation such as this.

Almost mated? He snorted at the thought and wondered who the hell to blame for it.

He finally decided on Jonas Wyatt, the infuriating director of the Bureau of Breed Affairs who had given him the job of tracking the wee lass down. No doubt, the interfering bastard was practicing his matchmaking habits again. His Enforcers swore he did it deliberately.

He crossed his arms over his chest, tilted his head and pursed his lips as he considered the benefits of his investigation into an almost mating with his courageous little mate.

One damned thing was certain, he'd not be bored.

Not that he was often bored. There'd been a whole world out there to investigate and to enjoy before he found her. He had a feeling she would challenge him far more than the world ever had though.

Moving into the bedroom, he checked her temperature, tucked the blankets around her again and gazed down at her sleeping face.

She looked at peace for a change.

The tranquilizer she had been shot with hadn't been a powerful one, but the exhaustion and physical weakness had taken their toll on her.

He was betting this was this first decent sleep she'd had in years.

"She's damned pretty."

Styx swung around, his weapon clearing the holster on instinct even as he realized who spoke behind him. He cursed his apparent absorption with his mate, and accepted it at the same time, and blamed it for the fact that he hadn't heard his "grandfather" slip into the cabin.

"You're gonna get yourself killed, my friend," he informed him as he holstered the weapon just as quickly.

A single gray brow lifted as mocking amusement filled Dougal Mackenzie's expression. "I hear there's some question of the mating?" he asked as he entered the bedroom.

"I met Nikki outside. She seems to think the mating heat is reacting to a distrust you have of the girl?"

Hell, the old man was going to nosy. That was just what he needed.

"Don't you have your own mate to worry about?" Styx grunted. He was still damned uncomfortable with the fact that his biological grandfather had mated one of the older Wolf Breed females.

Not that there were many of them. Animera had been in her forties when the lab she had been created in, in France, had been liberated. The small facility had housed four Breeds, all females, that were once trained and used as whores for the Council.

Animera was as beautiful as any Breed, though harder than many. Once she had met Dougal, that stony outer shell had cracked though, and the woman hiding within had emerged.

They were a good match, yet watching the man who called himself Styx's "grandfather" becoming younger as the years wore on was damned uncomfortable.

The mating phenomenon was complicated, confusing and had the potential to destroy the Breeds, especially if Dougal's unique reaction to it were ever learned.

"You're staring at me as though I'm a freak again," Dougal snapped. "Don't let's turn this into yelling match, boy."

Styx grunted. "I don't have time for you today." He moved to the door and motioned Dougal to the living room.

"Doesn't surprise me," Dougal grunted. "Ye've not had time for me since Animera and I mated."

Styx grimaced as he headed for the kitchen and the coffee. This man who had created him, called himself his grandfather and insisted on interfering in his life had the ability to make him damned nervous.

"I've been busy," he lied without so much as a twinge of guilt.

Dougal snorted at the excuse. "Ye've been runnin'. What makes ye so damned uncomfortable around me now, boy? The fact that I'm happy for a change?"

"The fact that in the past eight years you seem to have regressed in age a good ten?" Styx questioned him mockingly. "Sorry, Pops, I guess I'm just not used to it. It throws a mon off just a wee bit." Dougal ignored the comment. This was the way of every argument they had. Styx couldn't explain why he was having problems with it, he just knew he was. Give it another six to ten years and his grandfather would look more like his brother.

"I'm sending after the equipment we hid in Scotland," Dougal said then, changing the subject. "Animera and I will be settin' a lab up here to aid Dr. Armani. The equipment we hid is more specialized, some of the technology more advanced than what Vanderale and Lawrence Industries have been providing. I'd like to see if we can't do more to figure out the problem of conception with the Wolf Breeds."

"Perhaps we weren't meant to conceive," Styx growled as he turned to glare at the other man. "The Feline mates conceive fine without help. Hell, they need birth control rather than conception aids. Let nature figure it out herself."

"You don't have the luxury of time, Styx," Dougal retorted, as he had in the past.

"Then we'll make the luxury."

Styx shrugged. Hell, he didn't want to argue over this. He wanted to curl up in the bed with his mate and warm her, to ensure she was never cold again.

"That may not be possible," Dougal warned him, his tone far too somber now. "My contacts within the Council Directorate's ranks called this morning. The Coyote they had chasing her was found in his hotel room this morning, dead. He'd been shot in the back of the head. The weapon used was the same the Montague girl used last month when she wounded one of their soldiers. They're assembling a team to find her."

The bastard had been executed. It served Farce right, and Styx was pretty certain Dog had been the executioner.

"Any word on where they're concentrating their search?" Styx asked.

Dougal shook his head. "My contact said they're being

damned quiet about it, but they want that girl more now than they did a month ago."

They were more careful now. The Directorate ensured that they were never in any way associated with the Breeds or the trainers and scientists that still worked for their cause. World sentiment was currently strong enough against the Breeds that prison sentences were being passed down on the few that had gone to trial in the past years.

The Directorate was careful, but they were still lethal. The fact that a team had been assembled to bring Storme in worried Styx.

"I'll take care of it," he assured Dougal.

"Be careful, lad," Dougal sighed. "You may be uncomfortable with the fact that we're family, but that's what we are. You and your brothers and sister are still my life. Losing any of you would break my heart."

Dougal stepped closer and much to Styx's consternation wrapped his arms around his shoulders for a quick hug.

"You're important to us as well, dammit." Styx raked his fingers through his hair as he stepped back and glared at him. "Cannot ye keep the mushy stuff for your mate and just continue as we were? Hell, Pops, give her the hugs."

Dougal chuckled at the response. "Ye'll get used to it, lad. Now I'll head to the labs and see what Nikki and I can come up with on your mating problems. She's requesting Amburg's help on this as well; he worked with Wolf Breeds almost as much as the Felines. Between the three of us here and Drs. Morrey and Vanderale at Sanctuary, I believe we'll have this problem solved in no time."

One problem down, God only knew how many more to go, Styx thought irritably as his grandfather left the cabin. Styx had a feeling this problem wouldn't be so easily fixed though. Mating heat and the word "easy" never went hand in hand.

Hell, he didn't need this. Not his grandfather with his youth returning, not Jonas in child protective mode, not all that while he was in the middle of a mating heat that wasn't a mating heat, with a mate who smelled of fear more often than affection.

Hell, he should kill Jonas simply for waiting until he needed the information before pulling Storme into safety. She could have learned, easily, that the Breeds weren't the monsters they were made out to be.

He'd show her that here though. Show her now.

Returning to the kitchen, he pulled the ingredients for dinner out of the freezer. Chicken soup fixed everything, the Felina, the alpha female of the Feline prides, had once assured him. He had a feeling she wasn't talking about a delayed mating heat though.

He stared at the chicken he'd laid in the sink to defrost, turned the water on to flow over it and decided he'd finally found a problem chocolate couldn't fix.

Grinning at the thought, he laid vegetables on the cutting board by the sink, then pulled the chef's knife from the butcher block to begin chopping them.

He was on the first slice when his body tensed, and before he could even consider his actions he raced from the kitchen, out the front door and to the side of the house.

The bedroom window was shattered.

Glass lay spread out on the pristine grass, some tipped with blood, some still lodged and glittering in the long black hair that fell around Storme's features and emphasized those large, fear-ridden emerald green eyes.

She looked like a cat. Lithe, sensual, clawed and hissing.

But she wasn't a cat. She was a Wolf's mate. She was his mate. And by God he was growing tired of her hurting herself, endangering herself and generally refusing to care for her own health.

If this trick was anything to go by, taming her was going to be a full-time job and ensuring her place in Haven wasn't going to be easy.

One thing was for damned certain, she could well see an ass paddling in her future if it didn't come to an end.

Alarms were screaming, and the bud tucked into his ear

began filling with Breed reports even as Styx stared at the fearful vision crouched in front of him.

He felt his stomach clench with rage as a snarl of protective fury burst from his chest. Damn her, he'd not allow her to continue this habit of harming herself. He couldn't bear to see more wounds on her delicate, pale flesh.

"She went out the back window. She's contained and we've only to return her to her room," Styx reported into the sensitive mic attached to the ear bud. "All Enforcers stand down. I repeat, stand down." Weapons were held ready with more Enforcers racing for the area.

The last thing he needed was the circle of Breeds already forming around her, let alone what could happen if more joined.

Terror and shock were vivid on her pale face, her dark green eyes were wild, and her long, straight black hair fanned around her. Her slender body was crouched as his was, facing the Breeds that had slowly begun to surround her.

In her own mind she was a woman facing death.

A woman who would die before walking easily into the monster's embrace again.

And Styx decided in that moment that she would come, and come easily, to his every touch.

⋅ CHAPTER 5 ⋅

She was dead.

Storme remained crouched, her breathing harsh and irregular as she stared back into the clear, amused gaze of the red Wolf casually facing her, his arms crossed over his chest, his blue eyes glittering with irritation. Canines gleamed in the early morning light as long, burnished red hair feathered back in the breeze and tempted her fingers to dig in and grip fingerfuls as she pulled him into her kiss.

She swore she could almost taste his kiss. Chocolate and spice, a hint of coffee and peppermint. The taste of it was on her lips, against her tongue, and she couldn't get rid of it. She'd awakened with the taste of him tormenting her, pushing her to demand more. What she wanted was freedom, she assured herself, not some Breed's kiss.

Not this Breed. Not the possessiveness, the dominance glowing in his gaze.

Savagery reflected in his features. A brutal, too attractive sort of savagery that drew a woman even as her survival instincts kicked in with a scream.

This was the Breed she had slept with, the one that had

given her such pleasure. She'd managed over the years to do a vast amount of research by using the passwords to Council records she'd been able to hack. She knew many of the Breeds by face as well as by their lab reports.

"Styx," she whispered as dread threatened to overwhelm her. She had read that in mythology the word meant "hated," "detested." It was the river of death, and so this Breed was one known for his hatred of humans and his ability to kill in the most painful ways and always with a smile.

If she died, she was going to go down fighting. She would not willingly give this bastard her neck for to rip open.

But shouldn't she have thought of this before she fucked him? Before she gave in to her weakness, gave in to the need to relish his warmth rather than running another night?

"Ah, lass, would ye keep runnin' from me," he crooned, that devil's soft brogue stroking over her feminine senses as every muscle in her body tightened further in the demand that she run.

She wouldn't make it far. There were more than a dozen Breeds surrounding her, all Wolf and Coyote, with the exception of the director of the Bureau of Breed Affairs, who lounged casually at the corner of the cabin.

She swallowed tightly. "Let me leave."

"Give me wha' I want, lass, and the Breeds will give you free passage. I promise this."

And he sounded oh so sincere, but there was something in his gaze, some premonition that warned her he would never let her go so easily.

Styx, the charming Scots red Wolf. He could flow through the night and kill in ways that left his victims screaming long after he had disappeared. Among a very select group of Breed supporters, he was also known as the Scots lover. A man that took physical pleasure to its very limits and left a woman always begging for more.

And damn her, she had known that about him. Known and been intrigued by his reputation. Intrigued enough that she couldn't resist him herself.

And now she was paying for it.

"I don't have what you want." She infused her voice with desperation, lying, though she knew she couldn't completely hide the scent of that lie.

He chuckled, a low, rough sound filled with amusement and patience.

"Then I'm verra verra sorry to say, we'll have to step back into this cabin for a while," he stated as his gaze flicked to the Lion Breed at his side. "Jonas, could ye do me the small favor of having a few bars placed on the windows so the lass can't catapult through them so easily? It distresses me mightily to smell the scent of her blood when she wounds herself."

He gave her a heavy-lashed, wicked look. A look that assured her he wanted her in top physical form for a certain reason.

And damn her, she shouldn't be blushing at the thought of it, or the memory of his touch.

"Well now, Styx, you know how I hate to see you distressed. It will be taken care of within the hour." Jonas Wyatt grinned back at her as she threw him a glare.

There had to be a way out of this. In the past ten years she had escaped every time she had feared she was well and truly caught by either Council or Bureau. Surely there was a way to escape this time as well.

She gazed around desperately, seeing only marked cool purpose on the Breeds' faces, and the lack of an opening to slip through.

This couldn't happen. It couldn't end this way.

She'd awakened from the nightmares of the past. The sight of her brother's throat ripped out, her father begging for mercy, gleaming red eyes and a monster's smile as curved canines descended to her own vulnerable flesh.

She'd awaken, confused, sweating with fear, and the horrible realization that she couldn't escape whatever was happening to her now. Whatever was going to happen to her. The abnormal reaction, the sense of desperation clawed at her throat and left her gasping for air.

"Let me go!" She was surprised by the vehemence and

the desperation that tore through her voice and came out as an agonized scream.

All she could see were those wicked curved canines tearing out her brother's throat. All she could feel was the nightmarish touch of them against her neck and the sensation of her blood spurting, her body growing cold in death.

"Lass, letting you go isna a part of the bargain here." That smile, so charming, so dangerous, had fear cramping her stomach. "So let's be a wee bit reasonable and step into the cabin for a bit o' chocolate coffee and perhaps a bowl of the chicken soup I'm preparing to put on the stove, while we discuss this predicament we find ourselves a part of and perhaps reminisce about the night past."

Storme could do nothing but blink. Every muscle, every nerve and instinct in her body was demanding action, and the killer standing casually in front of her was suggesting chocolate coffee and sex? Had he lost his ever loving Wolf mind?

Did he think this was the Internet where he had yet another groupie fawning over his every abbreviated typed word? That she didn't know the training, the years of blood and death, that had created him?

She had no weapon, there was no way to escape. Her gaze went constantly around the forested area, tracking each Breed surrounding her as she fought to stay in place rather than run in panic.

"Lass, you can see you're not escapin'," he crooned. "Come on now, let's go chat about this. I bet I could even find a brownie or two to occupy us while we sip at the coffee and argue a bit about your present situation."

Oh yeah, a brownie was really going to convince her to just give in and cooperate with her own murder.

"Do I look seven to you? I am not a child to be led to my own murder by a fucking brownie."

Male appreciation filled his gaze then, a hungry glint of lust brightening the sea blue gaze as his grin shifted to one of anticipation.

"I must admit, love, you're no' seven. A lovely grown

woman you are, and I had hoped one that well understood that if you were gonna die, I'd have just taken care of that little job before bringin' you here. Why then would I wait until you awakened, all soft and warm, afore doing the deed?"

She snorted at that, her breathing still rough, panicked. "Because you think I have something you want? Because you know there's not a chance in hell I'll trust you now."

"And why would I kill you now, believin' you have this 'something' that I want?" he asked. "Wouldn't I be inclined to let you live a bit, to give me what I wanted?" His gaze flicked over her breasts, the tops of which were revealed by the low neckline of her T-shirt. "Or perhaps, a bit more." He smiled. A slow, sensual smile that struck at the very core of her sensuality.

Storme sneered back at him. "You don't have a chance. Enjoy the memories because it won't happen again, Wolf boy."

His grin widened. "I don't know, pretty girl, I've been planning the next seductive little session we might have. I'd be bettin' that creamy flesh would take the taste of chocolate as though it had been made for it. Should we give it a try?"

For a second, the image of him licking chocolate from her body flashed through her mind. Decadent dark chocolate that his tongue feasted on, his features twisted in pleasure.

God, she was as sick as every other groupie this bastard Wolf came across.

"Let's say not," she snapped.

The other Breeds should have been distracted, like any other male would be. They should have relaxed their guard and allowed her the second she needed to slip past one of them. Any one of them. She didn't care which.

"Ms. Montague, would it help if I gave you my personal assurance that you're going to come to no harm here?"

Storme's gaze flicked back to the director, Jonas Wyatt. There were rumors of this one as well. The one that had struck deepest was the whispered tale of a volcano and the disappearance of several Breed enemies.

"Made any trips close to volcanoes lately?" She smiled tightly.

His brows merely lifted, as several Breeds behind her chuckled. He remained comfortably propped against the corner of the cabin, his hands in his slacks, the white silk of his shirt stretched across a broad chest.

"Lass, I can see you think our director has a fine chest, but I promise you, I can be a rather possessive Breed, and I know you're rather fond of mine."

Surprise. Shock.

Bullshit—if Styx was known for anything, it was his lack of possessiveness where a woman was concerned.

This was not going exactly as she would have foreseen it if she had considered this situation for even a moment.

Her gaze shifted instinctively back to Styx, though she refused to consider his chest or how much she had enjoyed it the night before. His hair flowed around his face and shoulders like pictures she had seen of Scottish warriors of old. Like the lover that had given her such pleasure that even now her senses reeled from the memory of it.

Her pussy tightened, clenched. She could feel it creaming, growing slick and wet as the wicked glint in his gaze continued to remind her of his touch.

His face was hardened, tough, his expression lazily filled with the male knowledge of his own charm, hungers, and his effect on the female of both Breed and human species. Especially his effect on her.

Soft, scarred boots covered large feet, jeans cupped and molded heavily muscled legs and thighs, while a black T-shirt molded biceps, chest and an eight-pack most men would kill for.

"There you go, love, I like the attention much more than our fine director," he said and chuckled knowingly.

She would have no better chance. These Breeds weren't going to relax; the only chance she had was to throw them off guard. She had no weapon; she had nothing but her ability to move, to run, and there wasn't a chance in hell she would make it.

She jumped.

Moving to avoid the crouched Wolf Breed Storme sprinted to the side, kept low and thought to slide between two of the Breeds on the far end of the circle as they moved to block her.

They fell back, and she knew she was screwed.

The harsh growl behind her had the others backing away as she sped past them, racing for the narrow lane that led to the exit and the road away from Haven.

She didn't run for the forest; either way she went, she knew she didn't have a chance without divine intervention. And divine intervention wasn't coming.

She was weak. She was tired. She could feel her muscles giving out on her; weeks of exhaustion and too little food had caught up with her.

She had a million excuses, but what it came down to was the fact that she had known it was a useless effort. She had made it no more than perhaps thirty feet when she felt the hard manacled arm that came around her waist, restraining her, and felt herself lifted up and back against a hard, broad chest.

"No!" The rage that tore from her throat was harsh, tearing at her vocal chords as she felt tears of anger falling from her eyes.

"Lass, ease up." Gentle, crooning, his lips at her ear, the Scots Wolf restrained her arms at her side and turned to head back to the cabin.

She kicked, she screamed. Rage and terror whipped through her system as she tried to fight, only to find each move blocked, the training she had gained over the years ineffective in the face of her own weakness, and the strength of the Breed holding her.

"Tell you what, we'll get some food in you, a few cups of coffee, some rest, and you can try it again," he suggested, and she was certain the good-natured tone of his voice was no more than a lie.

He was enjoying this; she could feel it, sense it. Just as he would enjoy killing her.

"You bastard! Fucking monster," she screamed. "I hope you die. I hope all of you die. You should have never been created . . ." She sobbed as he stepped onto the porch and moved into the cabin. "Just kill me now."

"Would you stop the damned caterwauling, lass." He strode through the cabin before yelling behind him, "Jonas, get Nikki up here. She's bleedin'."

She tried to claw at his arms, his hands, but the hold he had on her kept her from scratching. She slammed her head back and only met his shoulder, not his chin or his face as she'd hoped.

She tried to kick, but he evaded each swing of her legs until he reached the bed and threw her onto it.

"Like hell!" Coming off the bed, her only thought was to go back through the window, to escape the only way she knew how.

With a casual little push against her shoulders, he effectively managed to put her on her back as she fell.

Rage was burning inside her like wildfire. It whipped through her exhausted mind, stealing her ability to do anything but to hate and to fear.

They were playing with her and she knew it.

She rolled to the other side of the bed. There was another window, another way out.

Hard fingers at her ankle jerked her back, holding her to the bed as she flipped to her back and tried to kick furiously at the restraining fingers locked around her, keeping her on the bed.

"You could always tie her to the bed," an amused male voice pointed out.

Storme's gaze sliced to the doorway. "You monster!" she screamed at the Bureau director. "You won't win. You won't be able to kill everyone who knows what you are."

"It's a very nice thought though." He shrugged as Storme collapsed in exhaustion, hatred still spilling through her as she regarded him with a bitter sneer.

"Jonas, you're no' helping matters," Styx muttered, her

lungs laboring as she fought to breathe through the panic assailing her.

"I'm not trying to help matters, Wolf." Irritation filled his voice as Storme kicked once again at the Breed holding her. "You're not going to be able to reason with her. Do you smell the terror rolling off her? She's beyond reason, Styx."

"Enough, Jonas."

She was not beyond reason. She was never beyond humanity.

"There's no reasoning with you," she sobbed, coming halfway off the bed to slap at the Breed holding her, only to have him push her back once again. "You're animals. Rabid, vicious animals that know nothing but killing. Nothing but death."

"Because we were given nothing but death." Styx was suddenly in her face, his lips pulled back from his teeth, canines sharp and wicked, snapping mere inches from her. "Your father helped create us. Your brother helped train us. We were given nothing but death, horror and pain, and you expect us to lie back and politely ask for more?"

"I expect you not to kill those helping you," she screamed.

"Call another Breed an animal again in front of me, and as God is my witness I will paddle your ass red." Those teeth snapped again. "You have no fear of death from me, you vicious little wretch. What you should fear though is being treated as the child you appear to be."

He released her.

Storme stared up at him in shock as he stood next to the bed, staring down at her as though he were no more than irritated over a child's antics.

"Dr. Armani's coming up the drive now, Styx," Jonas announced, the clear amusement in his voice drawing another glare from her. "You might want to get her out of those jeans before she gets here. I'd hate for Nikki to have to suffer those quick little feet for doing a good deed."

He didn't say a word. Before Storme could fight back, he tore apart the snap and zipper of her jeans, and before she could do more than rasp out a shocked "What . . . ," the jeans were coming off her legs, only to come to a stop at her boots.

Gripping the hem of the denim, she fought to cover the fact that she was completely naked beneath the jeans as he gripped one foot then the other and within seconds jerked the boots from her feet.

There was no way to fight him.

Furious tears rolled down her cheeks as she tried, only to find every move she made completely ineffective against him.

He didn't speak, he didn't argue with her, and he didn't demand she undress. He simply undressed her, as though she were the child he had accused her of being and he was tired of arguing the matter.

Storme found herself jerking the blanket from the bottom of the bed to cover the nakedness of her lower body as she sat on the mattress, glaring up at him with all the ineffective fury and fear that had ever raced through her system.

"Someone needs to do something about the stink of her fear," Jonas sighed. "Should I give her a reason to be afraid, do you think?"

"Shut up, Jonas." The muttered order drew Storme's gaze back to the irritated Wolf Breed that watched her with lush, heavily lashed eyes and a stern irritation in his gaze.

Her lips parted to throw a string of insults at him that would have withered even the worst of the filthy creatures that had been "created."

His finger came up with a sharp growl from his throat. "Don't make the mistake of thinking I'm joking about that paddling," he warned her. "It will happen."

As he stepped back, another, lower growl rumbled in his chest as the dark-skinned, braided doctor entered the room.

Storme stared at her silently. Dr. Nikki Armani. She was human. A child protégé for the Council when she had worked for them. She had learned Breed genetics at her father's knee as a young girl and trained under the best scientists at several labs. For a brief time, she had even been in the Andes lab, several years before the Breed rescues.

"Keep her away from me." She was the enemy, just as the Breeds were, just as the Council was.

Storme's gaze slashed back to the red Wolf, the overwhelming fury that enveloped her burning through her mind. "Don't let her touch me."

"Shall I hold you down while she repairs that gash you just tore into your hip?" he snapped. "Settle your ass down or that's exactly what I'll do."

The gash?

Her gaze went to the flesh burning high on her hip, and her eyes widened. It was deep and bleeding sluggishly, while the flesh around it appeared to be bruising heavily.

It was at least four inches long and, judging by the amount of blood soaking into the sheets, deep enough to have been dangerous.

This was why she was so weak, why she couldn't fight. She was losing too much blood to maintain her strength and energy. Storme bit at her lip and felt another sob as it trembled through her chest.

"How are you going to escape, Storme, if you don't allow yourself to heal first?" Nikki snapped, her dark brown gaze cool and at odds with the harsh sound of her voice.

"Let me go and I'll show you." She pushed between clenched teeth.

"Then it wouldn't be an escape, would it?" Nikki asked, the sarcasm in her tone raking against the anger surging through Storme. "Now, let me fix that wound, then we'll see if we can't do something to keep you from tearing it loose before it heals. Wasting my time isn't something I enjoy doing."

Storme remained still, silent. Turning to her side, she allowed the doctor access to her thigh, despite the fear shuddering through her system.

As the doctor leaned closer, Storme whispered, "They'll kill me," trying to appeal to whatever compassion or mercy might lurk beneath the appearance of competenance.

"If they were going to kill you, then you would be dead." The doctor's voice was harder now, lacking either mercy or sympathy.

Storme knew there were those people who believed the Breeds could do no wrong, who thought the trials they had suffered in those labs had given the Breeds license to kill as they chose.

The world was slowly becoming divided over Breed rights. Were they animal or human? Should they be allowed freedom or be contained once again?

As far as Storme was concerned, they should be shipped to another planet where they could never harm another human simply because they had the ability to do so.

She fought back the sobs that would have escaped her throat at the memory, still so vivid, of the Breed bending his head, his canines digging into her brother's throat before ripping it from his neck. The blood that covered his face, that spurted from her brother's neck. The rage and sorrow in her father's face and the desperation that filled his gaze.

Her father and brother had tried to help the Breeds. They had worked for years to deceive the Genetics Council and they had died for it. She had lost everything she loved, everything she had known of security in her life because of those monsters.

She ignored the pain at her thigh as the doctor cleaned the wound and repaired it once again. She held back the rage that screamed inside her, that tunneled through her muscles, tightening them, pulling at them, demanding that she do something, anything. That she hurt them as much as they had hurt her.

◆   ◆   ◆

Styx stared at the trembling young woman, her back to him, the soft bare curves of her lovely ass leading to the creamy, satin flesh of her bloodstained thigh.

This, unfortunately, was one of the side effects of the tranquilizers Ghost Team used. Styx had forgotten the paranoia that affected some humans when they were given the drug. A variety of conditions could make it worse, chief among them anemia, exhaustion, dehydration.

He could see her trying to fight it, but sweet wee lass, she was too tired, too weak to do much more than give in to the rage she kept bottled up the majority of the time.

Nikki blocked much of the sight of her, but nothing could block the scents that rolled from her. The smell of such bitter agony that it was almost acrid. Pain. Horror. Rage. They lay inside her like a festering wound as she fought to hold on to the control that restrained her trembling lips.

Breathing in deeply, he turned back to Jonas, giving a quick nod as the director jerked his head in the direction of the living room.

Styx followed him from the room, but only because he was aware of the Breeds outside the windows securing the black iron bars to the openings.

He hated being closed in, but damned if he was going to have her jumping out of windows every chance she had. At this rate, there wouldn't be a piece of glass left in his windows, and replacing them actually wasn't something he was looking forward to.

"I forgot about the fucking tranquilizer," he growled as they moved to the kitchen.

Jonas gave a hard nod. "And she evidently has all the weaknesses that make the symptoms worse. Though I have to give her credit." A grin tugged at his lips. "She's more restrained than some of the human soldiers stationed here at Haven and at Sanctuary. We dose them with it before they begin their duties, to accurately predict any resentment they harbor against the Breeds."

Styx could see where it would be a proper indicator.

"Her father's and brother's throats were ripped out by a Coyote Breed," Jonas muttered as he moved back to the coffeepot, the controlled fury that invaded his body making him appear more lethally dangerous than ever before. "I told you I suspect she was watching as they died." Jonas breathed out as he turned back to Styx. "She's been running from Council Coyotes for years, refusing to trust us, suffering the death of any friend she may have even considered having. They were brutal, Styx. Honestly, I'm surprised we're not having to restrain her."

She had suffered because of Jonas's pride where the Breeds were concerned. Because he had a basic resentment toward any human who feared them.

"And you didn't fucking pull her out of it?" he snarled back at the director. "You could have, at any time."

The thought of that enraged him. That Jonas had allowed such a young woman to live such a life. But hell, for two years Styx had chased after her, always standing back, protecting her yet never pulling her into the safety of Haven or forcing her to release her fears of the Breeds.

"I found her when she was nineteen, Styx. I've kept in contact with her; I've made offer after offer to protect her, to help her, with or without the information I know she has. She's refused. She's terrified of Breeds, and rightly so. It wasn't just Coyotes that the Council sent after her. They sent Lions, and they sent a Wolf." Jonas's expression hardened. "They reached her before I did. I was able to help her escape, but while I was dealing with the bastards sent after her, she slipped out of my grasp every time."

Styx bit off a snarl that would have easily carried into the other room had he not throttled it.

He could imagine the hell her life had been. For years after the rescues had begun, there were still those Breeds under Council control for one reason or another. Hell, even now, more than thirteen years later, there were rumors of a few shadow Breeds other than Coyotes that the Council retained.

"We captured her easily enough last night . . ."

"You were lucky last night," Jonas broke in. "If the woman that has continually stepped in and interfered with my efforts over the years whenever I was close enough to help her was there, then you wouldn't have had the chance to get close to her. We suspect Gena Waters is with the Council, but Storme doesn't know or want to believe that, and until she betrays Storme, there's nothing I can do."

Styx shook his head, before striding to the counter and the forgotten chocolate coffee. He pushed it into the microwave and nuked it, before drawing the steaming liquid from the appliance and sipping at it.

He could feel the anger building, brewing. Anger was something he tried to keep out of his little world. It served no purpose; getting even was far better. But there was no one here that he could get even with.

"Where is Waters, then? Have you found her?" he finally asked, knowing Jonas wasn't just standing there tormenting the hell out of him. He would have men searching for Gena Waters, tracking her, and learning where her orders originated from.

Gena Waters had latched onto Storme six years before, during a time when the Breeds had lost track of her. In those six years she had seemed to be slowly gaining Storme's trust. Though she hadn't yet gained enough of it to acquire the data chip the Council was so desperate to acquire.

"I have Rule and Lawe on her," Jonas said and nodded. "They should have something soon. But catching her won't ensure Storme's safety. Until she gives up that data chip her father gave her, then she'll never be safe, Styx."

And that was no less than the truth. The Council had been chasing her for ten years now; they weren't going to give up just because she was currently under Breed protection. They would wait, knowing that eventually the Breeds would have to blink. And when they blinked, the Council would strike.

"She's not going to give us that data chip," Styx said and sighed.

"No, she's not," Jonas agreed. "That leaves only one option."

Styx lifted a brow curiously. "There's an option?"

"One." Jonas nodded as a grin tugged at his lips.

Hell, seeing Jonas almost grin was damned scary. He'd only been doing it since his mating, and that just wasn't enough time to get used to it.

"So tell me what it is already," Styx growled.

"Show her who and what we are," Jonas stated. "Show her, Styx, the Wolf Breeds, the Coyotes, and the Felines here at Haven. Show her the good, let her see we're not all monsters."

Styx shook his head. "That's not enough."

She would need more.

"A woman who has been running since she was a teenager, no more than a child," he mused. "Her friends were killed or attacked before they were even friends. The Council left her no one but Gena Waters, a cold, unfeeling person who likely had no idea the affection a woman of Storme's temperament would need. There are few ways to get to the heart of such a woman."

Jonas nodded slowly. "Then give her affection, Styx. Give her warmth, and maybe, just maybe, in return, she'll give us the key to her own safety."

Styx stared back at him silently. "And you'll stay away from her until I've completed this."

"I didn't say that."

"I said you will," Styx demanded. "You won't harass my mate, Jonas."

Jonas rolled his eyes. "Wolf, you know the signs of mating heat. Do you have them?"

"The symptoms are there," Styx growled, the sensitivity of his tongue an itchy irritation, the need to kiss his mate, to share a hormone that refused to release from the glands, a frustration that would likely drive him crazy.

"The mating mark isn't there, the mating scent isn't there, therefore there is no mating," Jonas said and shrugged negligently, as though he could possibly have the final word.

"Don't piss me off, Jonas," Styx warned him as he picked up the chef's knife and began chopping the vegetables for the soup.

"It's been enough time, you've had skin-to-skin contact." Jonas shrugged again. "I refuse to accept a mating without it."

Styx grinned. A real grin. One of anticipation and challenge.

"Weel then, I'd guess we can be workin' with that, can't
we, Director?" he mused, feeling the playfulness returning. "We can work wi' that right well. I promise you, you'll
learn I don't accept threats to what's mine."

And to that, Jonas nodded, as he gave another of those
smiles that never failed to make Styx suspicious. "You
know, Styx, I had a feeling you were going to be difficult
about this."

Difficult didn't even come close.

CHAPTER 6

Haven wasn't much different from Sanctuary, Storme thought as she stood in the immaculate kitchen of the cabin she had awakened within after a heavy dose of Breed tranquilizer. She was still feeling the irritable, almost paranoid effects of the drug two days later, after the sleepiness had finally worn off. Of course, as Dr. Armani had told her with a smirk, if she hadn't been so exhausted, the effects wouldn't have been nearly so severe.

Added to it was a symptom the doctor hadn't told her about. A sensitivity to her flesh, a low-level aching need to rub at her skin, yet rubbing at it only seemed to make it worse. And her back itched in places she couldn't reach. Adding to the irritation was the fact that Styx was no place to be found.

If the Wolf was good for nothing else, maybe he could be a decent back scratcher.

She tried to ignore that little voice inside her that assured her there were other things Styx was definitely good at.

As midmorning approached and Styx still hadn't shown up, Storme paced to the kitchen door, stared into the huge courtyard that each cabin faced and felt like growling herself.

She was damned bored. Bored and curious. She knew the layout of the Feline prides' base, Sanctuary, from schematics that the pure blood societies had managed to attain from the Council. The historic old mansion that served as the main house in the compound had been renovated and owned by the Council at one time.

She had no idea where anything was at in Haven though, or even where she was located within it. Unlike Sanctuary, Haven was newly built, and the strict security within it had, so far, kept the pure blood societies from learning where the alpha of the packs' home was located, or his seconds in command.

From Styx's cabin all she could see was the main living community that Styx had brought her to. It rather resembled a large city block of cabins of various sizes that had been built beneath the shading limbs of oaks that had to be centuries old.

Spread out from the block, beneath the canopy of other heavy, camouflaging trees were other cabins of differing sizes and designs that she could see from several windows. There was a small store at the end of the block, what appeared to be a community center of sorts at the corner of the block behind the cabin, and a large secured bunker-type building set into the side of a cliff at the base of the mountain rising above the compound.

From the back door window of the kitchen, she could barely glimpse the steel and cement facade built into the mountain. It was set far enough from the cabins that if it were targeted, the residents would be safe, but it was close enough to provide shelter if needed.

A mountain lake surrounded by pines and heavy forest also held cabins that had been built to blend with the terrain rather than detract from it. In several areas there were home facings built into the mountain, just as the heavily secured steel bunker was set. Farther along the side of the lower slope of the mountain, more cabins were set. The soft gleam of lights shimmered within the trees, betraying the locations of a few, but not all, she knew.

It was serene.

As dawn brightened the night sky and gave the faintest hint of softness to the fog that filled the valley, Storme realized what made it so hard for Council assassins and pure blood terrorist groups to gain a foothold or information in Haven.

It was heavily shrouded by mountains and trees, blocked from satellite view, and every security measure had been taken to ensure that Council spies had no chance to reveal the locations of the homes.

The heavily guarded entrance to Haven was set back from the main compound, giving no opportunity to glimpse it from the road. Anyone with an intent to slip close enough to gain any detail had to first traverse the mountains that rose around the compound, also Wolf Breed and Coyote land, and had to slip past the sensitive noses of the teams of Enforcers that patrolled the land.

There were close to three hundred thousand acres of land that made up the Wolf Breed territory. The land had once been government owned, a wildlife preserve that had been accessible to tourists and nature lovers. It was now heavily guarded and closed to all but those who managed to gain special permission from the Wolf Breeds or the Bureau of Breed Affairs.

Haven was impossible to get into, according to the Council and pure blood societies that kept attempting to break past the security. And for Storme, impossible to get out of. Hell, the cabin itself was impossible to get out of.

The windows were barred, even the one at the back door. Enforcers patrolled the courtyard, as well as the front of the house. And as she had seen the morning she had gone through the bedroom window, dozens could be gathered within seconds of an alarm.

Finally, as her irritation seemed to reach peak level, the front door opened, a rush of fresh mountain air blowing into the house. Pine, the scent of freshly cut grass, and the smell of a fresh mountain lake. And it all seemed to wrap around him, making his shoulders look broader, his hair a fiery red as the sun glinted off it, the blue of his eyes deeper than an ocean.

She rubbed at her arms, the prickle beneath the skin seeming to intensify as he stalked across the room.

"The alpha and his lupina will be arriving this afternoon," Styx announced as he entered the kitchen and flashed her a flirtatious smile. "They've offered to bring any clothing or guest items you may need."

"I don't need their clothes," she muttered.

She'd prefer to wear nothing at the moment, maybe her flesh would stop tingling and itching as though the need for touch were driving her crazy.

"Fine, go naked." He shrugged as he shot her a wicked grin, then moved to the coffee he had made before he showered. "Suits me fine."

She just bet it would.

Before she could voice the sarcastic rejoinder, he strode to her, his hand curving beneath her hair to the back of her neck, surprising her as his head lowered.

Oh God. She almost moaned as his head slanted and his lips covered hers in a voracious, hungry kiss.

For a moment, panic and fear receded beneath an onslaught of such intense pleasure that her knees weakened.

Gripping his shoulders, Storme held on for the tumultuous ride, unable to do anything for heart-stopping seconds but meet his lips and tongue and draw as much of the pleasure around her as possible.

One hand lay at her hip, holding her to him as the other stroked up her side until his wide palm could cup and weight the curve of her breast.

An enterprising thumb stroked over the hard peak, sending spikes of dark, wicked sensation to spread through her body as she arched into him, suddenly hungry for more.

"No!" It was a moan rather than a demand as Storme jerked back from him.

She stumbled back against the wall, fighting a need that seemed to burn through her womb, into her pussy, and wrap around her clit like a lover's caress.

The itch beneath her flesh was turning to a burn. Until he touched her. Her entire body felt wrapped in static electricity, her skin humming in pleasure at the feel of him against her.

"No?" He stared at her from beneath heavily lashed lids, the glitter in his blue eyes heatedly sensual. "Sugar, I could eat you like chocolate you taste so damned good."

She would have delivered a scathing retort if a knock at the front door hadn't drawn her attention. She turned, staring across the room, over the open counter space to the heavy wood door on the opposite side of the living room.

With an amused arch of his brows Styx moved through the other room to open the door and greet the arrival.

"Jonas. Rachel. Welcome to my home," he said to greet the couple as they stepped into the living room and then moved to the kitchen, where Storme crossed her arms over her breasts and glared back at them. She didn't consider them welcome at all.

Storme fought to ignore them. She concentrated instead on the soft light that filled the area, bouncing off gleaming stone counters and shimmering wood cabinets that were obviously old and well polished.

Modern appliances filled the room along with an oval six-chair table that sat in the middle of a stone floor just a few shades lighter than the toasted cream color of the counters.

The open design of the cabin allowed Storme to see the large living area from there. An open fireplace gave a peek into a bedroom that seemed to fill one end of the cabin. The other end held two other bedrooms, with a shared bathroom and linen closet and small office between.

As Jonas and his wife entered the kitchen, the back door opened and Storme watched as Navarro Blaine and another Breed stepped into the room. There were too many Breeds here. She felt surrounded by them and it was terrifying.

She was still weak, unable to fight. The adhesive at her hip hadn't had time to seal the wound from her attempt to escape, and she could feel the additional bruises on her ribs from her contact with too many large rocks on the ground. She was sore, hungry, certain she was running a fever, and she just wanted to be left the hell alone to rest again and suffer in peace. If she was going to be stuck here, the least they could do was allow her to be miserable in peace.

As the Breeds filled the kitchen, Storme moved cautiously from the room and stepped into the living room, until she was standing in front of the fireplace staring at the wide, luxurious autumn brown leather couch. A heavy coffee table sat between her and the couch, and to the side of that was an autumn red recliner that looked large enough for three of her.

The electronic glass of the coffee table was darkened by the computerized components that likely ran and programmed the television, stereo system and holographic Internet and entertainment capabilities. It was state-of-the-art, and she would have loved to have gotten her hands on it and investigated the various options it was programmed with.

A wide-screen television hung over the fireplace, a compact music station on the wall over the opposite fireplace, the heavy front door and a wet bar in the wall next to the kitchen.

A Breed bachelor pad, perhaps, with all the amenities.

"Navarro, have the bars on the windows been checked for tampering?" Styx questioned the other Breed as they stared at her through the opening above the counter.

Storme crossed her arms over her breasts and stared back at both men mutinously.

"Everything's taken care of," Navarro said and nodded. "There was some slight tampering to the locks as well as few of the bars, where the bolts secure them. It seems we have enterprising wildlife of late. Surely your guest wouldn't have attempted anything so outrageous?" Mockery filled the other Wolf's voice as Storme glared back at him furiously.

Bastard. She had been certain no one could have detected the probing attempts she had made to check the security of the bars.

"I'm honored that y'all would go to all that trouble for little ole me," Storme drawled sarcastically as the nervous tension began to get the best of her. "Bars on the windows, guards at the door. Why, the next thing you know I'll be on a bread and water diet."

"We take care of all our guests similarly," Navarro assured her. "We're far more hospitable than the Council. They'd lock you in a cell and leave you to rot without the bread and water."

Storme glared back at him. Damned smart-ass. Even in the labs, under the rule of soldiers who enjoyed beating the hell out of him if they got the chance, Navarro had been a sarcastic bastard.

"Enough, Navarro," Styx ordered softly. "As long as she's here, she's mine."

"As long as she stinks of fear and prejudice, she's the enemy," Navarro stated matter-of-factly, his expression, voice and entire demeanor cool and unaffected. "It's hard to imagine JR having a child that hated something he loved as much as he loved the Breeds he helped create."

"More than he loved his children." The words passed her lips before she could call them back.

Navarro stared back at her silently for long moments. "Or perhaps he simply expected his children to understand the responsibility he felt he owed to those he'd helped create and imprison. It's too bad, Storme, that only one of his children understood that."

Why do you love them, Daddy? a young Storme had whispered painfully when her father arrived home too late to celebrate her tenth birthday with her. *Why are they more important?*

She had wanted to understand, to make sense of the fact that the animals held more of her father's affection than it seemed she did.

Her father had bent down to her, his hands heavy on her young shoulders, his gaze filled with somber remorse. *Because they're my children too, Storme. And they suffer where you don't.*

That admission had broken her heart. They were his children too, and they were more important than she was.

"They weren't his children," she whispered painfully. "He had a choice. He could have left at any time."

"As you left the day you caught a Council soldier beating one of the young?" Navarro asked then.

"And how did I pay for it?" she asked mockingly as she extended her arm to show the two small scars she still carried on the inside of her wrist. "Their canines may have been small, but they sure as hell knew how to use them. He attacked me like a rabid little dog."

The child had bit her, nearly slashing the veins in her wrists as she tried to pull him to safety after distracting the trainer that had been beating his back bloody.

"Stop!" Within a breath Styx moved into the room and swung her around, his head lowering, his gaze snaring hers with a gleam of command as that damned Wolf's growl in his voice rumbled in his chest. A warning to assure her that he meant what he said about calling any Breed an animal.

"That rabid little dog, as you call him, was out of his mind with fever and pain," Navarro informed her mercilessly as she stared up at Styx, her eyes wide.

Her heart slammed into her throat as she fought to hold back her surprise, the knowledge that the child might not have known what it was doing affecting her more than she wanted to admit. She had always believed the child had known, had been aware that he was attacking someone trying to help him.

She swallowed tightly, refusing to give any outward sign that she had heard him, agreed with him, or would obey Styx's order. She didn't dare give in to either of them, not now, not while so many eyes watched.

Slowly, deliberately, she pulled her wrist from Styx's grip, turned and walked around the coffee table before plopping onto the couch as though there wasn't a single individual in the cabin that concerned her.

Pulling the remote from the arm of the couch, she aimed it at the television and pushed the on button, determined to at least appear to enjoy a few rare moments of entertainment.

"I have to give her credit, if she didn't stink of terror

and remorse, I'd swear she was making herself at home," Navarro grunted.

The volume control was handy. Too bad the mute button didn't work on real people or Breeds. She turned the sound up instead, hoping that the *stink* that so seemed to offend him would dissipate soon.

"Jonas, will you be staying at Haven much longer?" Styx questioned him.

"For the time being," she heard the director answer. "Our scientist Ely Morrey and one of her 'assistants' will be arriving this afternoon to help Dr. Armani on a small project she seems to have acquired." The amusement in his voice made Storme wonder what the hell he was talking about. If she hadn't known better, she would have thought it concerned her.

The emphasis on "assistant" had her lips thinning. No doubt the assistant was Jeffrey Amburg, the captive scientist the Breeds were holding. Amburg had once been a close friend of her father and brother, until her father had disagreed with him over some subject that had severed that friendship. Storme had a feeling that subject was whatever project her father had been working on with her brother.

"Navarro, inform Nikki I'll need her back here as well," Styx ordered the other Wolf Breed. "And if Cassie is on-site, please let her know I'll have to reschedule the date we had planned for this evening."

Date?

Storme refused to look at him and prayed that the fear and prejudice Navarro had spoken of earlier was still strong enough to hide the fact that her first instinct was to protest any *date* Styx might have.

"I'll take care of it," Navarro promised. "And you should be aware that Alpha Gunnar and his lupina are making their way here now. Have fun, Styx."

◆   ◆   ◆

Have fun? Styx glared at Navarro before sighing heavily and turning back to Jonas and Rachel. The worry in their eyes wasn't easy to ignore. Their child was at risk here, and though Styx understood that more than he admitted to, still, he couldn't make himself frighten Storme further to reveal that information.

"Will you be staying in the alpha residence?" he asked the director, determined not to offer the spare room to Jonas and his mate.

"Rachel and I will be taking the guest cabin," Jonas informed him. "For the time being at least."

The director shot a look at Storme's back, his expression doubtful. She was damned stubborn, Styx could almost read what the other man was thinking. The hope that they would have that information soon was dwindling.

As Styx stepped from the front of the fireplace and shot his "near" mate a disgruntled look, the back door opened once more, to admit the alpha of the Wolf packs and leader of Haven, Wolfe Gunnar, and his mated wife Hope.

Hope still had the fresh, innocent look of the college student Wolfe had kidnapped almost thirteen years before.

As Wolfe stepped to the wide entrance into the kitchen, she stepped past him, the soft Asian flavor of her features still and quiet as she moved into the living room and stepped to the couch.

"Hello, Storme." The familiarity in her voice and the sudden scent of pain radiating from Storme had Styx's senses going on high alert. "It's been a long time. Aren't you going to say hello?"

Storme laid the remote down carefully, the tension in her body mixing with the fear, the pain and the anger.

Slowly, her head turned, the dark, emerald green of her eyes glittering with so many emotions Styx nearly winced at the sight of them.

"No," Storme stated, the low tone of her voice grating, "I'm not."

She rose from the couch, moved to his bedroom, opened the door and stepped inside before closing the door softly. Behind her, she left them staring at where she had disappeared, the men in the room too aware, too sensitive and too uncertain about the emotions that flowed between the two women.

One thing was for damned certain, they knew each other well, and Storme had just found another part of her past to run away from: the lupina, whose soft blue eyes shimmered with tears.

◆   ◆   ◆

"Storme wasn't very old when the first Breed rescues began," Hope stated as Styx set a pot of coffee on the kitchen table in front of his alpha and lupina almost an hour later. "That was fourteen years ago, so she would have been ten perhaps. I met her just after Wolfe and his pack escaped from Mexico. Delia, my mother, was sent to the Omega labs for nearly a year before we were transferred back to the States and she left me with my father's sister. Storme was there, lonely, always reaching out to a father and brother who had no real time for her."

"Navarro told me the labs there were worse than the others," Styx commented as he glanced back at her.

"They were horrendous," she agreed painfully as Jonas and Rachel watched her heavily. "I didn't know about whatever project was going on there. Mother didn't take me to the labs because she didn't want the Coyote Breeds there to sense whatever hormonal reaction had begun in my body. She wanted to study it for herself. But I know Storme was taken often to the labs where wounded and experimental Breeds were kept. It was a hellhole there. She saw only the worst of what the scientists had created the Breeds to be. The fury and the agonizing rage that filled them, a result of the pain they endured from the experiments or the wounds they carried."

"Were you close?" Jonas questioned her.

Hope shrugged. "At one time, perhaps. For years I've waited, hoping she would contact me, hoping she would trust me with whatever information her father gave her, but I never heard from her."

Wolfe spoke up then. "Jonas, what information does she

have that's so important to your child?" The Wolf Breed alpha leaned back in his chair and watched the director curiously. The fact that Dr. Armani was under orders by the Bureau not to reveal the details of the information she had found was known by the alpha. It was an order he wouldn't force her to break unless he had no other choice.

Jonas sighed. "I'm not certain of the parameters of Project Omega. What I'm certain of is that somehow it coincides with whatever Brandenmore was researching as well. A serum or virus that has halted his aging and begun regenerating his cellular structure. Organs are healing and rejuvenating, at a very slow rate, yet still it's happening. At the time Brandenmore kidnapped our daughter, Amber, he injected her with something we believed was a sedative until I nearly killed Brandenmore. He told me then it was an experimental drug and that if he died, the secret of saving her if the reaction became adverse would die with him. I have to admit, I didn't completely believe him until the night I heard her purr."

Styx blinked back at Jonas as Rachel's breath caught on a sob.

There were rumors of Council scientists attempting to create a virus that would alter the DNA of humans after birth. In each case, the test subject had died in horrible pain from the agony of the body attempting to both fight as well as accept the strange genetic virus.

The conflict within the test subjects had created horrifying stories of screaming, mindless humans who had survived until their hearts had finally ruptured from the stress of the genetic mutations.

"Are there any signs the baby is in distress?" Hope whispered, compassion and sympathy spilling from her eyes as she stared at Rachel.

Rachel, thankfully, shook her head. "The scientists can find no Breed genetics or hormones in her system to match those of Brandenmore. All we have are the odd purrs. It's happened twice now, and each time, Jonas has scented a hint of a Feline babe about her. Just as quickly, the scent as well as the purr is gone."

"Then you believe the information Storme has is somehow related to the genetic experimentations on humans?" Wolfe asked, his tone boarding the harsh growl of an angered Wolf.

Jonas nodded sharply. "I've let her run for ten years, hoping she would grow up, see the truth of the Council and the Breeds and accept my offer of help. Had I known her father had been insane enough to actually save the research conducted on Omega, then I would have captured her when she was fourteen. Unfortunately, I had no idea the full extent of the research the Montagues conducted."

The fact that he hadn't was lying heavily on his shoulders. Styx could sense the director's regret as well as his inner fury.

"What now, then?" Wolfe asked. "How do we force her to turn over the information?"

"We force nothing." Styx crossed his arms over his chest and stared back at the four of them implacably, aware of Navarro coming to attention behind him in the corner of the room.

Wolfe turned his head and narrowed his eyes. "Styx, you can't protect her from this. This is a woman and a battle you have to step away from."

He was known to love women. Styx did love women. He protected them whenever possible simply because of their soft flesh and lush sensuality. And the very fact that they were indeed gentler, softer, and weaker than men, let alone Breeds.

"He's acting as though he's mated her," Jonas stated. "But there's no mating scent, even after they've had sex. You need to advise your Breed a bit more firmly to back off, Alpha Gunnar."

To give Wolfe credit, he did nothing of the sort. Instead, he shot Jonas an irate look as Rachel, Jonas's mate, rolled her eyes. Such autocratic orders were Jonas's trademark.

"Styx?" Wolfe questioned him curiously. "What's going on?"

"She's my mate." He made the declaration, knowing the very arguments Jonas had just made.

The mating symptoms weren't strong yet, the scent of a mating was still undetectable. The scent of sex was far different from a mating scent.

Jonas shook his head. "Do you smell a mating, Alpha Gunnar?"

"Do you smell a lie, Director?" Wolfe shot back, his black eyes shifting to Jonas before returning to Styx. "Because I don't."

"That protective instinct of his is overreacting," Jonas argued. "We all know how he is with his lovers, Alpha Gunnar. He has some kind of overinflated need to protect them at all costs."

Bullshit.

"Shut him up before I find myself arrested for killing our director, Wolfe," Styx grunted, with a suspicion he wasn't completely joking.

"What makes you believe she's your mate?" Jonas breathed out roughly. "Come on, Styx, there are signs, and you know them. You have none of those signs."

"That you can tell, Director," Styx growled. "And what I have can wait for Dr. Armani's analysis. It's none of your damned business."

The signs of mating were still subtle. Itchy hormonal glands beneath his tongue that hadn't yet spilled the mating hormone. His skin was sensitive; each time he touched her he felt as though a static charge were building just beneath the flesh. The scent wasn't there though. He hadn't locked inside her when he had taken her the night before, and he wasn't out of his mind with the need for sex. More importantly, Storme wasn't out of her mind with the need for sex, which was one of the more well-known signs.

"This is very much my business," Jonas stated, his tone turning icy once more. "It's my intent, Styx, to enact Breed Law where Ms. Montague is concerned if she doesn't willingly turn over the information she has. You know what that means. She's killed Breeds and actively worked against Breed society . . ."

"She killed fucking Council Breeds," Styx snarled furiously as he felt that burning, protective rage rising inside him once again. "And how has she worked against Breed society other than in your mind when she refused to give you something you wanted?"

"Something that could save my child." Jonas came out of his chair, his hands flat on the table as his silver eyes flashed with deadly restraint. "She has worked against Breed society since she was eighteen years old and joined her first pure blood society. Shall I tell you the Breeds that group killed? Can you swear she had no part in those deaths?"

"I can and will swear it." Styx leaned against the table himself now as pure animal determination began to fill him. "And I tell you now, you will not take my mate, nor will you place her under Breed Law. Attempt to do so and I will disappear with her so fast it will make your autocratic, god-syndrome head fucking spin like a windmill out of control."

Once again, Jonas was nose to nose with someone, and this time, Styx determined, the director had bitten off more than he could chew.

"Styx, stand down," Wolfe suggested. Surprisingly, it wasn't an alpha order, one of those orders he was bound by vows and by blood to obey.

"She's my mate." His gaze never left Jonas's. "I am not required to obey any order that places my mate in harm's way. With all due respect, Alpha Gunnar, I will rip his throat out if he dares to attempt to take what is mine."

There were few things a Breed could call his or her own, other than a mate. A mate was considered God's gift, His acceptance of and determination to see to the survival of the Breeds. Without His acceptance, mating wouldn't occur, and there would not have been the natural conception and birth of the Breed children that now existed.

"You can try." Feline, furious, the growl in Jonas's voice had the hairs at the back of Styx's neck lifting in primal warning.

Styx tensed, preparing himself for a fight as Navarro moved in behind him and Wolfe stood slowly to his feet. No one would back him in going against his alpha over his mate. Understanding and approving were two different things.

"Styx, your mate will not be taken from Haven at any time," Wolfe stated as Styx narrowed his eyes in surprise.

"She has to test as his mate first." Jonas's lips lifted in a snarl. "And how much do you want to bet she won't test positive for the Breed mating hormone?"

Rachel and Hope moved away slowly. Not that Rachel did so easily, but Hope's whispered promise that Wolfe would handle it had her following the other woman, though she kept a wary eye on her husband.

"Then let me put it this way, Director," Wolfe stated. "Ms. Montague will not be leaving Haven until Styx makes a formal declaration, rescinding his protection of her. Don't turn this into a battle, Jonas, because I promise you, you won't win against me."

Alphas and their mates were sacred. Every Breed from Jonas down was beneath their rule, it didn't matter the species. If they were in Haven, then their very presence was their agreement to abide by the rules of the community and by the dictates Wolfe set out, until a formal complaint could be lodged and a tribunal of Breeds brought together. And Jonas knew it.

Jonas eased back before straightening. "Do I have your promise, Alpha Gunnar, that this Breed will not leave Haven with Ms. Montague? I would hate to lose my child because of his stubbornness, or your lack of foresight."

There weren't many Breeds or men that could get away with making such a statement to the powerful leader of the Wolf Breed community. The fact that Jonas did so, and would get away with it, was a testament to the sheer power he wielded as the director of the Washington, DC–based Bureau of Breed Affairs.

"I swear I have no intentions of removing her from the safety of Haven unless I feel her safety is endangered by being here." And that was the only promise he was willing to give at this point.

The fact that Jonas wasn't the least bit happy with it was apparent.

Leaning forward, his hands against the table, the director issued a warning snarl. "Don't make the mistake of pushing me too far in this, Styx. Make no mistake, my patience is wearing thin. If my daughter ends up paying for Ms. Montague's stubbornness and hatred, then have no fucking doubt I will demand her punishment. To the fullest extent of Breed Law."

And God help him, but there wasn't a Breed in Haven that would blame Jonas for it, even Styx.

They all tensed further at the sound of the bedroom door opening then.

"Wow, do I get to see a real catfight?" Storme questioned mockingly as she stepped into the kitchen and cast a look of disgust at Styx as well as Jonas. "And you Breeds wonder why I don't feel safe around any of you. All you want to do is fight. If not humans, then one another. Is there a pecking order for who gets to die first, or do you draw straws?"

For the briefest second, despite the sarcasm in her voice, Styx swore he could just detect the pain and remorse in her voice, but he also scented the slightest hint of it in the air.

Hope stepped forward at this point. "Ms. Montague, you are in the presence of an alpha of the Breed community. I demand that you show him the respect you would show any senator or congressman of this country." The cool and berating tone of her voice held no familiarity with the young woman she was speaking to now. Storme had offended her, and had broken an unwritten law of etiquette as far as the lupina was concerned. She had disrespected the alpha who had just willingly stood up for her.

That impacted Hope, as well as the concern and lack of understanding about the young woman withholding vital information needed to save a child. To most Breeds, actually, all Breeds but those still under the control of the

Genetics Council, there were few things more important than a child.

"You want me to spit on him?" Storme widened her eyes and stared back at Hope in mocking disbelief. "If you insist, Mrs. Gunnar, but honestly, considering the fact that I haven't had my throat ripped out yet, and I haven't been skinned alive, I thought I'd at least give him the benefit of the doubt."

"Unacceptable," Hope snapped. "Why don't you let us all know when you've grown up, Storme? Maybe then we'll begin to speak to you as we would an adult, rather than a child."

To which Storme grunted, "Get off your high horse, Hope. We both know I'm not going to kowtow to a single Breed in this place, and the first chance I have to escape, then I'm gone. Let's not pretend I like any of you, and certainly let's not pretend that any Breed deserves anything from me. If your precious Wolf wants my respect, then he can earn it, just like anyone else does." Her gaze flicked to Wolfe as he stared at her with cool intent.

When her lips opened to say more, Hope broke in with icy fury, her gaze glittering with the frustration and anger that brewed inside them all. "Say another disrespectful word in the presence of my mate and Haven's alpha, and I'll have you gagged if you're ever in his presence again," Hope stated, as her mate moved in closer. "Alpha Gunnar doesn't have to earn a damned thing from you, Storme. He earned it the day men like your father decided to create him to kill. The day he escaped rather than taking an innocent human life. Think of that one before you decide to insult him further."

This wasn't a world where insults to the leader of the community could be taken lightly, and there was nothing Styx could do to ease the chastisement his mate received at the moment.

It wasn't a democracy such as the one the nation had voted in so many centuries ago. But it wasn't corrupt, and it wasn't deserving of her disdain. If she was allowed to continue to offend Wolfe, no matter his friendship or the fairness he displayed, Wolfe would have no choice but to, at the very least, ostracize her, which would in turn bring the censure of the community against them both.

"Styx, Hope." Wolfe laid his hand against his mate's back and rubbed his chin against the top of her hair before standing tall beside her once again. "Ms. Montague is not a part of the community, and therefore I can understand her ignorance as to the etiquette we have in place here," Wolfe stated as he stared back at Storme, his gaze penetrating, commanding. "Nothing more will be said of this, and I'm certain it won't happen again." Wolfe continued to hold Storme's gaze.

Styx could feel the rigid set of her body and once again could smell her fear bleeding from her.

The smart-assed cracks, the deliberate disrespect were the only weapons she had to wield at the moment, and though he understood her reasons, he couldn't allow it to continue. Aside from the fact that Wolfe and Hope were his leaders, they were deserving of more than Storme's sharp tongue and deliberate insults.

"Perhaps it's time we leave, Wolfe." Hope leaned against her mate, her expression calm and no longer filled with compassion or warmth as she stared back at Storme. "Once Jonas and Styx have resolved this situation, then we can decide the measure of aid Haven will lend Ms. Montague should she decide to leave our community."

The implication that, at this moment, Hope really didn't give a damn what Storme did was clear.

"I think we'll join you, Alpha Gunnar, Lupina," Rachel stated carefully as she moved to Jonas's side. "I could use some rest."

The look she gave Storme was one filled with pain. No one knew for certain the information Storme carried, but Rachel was desperate to find a way to help her daughter before any problems arose.

Jonas said nothing. He stared back at Storme with silver-eyed contempt before turning and leaving the cabin behind Wolfe and Hope. Navarro followed, but not before he glared back at Storme in disgust. "Your father once told me you had the heart of the Lion, the courage of the Wolf, and the logic of the Coyote. Tell me, Storme, how did you manage to fool him into believing you could actually be trusted to know whom to give that information to?"

She flinched as the Wolf stepped out and closed the door softly behind him. For a moment, the room was filled with such agonizing indecision that it had a scent all its own.

"Well, if I had known it was that easy to get rid of them, I would have insulted them sooner." She jerked out of his grip before turning and facing him, the false bravado in her voice and in her expression painful to witness. "Are we doing breakfast or arguing the rest of the morning?" A slender black brow arched mockingly. "Personally, I think I prefer food."

Personally, he preferred doing her and showing her once and for all who dominated here and who would follow the orders. The Wolf inside him was pacing, snarling, demanding he do something to show her, to prove to her, that the contempt that poured out of her for him and his people would not be tolerated. Despite the pain and the indecision he knew she was fighting at the moment, no matter her fear or her battle to accept her present situation, he couldn't allow the disrespect to continue.

It wouldn't be tolerated and it wouldn't be allowed.

"I can make your stay here easy." He gave her a relaxed, confident smile. "Or I can show you how we treat those who want to consider themselves prisoners. Take your pick, Sugar, before I make the choice for you."

CHAPTER 7

Hope Bainesmith Gunnar.

Storme remembered the young woman who had be-friended her more than ten years before. Storme had been ten, Hope was now thirty years old. She didn't look thirty. She looked no different now than she had looked when she had been at the Omega compound and watched the Wolf Breeds as though searching for a familiar face, or a way to escape.

Or perhaps even both.

Storme remembered the day the news reports hit of the Wolf Breeds being granted the land in Colorado in recom-pense for America's part in funding the Genetics Council. She hadn't heard of the Wolf Breed alpha before then, but when a picture had flashed of Wolfe Gunnar and his new bride, the daughter of a Council scientist, Storme had felt her stomach clench in despair and fear for the young woman she had once looked up to.

Over the years, she had feared for Hope, worried for her, terrified she was locked in a marriage she couldn't have possibly wanted.

Yet the Hope she had seen when she arrived at Haven three days before wasn't a woman stuck in a relationship she didn't want. The woman she watched in the huge courtyard that was the center of the block of homes wasn't a woman unhappy with her life or with her husband.

Hope Bainesmith Gunnar was a woman well content with the life and the creature she seemed to love.

Standing at the back door now as dusk moved slowly over the mountain, arms crossed, a frown on her face, she watched as Hope played with an infant from the home next door.

The child belonged to Aiden and Charity Chance. Aiden was head of security at Haven if she remembered correctly. The two-story cabin to the right of the Gunnars' was the Chance home. There was nothing ostentatious or elite about the home, despite the hierarchical place the Chances held within the pack at Haven.

Like the Gunnar home, and the home belonging to Jacob and Faith Arlington to the left of it, it was two stories, a log cabin–style home that blended well with the trees that grew both in front of it and within the courtyard behind it.

Lights hung from the trees to create soft, effective lighting in the central yard. Each of the twenty or so homes was built far enough apart for privacy inside, but opened into the central design to allow for full socialization.

Wolves were far more social than the Felines, she had heard; in that case, it seemed that propaganda in favor of the Breeds was true.

Now, as the lights brightened the area between Styx's home and those across from it, she watched as those who lived within this centralized grouping came together.

Wolfe and Hope had come out first, followed by the Chances and the Arlingtons.

Charity Chance had walked beside her tall, dark husband, Aiden, as he carried their infant snuggly against his broad chest. They had joined Hope and Wolfe in one of the gathering spots outfitted with comfortable outdoor furnishings, a fire pit and grill and an attractive overhead covering that blended with the branches of the trees above in case of rain.

Jacob and Faith Arlington had followed. They carried food. Jacob with his dark coloring and the light auburn highlights to his hair had once been a part of several teams of Breeds sent out to locate hidden Council labs. He had been instrumental in locating and rescuing the rare, mysterious winged Breeds. His wife, Faith, liaison to the various packs and prides that were still spread out over the world, most in hiding, was tall and sleek, her long dark hair falling beneath her shoulders.

She stood next to her husband at the grill, laughing, seeming to bask in what appeared to be the pure adoration that filled her husband's face.

The three Breeds stared at their wives as though there was nothing on the Earth that could compare to them.

How could that be true? It was a far different picture than those of blood and atrocities practiced within the Breed communities, pictures that the pure blood societies circulated.

As food went on the grill, others began to arrive, until the area soon held more than two dozen Breeds and a few humans. There were a few American soldiers and technical support people who worked within Haven. But it was the Breeds she watched.

Many of them sat on the outer perimeter of the impromptu party, watching, chatting, slowly warming to the laughter and camaraderie that seemed to exist. She didn't know how long she stood there watching, but as she watched, others slowly moved closer and became a part of the laughter-filled group.

She had been there three days, and each evening she had stood here watching as the residents of Haven flowed in and out, moving within the acceptance their alpha gave so freely.

"You could be a part of it."

Storme swung around at the soft growl of Styx's voice behind her.

Dropping her arms, she tucked her hands into the pockets of her borrowed jeans and glared back at him.

"Just bring back some food if you don't mind." The smells alone were enough to tempt her to slip into the crowd of sharp-toothed creatures that still held the power to terrify her.

His eyes narrowed.

Each time he made the offer that she could accompany him, and each time she refused.

"You could make an effort to get to know us," he pointed out, his voice sharp.

Storme shrugged. "I just want the food, Styx, I don't want to become the meal."

A muscle at his jaw flexed sharply as she lifted her chin, defying him to retaliate. Storme had learned early on that she wasn't the cowering type, just as she had learned that often her smart-ass perseverance provided the distraction needed for a Coyote or Council soldier to drop his guard. She'd escaped many times using such a strategy.

And though she realized it wasn't going to work here, still, it was such an ingrained habit that it was almost natural. What wasn't natural though was the small pinprick of guilt this time.

"Do you think I'll allow you to get away with this much longer?" His head tilted to the side, the long strands of wicked red hair falling around the dark, savagely hewn features like a heavy curtain of flames.

Damn, he was too attractive, but then, all Breeds, male and female, were designed to create the image of sexual allure. There were no plain Breeds.

"I try really hard not to think period while I'm here," she informed him tightly. "If I actually allow myself to think, then I may lose my sanity in the bargain. This isn't exactly my idea of a vacation getaway, Wolf."

Irritation at the name flared in his eyes and pricked at

her conscience. She couldn't understand why she felt that flare of guilt though. So what if she managed to strike a tender spot. The Breed who had killed her brother hadn't cared how tender James's neck had been when he sliced it open with his teeth. Nor would these Breeds, supposedly more honorable, lose a moment's sleep over ripping her throat out if they thought she had betrayed them.

"Storme, you're creating a situation for yourself that you may not want to step into so easily," he warned her, his tone darkening. "I'd suggest watching that mouth if I were you."

A sharp, mocking laugh leapt to her lips. "Yeah, I'll get right on that, Wolf. While I'm doing that, why don't you fetch us some food?"

Perhaps she should have heeded his advice. Or left off the word fetch. Either one would have likely worked, she thought, as his hands suddenly gripped her shoulders and jerked her around to him, and his head lowered. He shut her up more effectively than if he had possessed a mute button on a remote control designed just for her.

He kissed her.

He stole her strength, her courage and her ability to protest by the simple act of possessing her lips.

Or maybe this was what she was attempting to find again, rather than face his ire.

His lips covering hers, the feel of his kiss, powerful and dominant as it stroked across her senses and brought to life the dreams she'd had in the past nights of those stolen hours they'd shared. Hours spent in the grip of a heated lust so impossible to deny that she had actually allowed a Wolf Breed to take her.

There was something more there than lust though. As his arms surrounded her, pulling her close to the harder, broader length of his body, she felt that something more wrapping around her.

A warmth, a heated emotion she didn't want to examine or know the cause of. Because looking too deeply into it could undermine everything she had ever believed in, everything she had fought for.

She wanted to live for this moment, for this kiss and the feel of his hands pushing beneath the loose T-shirt she wore, to caress her naked skin. The feel of his palms, roughened and calloused, stroking against her flesh even as he pulled her closer.

He kissed her with heated demand, ate at her lips with a male hunger that struck straight to the heart of the feminine heat building inside her.

The sensual side of her had never been pulled free the way Styx drew it from her. He opened a door inside her that she had never known existed. A part of her that she wished would lie dormant once again rather than awakening for a man she knew she could never truly have.

Except for this moment.

Burying her hands in his hair, she gripped the coarse strands, holding on to them as one hand curled beneath her bottom to lift her to him and the other cupped the side of her swollen, unbound breast. Using the hand at her rear for leverage, Storme lifted her knees to grip his hips and allowed the heavy, hard ridge of his cock to ride against the sensitive mound of her pussy through the thin summer denim she wore.

It was exquisite. Pleasure seared the swollen bud of her clit beneath the borrowed jeans and dampened the sensitive folds of her pussy as a feeling of lush sensuality overcame her.

"I can smell your heat," he groaned against her lips. "Like a soft spring rain, damp and sweet as it washes over me."

Her head fell back as his teeth raked along her neck. There should have been fear, and she couldn't quite figure out why there wasn't. Why didn't the horrifying image of her brother's death haunt her when he nipped at her neck and raked his teeth along the sensitive flesh?

She couldn't figure it out; all she knew was that rather than visions of pain, what she saw was an explosion of light and color behind her closed eyelids, as pleasure flooded her body.

As her knees gripped his hips, she was aware of him walking, moving, until he reached the living room and she felt the smooth, butter-soft leather of the couch beneath her back.

Her knees still gripped his hips, her hands still burrowed in his hair, as his lips moved back to hers. A little nip of his teeth and she opened to him, her tongue meeting his, licking, taking, exhilarating in the rush of sensations that came from it.

That subtle taste of cinnamon and chocolate met her taste buds and had her moaning at the sheer decadence of it. His tongue was heated and warm, licking against hers, spreading the taste of his kiss, teasing her until she surrounded it and fought to hold it in her mouth, sucking at it with greedy draws of her lips as he pumped it between her lips.

God, it was so good. She couldn't stand it, she wondered if she would ever be able to live without the regret of losing the pleasure, the taste and the feel of him once this was over and she left Haven.

Stretching beneath him, Storme felt the moan that vibrated in her own chest, a human counterpoint to the half-animal growl of pleasure that came from his.

Pressing her heel into the leather of the couch, she arched to him, breasts and hips pressing into him as her head fell back, giving him leave to caress the fragile line of her throat.

The material of her T-shirt eased up her torso. Releasing his hair, Storme stretched her arms over her head, allowing him to peel the shirt from her before he tossed it away and jerked his own over his head.

Opening her lashes, Storme stared up at the warrior poised above her. With the long red hair, the ocean blue eyes and the tough, hard contours of his chest and muscled biceps, he could have been a warrior of centuries past. A seductive, dominant warrior determined to possess.

Rising, moving back with one knee in the couch, the other on the floor, he trailed his fingers down her stomach to the snap of her jeans.

Within seconds they were both naked and Storme was reaching for him with all the desperate need for the warmth that was so much a part of him.

"Not yet," he growled, pushing her hands back as he spread her thighs and gazed down at the bare folds of her pussy. "I've dreamed of tasting you, Storme. Of licking that silken bare pussy like the precious treat I know it's going to be."

Her womb clenched in response, a punch of sensation vibrating through it as lust speared straight to the heart of her sex. Beneath his darkening gaze she felt the folds heat, become plumper as her clit swelled with responsive need.

"Touch yourself for me, lass," he whispered, his gaze flicking to hers before lowering once again between her thighs. "Let me see the pleasure you can give yourself first. Tease me, lass, until I'm ready to burn alive for ye."

She nearly lost her breath; definitely she was losing her senses. As Styx moved to kneel on the floor beside her, her fingers slipped down her stomach to the wet heat of her sex.

Never had she felt so sensual, so sexual. There was something about that wicked challenge in his gaze that called out to the temptress she'd always wondered if she could be.

Her breath caught as she circled her clit slowly and Styx's chest rumbled with a low vibration of pleasure. With one hand he gripped the hard, flushed shaft of his cock as he pressed her thighs farther apart with the other.

The bare folds beneath her fingers parted as the slick juices of her arousal clung to her fingers. The feel of her own fingers stroking the sensitive, intimate flesh rarely brought her to release. But as he watched, his gaze darker, his expression tight, she felt the pleasure beginning to burn along her flesh and settle in the sensitive tissue of her pussy.

Her touch moved to her clit as he parted the intimate folds with his fingers, parting her, sending swift flares of desperate heat exploding through her pussy and traveling through her body as he watched her caress herself.

"There, love," he crooned. "Stroke your pretty clit, show me your pleasure as I feel it trembling through you."

Her head twisted on the leather cushions as her hips arched, driving the penetration deeper. She wanted him inside her, wanted him filling her. Moving against her clit, her fingers elicited exquisite pleasure. Opening her eyes, she gazed back at him, a whimpering sound of agonizing need passing her lips.

"Tell me what you need, lass," he crooned as his fingers parted the swollen lips and caressed the edges of the clenched opening with firm, sensual strokes.

"You know what I need," she gasped, fighting to breathe as the hunger for it struck at her womb, clenching it almost violently.

"Nay, lass, not unless you tell me," he urged her, his voice tight, deep and rough. "Tell me, little Storme. Tell me what you need."

"Oh God!" She couldn't handle it. She needed it so bad it was like an addiction. "Fuck me, Styx."

"Ah, lass, then I'll no' be able to watch you stroke your wee clit. Soon, I promise."

She shook her head desperately as he rubbed the snug entrance to her pussy, playing with it, stroking it as she arched closer, tried to force his fingers inside her.

"Is there not something I can do for you instead, love?"

She stared back at him, her tongue running over her lips as she gathered her courage.

"Fuck me, Styx," she moaned again. "With your fingers." Sensation speared her clit as she stroked it, as she spoke the need tearing through her. "Fill me. Please, please fill me."

A cry tore from her. Her hips jerked, arching high as one finger thrust deep and hard inside the sensitive muscles, parting them with a swift, fiery thrust of pure pleasure.

She was burning out of control.

As her fingers moved over her clit, stroking against the side of the tender bud, and her thighs spread wider, she gasped, "More. Styx, please. Please more."

She needed that stretching burn. She needed the extremity of the pleasure-pain she knew he could give her.

Shards of heat pierced her vagina, wrapped around her clit and sent the heated dampness of her arousal to coat his fingers as her hips writhed beneath their combined touch.

She wanted to beg, but she could barely breathe for the need. She wanted to scream at him . . .

"Do it," she groaned roughly. "Please, Styx. More."

The next thrust was brutally hot, filling her, giving her a small measure of that pure heat she was begging for as two fingers surged inside her.

"Oh God, yes!" Her fingers moved faster, harder against the tender bud of her clit as she felt waves of impending release beginning to rise inside her.

She was so close. She could feel the hard nub of her clit throbbing in need, the aching demand for orgasm tearing through her as she whimpered in distress.

Never had she been so close yet found it so difficult to find release. Eyes closed, lips parted, she moved her fingers over the ultra-sensitive bud of nerves as a moan of desperation slipped past her lips.

She couldn't do it.

Breathing hard, each uneven gasp a battle to draw in air, Storme fought to find release. It hovered just out of reach, a temptation, a promise of lightning-swift, brutal pleasure, if she could just push herself over the edge.

"Styx!" Her hips churned, thrusting up into each impalement of his fingers as she felt tears filling her eyes.

Each stroke inside her only built the agony higher.

"Please. Please, Styx . . ." Her head tossed as her fingers fought to move faster, harder, against her clit. "I can't." Harsh and broken, the sound of her voice would have shocked her if she'd had the sense to understand the desperation in it. "Please. Please make me come . . ."

Staring up at him, she tried to find her way past whatever held that final pleasure back. Each thrust of his fingers, each stroke of her own built the sensations until she felt as though she could barely breathe. Until nothing mattered, not even a breath, except the waves of ecstasy building inside her.

Staring up at him, lips parted, she whispered, "Please, please make me come."

A growl tore from his chest, and a second later he brushed her fingers aside only to replace her touch with the heated warmth and suckling pressure of his lips.

His tongue flicked with fiery heat over the tight bud of her clit, stroked, licked, and within seconds threw Storme into a release that had her fighting back a scream of pure rapture.

Arching, her thighs tight, tremors racing over her body she felt the fiery explosions tearing through her as he rose over her with a hungry groan.

Before the last shudders of completion raced through her, the feel of the broad, hot head of his cock pressed between the slick folds of her pussy and began a firm, demanding rocking motion that stretched her flesh and buried him, inch by inch, inside the trembling muscles as they tightened and gripped the hardened flesh.

She felt the spurt of heated pre-cum, and fought against that nagging little voice in the back of her mind that warned her something wasn't normal. But hard on the heels of the warmth filling her, the pleasure intensified.

Heat rose inside her pussy, inundating the gripping flesh with ripples of sensation as it relaxed marginally, taking the iron-hard, wide cock with an exciting pleasure-pain.

Her hands gripped his biceps, her nails biting into the tough skin as he worked the hot shaft inside her, the spurts of pre-cum sensitizing her with each blast inside her pussy as the additional sensations sparked a wildfire of lust that rapidly burned out of control.

Ecstasy surged through her. The feel of his cock stretching her to her furthest limits, burning her with pleasure-pain, tore a whimpering cry from her lips.

She was burning for him. Aching for more. Destroying herself with a need for a man she knew she couldn't keep.

◆   ◆   ◆

Styx clenched his teeth and fought against the ever rising tide of pure, naked hunger unlike anything he had known before. The clench of her pussy around the agonizingly tight flesh of his dick was agony and ecstasy. The rippling of those muscles stroked and caressed, clenched on the sensitive crest and sent brutal fingers of sensation tearing through the shaft, his balls, then up his spine.

God help him, pleasure had never been so intense. It bordered on pain it was so overwhelming.

Beneath him, Storme arched closer, her legs lifting, knees gripping his hips as he stroked deeper inside her, lodging to the hilt and feeling his balls tighten in impending release.

Beneath the agonizingly tight flesh of his cock he could feel the pulse of the unique Breed mating physiology tightening, yet refusing to emerge. The knot was supposed to be a mating pleasure and was usually accompanied by the heated spurts of a pre-cum lubrication that eased the female muscles and sensitized them further.

Yet that response to his mate was held back. It pulsed and ached to be released, but refused to swell in response to the release building in his balls.

Never in his life had he wanted anything as he wanted to fill her, to experience that mating heat and bonding that came when two mates were locked together, unable to separate, pulsing in a pleasure they couldn't deny.

Moving against her, he clenched his teeth as he stroked inside her, harder, faster. The knot should emerge with release. Perhaps this time. If he fucked her past her release, held back as long as possible, gave in to the need to lock his teeth at her shoulder as he filled her with his come, then maybe the mating knot would emerge. Maybe the agony of the need would ease.

Pumping harder, his breathing harsh as he scented the impending release of his mate arching and crying beneath him, Styx felt her pussy tightening further, growing hotter, rippling, shuddering until she jerked in his arms and he felt the spill of her juices along the painful hardness of his dick.

There. His teeth locked in her shoulder as he felt her explosion rock her body again. Right there. God, he couldn't hold on any longer. He was losing his mind, losing his control.

His release spurted hard and with a blaze of ecstasy from the head of his cock, filling her, sending a surge of fiery heat racing through his body.

But the completion fell short of the need. His cock jerked and throbbed, semen spilling into her as pleasure raked across his nerve endings. But still, that something was missing. The ache of the throb in the center of his shaft refused to abate, refuse to allow him to forget that for some reason, he couldn't mate his mate.

◆   ◆   ◆

As night spread a black velvet cloak over the mountains, the fog lifting from the cool mountain lake to create a froth of mystery around the small community of Haven, Styx made his way to the base of the mountain and the cabin that sat close to the entrance of the Breed scientific facility. Trailing fingers of the shifting moisture eased into the trees, wrapped around them like a lover and created a sense of comfort as Styx moved along the path that led away from the main block of homes to the home of Dr. Nikki Armani.

The door was open, soft light spilling from the kitchen as Dr. Armani sat at the kitchen table surrounded by stacks and piles of hard copy files that had been taken from various labs during the Breed rescues.

The human doctor had worked with Breeds since she was barely more than a girl. A genius in genetic sequencing and the complications of merging human and animal DNA, she was considered a treasure by the Council, and the Wolf Breeds' only hope to understand their own unique DNA and the phenomenon of mating heat.

Unlike Feline Breeds, Wolf Breed mates rarely conceived. There were few children to compensate for the dangers of mating heat and the cost of hiding the decrease in aging that came with it.

"Styx?" She looked up, the darkened features of her face tightening in concern as she rose to her feet. "Is everything okay?"

Hell no, it wasn't.

"It's getting worse." He cleared his throat, uncertain how to actually voice the fact that he still couldn't seem to mate his mate.

"Come in, I'll fix a cup of decaf coffee and I'll tell you what I've been working on"

"No coffee, Nikki." He shook his head as he paused at the entrance to the kitchen. "You have to tell me what the hell is going on here before this need makes me insane."

She stared back at him as she stood at the table for long moments. Finally, she nodded slowly. "Have the symptoms grown worse yet? The tests we've done show compatibility for mate, and there are minute quantities of the mating hormone in your saliva and semen. It should have progressed by now."

"The glands beneath my tongue have gone from an itch to a damned ache, but they haven't swollen. I've a damned hard-on that's driving me fucking insane, and the pressure of the mating knot that never emerges during sex," he stated as she frowned back at him. "Nikki, this is wearing at my control here. It's all I can do not to lose my mind when I'm with her. Hell, I can barely think long enough to get our damned clothes off."

Hell, this was harder than he had thought it would be. He didn't want to stand here and state his continued failure to claim his mate to anyone, let alone the Breed scientist in charge of figuring out why there would be a failure to begin with.

"The glands ache?" She rubbed at her ear, a gesture that bespoke her confusion. "That's not common. The glands normally swell. Does she have any symptoms?"

"A few." Pushing his hands wearily through his hair, he breathed out roughly. "The faintest scent of chocolate and cinnamon. Tonight, there was a subtle scent of heat, but it receded before she found her release."

"Abstaining as I suggested didn't work then? Nor did it make the need greater?" she asked.

"For me." He grimaced. "She doesn't refuse me, but

damn, Nikki," he growled, "I can all but hear her cursing because the pleasure is more than she wants to reject. She wants me, but I feel she hates the fact that she does."

No matter how hard he'd tried, he couldn't quiet the need to take her, to come, to pump inside her until maybe he could force that final satisfaction free.

Tonight though, as she'd turned her back to him and wrapped her arms around herself, he'd wondered if she was lying there flaying herself for giving in to the hunger.

She hadn't cried, there had been no scent of pain, but what he had sensed, a dark, confused emotion, had tightened his chest with the need to ease her.

Nikki crossed her arms over her breasts, rather as he had seen Storme do when she was trying to figure something out, or when she was considering her next smart-assed crack.

"How far has intimacy gone?" she finally asked.

"As far as it can go," he growled, deciding to jump in rather than ease in painfully. "The glands ache as though they're blocked. My flesh is sensitive, like a slight tingle beneath the skin. The need for her is always present, but not painful, and I can feel the knot forming, but it never emerges. As far as I can tell, she has none of the symptoms."

Nikki blinked back at him in disbelief, and he was damned if he could blame her. He was confused as hell himself.

Pushing his fingers through his hair again, he blew out another hard, rough breath. "I don't know what the hell is going on, Nikki, but I know Jonas. He's making threats to go before the Breed Cabinet to place her under Breed Law. He's determined to force her to give up any information she has, and I can't allow him to take her. You have to prove the mating compatibility if nothing else."

Disbelief still filled her face.

"Proving compatibility isn't a problem, Styx, but none of this makes sense. According to the tests I've conducted, both of you should be in full mating heat." She shook her head. "You can't almost mate your mate."

"Then explain it," he snarled, feeling the imperative demand of the Wolf howling inside him. "She's mine, Nikki, I know she is. The animal senses it, but mating heat is just out of reach. Explain to me what the hell is going on before it makes me insane."

He had tried staying away from her. He had considered attempting to find another lover, but the thought of that brought nothing but distaste. He was spending the better part of his time trying to figure out how to block Jonas rather than figuring out what the hell was going on with his own body. Not that he had any answers there either.

"Hell," she finally breathed out roughly as she stared at the files piled around her. "I've gone through every file I have of experiments done in the labs for the phenomenon they called feral fever as well as mating fever. The only references I can find to anything like this are regarding some of the highest trained assassins, as well as a deep cover operative the Council used as a glorified prostitute. In each case, the Breeds were in positions where the mating heat would have risked the mate, or even those they were responsible for in the labs."

"A subconscious blocking of the heat then?" he mused thoughtfully. It was something he hadn't considered.

"This is going to be a hell of a mess, Styx," she said and sighed as she stared back at the stacks of files then turned back to him with a grimace. "I can prove compatibility, I can prove the mating hormone in your system, but only in minute quantities. I don't know if it's going to be enough to block Jonas if he calls to have her brought up on charges through Breed Law."

"Consider it a challenge," he growled. "I don't care what you have to do, Nikki, but if you don't help me here then I'm going to end up coming under Breed Law myself. I'll run with her. I won't let him take her from me."

That admission hadn't been easy to make. Styx took his oath of loyalty to the Breeds, to Wolfe and to the Bureau, which he had sworn when he accepted the position of

Enforcer, very seriously. The thought of breaking that oath filled him with pain, with a sense of loss.

Haven, the community Wolfe had built here was his family, was his home. Leaving it would never be done easily, but for his mate he would do so gladly. To protect his mate, he would break any vow, betray any oath that endangered her.

"One of these days someone is going to kill Jonas Wyatt and most likely give his mate a lifetime of peace," Nikki finally grunted as she propped one hand on her hip and rubbed at her jaw with the fingers of the other. "So we have to find a way to block Jonas while we work out the reasons why your Wolf is holding back."

Styx narrowed his eyes back at her. "My Wolf isn't holding back, Nikki. If anything, it's fighting for dominance. It's not my Breed genetics hesitating. I suspect it's Storme. My Wolf won't allow her to be forced. Perhaps at this moment mating heat is something she wouldn't be able to balance with the conflict her emotions are building inside her."

She nodded slowly, though her expression was one of pure confusion. The same confusion filling him.

"That could be possible, though I haven't been able to draw a conclusion based on the tests so far. When I take more samples in the morning, perhaps, if, as you say, you've detected the mating scent lately, they'll show more."

Styx shook his head. "Figure something out, Nikki. The hunger is raging inside me. I swear, it feels like a fever that's only growing more severe. If something doesn't give soon, then once it breaks loose I may not be able to control the more animalistic side fighting to be free."

The side that would terrify his mate. A hunger that wouldn't be relieved, a possession she might not understand, and might never forgive him for.

Dominance was a Breed trait, but Wolf Breeds in particular had it in double measure. Even Coyotes didn't have the same intense, burning need for dominance over their mates that Wolf Breeds did. A dominance that came out sexually, and often, when challenged, coalesced in a powerful need to force submission from their mates. When a mate endangered her own life, or the mating, then the animal genetics kicked in with a punch and turned into a burning hunger for an act that would imprint the Wolf's dominance on his mate's subconscious.

It wasn't something Styx liked to admit to, that the Wolf he was bred from could become so overwhelming. Hell, he'd never had it happen before, and he wasn't certain how to handle it now.

All he knew was that something had to be done.

"Let me get more samples from you tonight, then I'll see what they show in the morning as well." Nikki turned and rushed to a storage room at the side of the kitchen. She returned moments later with the heavy black bag she carried with her whenever leaving her cabin.

Setting the bag on the table, she opened it and lifted two sealed sample cups from inside. "Urine and semen." She pressed the sterilized cups into his hand. "We'll get blood and saliva when you get back."

She turned from him as he stared at the plastic cups with a sense of resignation. He could feel his bachelorhood draining from his body, but rather than the weakness he had thought he would feel, he could only feel a sense of impending danger.

If he didn't resolve this, if he didn't claim his mate, then he could lose her forever. And losing his smart-assed, vulnerable, outrageous Storme wasn't something he could imagine surviving.

CHAPTER 8

Storme watched Dr. Armani silently as she extracted the fourth vial of blood from the pressure syringe before storing the supplies she had used over the past several hours back into the heavy, old-fashioned black bag she carried.

She'd arrived as usual, but this morning, she seemed more intent than normal.

Saliva and vaginal swabs had been taken, a scrape of skin from Storme's inner thigh as well as her arm; the bite Styx had given her the night before was swabbed and four vials of blood were taken.

"Which Breed is contagious?" she asked as the doctor snapped the lid shut on the bag.

She couldn't imagine any other reason for the samples being taken every day. She'd lived long enough in the labs to know certain procedures. It may have been ten years since she was there, but she clearly remembered her father swabbing her inner cheek and taking blood when any of the Breeds in the labs had appeared to be ill.

The vaginal swab and skin scraping were something new,

but she made allowances for more thorough testing and better procedures having been developed in the past ten years.

"No one is contagious, Ms. Montague." The doctor gave her a cool smile as she stripped off the thin medical gloves she wore and pushed them into the pockets of her lab coat.

"Then why the examination and the samples every friggin' day?" She waved her hand toward the bag where the doctor had stored the various vials. "When we were in the labs, they only did this when they thought a Breed might be contagious."

"There are other reasons." The doctor brushed back the long mass of braids that swung over her shoulders, before sitting down in the plush chair next to the bed.

"And what would those other reasons be?" Storme crossed her arms over her breasts and stared back at the doctor inquisitively.

She didn't fully trust Nikki Armani. The other woman was a Breed doctor and, according to many reports from the pure blood societies, had worked against the Council even when she was a part of it.

"Have you been feeling uncomfortable? Had any unusual reactions to anything?" the doctor asked instead.

"Like what?" Storme frowned in surprise. "What are you looking for, Dr. Armani?"

"Some answers." The doctor remained cool and unflappable. "Everyone that comes into Haven is required to undergo testing, for your protection as well as ours."

"You talk as though you're a Breed," Storme commented. "You're not. You're human."

Nikki tilted her head and stared back at her curiously. "There's no distinction in my eyes, Storme, and according to the Breed mandates, there is no distinction in the eyes of the world courts."

That didn't mean there wasn't a distinction. It simply meant that the human parts of the Breeds were strong enough to encourage sympathy in the politically correct and politically distrustful world of the moment.

Not that what had been done to the Breeds could ever be considered right or just, but that didn't make them human either.

"But you know that it isn't true," she said softly. "You worked in the labs, Dr. Armani, you know they're not human."

Armani's gaze became thoughtful for a second before a glitter of condemnation filled them. "Storme, I pity you, and I pity those like you who refuse to acknowledge the very unique strength of Breed humanity."

"I respect their strength, Dr. Armani," she said softly. "Just as I respect the strength and intelligence of their animal cousins. But as with the creatures whose genetics they carry, I know better than to bare my throat to them. I learned better the hard way."

By watching her brother die at the sharp, bloodthirsty edge of a Coyote Breed's teeth.

The doctor leaned forward slowly. "When Styx kisses you, is there a difference, Ms. Montague, between his kiss and the kiss of a man who is not a Breed? When that man makes love to you, when he touches you, are you with a man or with an animal? Tell me." She glanced at the mark on Storme's neck. "Do you bare your neck for him?"

"There's still a difference," she whispered. "It's just one you don't want to acknowledge."

The other woman's smile was filled with pity and with anger. "I remember when my grandfather would tell us stories of the racial conflicts in the past century. How we as biracial children were considered less than human because of the color of our skin, or the color of our parents' skin. Courts debated, brothers separated, and a war was fought to uphold the value of our humanity. Simply because these men and women were forced to carry the genetics of proud, highly intelligent hunters doesn't make them any less human for it. If you want my opinion, it makes them far superior to us in the very fact that unlike us, they know the value of life."

The doctor didn't storm from the room, she rose slowly, shook her head at Storme in disgust, picked up her bag and walked calmly away.

And still, she hadn't answered Storme's questions. Why were the samples needed, and what were they testing for? But what she had left Storme with was a mind filled with even more conflicts than before.

There was nothing different in the sex with Styx, other than the pleasure. He could touch her, and her heart rate tripled, kiss her and she lost her senses to anything but the pleasure of that kiss, and when he made love to her, he made love to her with all the hungry, intense pleasure that a woman could dream of. There were times he made her feel her own femininity with such keen strength that it nearly overwhelmed her.

He made her feel like a woman that held her lover's complete attention, his absorption. And that was something she had never known before.

When he held her, she didn't consider him an animal. In the cold light of day she wondered just what the hell she was letting herself get involved in though, because she could feel her emotions and her feelings changing. And that terrified her, because she knew that would also change the entire course she had set for her life.

"Hello, anyone here?" The greeting came through the bedroom, from a voice she knew could belong to only one person. "Styx, come on, honey, I have the chocolate and the wine for you to check out."

Storme's head snapped around, eyes narrowing as a slender, svelte form stepped into the bedroom as though she were well used to being there.

Cassandra Sinclair. Nineteen years old, the only Coyote/Wolf mix created, and rumored to be the foremost authority on Breed Law, she stood in the doorway, leaning against the frame as though she owned the place. Her eyes narrowed on Storme, her expression smooth, but with a hint of condescension.

Dressed in skimpy jean shorts and a barely there racerback tank top, her full breasts pressing against the top, obviously unbound, while skeins of long, lush black curls tumbled to her hips and around her shoulders, she looked like a teenage Lolita dressed to seduce, rather than the legal genius she was rumored to be.

Cassandra Sinclair was highly sought after for the price the Genetics Council had placed on her head because of her unique Breed status, created in vitro and carried to term by her mother. The blending of Coyote and Wolf DNA had failed each time scientists had attempted, until the success with Cassandra's mother.

Pale blue eyes roved over Storme, assessed her, and if the message she saw in the girl's gaze was anything to go by, she definitely wasn't considered a threat to whatever plans the younger woman might have for Styx.

Chocolate and wine? Oh no, Storme didn't think so.

"Styx is not here." She rose from the side of the bed and confronted the girl warily. "And I think you're aware of the fact he isn't."

A black brow arched with feminine arrogance. "Well, if I knew he wasn't here, then I would have looked elsewhere." There was a vein of laughter, an edge of mockery, in Cassandra's tone as she stared around the bedroom. "Normally, he's fairly easy to find. I wonder why he's hiding." No doubt she believed he was hiding from Storme.

Storme tilted her head and stared back at her, wondering why the girl hadn't asked her where Styx was rather than why he wasn't there.

"Styx wouldn't have told you where he was," Cassandra said softly, that smile on her lips sending a rush of disbelief tearing through her. Cassandra couldn't have known what she was thinking. "It's obvious from the bars on the windows and the guards outside that you're a prisoner, so I guess it would be rather useless to inquire from you into his whereabouts?"

Posed as a question, but Storme couldn't shake the feeling that it was deliberate, any more than she could ignore the glitter in those light blue eyes. They were as eerie as Jonas Wyatt's silver gaze.

"If you know a prisoner is here, then why bother to come in looking for Styx?" Storme asked confrontationally as she crossed her arms over her borrowed T-shirt.

Cassandra's lips quirked again. "I'll have to talk to Styx about loaning my clothes out without my permission. That's one of my favorite T-shirts." There was an edge of anger in the girl's voice, an edge that said she wasn't pleased to learn that Styx had loaned Storme anything that belonged to her.

"I left those clothes here, come to think of it," Cassandra murmured. "They look much better on me."

The jeans were a little long. Cassandra was an inch or so taller than Storme, with a lithe, slimmer figure. Storme knew she was a bit hippy, and that made the jeans rather snug. Cassandra's breasts might be fuller, which explained why the T-shirt was just a bit loose.

Storme's lips tightened. "Would you like to have them back?" she asked with false sweetness.

"You could wash them first." Cassandra shrugged. "I hope you wear panties."

Storme breathed in deeply. The other girl was being damned catty for a Wolf Breed.

"Actually I don't," Storme drawled. "But I'll make sure the jeans get a nice rinse."

"Just keep them." Cassandra straightened, her gaze suddenly more intent, sharper. "I didn't mean to make you feel inferior, I was simply upset that Styx didn't ask for the clothing."

Was this woman deranged?

"You can have the clothes back," Storme assured her.

Cassandra shook her head. "I have more you can borrow if you need them. There are few Breed females here at Haven that will meet your size requirements. I would be closest."

Storme watched her warily. For a moment, Cassandra Sinclair looked like any teenager in the world, but she wasn't. Storme had never realized how difficult it must be for the Breeds to maintain the reality of what they were in the face of the illusion they presented to the world.

She was having sex with a Breed male, and now standing here in front of a Breed female that the Council would pay more than three million dollars to possess themselves, she found herself questioning many of the beliefs she'd had for years. Questions she shied quickly away from because she was terrified of the consequences of delving too deeply into them.

As she stared back at Storme, Cassandra didn't appear to be a miracle of genetic engineering, nor did she appear to possess the special, dangerous abilities the Genetics Council was rumored to have stated she possessed.

She looked like any normal teenager confronting someone she didn't understand, and who could possibly be a danger to her. And, Storme admitted, there were times when the anger and rage that filled her could have made her a danger to any Breed.

"You're watching me like Nikki watches her little specimen slides under a microscope," Cassandra laughed.

"You look a lot different than your pictures," Storme said quietly. "A little shorter, and definitely prettier."

The pictures the Council had of her gave her the appearance of cold intelligence. Black-and-white, they showed her with her hair pulled back from her face, her blue eyes appearing paler than they actually were.

Here, in real life, she looked fragile, vulnerable and full of energy. For a moment, she acted as though she weren't entirely certain of something, but she didn't look cold or dangerous and she sure as hell didn't look as though she would survive the cell labs Storme remembered from the Omega compound where she had been raised.

"Well thank you for the compliment, I guess." The smile Cassandra flashed her was at once uncomfortable as well as warm.

"So I guess Styx had things to do today," Cassandra said and sighed. "We've been looking for this really cool, rare chocolate and I finally found it. It arrived today along with the wine we ordered. I just thought he might like to know."

"I'll let him know you were here, Cassandra." Storme wished she could forget. The thought of Styx sharing chocolate and wine with this young woman wasn't a comfortable feeling.

"Call me Cassie. One of these days, we might be friends." Cassie tilted her head, her gaze at once mysterious as well as sharp, intent. As though she could see beyond the surface into part of Storme that Storme wanted no one to see, or to know. Especially Breeds. "If you ever decide we're not monsters, that is."

"We might be friends?" Storme questioned in confusion. "Hopefully, I'll be leaving soon, Cassie. I rather doubt you socialize much outside Breed society. As for monsters, no, I don't see you as a monster." At the moment. And that statement didn't apply to many of the Breeds she had met before Styx kidnapped her.

"Well, the socializing part is rather true. There's that whole nasty price-on-my-head thing," Cassie stated mockingly, though Storme could have sworn there was an edge of pain in her voice. "But the Breed social set is improving daily and we do enjoy our little parties."

Parties such as the one Cassie and her parents had attended on Lawrence Island several months past. The party where she, pride leader Callan Lyons, and an Enforcer had nearly died.

"The reports stated you nearly died at the Lawrence party," Storme said.

Cassie laughed, a bitter, mocking sound that sliced at the illusion of teenage perseverance. For a second, her expression was far too mature for her age, and far too frightened of the future.

"A former Council trainer, Jason Phelps." Cassie swallowed tightly. "He really wanted Dawn, Seth Lawrence's wife now. He was at the labs where she was created and decided that because he was given leave to terrorize and rape her as a child, he could do so now that she was an adult. I was just a little extra, I guess. Three million dollars is a lot of money to pass up, right?"

Jason Phelps. Storme had known Jason Phelps. He had been a friend of her brother's, for a while. For a moment, a flash of memory surfaced. Her brother stalking into the house late one night, furious, his expression tight and hard as Jason followed him inside.

She didn't remember the conversation, or rather the loud argument, that had awakened her and drawn her from her bed. Her brother had been so enraged he had ended up slamming his fist into Jason's face and throwing him out the door of the house.

"Three million dollars is a lot of money," Storme agreed as she fought the panicked feeling beginning to rise inside her. What this young woman had suffered, what she endured as her life had to be hell. Storme was alone, fighting to run from the Council for years. But in all fairness, they hadn't seriously tracked her, simply because until lately, no one had believed the importance of the information she had.

Unlike Cassandra Sinclair. Every move she made, every breath she took was with the knowledge that the Council was willing to pay a fortune to destroy her.

Cassie watched her curiously, a question in her gaze. No doubt she caught the response, the heavy hard thud of her heart before she could control it.

"Jason was killed wasn't he?" Storme asked when Cassie said nothing further.

"A sniper, we still haven't learned who it was." Cassie shoved her hands in the back pockets of her jeans as she drew in a hard breath. "Thankfully, I survived it. The alternative wouldn't have turned out nearly as well."

"And the alternative was?" Storme asked.

Cassie gave her a hard smile. "Standing order among the Breed community where I'm concerned. If I'm taken and rescue isn't possible, then I'll be killed by the very people who love me. And trust me, that is preferable to a life in a Breed lab."

Storme flinched. She remembered the Omega labs, the cells where wounded or experimental Breeds were kept. Cassie would be considered an experimental Breed. She would be caged, kept naked, tested, examined and forced to endure a life that even an animal shouldn't have to endure.

That realization had Storme's heart clenching, her stomach dropping. The Council had been wrong in the creation and the treatment of the Breeds. Storme had known that all along. So how right did that make her?

It was a question she pushed back, one she couldn't focus on quite yet.

"And it's okay for you that your own people would execute you?" she asked Cassie heavily, wondering how she could have lived with the knowledge if her father or brother would have been in that situation.

Cassie's smile was bitter. "Trust me, Storme, I'd rather die than suffer the rapes, the beatings, and the experiments the Council would conduct on me. Death would be a vacation."

Storme swung away from the other girl and paced to the barred window. She couldn't imagine living in such a way. Cassie at least had been raised as a human; for years she hadn't known what she was or how she had been created. Still, the scientists would strip her of her freedom, her very humanity, to find the animal they believed she was inside.

She was, at least mentally and psychologically, human. To have to live with the threat of death at the hands of the people she loved must be a horrifying weight. To be so young and to have to accept that the dreams that could have been hers, the future she could have had, would never be.

Cassandra Sinclair was a young woman who didn't have college to look forward to. The illusion of security, peace or happiness would never be hers. And yet she was here, she had been laughing, joking. She had actually fared far better than Storme had in the past ten years.

"I'm tired . . ." Storme needed to be alone. Only when she was alone could she sort out her emotions and her thoughts enough to remain true to the promise she had made to her father.

"No, you're not tired." Cassie mocked the excuse as Storme refused to turn and meet her gaze. "What's wrong, Storme, your idea of reality faltering somehow?"

It wasn't her idea of reality that was faltering. It was her idea of the past, the future and everything she had thought she believed in.

"You know who I am. I was raised in the labs. I saw what the Breeds were, what they were created to be," Storme whispered. "You know who my family was . . ."

Cassie waved through her words, her expression irritated as she shook her head in impatience.

"Your father and your brother were friends to the Breeds, and their deaths were a terrible tragedy, I know that," Cassie stated. "I came across their file when I was going over a case against another trainer. You however, are a different story, aren't you, Storme? If we all died tomorrow, you wouldn't give a damn."

"That's not true." She swung around, instinctive anger rising inside her.

"Oh, well, you might want to keep Styx around for a little while." Cassie laughed derisively. "To play pet stud perhaps? But the rest of us could go to hell, couldn't we?"

"No." She shook her head, though she knew it was a comment she had made often in regard to Breeds in general. That they could go to hell for all she cared.

The thought of Styx dying, of his laughter, his charm, and his wicked flirtatiousness being extinguished or locked in a cold cell, was more than she could bear.

And strangely, the thought of knowing that gatherings such as the one she'd glimpsed the night before would never happen again had her chest clenching in something resembling regret.

She knew for a fact that Breeds had never had such gatherings in the labs. There had been no warmth for them, no peace and no love. Even a human without Breed genetics could be turned into an animal. And if that human had animal genetics to begin with? Genetics taken from not just the most savage animals on the Earth, but also DNA gathered from some of the most criminal minds the world had ever known, what would then be produced?

That process produced Breeds.

"Look, you've been through hell, your dad and your brother were killed and I'm sure you saw it all, but you know what, Storme, they made a choice and stuck to it. Whatever your father gave you, he gave you for a reason. Because we may need it . . ."

"Stop." Storme couldn't hold back the word, or the demand that this end and this end now. "You don't know me, and you didn't know my father or my brother. I don't have anything to give you, it's that simple. You, Styx, Jonas Wyatt and your alpha are simply going to have to accept that."

"But Navarro did know you," Cassie broke in. "And Navarro remembers well the times your father and brother hid certain details, and worked with him to help certain Breeds escape. They risked their lives for the Breeds, and they told him you held the key to the secrets they were destroying."

"Then they lied to him. And they risked my life by telling him that," Storme bit out furiously. If Navarro had been such a friend, if her father had wanted the Breeds to have the data chip, then surely he would have said something. "I was there in those labs too, Cassie. Any risk they took on themselves, they placed me in the same line of fire. Tell me, would your father do the same?"

"Any battle my father took on would be my battle as well," Cassie told her fiercely. "We're not animals and we're not monsters, but that's not what you believe, is it? It's not what you want to see either. Styx is fine for you to fuck, but tell me, would you stand in front of him to protect him? Would you argue to the world that your lover is human and deserving of life? And if you did, would you argue for his friend as well? His pack mate? His alpha?"

Storme drew in a hard, shaky breath. "You need to leave."

"So you can wallow in your self-pity and judgmental racism?" Cassie's smiled was censorious and edged with disgust. "Sure, Storme, I'll leave now. Be sure to tell Styx I'm looking for him." Cassie paused then, a tight, confident smile filled with critical certainty crossing her face. "When you're gone, he'll be mine again. I can be patient. Right?"

For a second, Cassie's gaze gleamed with feminine confidence. She felt she had a hold on Styx for some reason, a hold that went far beyond sharing a little chocolate.

"Isn't Styx a little old for you?" Storme asked tightly. "I'd think you'd want someone closer to your own age, Cassie."

"I like older men," Cassie assured her. "I especially like Styx. He makes sure I have fun. He may have other lovers, but he always comes back to me. And we both know you have no intention of hanging around, don't we, Storme?"

She had to force herself to control her breathing, to keep from raging inside and out with anger. An anger she shouldn't feel. As Cassie had said, she had no intention of hanging around. Her only firm plan was to escape this place the moment she found her opening, and never look back.

She couldn't force herself to agree with Cassie though. There was something about the other girl that warned her to be wary, to be careful of what she thought, felt and said.

Cassie smiled slowly. "You're a bright woman, Storme. It's too bad you're so damned stubborn as well. Life might have been better for you if you had realized who your friends were, and what your enemies want from you."

"Meaning the Breeds are my friends?" Storme asked bitterly. "Should I just expose my neck with a smile and hope for the best?"

"It depends on the Breed you're exposing your neck to." Cassie was clearly laughing at her. "I believe there may be a few you've pissed off over the years. They might nip you just for the hell of it unless Styx declares you as belonging to him. And I'm certain the Council Coyotes would be more than happy to do some true damage, but until you actually threaten Haven, I don't think you have much to fear."

"And what would it take to threaten Haven?" Storme crossed her arms defensively over her breasts and glared back at Cassie.

Strangely, she had the feeling that Cassie was right, that under different circumstances, they might have been friends. But these weren't different circumstances, this was reality, and in this reality, they weren't friends. There was no chance of them being friends that she could see.

"Escape," Cassie answered thoughtfully. "That's what it would take, Storme. Because if you escape, then you escape with information no one else has, information that could be a danger to us. Be careful what you plan, be careful how determined you become to remain so very stubborn, Storme. Because if you escape, then as with me, we can't afford to allow the Council to take you."

"So your precious alpha would have me killed?" Storme bit out furiously.

"That job would fall to me."

Both Cassie and Storme whirled around, staring in surprise at the implacable expression on Styx's face and the cold, hard edge of determination that filled his eyes.

Panic, fear—they rose inside her like a whirlwind growing rapidly out of control. Like something she couldn't contain or control with the last ounce of determination inside her.

She could see the truth on his face. If she escaped, then she would have the knowledge that even the human soldiers working in Haven didn't have.

Humans were confined to the security areas only. The communications bunkers, the secured entrances. They didn't roam the small cluster of homes and likely only a few had any knowledge of the location of the alpha and his second's homes, except the most trusted ones.

She knew pure blood societies that would pay a hefty price for that information. For any information that would aid in even a quick suicide strike against the leaders of this community, a strike that would come even close to success.

She was a liability to Haven and to the Breeds in general, and the slow, icy knowledge of the danger that placed her in had her throat tightening.

She had slept with this Breed. She had curled against him, felt his arms around her, and she had felt safe.

Even here, safety was an illusion.

"Somehow, that doesn't surprise me." She forced the words past her lips as she turned away from both him as well as Cassie. "Could the two of you leave now? I'm tired of company. I rather enjoy the time I have here to stare at the walls."

To plot and to plan. Suddenly, the idea of escape had never seemed so imperative and yet so far out of reach.

"Like hell," Styx growled as he stalked into the room, then turned to Cassie. "What are you doing here? I sent word I'd meet you in the community center this evening."

Storme swung around and stared at him in disbelief as he spoke to Cassie.

"Strange," Cassie murmured. "I didn't get that message. I wanted to let you know the chocolate we ordered arrived today. Dr. Armani promised to have it tested by the party next week along with the wine we ordered to go with it. I thought we'd check it out tonight."

He glanced back at Storme. Catching his gaze, she made damned certain he didn't sense anything out of her but the anger and disgust she felt.

"Not tonight, Cassie," he growled as he turned back to her.

Cassie pouted prettily. "You promised, Styx."

"And things have happened since I promised," he stated, his tone firm, but still warm. There was a softness to his tone as he spoke to Cassie that set Storme's nerves on edge.

What was it that made her feel like clawing both their eyes out. That had her fingers curling in an effort to hold back that need.

"Styx, this chocolate cost me a month's allowance." Cassie propped her hands on her hips as irritation filled her voice. "And that wine? Do you remember how much that wine cost, Styx? We had a date. You are not allowed to break dates because of a current playmate. You promised me that."

"A current playmate?" Storme was all but choking on her anger now as Cassie shot her a glare and Styx turned, raked his fingers through his hair and grimaced helplessly; she lifted her hand and fought back the incredible urge to throw something at him. "Don't let me hold you back, Styx. And don't even imagine in any part of that tiny brain of yours that I'm some kind of playmate. Go eat your chocolate." Mockery filled her voice. "Drink your wine." Her eyes widened with an innocent concern that was patently false. "Have a really good time by all means. I'm sure I'll find some way to entertain myself." It was all she could do not to clench her teeth in fury.

She hoped they had fun. She hoped to hell that if he was fucking Cassie, then her father caught him. Better yet, she just might make damned certain Dash and Elizabeth

Sinclair found out about it straight from her. They were, after all, normally present in the gatherings each night in the courtyard.

And if she was really, really lucky, then Dash Sinclair would let her watch him neuter the bastard for touching his daughter.

"See, Styx." Cassie smiled in apparent excitement. "She doesn't care a bit. Come share the chocolate with me, you know you want to."

Styx turned back to her slowly.

"Some other time, Cassie." And no one was more shocked than Storme that he gave the refusal. "There are things I have to do this evening. Perhaps tomorrow evening though, since Storme is so determined to do without my company." He shot Storme another look as the flare of anger jumped out of her control and had her teeth snapping together.

"Great. No breaking the promise." Cassie gripped his shoulders, went to her tiptoes and delivered a loud, smacking kiss directly on his lips. "See you tomorrow, sweetie."

She bounced out of the room with all the exuberance of a young woman barely out of childhood, and for a second, Storme could do nothing but hate her.

Chocolate and wine. She breathed in deeply, feeling the edge of tremors of anger as they threatened to slip past her control. She was stuck in this damned house to stare at the walls for days on end. The television was blocked, the Internet didn't work even if they hadn't taken her PDA phone, and she hadn't had chocolate herself in months.

"Have fun," she bit out, her lips curling in distaste as he stared back at her with narrow-eyed suspicion.

"Cassie's always fun," he drawled softly. "But remember, Storme, you're the one that gave me permission."

With one last hard, disgusted look she turned and stomped out of the bedroom and away from the greatest threat she had faced since the night her father and brother died.

The allure of a Breed created to deceive, to seduce and to kill.

CHAPTER 9

Styx fought to replace the anger building inside him with the calm he'd always found centered him. He'd learned years ago that anger only clouded his judgment, it only led to decisions made in the heat of emotion rather than cool logic.

And in dealing with the situation at hand, cool logic was all that would prevail and still see his soul intact.

As Cassie left the house with a cheery wave, he couldn't help but grit his teeth. Cassie could be a bit of a trouble-maker when she felt the situation called for it, and she was definitely attempting to stir the pot of irritation at present.

But mixed with his exasperation at her was an edge of satisfaction as well. His wee Storme was madder than hell at the thought of him spending the next evening with Cassie, chocolate and a bottle of wine at the Point.

The Point being Cassie's name for the small gatherings that were held each evening for dinner. She had been calling it the Point for years now, and none yet knew why. The wine was a gift to her mother for her anniversary and the chocolate was the gourmet truffle cake Cassie had found for Styx to give her parents as a present.

Cassie had made it sound like an intimate, secluded date, and she'd pulled it off with a daring little smile. She'd finally managed to pull the fiery scent of jealousy from Storme's body in a fierce, hot wave.

It had lasted for only a few fragile moments, but it had been there, burning the senses and filling the air with feminine possession.

He rubbed at the back of his neck as he closed the door and moved into the kitchen. From the fridge he pulled a cold chocolate coffee drink, uncapped it and drained it in two solid gulps.

Sleeping was something he wasn't doing much of lately. Hopefully the caffeine would kick-start his energy level just enough to face the stubborn little minx still pouting in his bedroom.

Ah, he liked the sound of those words. Storme waiting in his bedroom. If only he had the right to stalk in there and demand his due as her mate. To demand her safety and convince her of the logic of handing over the data chip her father had given her.

Jonas wasn't going to leave Haven without it. He'd made his position clear that afternoon before the Wolf-Coyote Breed Ruling Cabinet. If Storme didn't produce the data chip, then she would be arrested under the tenants of Breed Law and confined in Sanctuary until such time as she did turn it over.

His teeth snapped together at the thought.

He wouldn't fucking allow it. His mate would not be confined in those windowless cells beneath the mountain, trapped in a small square of a room with no way out, no way to scent the breeze or feel the sunshine. And she sure as hell wouldn't be under the control of Jonas Wyatt.

As much as he respected Jonas, he'd kill the man before he allowed him to fly out of Haven with Storme.

On the heels of that thought his bedroom door was jerked open, and the object of his affection, his lust, and rapidly his heart, stepped into the living room to glare at him in irritation.

"You're still here?" she questioned him, the anger in her tone barely hidden. "I would have thought you'd have left by now."

"Well now, lass, it *is* my home." He gave her a toothy grin, one sure to flash the canines at the side of his mouth.

He wasn't going to hide who he was from her. There were times he got the impression that Storme fought to ignore the fact that he was a Breed, and wanted nothing more than to convince herself that he was as much human as she was.

"Well, I would gladly return your home to you," she muttered as she moved into the kitchen, hips swaying, nipples hard beneath the T-shirt and the long black hair flowing to her shoulders.

She was a wild, beautiful lass, he thought with a sigh. And so damned stubborn. She had the rounded tip of her nose lifted, her determined chin tilted, and those beautiful green eyes were narrowed with disdain and anger, and just that softest hint of jealousy wafted through the air.

That hint of possessive heat was the first sign he'd had that perhaps she felt something more for him than simply lust. It was hell, knowing this woman was his mate, feeling the edge of mating heat that had yet to flare to full life, and being without the satisfaction of knowing that all Breeds would scent his possession and see his mark, know her for the treasure she was to him.

Since Breed freedom had been achieved and mating heat realized, those male Breeds who were aware of the phenomenon waited with eager anticipation for their mate.

There were still those Breeds, both male and female, who were unaware of nature's gift to the Breeds, unless they had already mated. Knowledge of the biological bonding was kept in the strictest confidence, and any Breed who dared to tell the tale would face the combined fury of all Breeds.

"What are you thinking about so heavy? Your little date?" she said to mock him as she entered the kitchen and moved for the coffeepot.

Styx sighed. It would be his luck to be the only unmated

mated Breed in existence. Damn if the pressure of it wasn't ready to chip at his unflappable calm as well.

His cock was hard. He shifted his stance, wondering if there was some way to ease the pressure of it that she wouldn't notice.

"I've things to do, Sugar," he answered as he leaned back against the counter, propped his hands on the slate countertop behind him and just watched her. "The life of a Breed isn't all chocolate and fun, ye know."

He wondered what her flesh would taste like decorated in chocolate. Truly fine, dark and sweet with just a hint of the cocoa sharpness. Even the most decadent chocolate didn't come near to the taste of her flesh though.

"Yeah, its chocolate, wine and fun," she grunted as she made her coffee then went through the kitchen cabinets. "You need to buy groceries unless you intend to starve me."

Styx scratched at his cheek. "Aye, I need to buy a few tidbits to contribute to dinner as well. We're having a pig roast next week, and a few of our more musically talented will be playing for a wee bit of dancing."

He watched her back, watched as she took a deep, hard breath. Next week she would learn the true nature of the wine and chocolate if she cared to pay attention. All mated couples celebrated the anniversary of their matings with the community. They reveled in what they had been gifted with and the lives they were leading now versus the ones they had led in the labs.

She shot him a mutinous glare. "Who's taking me? One of my jailers? You're certainly never around in the evenings."

"You can join yourself, Storme," he told her gently. "You are not excluded from the activities in the square. But if you would like an escort, I can have Navarro accompany you if you prefer not to arrive with me."

He did have other duties for tomorrow night's celebration. He was in charge of roasting the pig, a project that would begin in the next few hours.

"Forget it." The mutinous set of her lips assured him that she would fight tooth and nail before she joined the celebration.

"Ah." He nodded seriously. "I assumed you'd be gettin' cabin fever by now, but I imagine not having to run at every opportunity and having space to rest is rather a novelty. I'll allow you to do that. For a while."

He turned away, watching out of the corner of his eye as she glared at him.

"I'll bring ye a plate tonight though, beauty," he promised her with a grin that he knew would set her teeth on edge. "I believe it's fried chicken night. Aiden Chance, our head of security, insists on a fried chicken night that includes macaroni and cheese with extra cheese." He patted his stomach and made a smacking sound with his lips to indicate the level of sheer cuisine excellence. "Let me tell you what, we have damned fine fried chicken when Hope, Charity and Jessica, Hawke's mate, get together around the fryer."

And he wasn't lying. Of course, the fried chicken preparation took more than the three women. Frying enough chicken for an evening meal at Haven was an all-day event, with volunteers packing the community house from dawn until dinner.

The cabin that served as a kitchen and gathering area in the colder months worked in the summer as a central location for preparation. The entire bottom floor was a kitchen, pantry and eating area.

"Have fun," she muttered as the coffee finished and she poured a cup of the steaming brew.

"Lass, there's no limit to the fun to be had if one is of a mind to join in," he laughed, enjoying these few moments to tease her, though he knew she was unaware of the jest behind the words.

She turned and moved to the glass window of the back door, staring into the courtyard square pensively as she sipped at the coffee.

"Must be a hell of a shock," he stated. "To learn us dirty animals live not so differently from the humans that created us."

She stiffened.

Oh, he was more than aware of her opinion on Breeds. He'd actually heard her mutter the comment several times over the past few years as he tracked her.

He'd forgiven her though. Lord above knew the nightmares she must have had since she had seen her da and brother killed. Their throats had been ripped out; the bloody mess the Coyotes had left behind would give a grown man nightmares, let alone a fragile teenager who feared Breeds to begin with.

"I haven't called you an animal," she denied softly.

"Ah lass, when ye call Navarro, or Wolfe, or any Breed that fights for freedom an animal, ye call me one as well," he chastised her, wondering where this particular conversation would take them.

They hadn't had time to talk much in the past few days. When he was with her, he was more of a mind to fuck her than to talk with her.

Hell, there was nothing he wanted more at the moment than to sample the sweet, feminine taste of her and feel her snug little pussy opening for his dick. But, he could almost sense the conflict raging in her at the same time. A conflict that would offer little time for sexual play. At least for the time being.

Watching her, he now knew why the Breeds who were mated became slavering fools for the tender touch of their mate. If she turned to him, gave him a smile free of mockery, one filled with warmth and love, then he would willingly walk into death for her.

Her head dipped as she stared beyond the door, obviously watching the preparation for the night's meal. Normally, meals were prepared in advance, with everyone bringing their particular dish to the party. Tonight was no exception but for the amount of time pan frying the trays of crispy chicken that would be carried to the picnic tables as everyone began arriving.

"What has ye so pensive, Storme?" he asked gently as she continued to stare into the shaded courtyard beyond.

"I want to leave." It was said so matter-of-factly, so cold

and chillingly polite that he swore he felt something tear a hole in his chest.

Never had a woman wanted to leave his company, be she human or Breed. To hear it from this one, the one that should be his, had the power to awaken the animal inside him with a snarl of rage.

He was normally a calm, easygoing Breed. Even in the heat of battle Styx wasn't one to get overly pissed off or to allow the savage side of his nature freedom.

"You know you can't leave." The brogue dropped; the easy joking and playful fun dissipated inside him.

"Because you won't let me," she snapped as she turned on him, setting the cup heavily on the table as she moved across the room. "Because you and Jonas Wyatt think you can direct anyone and everyone's life however you choose."

"I leave the directing to Jonas." He shrugged easily. "Too many lives and not enough days."

"This isn't a joke, Styx," she yelled back at him. The heat of her anger, pain and fear slapped his senses like a barbed whip.

"I agree with you, your life is a verra damned serious thing to me, woman," he growled back at her, almost wincing at the animalistic sound that had her backing away. "Damn you, Storme. You act as though I'm going to attack you, hurt you in some way. When have I ever harmed you?"

"That doesn't mean you won't," she argued forcefully, as if she were trying to convince herself more than anyone else. "I saw Breeds turn on their handlers in the labs as though they had nothing human inside them . . ."

"Oh well hell, excuse the fuck outta me," he exclaimed, suddenly so completely fed up with her fear that he felt as if he were sinking in it himself. "Let's just brand us all as monsters, Storme, because the horrors we lived with may have riled us a bit. I guess we should execute those who killed their handlers and trainers for fucking raping them, dissecting them alive, and sending others out to shed innocent blood or face the deaths of those they had to leave behind in the labs."

He moved until he was standing over her, staring down at her, watching her eyes dilate with naked misery as she watched him.

"It wasn't like that. I knew them. Those scientists, those trainers. They weren't like that." Tears filled her eyes, and in them Styx saw the lie she tried to make herself believe. She knew they had been like that. But to admit it, meant admitting her father and her brother had been a part of it.

"You think because he was your father, because he loved you, that he wouldn't stand aside and allow those Coyotes and soldiers and trainers to rape those wee young women before they ever knew what it was like to understand a man's touch? Do you think your brother didn't watch men and women screaming in agony as their organs were cut from their living bodies so some fat, diseased bastard with enough cash to buy their lives could live another day?"

"Stop." She jerked away from him, her face pale, her eyes like deep, dark bruises in her pale face. "You don't know what you're saying."

"Your da kept you out of the labs, didn't he, Storme?" he yelled back at her as she retreated across the room. "Your brother kept you from the trainers and the soldiers, didn't he?"

She shook her head, but he knew they had. It was one of the few things he truly respected the Montague men for.

"They kept you out of those labs but for the rare times that they had no choice because of orders from the Directorate," he snapped back at her. "Children were always shown only certain areas of the labs. The ones where the Breeds were little more than animals, so out of their minds with fever and pain that they had no concept of reality, and therefore those who knew no better had no concept of them as human. Deny it, Storme, I dare you."

She shook her head. There were no tears on her face, no horror in her eyes. Hell no, she had to know by now, had to have realized the reality of what she had been shown.

"We don't pretend to be saints." He stepped back from her, the scent of her pain far more than he could bear. "We're strong enough to protect ourselves, able enough to create our own lives and to live in peace, with an assurance of some measure of justice, and I swear to God I think you'd send every one of us right back there if you could."

"No." Instinctive, horrified, her voice slapped back at him. "I just want to be left alone. By the Breeds as well as the Council. That's all I want."

"Then give me the location of the data chip," he said wearily, knowing he could never keep a vow to release her. Even now, with the mating not even fully in effect, he couldn't bear the thought of watching her walk out of his life. He would gladly lie to her, give her any promise she asked for to ensure that Jonas could never touch her with Breed Law and that the Council could never harm another person, especially his mate, with whatever experimentation they had been researching in those labs.

"Give you the location of the data chip," she said, mocking him bitterly. "Just give you what you want." Disgust filled her expression. "You're no better than the Council, Styx. Just give you what you want and I can have my freedom. Maybe I don't like being locked away any more than you did."

"At least you have comfort," he stated as he forced back the fury threatening to claim him. "You're not held down daily and raped by whichever soldier walks past your door. You're fed well, kept in pleasant accommodations, and you're allowed to wear fucking clothes," he sneered back at her. "So I'd say I'm a hell of a lot better than those fuckers and I'd dare you to even suggest otherwise ever again."

Storme stared back at him, her chest tight with the fear and ragged pain she had fought since the night her father and brother died.

True, Coyotes had killed them. Coyotes who were controlled by the Genetics Council. But Wolf Breeds had been escaping; they had to have known her father and brother were in danger, and they had let them die.

She knew they had. She had heard their howls outside the house even as James's throat had been ripped out. They hadn't cared about the two scientists who had worked to save them. They hadn't cared about the fourteen-year-old girl who had been terrified and running for her life.

All they had cared about was their freedom and she couldn't forget it. She couldn't forgive any of them for it. Only animals cared only for their own safety and nothing for the innocents they left behind.

"Think what you want." Her voice was ragged, the tears she refused to shed trapped as always in the dark, nightmarish vacuum inside her soul. "I have nothing that belongs to the Breeds, and I have nothing that belongs to you, or to Jonas Wyatt."

"And what of his child?" he bit off. "Do you think he wants that information to satisfy his own fucking curiosity, Storme? That research could save his wife's infant daughter. A daughter injected with a genetic virus by a human sweetheart. One who thinks he can play God and cheat death."

She felt the breath leave her chest for precious seconds. For a moment, she was fourteen again, running through that darkened tunnel as the nightmarish images of her brother's death replayed itself over and over again. She was alone, cold and praying it was all a dream.

Storme shook her head desperately then. "They destroyed all their files," she whispered. "I watched them do it. I saw them destroy everything. I saw them die because that research wasn't there when the Council henchmen and their Coyotes came to collect it . . ."

"It was there before he copied it all to a data chip and gave it to you," he amended softly. "That's why the Council repeatedly sends those bastards after you. That's why the Breeds have busted their asses since you were eighteen to keep them off your back until you grew up enough to realize who the fuck the bad guys are, Storme." The look he gave her was one filled with disappointment. "And you still haven't grown up, have you?"

Before she could fight, before the anger inside her could light a fuse to the temper she could feel raging out of control inside her, Styx jerked her into his arms.

Almost as though he were helpless against the need that suddenly flamed in his eyes, helpless against the situation and the sense that there would never be a way to resolve it.

A hungry groan tore from his chest as he pulled her head back and covered her lips with enough fiery lust to blaze out of control.

She couldn't fight him. She couldn't fight the pleasure, the anger or the pain. She couldn't fight the need to be in his arms, or the futility that seemed to shackle her.

She could give herself to this though. To the inferno of pleasure and hopeless longing, for just a few seconds.

It wasn't as though he gave her a choice. His arms wrapped around her, lifted her to him, and his tongue sank inside her lips to find hers.

Here, she wasn't alone. There were no conflicts, there was no danger. Here, Storme could forget that everyone wanted the very thing from her that she was terrified to give. At this moment, all Styx wanted was her kiss and her touch. And at this moment there was nothing more in this world that she wanted to give him.

"Don't stop." The cry that tore from her lips as he pulled back shocked her.

The sound was rife with desperation, with needs and desires she didn't dare look too deeply into.

"Storme, sweet lass," he sighed against her lips before pressing a soft, gentle kiss at the corner. "If only this could break down the barriers in your mind so easily."

She shook her head. "Don't, Styx. Please let this go. I'm begging you."

"Please let you go?" His lashes lifted, revealing eyes so blue that for a moment she feared she would drown in them.

Her lips trembled. "Kiss me again first."

She was desperate for the taste of him. So hungry for him she felt as though she were drowning with it. Her flesh was sensitive, her pussy heated and wet, her clit so swollen and throbbing with such a need for release that she felt tortured by it.

"Fuck you first?" he asked, his expression drawn and

tight. "Give you one last taste of being with an animal before you return to whatever human lover you'll have after me?"

"No." She shook her head fiercely, her eyes widening in shock that he would say something so horrible. "No, Styx. Because this is the only place in the world I've ever been able to find peace." Her lips trembled. "Just in your kiss."

"Ahh, lass." He pushed her hair back before laying his forehead against hers and staring into her eyes. "And what peace does it leave me? To know the woman I would claim as my own will take my body, but refuses to accept my heart, or the part of me that isn't so human?"

Confusion filled her, rocked her entire being. "Claim me?" She could barely push the words from her lips. "Why would you want to even think such a thing, Styx? That's not how it was supposed to be."

If he wanted to claim her, then there were emotions. Ties were forming. Bonds could be building. She couldn't have that. Her future was too dark, too uncertain. There was no place in it for promises.

Struggling, pushing back, she tore from his arms and stared back at him in panic. "This isn't a claiming, Styx. We didn't discuss that. That's not what this is supposed to be."

"Ah yes, how remiss of me," he drawled, his tone rougher, darker as she watched his gaze begin to burn with anger. "I guess I should have paid more attention to Jonas when he advised me that you would never see a Breed as anything more than a pet at best." Cold derision filled his expression. "I guess that's why he made certain I understood exactly how you felt about a Breed."

He didn't give her time to argue. He stalked from the house, the door slamming behind him and causing her to flinch at the violent sound.

"No, Styx," she whispered into the sudden silence that filled the house. "That's why Jonas told you how I *should* feel."

She wished he would tell her now, because she had no idea what she felt, or what she was supposed to do with the unfamiliar emotions and the raw, burning pain inside her chest.

Jonas should have kept his mouth shut. Nothing else mattered to Jonas but getting what he wanted though, just as reports suggested. Yes, he had kept Breeds on her ass for ten years. He had chased off Council Coyotes and soldiers, but the only reason he hadn't captured her before now was because he'd known he couldn't force that information from her.

Just as the only reason he had reminded Styx of how she felt about Breeds was to ensure that Styx felt no loyalty to her.

Breathing in deeply, she moved to the back door again, staring into the courtyard with narrowed eyes.

She had to get out of here before she lost her mind. Before this need, before these unfamiliar emotions, destroyed her.

But how did one escape from a highly secured Breed compound?

The front of the cabin was watched diligently. At any time day or night she could look out and see a Breed stalking the area.

Here though, in the courtyard where they all gathered to play and to socialize, security was much lighter. There had been two Enforcers conducting rounds in the past two nights. They had mostly spent their time beneath the wooden canopy where the food was laid out each evening. They were a little less on guard here, trusting the Breeds on perimeter patrol to alert them of any danger.

She could slip through the courtyard and out the other side. Getting past the sentries wouldn't be easy, but she could pull it off. If she took the last scent-neutralizing capsule hidden in her bag, then as long as they didn't see her, they would never know she was there.

Some of her stuff had been brought in that morning before the doctor arrived. Her jeans were in the bag she had been forced to leave in the hotel, and no doubt the Coyote soldiers who had trashed it had taken the bag just to be certain what they wanted wasn't there. But her car had still been in the parking lot, and the small duffel bag with her boots, socks and winter jacket was still stuffed in the trunk. The tiny compartment built into the hole of that boot still held her last scent neutralizer. She'd checked just to be certain.

It would last twelve hours. Long enough for her to get the hell out of Haven and halfway to the nearest town. If she were lucky, she might be able to contact the only friend she had ever been able to depend on and hitch a ride clear out of Colorado.

She was going to have to escape. She needed to figure out what to do with that data chip, and the best way to keep it out of both Breed and Council control.

She should just destroy it.

She played with the ring on her finger, her thumb rubbing over the sapphire set within the ring of diamonds. The gem looked real, the outer shell actually was real. What lay beneath it was the true value of the jewelry though. It was there that her father had hidden the chip filled with information on Project Omega.

Only God knew what it said, or what was actually in the files. She couldn't decrypt them, and she had tried countless times over the years.

One thing was for certain—she was going to have to do something. Getting out of here was imperative. Even more imperative was figuring out who to give that chip to.

She couldn't give it to the Council. They had killed her father and brother, given the order to the Coyote to rip her brother's throat out. Nothing on Earth or in hell could convince her to give them the information they wanted. She would destroy it first.

Giving it to the Breeds was just as dangerous. She had no idea what the information was or what her father's research entailed. She knew though that he considered it so dangerous, so lethal in the hands of the Council that he and her brother had died to protect it.

He had promised her someone would come for the chip, but no one had ever come to her to tell her that he was the one her father had sent.

The Council demanded it. Coyote soldiers fought to

capture her and to force the information from her. Breeds shadowed her as though she would turn around and pass it to them in the shadows.

But no one had simply said, "Your father told me to come to you."

Running at fourteen hadn't been easy. There had been days, weeks at a time when she had hid in the deserts of the Southwest, trying to ensure no Breed caught her scent, trying to figure out how to survive.

It didn't matter where she hid though, she was always found.

On a snowy, frigidly cold night the year she turned eighteen, she had been at a breaking point. Dirty, sick, cold and hungry, she had huddled in an alley behind a loud, popular restaurant and nightclub. She couldn't have gone any farther. She couldn't have fought so much as one more battle.

Gena Waters, a rough-talking, tattooed biker, had found her. She had pulled Storme up and urged her to come to the apartment she rented over the restaurant. She'd helped her bathe, fed her, and given her a place to hide.

Over the years, Gena had pulled her ass out of more fires than Storme could count. Fires they had assumed the free Breeds had begun and Council Breeds had tried to follow through with.

Gena had asked for nothing. She'd always been there.

Even when Storme hadn't called her.

That thought pierced her mind, causing her to pause now as it had in the past, as she wondered how Gena had known she was in danger those times.

God, she was becoming so suspicious.

Moving through the house, she began to plot the best course out of Haven and the best way to contact Gena.

Sometimes it took a day or two, but she always managed to find a way to help Storme when there was no other recourse.

It was Storme's only option. Because God knew, if she stayed here much longer, then she was going to lose her mind. Or even worse, her heart.

Lips thin, Styx stalked to the guest house Jonas and his mate had taken while in Haven. The heli-jet had landed within the secured gates of the Wolf Breed community, which was rare. Normally, unless medical care was required, the heli-jet landed just outside the gates, on the three-story-high heli-pad, which housed a secured entrance into Haven.

Enforcers had reported that the heli-jet had arrived with Jonas and Rachel's infant daughter, Amber.

The child was human, she wasn't Jonas's child by blood, but Styx knew that sometimes blood wasn't all that mattered. Jonas would be more protective now, most likely even more determined to force Storme into giving up the information she had. Unfortunately, Styx had a bad feeling Storme would fight to the death, or the last measure of strength, to hold on to whatever her father had given her to hide.

Stepping to the wide front porch, Styx laid his knuckles to the wood door and waited.

Jonas didn't make him wait long.

The door opened to the hard, savage expression of the director of the Bureau of Breed Affairs.

"We need to talk," Styx informed the other man.

Jonas blinked once before stepping back and allowing Styx to move into the house.

"I've already received Dr. Armani's report." Jonas's voice was graveled, hard. "I've requested a second set of tests to be run."

Styx gave a short nod.

He knew the results as well. Just as he knew Nikki was presently in her lab scratching her head, cussing and trying to figure out how a Breed could be an "almost" mate.

The hormone was in his system, there were minute amounts in Storme's system, and the mating compatibility had been established between the two of them. Nikki had pulled off the impossible and gotten him just enough evidence to ensure that Jonas couldn't move to pull Storme from Haven without the express permission of the alpha.

Mating compatibility was high. The hormone in Styx's and Storme's blood was even higher. Saliva and semen were showing a marked increase in the mating hormone, and the glands beneath his tongue were enflamed just enough to make him aware of it.

All the proof was there, but something held back the full, burning effects of the biological bonding between mates.

"I need you to back off, Jonas." Styx got straight to the point as the director led him into the modest office off the large living room.

"I'm sure you do." Jonas moved to his wide, old-fashioned wood desk and sat down in the leather chair behind it.

"There's enough evidence to support the request for examination that I've submitted with Wolfe," Styx informed the director.

Because the other man was his director, Styx felt he deserved the warning that Styx wasn't going to stand back and allow Jonas to run over his mate.

"A request for examination is not a mating, Styx," Jonas said and sighed. "All this will grant you is, at best, six weeks. If mating heat hasn't been established yet, then it isn't going to be. You're wasting your time, and your emotions, my friend."

There was an edge of weariness in Jonas's voice that sliced at Styx's feelings of guilt.

"How is the babe?" he asked, knowing Jonas's desperation to find a way to neutralize the threat Brandenmore had brought to the baby.

"She's all smiles and wonder." Jonas sighed as he shook his head. "But there's a difference to the baby scent of her. Something no one within Sanctuary can put a finger on. I've brought her here with Amburg and Dr. Morrey to consult with Nikki and the Coyote Breed specialist Del Rey has in the mountain. Hopefully, tighter, they can figure it out."

"And Brandenmore still isn't talking?"

"He still isn't talking," Jonas agreed. "Half the time he's not even in his right mind. Whatever he injected himself with has begun affecting logic and memory. He's currently confined to one of the cells the scientists had built in Sanctuary for Breeds suspected of having feral fever."

A small, padded cell reinforced to ensure the captives held there couldn't hurt themselves.

"There have to be files, Jonas," Styx urged him. "Like Montague, he wouldn't have destroyed them."

"Unlike Montague, Brandenmore was a paranoid nutcase before we ever managed to capture him," Jonas cursed. "Whatever he's been taking to mimic the hormone that slows down aging in mating heat has literally begun rotting his brain."

"I believe Storme will give up the information she has, Jonas," Styx stated, as he wished he could give Jonas more to believe in. "I don't believe Storme is holding the data chip back out of malice. Fear perhaps, but not any true desire to bring harm."

"Whatever the reason, she is endangering Amber," Jonas growled, his silver eyes flashing in momentary rage before it was hidden once again. "How much longer do you believe I will tolerate this, Styx?"

Styx fought back the challenging snarl he would have emitted with any other Breed making such a statement of intent.

"Do you believe I'll tolerate a threat to her, Jonas?" Styx asked, his tone smooth, dark. "Never doubt, I will not. But I am willing to work with you on this. If you can work with another refusing to obey your every command that is." The last words were mocking, doubtful.

There wasn't a Breed or human that knew Jonas who wasn't well aware of his penchant for insisting on giving the orders.

Jonas stared back at him silently for long moments before saying, "What do you have in mind?"

What he had in mind might not be possible. He could be counting too much on a heart Storme might well not possess.

"She's stubborn," he finally said and sighed. "It's her loyalty and her fear that are making her hold on to this. She has heart, Jonas. I want to find that heart. If I can convince her to accept the need to give us the location of the data chip, then I think it may solve the problem of a mating that isn't."

It was only a thought, a feeling. Styx was well aware he could be grasping at straws here, but he was willing to try anything at this point.

Jonas narrowed his gaze back at him. "Explain," he commanded, his voice low.

"Storme is fighting a battle within herself, Jonas," he said. "I gave her something she never believed she could find with a Breed. Safety, and warmth. Storme is a woman who fears the very thing she craves."

"You," Jonas stated.

Styx gave an abrupt nod. "Me. What she's finding with me is something I believe she is fighting even as she's drawn to it. If I'm right, until she accepts it, then the mating heat won't fully begin."

Jonas stared back at him almost blankly for long moments before his gaze flickered with a sense of recognition. "Your hypothesis is that mating heat begins with love, not the other way around?"

Styx nodded. "Hormones, pheromones and chemical

reactions have been proven to contribute heavily to the state of love. All the ingredients for it are there, Jonas. I believe fear is holding her back. Fear and whatever emotion keeps her holding on to something so dangerous as that damned information."

"You could be wrong," Jonas warned him.

Styx blew out a hard, heavy breath. "And I could die tomorrow, but she's worth it."

"Is she?" Jonas leaned forward slowly. "She hates Breeds, Styx. We're animals to her, nothing more. As far as she's concerned, we have no right to our freedoms and no right to our lives."

Styx shook his head as he allowed a small smile to tug at his lips. "No, Jonas, that's what comes from the fear and the anger that fills her. That's not what Storme feels. If she felt it, then I would never hold her in my bed each night."

"You're setting yourself up, Styx." Jonas sighed then. "The steps you're taking will place your status here at Haven, as well as your life, in jeopardy when she betrays you. If a single Breed dies from her actions, then you'll be under Breed Law along with her."

The laws listed in the public archives and law books were discreet, not easily discernible. Those that every Breed and human signed before entering to work in Haven or in Sanctuary were clear-cut and concise.

In this area, mating law ruled every Breed that had mated, especially those who had mated a human. If that human was proven to have deliberately betrayed either community or a Breed of the human's own free will, then punishment could be severe. That punishment extended to the Breed who had mated that human. If the mated pair had produced children, then those children could be taken by the community they were aligned with and raised within that community rather than by the parents they were born to.

The laws were strict, although the harsher punishments were used only in the most extreme circumstances and were at the discretion of the full twelve-member Breed Ruling Cabinet.

Styx found himself staring in the face of the knowledge that if Storme betrayed Breed Law, then he too could be, at the very least, exiled.

For a Wolf Breed especially, that could be hell. In many ways Haven was more social, more interactive than the Feline Breed Sanctuary. Felines were by nature more self-sufficient and less inclined to interact on a more personal basis.

"She's my mate." The animal part of him refused to accept anything less than his mate, and the human side could do nothing but long for that bond, that connection that he would never know with another woman.

Jonas breathed out heavily. "Hell, Styx." He rubbed wearily at the back of his neck. "I hate losing you as an Enforcer, and I know you, if she betrays the Breeds, then being exiled would kill you."

It would kill a part of him, he admitted. The fury he would feel at his mate would likely destroy them both, but she was his. He had to believe in the innate justice he sensed within her.

"Give me the six weeks I require, Jonas," he demanded. "I believe once Storme sees us as we are, versus what she's seen and what she's been taught, then she'll give us the research. If we force it from her, she will never forgive the Breeds, and she could become an enemy none of us can control."

"I'd hate to have to kill her, Styx." Jonas's voice hardened at the thought of Storme becoming an enemy.

"That's not a duty that would fall to your shoulders," Styx reminded him.

It was a duty Styx would have to carry out.

"Do you think I would allow that?" Jonas came slowly to his feet, his hands flat on the desk as he glared back at Styx. "I would not allow that any more than I would allow Dash to kill that precious child, Cassie, that we all had a hand in raising. Fuck Breed Law in that instance, Styx. Have no doubt, no fear, that measures are already in place to have this taken care of if Storme decides to betray us, or if the Council manages to take Cassie with no hope of rescuing her. I won't allow that."

"So you take it on your shoulders?" Styx narrowed his eyes back at the other man, suddenly seeing another side of Jonas that was kept well hidden. "Don't you worry that one day you'll stumble and drop the weights you hold?"

For a second, those eerie silver eyes flashed with a strength, a hidden core of pure titanium that Styx hadn't suspected.

"There is nothing I wouldn't do to ensure the survival of the Breeds," Jonas growled. "There's nothing I wouldn't do to make damned fucking certain my mate and my children live in a world where they won't experience the atrocities, the pure hell we suffered in our creation. Have no doubt, Styx, I would never allow a mate or a father to hesitate in such duties, as I know you would. Our people will not be destroyed because of one woman's or one man's prejudice any more than I would allow a child such as Cassie to suffer the hell I know she would suffer if she were taken. And if I stumble, then there are safeguards in place to ensure my orders are carried out."

Ghost Team. Styx had heard a vague rumor of the specially trained, select team of Breeds Jonas had put together well before he had been elected as director of the Bureau of Breed Affairs.

Like most Breeds, Styx had believed it was no more than a fable. But that fable was the only thing he could think of that could possibly carry out such an order.

"If your hand or your order takes the life of my mate, then watch your back, Jonas," Styx warned him as he felt the animal genetics that created him kicking in place at the thought of any risk to Storme. "Be damned sure you watch your back."

Turning, Styx stalked from the office and back to the front door. He ignored Rachel's questioning voice as she stepped from the kitchen and saw him leave. He didn't slam the door, not a sound was made as it closed. A clear indication to Jonas as he watched from the office door that the Wolf, the warrior Breed Styx was created to be, was fully dominant.

He fought back a smile, slid his hands in the pockets of his slacks and glanced back at his mate as she frowned at him suspiciously.

"What are you up to, Jonas?" Ah, how well she knew him. She was the other half of him just as he had always known she would be.

"Sometimes, human and Breed alike need a subtle little push to do what I feel they should do," he told her as he leaned against the door frame and allowed his gaze to rove over her slowly.

Her body was nearing the "heat" again. He could sense it, scent it as she watched him with those beautiful, suspicious blue eyes.

"What you feel they should do." Her brows lifted at the statement. "Jonas, do you ever worry that one day one of these Breeds you maneuver may decide to kill you rather than tolerate your interference any longer?"

It was a question she posed to him often.

Jonas grinned, as he always did. "They like you too much, mate. They wouldn't see you suffer for my sins."

And there were days he suspected that was much too close to the truth. His Enforcers went to her to complain, to rail, to rage and to threaten him. She soothed their ruffled fur, commiserated with them and generally kept him alive from one day to the next, he had no doubt.

Rachel crossed her arms over her breasts, cocked her curvy little hip and arched a brow mockingly. "One of these days, I just might help them."

She found a way out.

Storme watched late that evening as the Breed Enforcers guarding the house crossed paths, stopped and chatted. After the weeks she had been here, they were doing something she hadn't expected. They were growing complacent.

The night was cloudy, storm clouds brewing over the mountains to block the emerging moon and dim the light shining down on Haven.

She had to run.

Her emotions were in such conflict, the needs, the realities she had always known under attack. She couldn't fight this much longer. If she didn't get away from Haven, then she would never feel that the decision she was close to making was the right one to make.

As long as she was here in Styx's home, surrounded by the humanity and the joy of life and freedom she glimpsed in the Breeds, then her emotions were in such conflict that making the decision was becoming impossible.

Just as the thought of doing without Styx, of being without him, was beginning to become an agonizing choice.

It was a choice she would have to make eventually though. There was no future to a life here, no matter how much she was beginning to wish there were.

Checking the clock, she laced the hiking boots she had slid her feet into and pulled on the long-sleeved denim shirt she had stolen from Styx. When she retrieved the capsule, a grimace tightened her lips. It was crushed, the capsule no more than a fine powder now.

She could only pray she could mask her scent now.

Scent was everything when the Breeds tracked. If she covered her scent with his, it would make it easier to slip away and hike around the base of the Coyote rise to the other side, where she could slip through the security fence easier.

They would detect the break and move immediately to secure the perimeter. They might even be aware it was her breaking through, but she would be close enough to the main road that they wouldn't know if she had caught a ride or not. She knew how to hide from Breeds. She had been doing it for years, until Styx had captured her.

But that was Styx. She was convinced it had been the man combined with the situation that had led to her capture by her fun-loving, too charming Scots Wolf.

And now walking away from him was killing her.

Rubbing at her arms, she grimaced at the irritation she could feel just below the flesh. It was becoming more prominent now than it had been before. It was directly related to Styx, she knew, because if he touched her, if he kissed her, if she tasted that erotic, elusive flavor of chocolate and cinnamon, then the irritation eased. The arousal grew, became heated and hot, but that irritating, frustrating tingle beneath her skin went away.

The hunger for his kiss became sated, for a while at least.

She almost grinned at the thought. Who could have imagined that she, who had believed she hated Breeds for so long, could crave one's kiss?

But a part of her had always known it hadn't been Breeds in general she hated, but the fact that they were the reason her father had died. Protecting them had meant more to her father than protecting his daughter had. The knowledge of that had hurt.

Pulling the edges of the denim shirt closer about her, she stared out the barred window and watched as the Breed guards moved closer to position.

She bit her lip as she felt her throat tightening with emotion. Tears threatened to fill her eyes as she fought the instinctive need to stay rather than to run.

She had no business here, she told herself.

The longer she stayed, the closer she was coming to risking a part of herself she had never risked in her life. Her heart.

Styx was coming dangerously close to making her love him.

Her breath hitched as a sob caught in her chest.

She was not going to cry.

She was going to run, and she was going to hide until she could figure out what the hell she was going to do with the information her father had given her.

One thing was for damned sure, she couldn't keep it any longer. She couldn't risk her own life for something she was beginning to believe to the depths of her soul her father would have wanted the Breeds to have.

As the two Enforcers crossed the line she had marked with her line of sight over the past evenings, Storme moved.

Within seconds she was slipping out the front door and closing it silently.

The natural borders, trees and greenery that the Breeds left for privacy and seclusion worked to her advantage now.

With her gaze trained on the ground, she sidestepped the monitors built into the stone pathway that led to the narrow graveled road, and ducked beneath the motion sensor cameras.

Moving low and fast, she skirted the trees, crossed the road at a fast run then entered the forest as sirens began to sound behind her.

She must have missed a sensor or a camera, she thought.

How unusual. She had always been able to detect the traps laid for her thoroughout the years.

As Styx had said before, she was growing weak, soft.

She didn't bother to look behind her, didn't bother to attempt to see if she was being followed. Her only chance lay in keeping as much distance between her and Styx and the Enforcers as possible.

The farther she ran from him, the harder it became to hold back the tears, or to keep her breathing even enough to allow her to run.

Her vision became dazed and watery, her breathing short, choppy, as she fought back a regret that threatened to overwhelm her.

She didn't want to run from him.

She didn't want to leave, and she didn't want to stay to have her heart ripped from her chest.

She didn't want to ever lose anyone else she loved.

She stumbled, almost going to her knees at the thought.

She couldn't love him. She wouldn't allow herself to love him.

She cared for him. That's what it was. She cared for him and she wasn't used to caring for anyone. Other than Gena, she'd had no friends; they made her vulnerable. They frightened her.

Bracing herself against the trunk of a tree, she wiped her face and looked up as lightning streaked across the sky, illuminating the trees, and the rain began to fall in a hard, steady downpour.

How perfectly fitting, she thought as she drew in a hard, ragged breath and stared around the darkened night.

She could still hear the sirens blaring behind her and knew the Breeds already had teams scouring the forest. They were growing closer by the second and she was just standing there.

"Damn you," she whispered desperately as she fought the sobs that wanted to tear at her chest. "Damn you, Styx."

He was breaking her, she could feel it. She had never had a problem escaping the Council or the Breeds sent after her. She knew their tricks; her brother had taught her how to evade the training they were given. She knew them as only one who had been raised around them could know them. And yet here she stood, as though she couldn't force her legs to move, couldn't force the will to run.

Thunder shook the ground as lightning lit up the sky.

Flinching, Storme pushed herself from the tree as she forced herself to keep going, to keep running.

It was damned hard to run and to cry at the same time though. And why the hell she was crying she couldn't figure out. It wasn't as though she had allowed herself to get close to anyone here, besides Styx. She'd stayed secluded, refraining from joining the evening community meals or responding to any of the invitations issued by the mated couples along the "block."

But she had wanted to visit. She'd wanted to see Chance's child, talk to Faith Arlington about the recent negotiations in Russia concerning a discovery of gold on land ceded to a small Wolf Breed pack years before.

She'd wanted to see Jonas Wyatt and Rachel Broen's child, the one they feared Brandenmore had somehow infected with a potential Breed virus.

What was she doing?

Fists clenched, she added speed to her legs, forcing herself to push faster, farther. She had to get out of Haven if she was going to escape. There was no way she could manage to protect her heart this way, or the information her father had given her.

As another crash of lightning lit the sky, followed by a Wolf's howl that echoed through the trees as though it had been dragged from hell and was rushing up her ass.

She couldn't help turning to look, eyes wide, her lips parting in a surprised scream at the vision behind her.

Lightning flashed, turning a mane of red gold hair to the color of flames as blue eyes gleamed like unearthly lights in the darkness.

Narrowed and glittering with fury, they pierced the darkness as Styx stalked her, moving fast enough to assure her that she wasn't going to lose him, while staying far enough back to give her a sense of hope. If she were insane enough to believe there was any chance of hope where escaping him was concerned.

It was her own fault, just as it had been the first time.

With him behind her now, it seemed her legs filled with energy, with speed. She sprinted through the night, the wind whipping through her hair, excitement churning through her bloodstream as she raced forward.

There was an exhilaration pushing her now, a challenge that added not just the energy to run, but a strength, a surge of adrenaline that had her heart racing and a sense of wildness invading her.

Glancing quickly behind her, she assured herself he was still there, pacing, stalking her through the night as thunder crashed overhead and lightning split the heavens with a display of brilliant yellow streaks of lights.

Behind her, she heard him growl, a warning, deep-throated sound that sent waves of clenching need rushing through her pussy. She felt her juices gathering between her thighs even as she ran through the rain, glancing behind her, making certain he was still there, that he was still following her.

He let her run until her legs grew weak, trembling. As she stumbled against a hidden limb in the dark, lightning flared and she caught herself on a thick fallen tree, gasping for breath.

Instantly, he was there. Behind her, the warmth of his body, the heavy strength of his arms bracketed her, pressing her against the tree as she forced back a moan of pure lust that rose in her throat.

"You will not run from me." Animalistic, so rough and thick with lust, he growled the words at her ear before nipping the tender tip with an exquisite bite.

"I will not let you hold me." Yet she was leaning into him, her rear cushioning the straining length of his cock as he growled against her neck.

"You are mine!"

She shuddered at the declaration, feeling him behind her, his hips rocking against her rear as he pressed her farther over the fallen log.

The wind howled around them, rain beating down on them and soaking her to the skin, yet there was no chill. There was only the heat of his body behind her, his arms around her, the feel of his hands moving to the snap of her jeans, jerking them apart, releasing the zipper and tearing the denim down her thighs.

She wore no panties. She'd long ago forgone the underclothing, leaving her naked beneath the denim.

Against her neck he growled again, his canines raking against her sensitive flesh and sending flares of heated sensation racing through her body.

Was this why she couldn't run from him? Why she couldn't leave him?

With her hands braced on the log, she panted in front of him, feeling his fingers moving between her thighs, finding the swollen bud of her clit as the other hand pushed beneath her borrowed T-shirt to cup the mound of an unbound breast.

Her nipple hardened further, reaching out for his fingers as they found it and burning at the contact.

Storme arched, crying out at each touch as her body began to hum with pleasure. There was nothing as incredible as Styx's touch. As having his lips at her throat, his canines raking over the sensitive cords of her neck and his fingers pressing into the needy depths of her pussy.

"Yes," she hissed in desperation, pressing into the penetration of two strong, wide fingers as they worked their way inside the slick, greedy depths of her sex.

"I won't let you run." He nipped at her neck as she cried out at the deep, penetrating thrust of his fingers inside her. "I'll be damned if I'll lose you to your own damned stubbornness."

Her head fell back against his shoulder as he removed his hand from her breast. A second later she felt him working loose his jeans, releasing the hard, thick length of his cock.

She twisted against him then, a hunger she couldn't control rising inside her.

He let her move, let her turn to face him, only to brace his hands on his shoulders and push her to her knees on the ground.

Her hand went to his thigh, gripping the sides of the impossibly hard muscle with one hand as the fingers of the other curled around his cock.

There were few preliminaries. The desperation riding inside her threatened to steal her mind. She wanted to enjoy every second, every touch until she lost herself to it.

Her lips parted.

Styx's fingers threaded into her hair and gripped the strands as he wrapped the fingers of one hand around the base of the heavy shaft.

Lightning flashed again, sending flares of light flickering over the savage planes of his face. Taut, hard, his expression was filled with lust, with hunger, as he pressed the wide crest to her parted lips.

"Suck it, Sugar," he groaned. "Give me that tight little mouth, love."

A slow, shallow thrust buried the hard, burning head of his cock inside her mouth and dragged a low, hard groan from his chest.

Storme could sense the hunger flowing from him. He burned with it, his cock throbbed hard and tight with it as her tongue curled over the head, stroking as she licked, loving the taste of him, the feel of him.

As he held the hard flesh for her to work her mouth over the engorged tip, Storme's hands were free to roam. As rain poured over them, ran down his chest, to his thighs and around the thrusting length of his dick, her hands caressed and stroked the warmth of his thighs.

Dipping between them, she found the tight, drawn sac of his balls, caressed them and shivered at the sound of the harsh, rough rumble of pleasure that reached her ears.

The hand that held tight to her hair moved her head as he fucked her lips, while he held the base of the shaft with the other. Storme could feel the heavy pulse and throb of blood beneath the heavily veined flesh. Each minute pulse of pre-cum that shot into her mouth was filled with the taste of cinnamon and male heat.

Unique. Heated, the taste of him seemed to fill her senses with the flush and power of a narcotic. It rushed to her head with each pulse of blood to her brain and struck a match to the intoxicating, explosive power of the arousal that flooded her.

She was drowning in him.

Her tongue licked and stroked over the engorged cock as each heavy throb of the unusual ejaculation spurted against her tongue. She tasted and relished. She suckled at the hard flesh, moaning as her fingers slid to the swollen, sensitive bud of her clit.

It burned, throbbed. The swollen bud was so tight and hard it was nearly painful as she stroked and rubbed against the side of the sensitive knot of nerve endings.

"Such a sweet fucking mouth," he groaned, his voice as harsh, as deep as the sound of thunder, muted and low in the distance now. "Suck it hard, baby. Let me feel that hot little tongue loving the hell out of my dick."

And she was loving it. She was intoxicated with it.

She took it as deep as possible, feeling the hard pulse of the wide crest at the back of her throat before retreating to lick at the head once again.

His fingers kneaded her scalp as his thighs bunched and tightened and his cock seemed to harden further, the crest throbbing as though swelling further between her already stretched lips.

"Damn. Enough baby."

Styx jerked back. He could feel the knot pulsing in the tight flesh of his cock, closer to the surface, threatening to expand and swell with each hard pulse of pre-cum he released into her mouth.

He could feel her heat rising, smell it in the storm-drenched air around them.

It wasn't mating heat, but it was damned close. Rich, filled with spice, heated and tempting, it went to his head. Staring down at her, he watched as she pulled back, staring up at him as she licked over the head of his dick, the illumination of the slowly emerging moon gleaming over her pale face and the long, sodden silk of her hair as it flowed down her back.

She looked like a wood nymph, a sexy, sensual little temptress dragging him into a lust-filled adventure that threatened to destroy his self-control.

"Ah, lass," he groaned, unable to hold back the words as she sucked the head of his cock back into her mouth. "That's my sweet Storme."

Never had he known such pleasure. Never had he scented such need and hunger from his lover, and it wasn't even mating heat.

This was pure need, rich and hot, tightening his balls and sending fingers of electric sensation racing up his spine.

As she cupped his balls with one hand, the tips of her fingers playing over the taut sac, he was aware of her stroking herself, the smell of her rich cream filling his senses until he wondered if he could survive the pressure.

One damned thing was for sure, another minute in her mouth and he was going to come for her.

It took all the self-control he possessed to pull her head back and draw her to her feet. Swaying in front of him, her lips reddened and swollen, green eyes darkened and glittering with hunger, she looked like a woman lost in the pleasure she was giving her lover.

"Lass, give to me," he groaned as he turned her again, pressing against her back to bend her over the high trunk of the tree.

Her breath caught, but it was in excitement rather than fear as he tucked the head of his cock against the swollen, saturated folds of her pussy.

"There, love," he crooned, aware of the rough, deepened sound of his voice. "Let me have you. If I don't bury my dick in your sweet wee pussy, then I may not survive the night."

He would have preferred their bed, but there was no

way he would last the time it would take to return her to the cabin before fucking her.

The attempted escape, the chase, the storm that had raged around them and the one that raged inside him were too damned powerful to resist.

Gripping her hip with one hand, he braced his other hand next to hers on the fallen log.

"Storme, forgive me, lass." Because he couldn't go slow. Because he couldn't ease into her as he wanted. Because the need to fill her was riding him like a hard fever and he couldn't hold back any longer.

Storme felt the pressure of his cock against the entrance of her pussy, caught her breath, then let it out in a hard rush of air that should have been a scream.

Her entire body tensed at the first hard, determined thrust. It parted the clenched muscles of her pussy, lodged the head of his cock inside her with shocking swiftness and stole her breath as pleasure erupted within her.

"Styx!" Crying his name out, she arched into the thrust, trying to bury him deeper, harder, pleading for more of the intense, striking sensations that flooded her body at that first, abrupt entrance.

There was no need to beg. As desperate as she was for it, it was possible he was more so.

Storme barely had time to breathe in roughly before he was moving again, retreating, then thrusting in farther, deeper, the burning pleasure-pain of each thrust threatening to throw her over the edge of release with each fiery impalement, until he lodged deep inside her. The fierce, heavy pulses of the pre-cum throbbed from his cock, filling her, and each time she knew beyond a shadow of a doubt that it eased the fierce clench of her pussy around his cock while sensitizing the inner walls further.

A whimpering cry left her lips at the distant realization.

There were rumors, tabloid stories and whispered warnings to all female members of the pure blood societies about a phenomenon known as mating heat.

An uncontrollable lust that stole a woman's mind and made her a willing sensual slave to her Breed lover.

There were reports of the symptoms that she had never believed. The pre-cum that eased a woman's inner flesh and allowed her to easily take the overly thick width of the Wolf Breed cock. There were also rumors of the mating knot, the swelling in the cock.

She hadn't felt that, but she could feel the heavy thunder of his pulse thicker where her pussy was narrower, as though something just beneath the flesh throbbed to be free.

If this was what it was, then she well understood why the women were warned. Someone should have warned her of the pleasure, the heat and the sheer sensuality of it.

If she'd known this was it, then she couldn't say that she wouldn't have rushed into Styx's arms sooner.

"Styx," she whispered his name again as he thrust inside her fully once again before holding himself still inside her.

She could feel it more fully then. That hard throb in the middle of his cock, as though the flesh were fighting to expand, to lock him inside her.

"Ah, lass, I could die a happy man at this moment," he groaned. "Let me just linger a bit here. Let me feel that wee tight pussy wrapped around my dick. Storme, love, you could drive a man mad for hunger of you."

His voice was rougher, the hand at her hip tightening, flexing as his hips shifted, pressing his shaft deeper inside her as she felt her pussy clenching, tightening on him in increasing pleasure.

"Fuck me," she moaned. "Please, Styx. Oh God, please do something." She was trying to move, to shift her hips, to force him to move inside her when he gave a low, growling moan and began to move.

She felt the pleasure tearing through her at each hard thrust, each shocking penetration by the fiery heat of his cock. Electricity seemed to race over her body as her clit burned and swelled further and his fingers moved from her hip to between her thighs.

His fingers found her clit, and there she lost the ability

to think. The calloused tips of his fingers stroked and tormented as his cock thrust inside her with rapid strokes of ecstasy.

She was going to explode. She could feel it. She would die in his arms tonight and there was nothing she could do to stop it. She didn't want to stop it. Here, there was peace, there was a sense of security that she had never known in her life.

There was Styx.

"Ah, lass, you're so close," he groaned at her ear as his teeth raked over her shoulder. "I can't wait to feel it. Feel your wee sweet pussy clenching on my dick. Give it to me, love. Give me your pleasure."

His fingers moved against her clit then, stroking against it as his hips moved harder, faster. He fucked her with hard, powerful strokes, each penetration raking over nerve endings so sensitive, so hot and brutally responsive that she knew she was lost.

His fingers moved over her clit, rubbing, stroking. His cock moved inside her, stretching her, sending a fiery riot of sensations straight to her womb as the building explosion detonated inside her.

She screamed his name, she knew she did. Her body tightened to the breaking point, sizzling fingers of sensation erupted across her nerve endings, and a tidal wave of ecstasy overtook her, shuddering through her body, shaking her, marking her even as Styx marked her shoulder with the sharp, once feared canines he buried in it as he gave himself up to his own release.

And in his arms, Storme knew that somehow, somewhere, she had lost a part of herself and her heart to the Breed that held her.

• C H A P T E R 1 2 •

For the first time since aiding the development of the Wolf Breed community, a week later Styx almost regretted one of the few responsibilities he had toward it. One such duty was the occasional pig roast for mated anniversaries.

Dash Sinclair and his mate, Elizabeth, were celebrating the ten-year mark of their mating on the next evening, and the surprise celebration had been planned for months. Cassie had planned most of the event, and Styx knew this gift to them was very important to her. She wanted to show her parents the value of what they had done for her. Getting her to understand it was no more than any parent would do wasn't easy.

Her life hadn't been an easy one. When she had come to Wolfe and Hope with the idea of the celebration, the alpha pair had wholeheartedly embraced it because Dash had been instrumental in many of the advancements and contacts the Wolf Breed society had gained since the former Army Ranger had declared his Breed status.

Prepping the pig was time-consuming, but a project Styx could do while he thought about things. The fire pit was already prepared, lined, and the coals were glowing red hot as he wrapped the prepared pork in heavy baking foil and set it in the cast iron carrier that would be used to lower it into the pit and to retrieve it when it was ready.

But the activity separated him from Storme, and in the past days, since her attempted escape, something had changed within her. Something he couldn't quite put his finger on or explain.

She seemed quieter, more thoughtful. She still hadn't yet joined the community dinners in the evenings, but now he could see the hunger to do so in her eyes.

There were times he would have given anything to see or to hear what she was thinking when she sat on the back deck of the cabin each evening and watched the hilarity that ensued when they all came together.

Once or twice, he swore he had even caught her on the verge of laughing as the evening progressed and the men attempted to get the hang of a game of touch football or soccer.

They were accomplished athletes, but male Breeds were highly competitive and could become snarling, sweat-soaked friendly adversaries as the games progressed.

Still though, she hadn't joined the fun, nor had she come from the deck to draw closer to it. And her expressions had the power to worry him now.

She seemed almost saddened, as though a part of her just couldn't fight something anymore, and he feared she was giving up on some part of herself.

The mating heat hadn't progressed; he was still tortured by a mating that wasn't. He'd marked her, he could smell his scent on her, but the full heat still remained just out of reach.

Nodding to Navarro to take the other side of the heavy burden, Styx lifted the guest pork and helped carry it to the pit prepared in the middle of the courtyard. Chains attached to the sides of the carrier were then attached to a large hook used to maneuver it and lower it into the hot coals. It was then covered and all they had to do now was wait for the succulent meat to cook.

"It's going to be a hell of a party," Navarro commented as he stepped back and carefully dusted off his hands.

Styx nearly grinned at the Breed's fastidiousness. Navarro was a Custom Class Breed, a Breed created and trained to infiltrate political, social or elite influential societies. Styx called him the "pretty boy" of Haven. He preferred not to get his hands dirty, his hair was always perfectly cut and styled, his clothing always tailored to perfectly fit his tall, corded frame.

"Cassie has it planned to the last minute," Styx murmured in amusement.

"Will your woman be attending?" Navarro asked, surprising Styx with the question.

The other Breed called her his "woman," not his mate. The knowledge of the fact that every Breed in Haven could sense that he hadn't marked her, had his back teeth gritting in anger.

"Perhaps," he answered shortly.

"I can sense the bond there, Styx," Navarro commented. "But you haven't yet mated her. What's holding your Wolf back?"

Styx stared back at the other Breed. "It's not the Wolf holding back, it's the woman."

Navarro grunted at that. "The woman doesn't produce the mating hormone, my friend," Navarro informed him. "She's only subject to it. Therefore, it seems to me it's your Wolf holding back."

"Or her acceptance," Styx growled. "I always wondered at the impression of force the mating hormone gave. That it took choice from the female's hands. I believe Storme is retaining control by refusing to accept . . ."

"Or you are."

Styx gave a low, warning growl. "She's my mate. I accept that."

"But does your Wolf?" Navarro posed the question curiously. "This mating phenomenon intrigues me, Styx. This is the first time a Breed has been held back from his mate in such a way. Perhaps you are the one who refuses to accept a mate that feels such prejudice toward you. A mate that refuses to accept her lover is human as well as animal."

Styx forced himself to hold back the anger that demanded a physical repercussion for the slight toward his acceptance of his mate.

The Wolf inside him was going crazy at the fact that he couldn't mark her properly, that the mating hormone was just out of reach, irritating the glands but refusing to release.

It had to be an unconscious reaction to the fact that his mate didn't accept him, because he sure as hell had no problem accepting his mate. He couldn't and wouldn't accept that the problem lay with him.

"I would rescind the mating acceptance I understand you have given your alpha in regards to the woman," Navarro stated then. "Perhaps a part of you realizes she's going to betray you, or Haven. The consequences of that could be disastrous."

"Did I ask your opinion?" Styx all but snarled back.

"You didn't have to ask my opinion," Navarro assured him. "It was volunteered."

"Then stop fucking volunteering," Styx snapped.

Navarro grunted at the order. "You refuse to even see the truth then? To recognize the fact that this woman is being rejected by your genetics not because of her feelings, but because of your mistrust of her?"

"Exactly." Styx punctuated the statement with a hard growl. "Because unlike you, Navarro, I know my Wolf well. When you understand yours as well, then you can come chat with me."

He turned on his heel and stalked from the fire pit, through the sheltering trees that surrounded it and back to his own home and his own woman.

He'd be damned if he would allow the other Breed to question something so significant as his trust in Storme's innate honesty. She wasn't a cruel person, as much as she wanted to pretend. He could sense the goodness in her, just as he sensed her fear and her confusion.

He wasn't certain why the mating heat wasn't active;

all he knew were his feelings, his belief, that nothing or no one could force love, even mating heat. And thus far, no mating had occurred where there hadn't been the potential for love. Until now.

Storme was intrigued. She wanted him, ached for him. But until she let go of the past, she would never be able to love anyone. Not Breed or human.

Pushing the door open, he caught her scent immediately. His already hardened cock became pure iron, throbbing in need as his balls tightened.

Taking a deep, hard breath, he controlled the impulse to follow the scent to the living room and take her immediately.

His cock was so hard it was painful. His tongue throbbed and itched, though a quick check against the sides of his teeth assured him that the glands hadn't swelled, the mating hormone wasn't filling them.

"I need your help in here." Resignation filled her tone as it echoed from the living room.

Frowning, he moved into the living room before coming to a surprised stop just inside the door.

Storme sat on the floor, her head beneath the living room table where the television controls, the glass top's internal computer display and the room temperature and lighting controls were accessed and wired into.

The sensitive electronic tabletop lifted for easier view, with a holographic keyboard that moved and angled to fit any position on the couch in front of it.

At least, it had. At the moment, Storme seemed to have several components to the wireless receivers as well as the main control board disassembled.

He felt his stomach fall in acute disappointment. Damn, he loved that system. It controlled not just his ability to access the Internet and Bureau files, but also his television, satellite links, security details and his state-of-the-art audio system on the far wall.

"May I ask what you're doing?" He stepped to her, keeping his hands carefully from around her neck.

He was in love with her. If he wasn't in love with her

before, then in that moment, he fell head over heels as she reached for the slender electronic adjustment wand at her side and expertly applied it to the sensor in the control module that had been giving him hell for months.

"Well, I was trying to bypass the security protocols on the system so I could watch the damned television," she muttered. "While I was in there, I found about a dozen shorts in the system and several hardware vulnerabilities. I thought I'd just fix everything."

"Bored, Storme?" he drawled in amusement as he hunched down beside her.

"Just hold this." Feigned disgust filled her tone as she indicated the long, awkwardly mounted control board beneath the table. "Whoever installed this should be shot. It's a freakin' mess. Do you realize hardware vulnerabilities can screw your entire firewall system? What? You want someone to slip into your system and fuck with it?"

No, he didn't, but he had suspected Storme's talents based on the files the Bureau had on her. He'd deliberately left the problems in place and had the communications bunker closely monitoring it as he waited on her to get tired of roaming the house like a ghost and do something about it when one of the shorts caused the television to stop working.

"I appreciate your concern," he murmured as his gaze drifted to where the shirt she wore gapped at her stomach, several buttons having slipped free.

She was wearing one of his shirts now. Bare, tanned flesh tempted him to take a taste as he reached in and held the control board in place for her.

"My concern or my boredom?" she questioned crisply as she reached for another of the electronic tools, her fingers feeling around against the sheet until he pushed it in her path silently.

She picked up the slender needle-nosed wire adjuster and soldering tool, and he watched as she gripped two minute wires, set them in place and activated the tool to set the wires.

So much for Jonas and Navarro's opinion that she would

betray them at first opportunity. She could have kept her mouth shut about the hardware problems, likely believing he was unaware of them, and tried to find a way to hurt Haven.

She hadn't. She had warned him of the problem instead. That knowledge sent a surge of pure emotion slamming through his gut, nearly causing him to lose his grip on the control board.

"Geez, Styx, don't get fumble fingers on me," she muttered as she pulled the pliers back and checked her work with a small electronic surge light.

Thumbing the switch to the light, she activated the testing system and began running the white light over each component and wire.

"Where did you learn how to work on these systems?" Styx asked as she frowned up at the internal system fiercely.

"Tinkering some," she answered absently. "I had some training at the Omega lab, with one of their computer experts, before the rescues."

"You have a knack for it," he stated.

"It's a talent." She reached for another slender tool and made an adjustment in the wireless modules that connected the system to the various electronics it controlled.

"I would have imagined you would lean toward medical or genetic engineering. I wouldn't have guessed a talent in computerized systems."

She paused, glared at the system then sighed heavily. "I thank God I didn't lean toward anything medical in any way. The thought of it sickens me."

"Because of the work your father and brother did?"

She pushed herself from beneath the table and glared up at him now. "Would you like to know, Styx, why I hate Breeds with a depth that frightens me at times?"

His teeth clenched. She was admitting it, and he hated that.

"Why, Storme?" he asked softly.

"Because they sent my father and my brother to hell before I was ready to let them go. My father and brother broke the laws of nature, and the laws of decency, in what they helped the Council to do. And then they broke my heart when they showed their loyalty to their work over their loyalty to me. I hated them for it, I hated the Breeds for it, and I hate that fucking Council so bad I'd kill every one of those bastards if I could. So the Breeds can count themselves lucky. At least I don't wish I could murder them to their faces. Now, excuse me, but I don't need your help any longer. You can leave now."

She pushed her back beneath the table and ignored him as though he wasn't there, while she went back to work on reassembling the electronics she had taken apart.

At least, she appeared to ignore him; what he sensed was far different. He could feel her pain, tears unshed and a sudden desperation that tore at his chest.

Storme was fighting more than the past or her emotions. She was fighting the desertion of her father and brother, and the suspicion that they had loved the Breeds far more than they had loved her.

Unfortunately, Styx agreed with her.

Styx retreated, hoping that the very fact of the battle waging inside her now boded well for her realization that the Breeds weren't at fault for what she'd lost, but rather her father and brother were.

Moving to the kitchen, he pulled coffee beans from the cabinet along with an old-fashioned hand grinder and dark chocolate. He had a system he liked for coffee. The fresh beans hand ground with the dark chocolate.

He was a chocolate fanatic, he admitted to that. The first time he had tasted chocolate was after the Breed rescues. Despite the fact that his training had been easier than most Breeds', still, chocolate had been something denied him until he had the choice to indulge in it after the rescue.

Storme reminded him of his favorite chocolate, he thought with a brief grin. A little sharp, with all the sweetness hid beneath that first sharp bite.

"Now I can watch television." Satisfaction filled her tone as she entered the kitchen. "And that's a hell of an audio system."

Her voice was deliberately light; he could feel it, sense

it. She was trying to ignore the fact that she had admitted to hating the Breeds, that she had admitted, in effect, to hating him.

The softened amusement of moments before had dissipated.

Turning back to the coffeemaker, he poured the coffee into cups. As she sat down at the old-fashioned country kitchen table, he set the cup in front of her then retreated back to the cabinets to sip his own.

He could show her a thing or two about how she didn't hate him, how she didn't hate Breeds period. He could show her, force her to acknowledge that at least where he was concerned, what she felt was the furthest thing possible from hatred.

She lifted the cup to her lips, and his dick tightened impossibly further.

When he didn't comment, she glanced back at him and breathed in deeply, with a slow, subtle movement.

She had obviously said what she had earlier without truly considering the implications of her words.

"The system should be working properly now," she stated. "I'm certain you'll want to ensure that the firewall is working within standards."

"I'll be sure to do that," he assured her.

He would be replacing the firewall soon if this situation didn't change. If the mating heat didn't slip into place soon. If he didn't win his mate's heart.

She sipped at the coffee again before replacing the cup on the table, her fingers playing absently with the handle as she stared into the cup's depths.

"I don't hate you," she finally said softly, her voice torn with confusion and pain. "I didn't mean that as it came out."

"Of course you did," he retorted lightly. "What you said, you said in anger, and in self-defense. You've likely never been more truthful."

"Don't put words or feelings into my mouth." She glared back at him as her lips tightened angrily. "Fine, I feel animosity, and a hell of a lot of anger where the Breeds are concerned.

If Dad and James hadn't been so in love with their research and what they were creating, then they wouldn't have died and I wouldn't have been forced to run to live."

The pain in her voice struck at his heart, clenching his chest and his emotions. The pressure she had lived under for the past ten years had been incredible, and he didn't blame her for being angry. But the anger was misdirected.

"You wouldn't have been forced to run in order to live if you had come to us when you first escaped Omega," he informed her before taking another sip of the coffee and setting the cup aside.

He could feel the confrontation coming like a tingle of electricity over his flesh. Anger was the product of denied hunger, of cross-purposes and emotions without outlet. And if anyone needed to let emotions out, then it was Storme. She was like her name, raging inside, crashing like thunder in the heavens as the past and the present came in conflict with what she wanted, needed and denied herself for the future.

"Yeah, I really wanted to face a Breed then." The hard, bitter smile that crossed her face had nothing to do with amusement and everything to do with the pain raging inside her. "I was fourteen, Styx . . ."

"And you're twenty-four now," he reminded her caustically. "Tell me, Storme, have you managed to grow up in anything but body?"

Storme rose slowly from the chair, feeling a shudder of intense emotion tear through her as she fought to hold back a sudden, wrenching sob.

His expression was stoic, his blue eyes almost darker, brighter.

"What do you want me to say?" she demanded, almost wincing at the harsh sound of her own voice. "What do you want from me, Styx?"

"Your safety," he snarled back at her, his canines flashing as his lips pulled back from his teeth. "I want that fucking data chip."

"For my safety?" Her words were suffused with bitter

mockery. "And of course your motives are completely altruistic, aren't they, Styx? It has nothing to do with the fact that you fucked me to attain that damned chip, does it? That you and Jonas Wyatt would willingly throw me to the Council if it achieved your ends?"

Her pain swirled around him then.

"Is this what you think?" The growl that vibrated in his chest was deeper, harsher than he'd expected, as incredulity flared inside him. "You believe I took you to my bed to get that damned chip? That I would betray you in such a manner if I don't get it?"

"What else should I think? Orders to kill me if I escape and can't be recovered before the Council gets to me?" she sneered back at him. "I guess those orders come from love? From an overwhelming desire for me alone? Don't bother lying to me because I know better."

"And how do you know better?" This was it. Damn her, she was pushing him past reason, and holding back from her wasn't easy to begin with. The need to have her, to possess her, to imprint upon her body, her sensuality, the dominant possessiveness raging inside him was becoming quickly overwhelming. "Tell me, Storme, if the only reason I fucked you was for that chip, do you truly believe that's why I kept fucking you?"

"Why else?" Her arms opened wide in an indication of resignation. "Do you have the chip? If you kill me, you can't locate it. What other recourse is left but to fuck me and attempt to convince me there's some emotion involved. Tell me, Styx, do you love me?" she sneered mockingly.

Storme could feel the anger surging through her now; the aching, torn emotions that ripped through her were harder to define, but the anger was clearly recognizable.

As she stared back at him, seeing the seeming sincerity in his gaze, the urge for violence rose inside her like a dark, vicious cloud.

Fists clenched, she swung away from him, turned and tried to race from the kitchen, from the man, the Breed. She'd spent the past week hiding, running, avoiding this

Breed that made her feel emotions and sensations she didn't want to feel.

He made her feel guilty, regretful, and he made her wish things were different, made her want to find reasons to trust him. And Storme knew there was no trusting a Breed.

How many had taught her that lesson, beginning the night her father and brother had died.

"By God, I'm sick of you running from me." Before she reached the door, his arm latched around her waist and she found herself pulled flush against his chest, his hold firm, possessive, as she felt his heart thundering at her back.

"And I'm sick of being locked up and made a prisoner," she cried out furiously. "I'm sick of being used by you and I'm sick of being lied to."

She was turned before she could fight. His fingers threaded through her hair, pulled her head back, and his lips covered hers as she parted them to scream.

At least, she told herself she meant to scream. Instead her tongue met his, licked and stroked until she tempted it inside, where her mouth enclosed it and she suckled it with sharp, demanding movements of her lips.

A harsh growl echoed around her as her hands moved over his chest, his shoulders, pulling at the dark gray shirt that had complemented the long red hair and vivid blue eyes. She wanted it off his body. She wanted to feel him against her, the warmth and the strength she craved wrapped around her.

She tasted the softest hint of cinnamon before it was gone. The taste drew at her senses and had her reaching for more of him, the kiss growing deeper, stronger as she pulled at the edge of the shirt.

Her fingers fumbled as she tried to unbutton it. A ragged groan tore from her throat as she tried to pull the hem of the shirt from his pants.

Storme gave a groan herself as he pulled back, nipping his lips in retaliation as she tried to draw him to her.

There was something desperate, something ecstatic

about being in his arms, feeling his touch, touching him and relishing the excitement that began to surge through her.

As his lips moved along her jaw and down her neck, Storme found her head tipping back in invitation. The thought of pain never entered her mind. Only pleasure could come from his touch there.

And only pleasure came. The rake of his teeth, the lick of his tongue, the feel of his lips smoothing along the column pulled a desperate mewl of pleasure from her lips.

"Come here." The demand was followed by his arm hooking beneath her knees as he lifted her against him, turned and strode through the living room and into the bedroom. To the bed.

Storme felt her back meet the mattress as Styx came over her, his hands going instantly to the edges of the shirt she had borrowed from him, to rip the buttons from their moorings with a quick jerk.

She tried to follow suit, but his lips returned to hers, kissing her mindless as she felt him moving. His shirt was gone, giving the bare expanse of his flesh to her eager touch.

His fingers were at her jeans, tearing at the metal buttons, pushing the denim down her hips as her legs lifted and moved, her hips shifting, helping him undress her as their lips and tongues mated and dueled with a hunger that flared hotter, brighter than ever before.

Within minutes she was naked, then crying out hoarsely as he jerked back from her.

Moving to the edge of the bed, he yanked his boots from his feet, rose and stripped off his jeans, then turned back to her.

Storme felt the breath leave her chest at the sight of his cock, so thick and hard, the crest flushed nearly purple as it throbbed in lust, a sheen of pre-cum glistening on the tip as he hovered over her.

Her thighs parted for him, but he didn't fit his hips between them. Instead, before her astounded gaze, his head lowered and his tongue swiped through the hot, slick folds of flesh that ached in fiery need for his touch.

Storme shuddered as pleasure whipped through her. His tongue licked and stroked, flickered around her clit and ignored the desperate arch and shudder in her thighs.

"Styx, oh God, I can't stand it," she cried out, her voice hoarse as the need burned like wildfire through her sex.

Storme could feel her juices gathering inside before rushing to meet his licking tongue. His fingers parted the swollen slips as his tongue lapped at the sensitive flesh before circling her clit with fiery hunger.

"So good," she panted, unable to keep her silence, unable to hold back the pleasure she was feeling. "Oh God, Styx. It's so good. So hot."

His tongue flicked around her clit in a lash of fiery sensation and incredible pleasure.

A hungry growl met the words, speeding up her heart rate and spurring her arousal.

Her knees bent, her thighs parting farther as her hips arched to lift closer.

"Styx." Desperation began to fill her at the ache centered in her pussy, the clenching, heated hunger that radiated from the very heart of her femininity.

Storme felt his fingers moving as though he sensed the need, two pressing at the greedy entrance as his lips surrounded the bud of her clit and began to suckle it with tempting, firm pressure.

Her fingers fisted in the comforter beneath her. As her head whirled with sensation, the need to find something to hold on to became overwhelming.

As his lips and tongue tormented and tortured her clit, his fingers worked slowly inside her pussy, parting the tender tissue, stretching it as burning flares of impending orgasm began to race through her.

This wasn't love, she thought desperately. This was just pleasure, it was just hunger. She could still walk away without regrets, she was convinced of it.

That thought was distant though, without conviction,

and shrouded with such intense pleasure she was on the verge of screaming.

Strong, masculine fingers moved inside her, stroking, caressing tender tissue and ultrasensitive nerve endings. Thrusting her hips upward, she wedged his fingers in deeper, a cry falling from her lips as he chose that moment to cover the tender bundle of nerves with his lips.

Her clit, throbbing and swollen, lifted to the damp heat of his mouth. Fire and ice seemed to wash through her system, tear across her nerve endings, and pleasure stormed her senses with hard bursts of electric sensation.

Her hips jerked against the impalements, the sliding of his fingers inside her, the retreat, the sudden fullness of the inner thrust that sent fiery waves of pleasure rushing through her womb.

Shaking, trembling from the excess pleasure, Storme lifted her hands from the comforter and tangled her fingers in the long, coarse strands of his hair. Bunching in the heavy warmth, she held his head in place, her hips rising and falling, forcing his fingers harder, deeper inside her as ragged cries began to tear from her throat.

She could feel the force of the impending ecstasy beginning to burn inside her. Felt the sensations multiply, racing across her nerve endings and screaming through her senses.

"Styx!" She moaned his name desperately. "Harder." Her hips churned on his fingers. "Oh God, fuck me harder, Styx. Harder . . ."

The pace of his fingers quickened, moving inside the slick recesses of her pussy as she felt that tight, burning ball of need explode in her clit, her womb, and throw her into rapture.

A muffled, weak scream tore from her lips as her hips jerked up, her thighs shaking, her clit radiating with a wildfire of pleasure as her orgasm overtook her and threw her into a brilliant fire burst of light, color and screaming pleasure.

◆　　◆　　◆

Styx was desperate. An agony of hunger and lust throbbed through his entire body. His cock was harder than he could ever remember it being. It throbbed and pulsed, pre-cum dampening the crest and slickening the bulging flesh as he came to his knees and positioned himself between her thighs.

The bare flesh of the folds of her pussy flowered open, glistening and shimmering slick and wet as he gripped the shaft of this thick flesh and placed the head at the heated entrance.

The shock of pleasure clenched his teeth as he stared down at the swollen, silken folds as he began to press inside.

"Styx." Her thighs parted farther as she whispered his name, her voice hoarse, drawing his gaze.

Her face was awash with ecstasy, her green eyes gleaming like living emeralds as she stared back at him.

He felt the snug entrance begin to stretch over the flared crest of his dick. The heated, slick flesh sent sharp shards of dark pleasure racing through him.

"Sweet Storme," he groaned, his voice rougher, more of a growl than before as he grimaced, feeling the ultratight flesh stretching around his cock.

"So good," she moaned, her neck arching, perspiration dampening the fragile column of her neck as her lips parted and her drowsy gaze locked with his. "It's so good, Styx."

It was so good. It was like heaven and hell. The most exquisite ecstasy he had ever known. The pleasure was white hot, brilliant, as close to pain as pleasure could get, as the tight muscles of her pussy gripped and rippled over the flared head of his dick.

A rumbling growl echoed in his chest as he worked the swollen, heavy flesh into the slick recesses of her pussy. The ripple of her inner flesh over the sensitive crest was like electric rapture. The surging sensations raced over his body and sizzled up his spine as he surged those last inches and buried himself to the hilt inside her.

"Ah God!" He couldn't hold back the growl. "Fuck, Sugar. So sweet and fucking hot."

He was in agony the pleasure was so brilliant. Seated fully inside her, he lingered for seconds, a lifetime, feeling the clench of her stretched flesh around his cock, feeling the liquid heat of her arousal.

In the center of the shaft that agonizing throb began to pulse, the Wolf Breed knot flexing as he began to move, to thrust inside her as he worked in and out, stroking the pleasure higher, hotter.

One hand gripped her hip as he set the opposite elbow on the mattress at her shoulder and rose over her. His lips touched hers, the need for breath holding back the kiss they both longed for.

A growl surged from his chest again as he felt her hips elevate, her legs wrap around his hips as she took him impossibly deeper.

God, she was tight. So fucking tight he could feel every ripple of response, every little throb of pulsing need that shuddered through her hot little pussy.

Fucking her was incredible. It was living, breathing ecstasy. It was being surrounded by pure sensation and drowning in the slick heat of each thrust inside the velvety depths of her sex.

Never had he known pleasure so brilliantly hot. It was the most pleasure any man could ever know and survive.

Holding her close, Styx rose farther over her, his lips moving to the bend of her shoulder, close to her neck, instinct and need combining as his tongue licked over the tender flesh there.

The glands beneath his tongue itched with a torturous irritation. His body became sensitive, each cell atuned to each stroke of her hands as they clenched on his back, her little nails digging into his flesh.

Hunger surged with incredible force inside them both. The scent of her need filled his senses as the silken perspiration on her damp flesh stroked against his. His hand clenched on her hip, his teeth gripped the flesh between shoulder blade and neck, and as he felt her explode beneath him, Styx gave in to the need clawing up his back.

As the heated, tight muscles of her pussy clenched further and began to flex, to throb as she cried out below him, Styx moved harder against her, fucking into her with heavy thrusts until he felt the fiery heat of release began to explode in his tortured balls.

The snarling growl that tore from his chest was accompanied by his teeth locking into her shoulder, his hand pressing her hips closer, and Storme's ragged cry and second orgasm exploding around him.

She cried out his name, lifted and shuddered in hard, deep tremors as Styx jerked his head back, locked his teeth together and rode the fierce, desperate waves of a release that tore through him.

The mating knot flexed beneath the shaft of his dick, heated, and as the hard pulses of semen spurted from the tip of his cock, it once again retreated without swelling, without locking him inside her or marking her as his mate.

Collapsing over her, Styx rested his head on the pillow beside hers, his forehead pressing into the cool material as the ache of regret ripped at his soul.

She was his mate. He knew it. She belonged to him, yet something kept her from him, whether her inability to fight past her fear, as he believed, or his lack of trust, as Navarro believed, he didn't know. What he knew was that something had to give. One way or the other, this problem had to be resolved.

He had only six weeks, if he was lucky, to prove she was his mate, or to mark her as such. There was no way to prove the bonding without a full mating. Without it, there would be no way to save her from Jonas's plans unless she gave up the data chip.

He didn't worry about proving shit if the mating happened. Mating didn't happen without love. It didn't happen without the most vital elements of that emotional bonding. If the mating occurred, then there was no doubt in his mind that she would trust him with the secrets she hid and, in turn, trust Jonas with them.

"Styx?" she whispered, her voice sated and drowsy as he brushed his lips over the edge of her shoulder.

"Yes, love?" What more could he give her? What would it take to convince her wary heart to trust him?

"You taste like chocolate," she said with a sigh, a hint of amusement in her voice. "A woman wouldn't have to gain weight to get her fix, all she would have to do is kiss you."

Styx closed his eyes as bitterness threatened to overwhelm him. If only it was something other than chocolate that she tasted. Each Breed had a distinctive "taste" to the mating hormone. A taste their mate craved, a kiss as addictive as it was pleasurable.

"Perhaps you should kiss me often then," he finally whispered as he lifted himself from her, grimacing as his sensitive cock eased from the tight depths of her pussy.

"Perhaps I should." She was soft now, sweet. Satiation filled her body and mind, stole the suspicion from her gaze and left her relaxed and lazy in his arms as he lay beside her and pulled her against his chest.

The wealth of black hair that flowed to the middle of her back spread over her shoulder and his arm. It glistened like a raven's wing, a blue black, silky and lustrous.

He rubbed the silky stuff between his thumb and forefinger, marveling at the softness and thickness of it.

"Everything's very quiet here," she murmured as she continued to lie against him, warm and naked, one leg layed over his. "I didn't think Haven would be so quiet."

"What did ye expect then, lass?" he murmured. "Revelry and orgies?" He laughed at that. The latest stories in the tabloids never failed to amuse him.

"Gunfire. Howls. Maybe screams." There was no fear coming from her, but there was an edge of confusion. The scent of her was distressed, as though a conflict waged inside her. He hoped that conflict involved emotions for him that she couldn't deny.

He could sense the emotions there, but he also sensed the battle against them.

"Gunfire, howls and screams?" He almost laughed, but he held the response back. "Storme, we've shadowed you for years and never attacked. What made you believe there would be such things here?"

She breathed out heavily. "I knew I was being shadowed. I believed it was my father's friends doing it."

Storme knew she should move. She knew she should force herself to get out of the bed, to dress, to put some distance between then. She couldn't make herself do it though. She was comfortable, she was warm. Lying there naked against him, there was a feeling she didn't know or understand. A feeling that held her in place, that kept her against him and refused to allow her to move.

"Council scientists?" he snorted.

"No." She frowned, remembering the past ten years, knowing Styx was telling her the truth. It wasn't her father's friends who had protected her, as she had believed, but it was the Breeds. She knew it was, and the sense of bitterness that welled inside her was like a dark cloud over the contentment of moments past.

"Who then, lass?" His fingers stroked down her spine, calloused and warm, easing the tension from her before it really had a chance to take hold.

"Friends." She breathed out roughly. "Dad told me someone would find me, and protect me. That he hadn't left me alone. I guess I always hoped that was who it was, and that they would reveal themselves when it was safe enough. I thought perhaps they couldn't risk the Council recognizing or identifying them."

She'd lived in a dreamworld for so many years. For so long she had believed someone would truly come for her to claim the data chip and wipe away the danger she faced.

As she lay there, she realized that there was no white knight. There was no one to ride to her rescue. But she realized that there never had been, and she had managed to stay alive anyway.

But how much longer would she have managed that?

"Your da did send someone for you," he stated heavily, causing her to lift from the warm comfort she had found, to stare back at him in suspicion.

"Lass." He shook his head. "The suspicion in your gaze breaks my heart. Jonas was part of the team that rescued the Breeds at the Omega lab. He was racing to your da's small home, but he arrived too late. You were to await him at an abandoned mountain cottage where your da had hidden a vehicle whose engine Jonas had provided in case of emergency. But he arrived there too late as well. You had already run."

"So you're telling me Jonas was the person my father meant to meet me?" She held back her mockery and disbelief.

"The one he meant to have the data chip," he clarified. "And that's no lie, lass, no matter your suspicions."

And her suspicions were great, but she didn't totally disbelieve it. She found herself wanting to believe though, and that terrified her.

"Dad said he would come to me and tell me." Forcing herself from the bed, she wrapped the sheet around her and stared back at him, as a sense of betrayal pricked at her heart.

He had to be lying to her. If Jonas was the man her father had wanted to have that information, then her father would have given her some indication, or at the very least Jonas would have told her. The man was not lacking in daring.

"Jonas didn't know the importance of the information," he revealed, as though he regretted that fact. "You were eighteen before he found you, and by then you were already outspoken against the Breeds. He wanted you to come to us willingly. To trust us. He didn't want to make your distrust worse. So he sent Enforcers to shadow you, to protect you, hoping you would see that you could trust us with the information your da gave you."

"How convenient," she murmured as she fought back the anger, the fear that he would lie to her so easily and make her want to believe it so desperately.

"Aye, I agree, lass." He rose from the bed, tall, powerful, his muscular body darkly tanned and ripped with lean muscle. "And disbelief and suspicion are all you know. I can't blame you for it, but I can ask you to look at what I say with an open mind."

"I lost my open mind ten years ago," she informed him, her fists clenching in the sheet as she fought with herself and became angrier each minute that she ached to believe in him.

She didn't believe in anyone. She couldn't believe in anyone.

The look he gave her was filled with pity. "And that's too bad, lass. Because sometimes, an open mind is all we have to keep our hearts open."

This time, her smile was mocking and bitter. "An open heart as well? Is that what you're counting on? No, Styx, I don't have a heart. It was cut out of my chest the last time a lover died and a friend paid for what others wanted from me. Breeds, Council. It doesn't matter which, I had nothing for either of you."

She turned and walked slowly to the bathroom, then to the shower.

She couldn't afford to have a heart, and if she did, she couldn't afford to allow Styx into it.

One thing was for damned sure though, if she didn't get the hell out of Haven, then she would end up losing what she claimed she didn't have, and trusting the very people she swore she would never trust.

If she didn't get out of Haven, she was going to fall in love with her Breed.

"Come on, you're going to dinner wi' me." Styx stood in the bedroom as Storme walked from the shower later the next evening, his arms crossed over his chest as he stared back at her impassively.

The past twenty-four hours hadn't been easy ones for her. A sense of impending doom, of disaster, had settled over her, warning her it was time to go.

Over the years she had developed an uncanny sense of danger, a premonition of coming disaster, and that self-preservation instinct was riding her hard to run.

"I'm not hungry." Tightening her fingers on the towel, she stared back at him with a sense of trepidation. She couldn't leave the house, not yet. Not until she had a plan in place and an idea where to run.

Each time she had moved for the back door since the evening before, she had felt a bull's-eye painted on her chest. When Styx had walked from the house, she could have sworn she saw it painted on him as well.

And it scared her. It scared her more than her own

emotions scared her, and those emotions made her damned nervous.

"Too bad." He shrugged, as though it didn't matter. "Get dressed, lass. I've grown weary of your stubbornness now. You're going with me."

Storme's lips tightened. "You don't want to force this, Styx. I'll only embarrass you."

A red brow arched in mockery as his blue eyes gleamed with confident arrogance. An arrogance she hadn't really glimpsed until now. That look had her stomach clenching, her pussy creaming, and something softening in her chest that shouldn't be softening.

Had she been so busy surviving that she had missed out on more than she had ever imagined? Was she only a woman who could sense danger, but had no idea what her own emotions were? All she had was the knowledge that it was time to run.

"Then I'll only embarrass you back by turning you over my knee and paddling that cute little arse of yours," he informed her, his voice hard as she watched him, wishing things were different, wishing the past ten years hadn't been as they were. That she had learned what other women had learned by now. That she had deciphered her emotions as a teenager, like most women did. Instead of standing here wondering if he would truly paddle her for embarrassing him, and wondering why her butt cheeks were clenching as though it might be enjoyable.

Storme had a very bad feeling he wasn't joking about the spanking, just as she had a feeling he might have scented the sudden rush of excitement that heated her clit and the inner depths of her pussy.

There was a strange look in his eyes. One of pure male determination and male lust, and that look was frankly terrifying to some hidden, feminine part of her psyche. That look had warning signals flaring in her brain that were nearly as imperative as the self-preservation instinct urging her to run.

"I'm not much of a social person, Styx. Besides, I get

damned tired of watching you and Cassandra Sinclair fawn all over each other," she informed him as she dropped the towel and padded to the small dresser where he had deposited what appeared to be some rather sinful underclothes earlier. New ones. She loved new under pretties. She'd been forced to stop wearing them years ago because she just couldn't afford them. But these, damn, she couldn't resist.

Pulling the drawer open, she lifted a pair of violet silk panties from inside and paired them with the matching silk camisole.

Pulling the underclothes on, she ignored the hunger that tightened his face, or she tried to. There was no way to halt the slick dampness that eased from her sex, or the hardening of her nipples that pressed against the cool silk.

When she felt his fingers curling around her upper arm to turn her to face him, she also felt the weakness that suffused her, the feminine sexual submission that flooded her entire being.

If sexual submission threatened to overwhelm her, then male sexual dominance burned in him. His expression was tight with it, his entire body tense, aroused as he faced her.

"Tonight is a very important celebration," he growled down at her. "You will dress as you would dress to celebrate a friend's special night. You will be polite, and by God, Storme, you will stand at my side as my woman, or I promise you, it will be something we'll both regret."

"What's going on, Styx?" Her voice trembled, an indication even to herself that she had no idea how to handle this situation, or the relationship developing between them.

He stared at her as though a question plagued him, a suspicion he couldn't fully release.

"I know when to behave myself," she assured him mockingly. "But it rather helps if I'm given the truth of a situation I'm about to enter into."

His lips tightened for long moments. "Do you want to avoid Breed Law for a little while longer, Storme?"

Breed Law. Storme stared back at him as her heart seemed to drop to the pit of her stomach. She couldn't afford to face Breed Law and she knew it. The years she had spent speaking out against the Breeds would only come back to haunt her.

"I haven't committed a crime against Breed Law since coming here." She swallowed tightly. "I make certain of it. I didn't even seriously try to escape last week. I don't leave the cabin, I don't socialize . . ."

"And you're holding information vital to a member of the Breed Ruling Cabinet," he reminded her. "Information you're refusing to hand over. Very carefully placed, very subtly written in the public laws, but clearly spelled out in the Breed version, such an act committed by Breed, human, a member of Haven or Sanctuary or not, is an offense against Breed Law."

She hadn't considered that. She remembered now listening during several pure blood society meetings as Breed laws, the public ones, were discussed. That particular law had come into question as the members of that society had tried to define it. There had been no other way to understand it other than as Styx just explained it.

"Okay, so I want to avoid Breed Law a bit longer," she stated with an attempt at flippancy. "What do I have to do?"

"Just as I said." He released her as though her flesh burned. "Stay at my side and at least try to pretend that you consider yourself my woman. That's the only way I can protect you at the moment."

His woman.

God, what would it mean to be his woman? To bask in the security of his hold each night, to live the life he lived, to soak in the peace and camaraderie she witnessed in the courtyard each night.

But she wasn't his woman, and as she stared back at him, another memory of the discussions over Breed Law surfaced. A discreetly worded law concerning Breed wives or lovers. Something to the effect that should a Breed take a wife or husband who had committed crimes against Breed Law, then the crimes committed would be erased unless the individual broke Breed Law after the "joining." Not the marriage, but the "joining."

So, essentially, becoming a Breed's lover, partner or wife, was a "get out of jail free" card. Which made no sense whatsoever, but whatever, she could go along with that for a while.

"Fine." She shrugged, though that memory had the power to only intensify the feeling of impending doom she couldn't shake. "But I still don't understand why my presence is so required."

"The nature of the celebration," he informed her. "To allow your guards to attend the celebration, you must be there as well."

"Ah." She nodded, her tone sarcastic. "It all makes sense now. Fine, Styx, I'll be there and I'll be a good girl, just for you."

And she would try desperately to make sense of the emotions, the fears and all the assorted needs that were suddenly rising inside her as she attempted to figure out where the sense of danger was coming from.

"I simply can't see you as being a good girl," he grunted. "But I'll settle for polite non-interference."

"Polite non-interference I can handle," she assured him with a patently false smile. "Polite interference is so much more fun though. Are you sure you wouldn't prefer that? I could really liven your party up, Wolf."

Polite interference was her motto where the Breeds were concerned. Or at least, it had been before her arrival at Haven.

His head tilted to the side as though he were considering the option. Slowly, his arms crossed over his chest and his eyes narrowed on her.

"I would remember one thing, Sugar," he drawled, his voice a rasped, husky croon of invitation. "I know how to tame that little wild streak you enjoy allowing free occasionally."

He was teasing her back. Somehow, he had figured out that beneath the anger and the fear lay a small, untapped reservoir of teasing amusement. She rarely had the opportunity to share it, or to enjoy it, but the thought of playing, just for a few moments, with Styx was too exciting to resist.

It was a spur-of-the-moment pleasure. An opportunity to save a memory, because she knew the time was going to come, very soon, when she would have to run from him. When staying here would become such a hazard, not just for her, but for him as well, that she would have no option but to escape.

"I wouldn't say you tame it," she murmured, holding back her smile as she pulled a pair of jeans from the dresser and paired them with a violet tank top with thin straps.

"I would say I definitely tame it," he assured her as she adjusted the tank top over the camisole before taking a seat on the bed and pulling on socks. "Maybe you simply exhaust it for a minute?"

She shouldn't be doing this. That sudden thought blazed through her mind as his low, deep chuckle stroked across her senses. They had barely spoken since the night before. He'd held her in his arms as she slept, his head tucked above her as he pulled her back against his chest.

He'd been up and out of there before she awoke, and he'd been gone most of the day. And instead of remaining angry, instead of holding to her promise to herself to remain aloof, instead she was flirting with him.

"Just for a minute?" he teased her.

"Maybe two." She adjusted the socks on her feet then pulled the low, lace-up boots from beneath the bed and pushed them on.

She had sneakers. She had a single pair of nice sandals, but it was the boots she was reaching for.

"You should smile more often, Storme," he stated as she lost the curve of her lips and stared down at the boots. "I sense a woman that longs to live rather than survive, yet if I let you walk out the gates of Haven today, then once clear of them you would run harder and faster than ever before."

She laced up her boots, wishing she hadn't allowed him to see that loss of amusement. But he would have known, she reminded herself. He could sense it, smell it. He likely knew her body better than she knew it herself.

"I take my amusement where I can," she assured him as she finished lacing her boots and rose to her feet. "So tell me, when am I required to attend your little celebration this evening?"

She should have ignored his gaze. She should have never allowed him to gaze so intently into her eyes. Before she could stop him, his gaze had hers though, the sea blue snaring her, mesmerizing her as his hand lifted to cup her cheek.

"Tell me what to do, Storme," he stated as he ignored her question. "Tell me how to gain your trust."

She came to her feet, feeling a moment's regret as his hand fell to his side.

"Now, that would just be too easy," she told him flippantly. "A girl has to maintain a little mystery, you know."

The ring was suddenly like a heavy weight on her finger now. For the first time since her father had pushed it on, Storme wanted to take it off.

It was no longer a reminder of her father, it was now a reminder of everything she didn't have, and everything she wouldn't have in her life.

"A little mystery, or as much resentment as possible?" he asked and sighed.

"Hey, whichever works at the moment," she assured him as she grabbed the heavy weight of her backpack and headed for the kitchen.

"You won't need the bag," he assured her.

"My bag goes where I go," she told him firmly. "If it stays, I stay."

"Why? What's in it, Storme, that you feel you have to have?"

For a second, her gaze flickered with a vulnerability he hadn't expected.

"You never know what can happen, Styx," she finally stated, the edge of discomfort in her voice reflecting in her scent.

Styx realized that her statement, that one never knew

what could happen, was far too true in her life. For ten years she had never known where safety lay, or if the next day would be her last.

Styx watched her back as she disappeared out of the bedroom, and he breathed out a heavy sigh.

The backpack was a symbol of security, perhaps. As she had said, she was never seen without it. But that didn't mean she would need it here in Haven. There were no longer any weapons in it, and there was nothing that would indicate the data chip was hidden there.

The backpack and its contents had been scanned, run through an x-ray and every conceivable electronic imaging device that would have revealed the data chip.

There was nothing hidden there, he was willing to bet his ass on it. Nothing but her need to ensure that no matter what happened, she was prepared. He could live with that.

Shaking his head at the wonder and the confusion this woman brought to his life, Styx followed behind her to the kitchen and watched as she poured herself a cup of coffee.

The backpack rested on a kitchen chair, the faded olive green canvas nicked and frayed in places. For a moment, he was damned jealous of the pack's importance in her life. She held on to it as a talisman of some kind. The way he wished she would accept him into her life. Perhaps then the torturous arousal burning in his cock and balls would stop driving him insane. The mating knot refused to swell and release the hormone-rich semen that would begin the full mating process.

As Styx moved to the long drawer at the side of the ceramic sink and pulled it open, he wondered at the jokes nature seemed to enjoy playing on the Breeds.

He grabbed a milk chocolate bar from the drawer and opened it and as he watched her sip at her coffee, he took a bite of the smooth, rich sweet.

Damn, he loved chocolate, but he'd give it up easily if it meant having Storme as he needed her.

"That has to be the third bar of chocolate I've seen you

eat in the past three days." She stared at the chocolate with a hint of jealousy.

"It's actually most likely the twelfth or better," he drawled, allowing the smooth edge of the brogue back into his voice.

She reacted to it instantly. The soft edge of liquid heat wafted from her, tempting his senses and making his cock throb harder. Damn, at this rate, the pigs might overcook while he satisfied a far different hunger.

"Twelve?" Her gaze flicked to the chocolate bar again as he parted his lips for another bite.

"At least." He nodded. "I'm rather fond of the sweet."

"You're going to get fat," she muttered, her gaze flicking to his stomach.

Styx grinned. "Breeds have a very high metabolism, lass. It burns off near as fast as I eat it."

Yep, that was pure envy that lit her green eyes. She wanted the chocolate.

Stepping closer, he moved his hand to allow the chocolate to glance off her lips. The smear of the dark sweet was immediately collected by her little pink tongue.

"Do ye want a bit, lass?" he asked, teasing her again, brushing the soft chocolate against her lips once more. "I've no problem sharin' my chocolate wi' ya."

The soft scent of arousal peaked in her delicate body. Her tongue collected the taste before it seemed she had to force herself to step back from it.

"A minute on the lips, a lifetime on the hips," she sighed. "Normal people don't burn the fat that fast."

"Aye, being a Breed has its advantages, I must say, love." He finished off the treat before smacking his lips in pleasure. "Doesn't taste near as luscious as your sweet pussy, but it will do."

Her face flamed, though not in embarrassment. The flush raced up her neck and across her face as the heat in the soft flesh between her thighs intensified.

Damn, he'd love to stretch her across the kitchen table and lap at the honey of her heat. Doing so would ensure the pigs were tough, however. It was nearly time to take them out. He could smell the meat cooking and knew he hadn't much time before they would begin pulling it from the ground.

"What time do we head out?" Despite her attempt to appear nonchalant, he could sense the excitement beginning to rise within her.

Each evening he'd sensed her regret at not joining the activities. He'd been reluctant to force her, until tonight. Tonight, he wanted her to see the warmth, the affection and sense of family that existed at Haven. The mating anniversaries reflected that full sense of joy that radiated through the community with a mating. With the knowledge that Breeds were evolving despite man's determination to destroy them. That some higher force had deemed them worthy and granted them the ability to be loved, to have children, to survive.

"You know, Storme, you could eat the chocolate. You could be a part of Haven. And here, ye could have friends and family," he stated without answering her question. "I think ye know well now that what ye believed as a child wasn't the truth. That what the pure blood societies teach is a far cry from what the Breeds truly are."

She turned away from him, inhaling deeply, quietly, as he felt that regret rushing through her again.

"What I believe isn't what's important," she finally stated.

"Storme, is that information worth having the Council soldiers torture you for it if they catch you?" he asked. "It's information gained by the experimentation and torture of Breeds. Beyond the fact that this information could save Jonas's stepdaughter's life, aren't the Breeds more entitled to that research than the Council?"

Storme breathed in roughly.

"I don't deny the Breeds' right to the research," she finally whispered.

"Then why do ye hold back, lass?" She hated the sound of disappointment in his tone, the chastisement, as though he couldn't understand why she would be so cruel.

It wasn't cruelty. She wished it were something so simple as that, so simple as merely being a bitch, or wanting to make the Breeds pay for what had happened to her family.

"It's complicated," she finally whispered, before realizing that for first time in ten years, she had admitted to having the data chip.

She should have been surprised, but she wasn't. Lying to Styx wasn't something she could make herself do any longer. Looking into his clear blue eyes, seeing his appearance, at least, of attempting to give her time, attempting to save her from Breed Law and from Jonas.

"What's so complicated, lass?" he asked her gently. "Tell me what demons I must fight. Tell me, Storme, how to help ye make your decision."

She felt her lips tremble. The conflict inside her was tearing at her, confusing her. She hated feeling this way. Hated having her loyalties torn and divided.

"Conquer the past." She turned back to him, her chest aching as she felt a sizzle of some sensation race over her flesh. As though her body ached for his touch. "Bring my father and my brother back so they can release me from the promise I made."

Her voice thickened as she felt moisture threaten to gather in her eyes. Her father and her brother were dead. How many times had her friend Gena told her that the dead wouldn't know what choices she made?

She didn't believe that. Sometimes she felt as though that promise chained her, locked her into a world that she would have given anything to escape.

"Your da said you would know the one he sent for the information?" Styx asked.

Storme nodded in reply. "No one came, Styx." Her breathing hitched as she fought against the pain that began to radiate inside her. "I waited for so many years. I even answered Jonas Wyatt's phone calls each time he reached my cell phone. I always answered the Council, I never refused to talk to the former friends of my father's when they managed to reach me. But no one ever had the words that would even make me suspect they could have been the one my father meant."

She watched as he moved slowly to her, his arms circling her shoulders to pull her against his chest.

Closing her eyes tightly, Storme fought against the need to cry, to shed the aching pain that seemed to build by the day.

"I wish I had the words for ye, lass," he whispered as she felt him kiss the top of her head. "I wish I could ease that conscience that seems to torture ye far into the night. Perhaps though, like your da, the one he thought would come to you may have died before he could complete his task. Remember, Storme, so many Breeds perished in the rescues. Perhaps the one to collect it was one of those Breeds."

And what should she say to that? In the past days as she sat in the cabin alone, she had considered it. She had fought to convince herself of it. The more she was with Styx, the less she cared if perhaps he was merely playing her, working her for the data chip.

This time at Haven had shown her that there could be peace. She could find a life somewhere. She could be safe. Without the data chip hampering her, there would be no reason to strike at her, would there?

Wrapped in his embrace now, she swore she could taste his kiss. That hint of cinnamon and chocolate she always tasted when they kissed. As his hands stroked over her back, her thighs tensed, her clit ached, and the need to have him take her almost overwhelmed her.

She hadn't wanted this. She hadn't wanted to need him, and that was what was happening. She wanted to hate him. She wanted to hate all Breeds, just as she had done for the past ten years. It made it easier to keep the promise she had given her father, the one he had feared she would break.

"Dad told James he couldn't trust me," she whispered as he continued to hold her. "Once, Scheme Tallant came to Omega, and I caught her talking to several Breeds secretly. I told Dad and James she was up to something, and they didn't say anything then. Later, I heard them talking. Dad told my brother that I wasn't loyal enough."

She pulled back from him as she wrapped her arms across her breasts and moved to the back door, where she gazed through the window into the courtyard.

"I was loyal," she whispered. "If I hadn't been, I wouldn't have told him about Scheme. I was loyal to my father and my brother. I wasn't old enough and didn't know enough to give my loyalty to anyone else."

And this was the battle she fought, Styx thought heavily. A battle that would be impossible for Storme to turn her back on. As the only daughter living in the Omega labs, facing the monsters the Council wanted to turn the Breeds into, seeing their savagery and their agony, she could have easily mistaken it for animal brutality.

The same type of animal that killed her family, the ones that shadowed her for years, pressuring her into giving up the information her father had made her swear she would protect.

She would protect it with her life, he thought. And it might very well come to her life.

"Your da loved you, Storme," he promised her softly. "He knew you were young, he knew you feared the Breeds and giving them your loyalty wouldn't be easy. Perhaps this was what he meant."

She turned back to him, a bitter smile curving her lips as she rubbed at her arms. "Perhaps," she whispered, then fought to shake off the pain, and the past. "You didn't answer me, when are we leaving?"

Styx almost sighed in regret. For a moment, for just a moment, he had felt as though, at the least, she was prepared to discuss the possibility of giving him the data chip. Now he could feel, smell, the refusal in her.

She had pulled back with an inner strength and determination that was integral to woman she was.

"I'll give my life to protect you, Storme, whether against Breeds or against the Council."

Shock flashed in her eyes. He had heard his own voice,

the animal inside him coming to the fore and revealing itself in the growl.

"What?" She shook her head as though what he were saying made no sense to her.

"My loyalty is to you," he stated, knowing he would not attempt to hide that from her any longer. She was his mate, and she might not have accepted him, but he had accepted her the moment he tasted her first kiss.

"Exactly what I said, lass. My loyalty is yours. I'd die to protect you, whether from Council soldiers, scientists or Breed Law and Jonas Wyatt. I'll no longer allow anyone or anything to steal the security I can give you. I'd prefer to make it easy." He gave her a soft smile. "I do rather enjoy my lazier side. For you though, I'll deal with whatever I must, unless you make the choice to give the information to anyone other than myself or Jonas."

The line was drawn, but it wasn't a line she had a problem with. Until she could decide the consequences to herself, and perhaps to the world, of breaking her promise, then it was all she had.

"We're not as bad as the pure blood societies would have you believe, love." He chided her as she continued to stare back at him.

She smiled. Tentative, soft. A curve of her lips that blended with the soft scent of . . . His head tilted as he drew that scent in. It was darker than affection, but nowhere close to the scent of mates that he had known from what others experienced.

But it was a start, a sliver of hope. And he would take what he could get until he had the time to steal her heart fully.

◆ CHAPTER 15 ◆

Styx gave Storme a reprieve. A few minutes to pull together the emotions raging through her as she fought the realizations he knew she was coming to.

He was making headway. There came a time in a man's, or a Breed's, life, when he had his own realizations. One of those was the knowledge that pushing Storme further could be more detrimental than simply walking away and allowing her to consider her options.

The first pig he and Navarro had placed in the fire pit had come out more than an hour before. That was the ceremonial roasted pig served to the mated couple's table, where the special guests of the couple sat.

The rest of the pork for the pig roast was ready to come off the spits now. It would be laid on the large banquet tables set up to hold bowls and platters of other contributions to the feast as well.

As he and several of the Enforcers extracted the roasted pork and laid each pig on one of the specially made wooden platters, Styx turned and caught sight of one of the Coyote Breeds currently working outside Haven.

"Marx, good to see you." Styx nodded to the Coyote as he strolled into the banquet area.

Marx Whitman was one of the rougher cut Coyote Breeds. As though the genetics for exceptional good looks and grace had somehow gone awry.

At five feet, eight inches, stocky, with a heavily muscular chest and arms, the quiet, normally antisocial Breed walked slowly to him.

"The Sinclair mating anniversary." Marx looked over the heavily laden tables. "You can smell that pig roasting all the way to the main gates."

"Aye, the Breeds on duty this evening have already called, bitching. The scent they say is starving them to death."

Marx chuckled at the comment before standing awkwardly for long moments.

"I hear you have a captive," he drawled. "Something about a woman that's leading you a merry little chase."

Styx grinned. "She is at that."

Marx shook his head, his brown eyes filling with amusement as he inhaled slowly. "There's no mating scent, man. What the hell is going on with that?"

Styx lifted his hand to rub at the back of his neck as he gave Marx a confused look. The other man rarely poked his nose into anyone else's business. Hell, when he wasn't on assignment he rarely came down from the mountain the Coyotes used as their home base, unless he had to.

"No one said it was a mating," Styx informed him.

Styx was unwilling to discuss the details or the problems associated with this particular mating.

"True." Marx inclined his head in agreement as he looked around at the food once again.

Most Breeds were difficult to read at the best of times. They learned to control their emotions and therefore their hormonal scents, making it harder to sense if a Breed were lying, telling the truth, or perhaps hungry and needing to join a celebration he wasn't familiar with.

"Are you going back to Haven for a while?" Styx asked as

he covered the last roast pig with a large sheet of foil, aware of other Breeds beginning to move into the courtyard.

"For a while," Marx answered absently. "Hey, have you seen Wolfe and Hope around? I wanted to say hello while I was here."

Talking to Marx was never easy. He shifted from one conversation to the next without warning and normally without finishing the previous conversation.

"They're visiting with Dash and Elizabeth," Styx informed him.

Dash didn't normally keep his family in Haven on a full-time basis. Cassie actually spent much of her time in Sanctuary. At the time that Dash had needed Breed help in protecting his new mate and her child, Haven had been a carefully guarded secret. Sanctuary, the Feline Breed compound, had been fully operational, with the Breeds of all species arriving almost daily from rescues and escapes. Dash had called the Felines, and Cassie had stayed there while Dash and her mother neutralized that first of many threats to the child.

"I'll catch up with them." Marx nodded. "See ya later, Styx."

Styx watched the other man leave, a frown on his brow before he shook his head. Marx had always been an odd one.

"Faith, the pork is perfect and ready." He turned to the Wolf Breed liaison to the Bureau of Breed Affairs.

Vivid black eyes, shoulder-length reddish brown hair and a creamy, satiny complexion. Tall and lithe, competent and deadly when she had to be, and still, she managed to look soft, gentle and without a merciless bone in her body.

Styx knew for a fact that Faith could and would kill as fast as any Breed male. Perhaps faster. Breed females were hardened in the labs in ways the males weren't. In many cases they were considered no more than toys to the soldiers and Council trainers. The fact that they had managed to maintain the innocence of their hearts amazed Styx.

Faith had escaped the worst of it, but still, life had been brutal for her there.

"Great." A ready smile crossed Faith's lips as she moved from the vegetable table to the roast pork. "It smells wonderful."

"Aye, a'course it does." Styx winked. "I did the deed myself."

Faith laughed, those unusual black eyes twinkling in delight.

"Is your captive coming to the feast?" she teased him then. "She's stayed hidden in the past weeks. I was hoping to get to meet her."

"Aye, tonight she'll be here." He nodded. "I wanted to get the pork from the pit and finish preparations before escorting her to the party."

Faith nodded. "Nikki mentioned the tests she's been doing." Her gaze flashed in concern. "Have there been any answers there?"

Styx shook his head. "And they're beginnin' to piss me off, Faith," he growled.

Where he had been unwilling to discuss the "almost" mating with Marx, he found himself able to talk to Faith about it.

"Mating heat makes you crazy anyway." She grinned, obviously not too crazy yet. "Once it hits, you'll be praying for a break." A teasing wink belied her words; her smile assured him she was perfectly content with the life and the heat she shared with her mate.

"Lass, at the moment, I'm just prayin' for the damned heat to make up its mind when tae begin burnin'. A Breed can only take so much pressure, ya know."

Laughter slipped past her lips, bringing a smile to his face. He'd known her before she and Jacob Arlington had completed their mating, when mating heat had taken its grip on the pair at a very inconvenient time, during a mission that had revealed another species of Breed. One that still caused disbelief and remained a mystery to the general population. But Styx had been there when Jacob and Faith reunited after several years apart, and he had seen not just the love, but also the fiery, dedicated hunger they shared.

"Lass, before your havin' me believin' I should commit myself to an asylum afore mating, I believe I'll go find my almost mate and see if the wee thing is ready tae eat yet."

Faith arched a brow, the amusement in her gaze contagious and causing the smile to linger on his lips even as he headed back to his cabin.

Breeds were beginning to enter the courtyard slowly, all navigating first to the appetizer table and the seating spread around the courtyard that allowed for different sizes of groups to congregate.

The lights strung in the trees would flicker on as dark began to fall soon, casting shadows among the artfully landscaped courtyard and shining down on those men and women who had never known laughter, camaraderie and joy until the past decade.

And even now it was rife with danger.

That danger might not end anytime soon, Styx feared as he reached the cabin. But each battle, each missing piece to the Breed puzzle brought them ever closer to the security they craved. The freedom they prayed to give their children.

And wasn't that why any species fought? To survive? To preserve the future of their species for those they loved?

Stepping into the cabin, Styx came to a slow stop, his senses exploding at the soft, almost-not-there scent that crossed his senses.

It wasn't mating heat, but it was similar perhaps, at the least familiar, though he couldn't quite place it.

It was a scent of cinnamon candy. Sweet and tinged with heat, but so subtle, so barely there, that he couldn't be certain if it was the scent of the woman or the scent of candy. Except, Styx kept chocolate in the house rather than cinnamon. Other than a hint of it in the coffee, it wasn't a sweet he bought often.

He would be buying it more often now though. A scent that would always remind him of this.

Storme stepped from the bedroom, her long black hair pinned to the top of her head, a small frown on her forehead, her face flushed.

"I can't find anything wrong with the air-conditioning, but you have a problem. It got damned hot in here after you left," she told him irritably.

It wasn't mating heat, but it was damned close. As though the slow simmer had finally heated marginally.

Styx tilted his head and watched her intently as he drew in the scents emanating from her.

His hardened cock and tight balls pulsed, throbbed. Shards of sensation wrapped around the sensitive shaft, tightening in the need to fuck.

For a second, for just a second, he tasted cinnamon.

Running his tongue over the edge of his teeth, he felt the slightest swelling. It was more than an irritation, but it wasn't quite the hormone-enflamed mating scent other Breed males had experienced.

She propped her hands on her hips and her frown deepened as she stopped just inside the kitchen and glared at him. "Did you hear me?"

"Aye." He cleared his throat. "I heard ye, lass."

"Power cells are testing full, the diagnostic came up clear." She shook her head. "But it's hotter than hell."

A fine sheen of perspiration glistened on her forehead and at her neck, and her pussy was hot. Sweet and hot and the scent of it was tinged with cinnamon.

He should call Nikki. Hell, he'd sworn he would call Nikki the minute anything changed. That he wouldn't touch Storme, wouldn't dare be tempted to forget his promise. Nikki had threatened to neuter him if he did.

"Why are you looking at me like that?" she asked as he watched her breathe in deeply, trying to hide it by doing it slow and easy.

Her heart was racing though. He could see the vein pounding in her neck, almost in time to the pounding in his cock.

Hell, he wasn't going to be able to get to a phone to call Nikki, let alone wait for her to actually get here to do whatever the hell it was she had to do.

"You're beautiful, lass," he growled.

He couldn't exactly tell her the truth. That the sweet, soft scent of her as she neared mating heat was driving him insane. And that was what it was. He knew it was. He could sense it. She was almost a mate. A closer "almost" than she had been before he left the cabin earlier.

"I know that look," she muttered.

Aye, she knew it, and she reciprocated the need pulsing through him.

She was sweet and soft and so ready for him.

"Take those jeans off, lass." If he had to take them off himself then he would likely end up tearing them off.

Perhaps he should warn her what could be coming, but if the heat still hadn't progressed to the point that the mating knot emerged, then warning her could be useless, and would likely scare the hell out of her.

Her face flushed further. Beneath the camisole top she wore her nipples puckered tighter than seconds before. The delicate, soft scent of her heat washed through the room as he inhaled deeply.

He felt as though he could become drunk on her.

"You're joking," she whispered breathlessly as she glanced toward the door. "I thought you had to be outside for your little get-together? Don't you have a date with Cassie or something?"

Ahh, she hadn't forgotten, and her jealous reaction had only grown stronger at the idea of him having an evening with the charming little sprite Cassie. Not that anyone could be as charming as his wee little "near" mate.

He'd seen her as he chased her over the past two years with that sparkle of humor, those timid smiles.

"Not tonight." He wasn't going to argue over this and he wasn't playing this game any longer. "There's no other woman, lass, you've no reason to fear."

He belonged to her. Not that he would tell her that at this moment. Something that he feared his lovely little "almost" mate might not be ready to hear.

But there were other things, such as the male Wolf Breed mating knot, that there would be no way to hide.

Her fingers moved to the metal buttons of her jeans.

Styx followed suit. His belt loosened. As she pushed the jeans and panties over her thighs and stepped out of them, he pulled the buttons of his own jeans free and allowed the heavy wedge of his cock to slip from the parted material.

The camisole and tank top came over her head, leaving her gloriously, beautifully naked.

The soft, swollen flesh of her pussy was glazed with her syrup.

Stroking his dick, Styx grimaced at the electric sensations racing through the shaft to pierce the mushroomed crest. The middle of the shaft pulsed and throbbed, the burning presence of the unrevealed knot ached with need.

Moving to her, Styx gripped her waist and lifted her to the open counter between the living room and the kitchen. There were going to be few preliminaries, he thought hazily. The need heating her flesh was brighter than ever, hotter. His fingers smoothed through the heavy glaze covering her pussy, the soft, rich cream heating the tips of his fingers before he tucked two in at the entrance and thrust.

At the same moment his lips covered hers, taking the whimpering cry that fell from her mouth. And there was that taste of cinnamon. Where the hell had it come from? He could taste it, but the glands at his tongue still weren't fully swollen.

Still, the hint of the taste of chocolate and cinnamon teased his senses as he pushed his tongue between her lips and groaned as her lips closed around it, sucking it inside.

She would burn him alive.

Storme moaned again as she tasted that distinctive taste of Styx. Chocolate and cinnamon. She could so easily become addicted. Hell, she was terribly afraid she was already addicted.

She took his tongue into her mouth as she took his fingers into her pussy. Eagerly. The penetration between her thighs stroked deeper, working fully inside her with shallow thrusts as he stretched muscles that seemed too tight to accommodate him. She had never felt so feminine, so aroused. Even with Styx, who had stoked her arousal higher than any other man in her life.

She wanted more.

Her fingers fumbled at the buttons of his shirt, managing to release enough that she could part the material and reach the broad expanse of his hairless chest.

She loved the tough, smooth expanse of flesh. Beneath her palms she could feel the tiny hairs, so light they were mostly invisible as she stroked his chest.

"Don't stop," she moaned weakly as he pulled back, breaking the kiss as his fingers slid free of her pussy.

"Never," he growled. God she loved that rough, animal sound that deepened as he grew hungrier.

His lips moved down her neck, then to her upthrust breasts. As his lips covered a tight, hard nipple, his thumb stroked over the swollen bud of her clit. He caressed the little bundle of nerves, stroking around it, flickering against it as his tongue flicked over her nipple, his teeth raking against it.

This was wild. Incredible.

Storme swore she could feel hidden flames burning deep in her vagina. Flames that demanded, that burned in agony for the hard thrust of his cock.

She didn't want foreplay.

She wanted Styx. She wanted him inside her, stretching her, burning her. She wanted to feel the iron-hard heat of the wide crest parting her, forging within her.

"Fuck, lass," he seemed to snarl, the brogue and the growl both heavy in his voice now. "We'll burn down the night afore it's done."

Back arching, she moved closer.

Wrapping her legs around his hips, Storme fought to align her hips with his, to thrust against him, to experience the burning impalement before she went crazy for it.

"Styx, I don't know what you do to me," she moaned, her hand smoothing down his tight, hard stomach to the thick shaft beyond.

Her fingers didn't have a hope of wrapping around it.

The shaft was too wide, too heavily veined and throbbing with power.

Stroking her fingers to the damp tip, Storme fought to pull enough of her senses together to keep from melting in a mass of pure sensation before he ever got around to fucking her.

"I know what ye do to me." Pulling back, he lifted her to his chest and strode to the living room. "Ye make me crazy for ye, Sugar. Ye make me forget everything but the pleasure ye bring me. Come, little Storme, give me this pleasure I need. I need it until I feel I'm burnin' inside for ye."

He moved to the couch, set her on her feet, turned her, then pressed her down until her knees hit the cushions. With his hand at the back of her shoulders, he pressed her over.

Storme trembled. She rested her folded arms against the arm of the couch before staring back at him nervously.

At any other time she would have protested. She would have never allowed him to take her like this, to come behind her undefended back.

"So fuckin' pretty." His hand smoothed down her spine, then to the curve of her buttocks.

The feel of his calloused fingertips stroking with demanding warmth sent her juices flowing from her pussy. The inner muscles pulsed and throbbed as she pressed back, so eager, so desperate to feel him thrusting inside her she could barely stand it.

"Do it already," she demanded, her voice hoarse as his fingers slid between her thighs to test the slick wetness once again. "God, Styx, what have you done to me?"

"Loved ye well, lass. Ah hell, I'll always love ye well."

Did he realize what he had said? Storme felt her chest tighten, her heart aching as the swollen head of his cock pressed between the swollen folds of her sex.

"Love me well." She couldn't believe she was demanding it. That she knew in her heart and soul that she was demanding more than the sex, more than the physical love he was always so ready to give her. "Oh God, Styx, I don't know if I can bear it."

He pressed inside, parting her, stretching her. She felt so tight, too snug for the width of the shaft easing inside her.

"Sweet Storme." He hovered over her, one hand gripping her hip, the other hand pressing to the arm of the couch as he began working his cock slowly inside the clenched depths of her pussy.

Each shallow thrust worked him farther inside the burning depths of her pussy, as she felt the pleasure-pain of the muscles parting, stretching, accommodating the heated shaft as the bulging crest pulsed and throbbed inside her.

She could feel it. The flex of each pulse of blood thundering in his cock seemed to echo inside her overstretched flesh.

Her head tossed, her nails clawed at the upholstery of the couch arm as she pressed back, fighting to take more, to force him to take possession of her before she went insane for it.

"Ah lass, how sweet and hot ye are," he groaned, his lips at her ear as she whimpered in rising pleasure. "Feel how tight ye are, lass. How ye grip my dick, sucking it inside your sweet little pussy."

The clenching, uncontrollable tremors that shook her body seemed centered there in the muscles surrounding no more than a few inches of the thick flesh.

"Fuck me, Styx," she moaned in rising heat. "Oh God, please fuck me."

His hips jerked, and buried in deeper, his cock throbbed as though he were only seconds from ejaculation.

"Storme, love," he groaned harshly, his hips pulling back, the next thrust harder, inches deeper. "Ye surround my dick the way I want ye to take my heart," he whispered at her ear. "Take me, Storme. Trust me, love."

Her eyes closed tight as she fought back the tears that wanted to flood them. Dropping her head against the arm of the couch, she couldn't hold back the whimper, the desperate little cry that escaped her throat.

"Don't," she whispered, unable to remain silent. "Please, Styx. Please don't."

Don't ask for what she couldn't give. Don't make her

choose. Don't make her betray herself before she could even figure out if that betrayal was for the best.

"Hell yes I will." His voice deepened as he pressed deeper, stronger inside her. He was taking her as though each thrust inside her, each burning impalement would somehow tie her closer to him.

And it did. She could feel it, though she couldn't understand it. Something had been tying them together from the start and she hadn't wanted to admit it.

Denying it was the only way to survive, the only way to hold on to her soul until she could navigate her way through the morass of emotions she could feel tearing her apart.

"I'll demand it." His teeth nipped at her ear as she thrust back to him, forcing him deeper as a white-hot shaft of pure sensation blazed inside her vagina.

Pleasure or pain. She didn't know which, she didn't care, as long as he didn't stop. As long as she didn't have to face anything but the pleasure, the pure sensation racing through her.

"You're mine!" The next thrust buried him to the hilt.

Storme screamed in agonizing pleasure.

Throwing her head back, she felt his teeth at her neck and didn't even give a damn. They scraped her flesh, sent shivers tearing down her spine, tremors racing through her pussy.

Inside her, his cock throbbed hard and heated for just a second before he began moving. Before he tore her mind from her body with a pleasure she couldn't fight, a pleasure that whipped through her like a living flame and pierced her feminine soul. Tore past her shields.

His hands moved over hers, his fingers lacing with hers as she gripped the couch arm. As his fingers curled beneath hers, she clenched on them, as her pussy tightened around his cock.

She couldn't control it. She couldn't fight it.

"Mine, Storme!" he snarled at her ear.

Her womb convulsed as a spear of burning sensation raced through the sensitive tissue and snug muscles.

She had never belonged to anyone. She had never accepted

that responsibility. She had never allowed herself to believe it was something she could ever have.

Until now.

Until Styx.

Groaning, pressing his chest against her back, he buried deep inside her, thrusting, fucking her with hard, measured strokes as she felt the blazing need rushing higher and burning hotter.

So close. She could feel her orgasm tightening in her clit, in her womb.

"Tell me, Storme!" he demanded as he burned her, thrusting inside her with a strength and power that pulled a whimpering cry from her lips.

Shaking her head, she fought the demand. "No." The cry was weak, as weak as any resistance she could have put between them to begin with.

"Then let me tell you," he snarled as he nipped at her shoulder. "Mine, lass. My woman." Deep, hot, he thrust inside her again, a long, hard thrust that burned across ultra-sensitive nerve endings and pulled a harsh cry from her lips. "I'll no' let you go. I'll no' let another tear you from me." His voice strengthened. "Damn you, I'll not let you tear yourself from me!"

She exploded.

A scream built in her throat as he fucked her harder, faster, sending her hurtling through a release that tore her from any hold reality might have had on her and threw her into a brilliant, sensation-searing orgasm she knew would bind her to him whether she wanted it or not.

She was only vaguely aware of his release spurting inside her. Burning jets of semen filled her as he bit her shoulder, his teeth holding her in place, a pure, primal growl echoing around her as the pleasure sent her imploding into herself and burning through the last of the barriers she had built to protect her soul.

CHAPTER 16

Storme left the cabin, forcing herself to keep her head high, her gaze searching the shadows that lengthened at the edge of the fluttering lights hanging from the trees.

The courtyard was huge. Nearly twenty cabins plus the community center surrounded it, with the long tables filled with food, while others were surrounded by chairs.

Heart racing, she moved across the courtyard with Styx, hiding her shaking hands and staring boldly at the curious gazes that focused on her.

"Several of the Breeds have hearing so acute they can actually hear the racing of your heart," Styx murmured in amusement. "They can smell the suspicion, but I'm certain they'll be pleased to know that before the suspicion was the fear."

"I'm terrified," she muttered back, and her lips almost twitched.

She was nervous, wary. These were Wolf Breeds, and mixed with them was a healthy number of Coyote Breeds. It was impossible to tell them apart, but it was the Coyotes that made her suspicious.

Changing a lifetime of beliefs and fears wasn't easy. She

had avoided these little community get-togethers for the
past weeks for a reason. She'd refused to socialize with the
enemy, except Styx.

From that first night, the image of him ever being anything but her lover had refused to come to mind.

"It's different tonight," she stated as they began to move
into the heavily populated area. "There are more Breeds
here tonight."

"Tonight's a special night," he told her, the deep edge of
the brogue stroking her senses. There was a tone of affection, of easy amusement, in his voice as his fingers brushed
against the small of her back while leading her toward a
table where Cassie Sinclair and her parents sat.

Dash Sinclair was just as handsome today as he had
been nearly a decade before when he and his wife, Elizabeth, had first come to the notice of the world. Sinclair,
a former Special Forces soldier, had been suspected and
questioned in the murder of a leading crime figure who
had threatened Cassie when she was a child.

Sinclair had been, and still was, a formidable figure.
Storme had no doubt in her mind that he could kill, and
kill easily, where the protection of his child was concerned.

And amazingly, just like Wolfe and Hope, Jacob and
Faith, Aiden and Charity, and the other married couples
within the Breed community, he and Elizabeth didn't
appear to have aged in the least.

There were rumors that somehow the Breeds had stopped
aging beyond a certain point, and that they had infected
their wives and husbands with some unknown virus that
caused the phenomenon.

Gossip magazines ran such stories on a nearly weekly
basis.

"You're thinking too hard, lass," Styx commented as
they moved to the head table. "Come, Storme, be a part
of my world for one night. I promise, you won't regret it."

And that was what worried her.

Moving to the head table, Styx drew a chair out for her,
helped her sit, then took his own seat.

"Ladies and gentlemen." Cassie stood to her feet, her voice amplified by the small mic that hooked over her ear.

The murmur of laughter and conversation stilled.

Cassie stood tall between her seated parents and gazed on the tables filled with Breeds and, as Storme had noticed, a number of humans and Feline Breeds as well. The Feline alpha and his felina were there, as well the Coyote alpha and his coya. If the pure blood societies had known about this little party, they would have been unable to resist the opportunity to strike.

"Tonight," she continued, "we celebrate my parents' tenth anniversary." A cheer went out. "Dash and Elizabeth Sinclair." She picked up the wineglass beside her plate as everyone followed suit.

Storme picked up her glass hesitantly, her gaze flicking to Styx as he picked up his as well.

Cassie stood to her father's side then, turned and faced her parents. "Your support and your love saved me." Her voice thickened as her parents held hands and Elizabeth's eyes filled with tears. "Your dedication and your loyalty to your friends, your family and the world we strive to be a part of is an example to everyone. May your love, your warmth and compassion continue to shine the way for us all."

A tear eased down Cassie's cheek as she lifted the wine to her lips and completed the toast.

Storme found herself toasting the couple as well, sipping and feeling her chest tighten at the emotion that reflected in the parents' expressions, in the child's and in the faces of those who occupied what appeared to be the celebratory couple's table.

Cheers went out, interspersed with howls and Feline roars.

Storme watched as the alphas and their wives came to the couple, congratulated them and laid in their hands on what appeared to be a sterling silver, or perhaps a white gold, charm or coin of some kind.

The males shook hands, the wives hugged warmly, but Storme noticed that the male alphas didn't touch Elizabeth

Sinclair in any way. And Dash, in thanking the alphas' wives, touched nothing but their hair. A tender, light stroke of the backs of his fingers against the right side of their heads. The male alphas did the same with Elizabeth. At no time did a Breed male touch a mated-female's flesh.

And though it appeared odd, there also seemed to be an immeasurable sense of respect and affection in the slight caress.

Dash turned to the crowd. "We have our trials," he stated, his tone rough, a hard rumble of sound softened with camaraderie and a vein of warmth that matched the gleam of purpose and determination in his gaze. "We also have our joys." He glanced to his wife and then to his daughter. "Tonight, the celebration isn't just for Elizabeth and me. It's for all of us." He lifted his glass then and toasted the others, and the cheers that went up were almost deafening.

It was more than a celebration. It was an affirmation.

As Storme stared around the table at the others, she caught Hope Gunnar's gaze and felt that first raw shaft of guilt since the night she had sworn the Breeds would pay for what had happened to her father and brother.

They were to blame, she had believed. The Coyotes, the escaping Breeds who hadn't thought to protect her father and brother when they had gone so far to help them achieve the freedom they had gained that night.

She had blamed the scientists, she had blamed the soldiers and the Council. And until Styx, she had refused to see the humanity that was such an integral part of the Breeds.

Now, watching as they ate, laughed and celebrated this anniversary with such a sense of thanksgiving, she had no choice but to face the rage and the pain that had driven her to blame an entire species for what one Breed had done.

And she didn't like seeing that part of herself. She didn't like seeing that it had been more than just loyalty to her father, or her determination to do as he would have wanted her to do.

He would have wanted her to give the Breeds that information. The very fact that he had hidden it from his fellow scientists assured her of that, and she had known it all along.

Lowering her gaze, she focused on the antique ring. She had worn it for ten years, refusing to take it off. All that time she had told herself she couldn't reveal it, couldn't allow herself to be caught, couldn't trust anyone, because her father hadn't told her who to trust.

But he had.

As plates were emptied and the music began to fill the clearing, Storme stood as Styx did and watched as Wolfe and Hope approached them.

Hope hadn't come to the cabin since that first night. She hadn't extended her friendship again, and she hadn't made an effort to give Storme the opportunity to apologize.

Standing silently, aware of the gazes that settled on them, and stayed, Storme met Hope's gaze as she and Wolfe came to a stop in front of Styx.

"Once again, Styx, the pork was perfection." Wolfe Gunnar inclined his head in thanks as a smile tugged at his lips. "Keep it up and we'll see about making you head chef."

Styx laughed. "Over my dead body, Alpha. I wouldn't take that job on a bet."

Wolfe laughed as he turned to Storme. "Styx insists on personally roasting the pig that sits on the anniversary table, Ms. Montague. He considers it his gift to the couple."

"It was perfect," Storme agreed. "I have to admit, the food he's prepared while I've been with him has been excellent," she admitted as she glanced at Hope once again. "Hello, Hope."

The lupina of the Wolf packs watched her closely.

"Hello, Storme, I trust Styx has kept you comfortable while you've been in Haven?" She was proud, but she always had been. Compassion and mercy had always tempered it, but Storme realized she had made a grave mistake when she had insulted the man Hope was in love with.

And it was love. She hadn't been forced, she wasn't there out of guilt. She was there because Wolfe Gunnar was her other half, the vision of love Storme had overheard her discussing with James so very long ago.

"My father once told me I spent too much time focusing on what wasn't important," Storme admitted to the other woman. "He said one of these days I would end up tripping and pushing my foot into my mouth at a time when I would regret it. It's unfortunate he was right."

Surprise flickered in Hope's blue eyes. "The good thing about stumbling is that you can stand back up and continue more carefully," she expressed coolly.

"Only if you don't manage to break anything," Storme stated regretfully. "I apologize for the insult to your husband and to the alpha, Hope. There's no excuse for it, and if I could retract my behavior, then I would do so."

She wouldn't grovel, but the Hope she remembered would have never expected her to.

"Nothing was broken, Storme," Hope assured her, the cool gleam in her gaze warming marginally, enough to give Storme hope.

She nodded before turning to Wolfe once again. "If you and Director Wyatt could meet with me tonight, Alpha Gunnar, I believe we have some business to discuss."

Styx stiffened at her side. For a moment, she swore she could feel his tension wrapping around her. His hand moved from the small of her back to her hip, his fingers curling over it firmly.

"I'll be there as well," Styx stated, his voice firm.

Wolfe nodded, his gaze still on Storme. "I look forward to the meeting. Let's enjoy the party for now, and enjoy all our freedoms." He glanced to Styx before his arm lifted, his hand clapping on Styx's shoulder. "As Hope said, once again, you've outdone yourself."

"Of course I did," Styx answered with a grin. "If it's worth doing, it's worth doing with excellence."

Storme turned to him, as always amazed at the easy, smooth charm and easy conceit he seemed to possess.

A subtle wink in her direction nearly had her shaking her head in exasperation.

"I guess I've lost my dance now." Cassie chose that moment to step forward.

Storme felt like a dowdy peon in the presence of a princess. The other girl's waist-length black curls and vivid blue eyes were amazing enough, but she managed to make even jeans and boots paired with a sleeveless camisole look like royal threads.

There was laughter in her gaze though, a smile on her lips, and Storme could see that the certain affection she felt for Styx went no further than a familial bond. There was no jealousy in Cassie's eyes, and no anger in her tone despite the fact that she propped her hands on her hips and gave Styx a mock glare.

"You have a lot of dance partners here, Cassie," Styx assured her with an easy laugh as his hand settled at Storme's hip once again. "If nothing else, you can torture Navarro."

Storme saw the look that crossed Cassie's face and filled her gaze. A mysterious, knowing look filled with concern.

"Navarro isn't available anymore," she said regretfully.

The tightness in Storme's chest increased. It wasn't what she said, or even the way she said it. It was that look in her eyes, the concern and the regret.

Something that even Styx and the others seemed to sense.

"What's happening, Cass?" It was her father that asked the question.

Cassie turned back to her father, breathed out roughly and shook her head. "I don't know, Dad. All I know is something is going to happen, and we all need to be ready for it."

"How long have you felt it?" Wolfe questioned her.

"The moment Navarro was introduced to my friend Micca this evening."

"The rumors are true," Storme injected softly. "You're psychic."

"Actually, no, I'm not." Cassie grimaced. "It's more complicated and not nearly so sane as being psychic." Her head tilted then, a light frown edging her forehead as she blinked slowly.

Her face seemed to pale before she shook that off and inhaled slowly, evenly.

As her lips parted to speak, another voice, a voice from the past, from a nightmare, spoke behind them.

"Dash, Elizabeth, congratulations."

Storme turned slowly.

She didn't know what Styx sensed, didn't understand the sudden, warning growl that came from his chest or the way his hand settled on the weapon he wore at his thigh, the one she hadn't noticed him strapping on before they left.

But she knew the voice, and she knew the Breed.

Almost in slow motion she turned and faced the nightmare she had been running from for so long. A nightmare she had always known, she realized, that she would come face-to-face with sooner or later.

The Breed wasn't expecting her any more than she was expecting him. She watched the shock that flickered in his cold brown eyes. Those eyes were carefully blank, as though he knew to hide the malicious, bloodthirsty nature that had once glowed almost red in them.

Curved canines that looked a bit dark. They weren't nice and pristine white as most Breeds' were. Storme imagined that the taste he had for blood had stained them, just as it had stained his soul.

As she stared back at him in shock and horror, his lips curled back, flashing the canines predominantly in a vicious snarl.

Storme shook her head, trying to deny that she was seeing who she was seeing, what she was seeing. He couldn't be here. Styx would have never allowed her brother and father's murderer to be here.

"Storme?" Styx stepped into a defensive stance next to her, pulling her partially behind him as she and the Coyote locked gazes.

"There's nothing you can do," the Coyote said with a smirk. "There's nothing they can do." He nodded to the Breeds gathered around her. "Breed Law protects me as well. Had I known you were Styx's captive, I would have ensured my absence." As though it mattered. As though he felt some remorse. There was no remorse, and she knew it, she could see it in his eyes.

She was shaking. Storme could feel her body shaking, shuddering as agony began to tear through her.

"Storme." Styx's voice was hard, demanding.

"Storme, what's going on?" Hope moved in beside her, her husband, Wolfe, moving protectively to flank her as Styx flanked Storme.

"He killed her family." It was Cassie that spoke, her voice eerie, lacking any emotion, any fear, compassion, mercy or pain. "He's the Breed that tore her brother's and father's throats out."

It was said so matter-of-factly. As though those deaths were little or nothing in the total scheme of life. But they were everything to Storme.

"Marx Whitman," Cassie continued, her voice turning slightly hoarse, strained. "Dad. Do something."

"There's nothing he can fucking do," Marx snapped back at her, his teeth flashing dangerously. "I'm under Breed Law as well where my protection is concerned, you stupid little girl. I can't be punished for anything. I have committed no crimes since I joined Haven."

As though the crimes he committed before could be wiped away so easily.

Dash stepped forward, his larger body keeping his wife as well as Cassie pushed behind him. Storme was aware of them surrounding her, the males positioned to ensure that the Coyote came no closer.

"We may not be able to punish you, but you won't be allowed to torture Storme with your presence either," Wolfe snapped back.

Storme would have been surprised if it weren't for the fact that it took all she could do to control the rage tearing through her, demanding justice, vindication.

"He killed them," she whispered through numb lips. "And he enjoyed it."

"I haven't killed since accepting Breed Law, outside my capacity as an Enforcer." Triumph glittered in his brown eyes. "I do what I'm told. I'm a good little Coyote now, Ms. Montague."

She wanted to scream. Her fingers curled into claws as she fought back the need to jump for him, to rip the smirk off his face.

"Find his alpha," Dash demanded, his voice low.

"Have him held," Styx demanded furiously as Marx's gaze glittered with surprise and his lips twisted into a snarl of disgust.

"Your precious princess, Cassie, can tell you that arresting me would be a mistake."

Cassie flinched as his gaze raked over her.

"Cassie?" Her father questioned her.

"There are always loopholes," Cassie drawled, though her voice was strained and hinted at indecision. "Unless we can prove he's committed an act of aggression against Breed Law, then there's nothing we can do. And I can't prove it." Her eyes glowed within her paperwhite face. "Even though I know he has."

Marx laughed bitterly at that. "Look around you, Alpha Gunnar. Arrest me, hold me for crimes committed while in the labs, and you'll lose the trust of every Breed here. Just because your little witch"—he flicked his fingers to Storme—"wants to believe I've done something, doesn't mean I have."

He was right. Even Storme knew he was right. There was no way for Styx or Wolfe to punish the Coyote for the crimes he had committed that night, because he had technically been under the control of the trainers, Council scientists and soldiers he had been trained to obey.

"Get her out of here, Styx," Wolfe ordered from Styx's side as Storme continued to stare at the monster from her past. "We'll find Jonas and handle this."

"What is there to handle, Alpha Gunnar?" Marx gave a sneering laugh. "There's nothing to handle. I'm a resident of Haven, you can't change that without breaking the laws you made."

Silence descended. Even the music that had been playing

before the Breed showed up had eased. All eyes were trained on them now. Hundreds of eyes, Breed and human alike.

"The Mating Articles," Cassie stated then.

"She's no fucking mate of his!" Marx exclaimed contemptuously then. "She stinks of her fear and hatred of us, just as her father did. He wanted nothing more than to destroy every Breed he ever created, and she knows it."

Storme stared, waiting, watching, her eyes narrowing on the hated, squared face of the Coyote that had destroyed her life.

He wasn't handsome, graceful, or charming as the other Breeds were. His features were out of sync, as though his genetics had somehow attempted to merge physically as well as psychologically.

"You can't do anything to me as the situation stands." Marx shrugged his shoulders as though what any of them might want to do didn't really matter. "Now, I came to enjoy the party and to discuss a few things with Alpha Gunnar. Standing here with this Breed hater in my face wasn't part of the plan."

"I never hated Breeds," Storme bit out, fighting to contain her rage as she glared back at him. "I hated you."

He laughed at that, as Styx growled, a low, violent sound that had Storme flinching. The tension was tightening around them now, low mumblings from the Breeds and humans filtering through the veil of disbelief and rage that surrounded Storme.

"Hate me all you want to." He rolled his eyes, obviously laughing at her now. "Hate me until hell freezes over, little girl. It won't matter. You can't touch me and neither can your lover."

"He killed them." She turned on Styx, certain there had to be a mistake. They couldn't allow this Breed to run around free, to laugh, to gloat that he had won, while her father and brother were dead.

"There's nothing we can do." Styx seemed to push the words from between his lips. "He's right. He signed Breed Law, and it protects him as well as you."

Marx grinned, his gaze flicking over Storme once more. "They can't even order me away from you. You're not his mate, which means there's no Breed loyalty to you, Ms. Montague. All you have is Styx." He shook his head as he made a tsking sound. "But look on the bright side, at least you won't be looking over your shoulder for me anymore." His spread his arms wide. "I'm right here."

Styx jumped for him.

Before his fist could make contact with the snide mockery in Marx's face, Dash, Wolfe, Navarro, and Jonas were there to pull him back, their voices raised, their hold unbreakable as Marx sneered at him.

More Breeds moved in then. A small contingent of Coyotes backed Marx as the majority of the Breeds moved in behind the Wolf Breed alpha and snarled back at the Coyotes watching them warily.

"Where is your alpha?" Wolfe snarled as Styx fought their hold.

Storme stared back at Marx, hatred filling her to the point that she could barely hold on to the need to kill.

"It doesn't matter where my alpha is," Marx snapped back. "You can't order me from Haven and neither can he."

"The hell I can't." Wolfe stepped forward, his voice lowering, deepening. "You have just deliberately instigated a confrontation with a higher ranking enforcement officer than yourself. I can and I will penalize you the full length of time possible until this situation is resolved. If I see you in Haven before the allotted fourteen days is up, then you will be locked up."

Marx laughed. Brown eyes glittered with such triumph, with such brutal mercilessness that Storme felt that tightening in her chest increase, the feeling of impending doom nearly choking her as she fought to get hold of her control.

"Dad, get Mom out of here," Cassie suddenly whispered.

Dash turned to her, shock lining his face.

"Dash, get her and Elizabeth to the heli-jet." Jonas was moving, calling Enforcers to him, attaching a comm set to his ear and ordering the heli-jet prepared.

"What have you done?" Wolfe advanced on Marx as Storme watched the Breeds behind Marx quickly dissipating, eager to place distance between themselves and whatever they sensed preparing to explode between the alpha and the Breed.

"Me?" False innocence filled the Coyote's face then. "What could I have done?"

"Contain him," Wolfe ordered several of the Breeds behind him.

Storme fought to breathe. That choked, panicked feeling always came just before . . .

The explosion shook the courtyard.

Storme felt herself flying, the blast of heated air that swept her off her feet tossing her onto the thick lawn as chaos started to fill the compound.

Roars, snarls, and furious screams began to erupt, and just when Storme thought she could jump to her feet, another explosion ripped through the night and sent her to her knees.

Lifting her head, Storme stared at the flames and the night erupting around them.

Carefully placed explosions had been laid in the courtyard, hidden and detonated at the moment when everyone would have been dancing had it not been for the confrontation with Marx.

"Let's go!" Styx's yell was accompanied by his arm wrapping around her waist as he dragged her from the ground.

"Cassie," she cried out, staring around desperately. "Where's Cassie?"

"Dash and Jonas's Enforcers have her," he yelled back as another explosion shook the ground and ripped through the alpha's home. "Move. Let's go."

He all but dragged her from the force of Breeds running through the flame-shrouded night, arming themselves, rushing Wolfe and Hope, Dash and his wife and daughter, and the wives of the other Breeds that had attended.

The Feline Breeds' alpha was holding a baby, her

teenage son at her side, snarling in rage as Enforcers moved to get them out of the line of fire.

"Get them out of the fucking courtyard," Styx screamed at the group. "This way."

Turning, Styx led the way through the dense foliage at the center of the courtyard as gun and laser fire began to erupt behind them.

"Haven's under attack. We're under attack!" Storme heard Enforcers behind them yelling while overhead the sound of a distinctive hum could be heard.

"Get them the fuck out of here. Move. Move!"

They were rushing between two cabins, shadows enfolding them as Styx raced to get out of the clearing.

As they cleared the cabins, it was as though hell opened up around them. Heavy machine gun fire powered by overhead helicopters began ripping along the ground.

A baby wailed. The sound of a frightened, pained scream could be heard. And before Storme could make sense of any of it, another explosion rocked the night, throwing debris, flames and destruction around them.

◆　◆　◆

"Bitch!" Storme found herself being jerked from the ground by her hair, agony screaming through her head as she fought, clawed at the fingers tangled in the thick strands to drag her to her feet. "You should be fucking dead."

Fighting to lock her knees in place, she tried to remain on her feet, only to stumble as she was jerked again, an agonizing cry leaving her lips as the searing pain tore through her head once more.

Where was Styx?

She tried to gaze around, but the group that had been together when the final explosion rocked the night was nowhere to be seen now.

He wouldn't leave her alone, she told herself. He wouldn't have taken the others and left her to protect herself. She knew he wouldn't.

Tears filled her eyes as that horrible premonition struck

her chest again. Her breathing hitched; she gasped for air and then lost the ability to breathe at the sight of his hard, broad form sprawled out on the ground several feet from her.

"Styx!" She screamed his name as the harsh fingers jerked her around, shook her, then a hard, heavy fist slammed into her face, turning the world black.

CHAPTER 17

"Well, it looks like the little bitch is finally awake."

Storme stared back at the faces watching her, and wondered why she should even bother with shock or surprise at this point.

Or betrayal.

Still, it was betrayal she felt as she stared back at the other woman, the one person in the world that she had once believed to be a friend.

Fear was a terrible, destructive sense. It was a panic attack in the darkest hours of the night. It was smothering, feeling the breath leave the body, unable to catch it back quickly at the sight of the monsters facing her.

The monsters that were human as well as Breed.

These were the eyes watching her through the darkness of her nightmares. Eyes that might not have glowed red in the low light, but they might as well have. She could still feel the danger, the merciless intent. She could still feel and remember the death that came with them, as well as the recrimination and the consequences that would come when Styx caught up with her. If he caught up with her.

If he was even out there. How could he be though? Marx and Gena had taken her from Haven so easily. She remembered bits and pieces. Being thrown over Marx's shoulder and toted through the night like a sack of potatoes while it seemed that Haven was burning down behind her.

They'd thrown her in the trunk of a car, where she'd blacked out again, and when she awoke, she was in the home she had known before her mother's death, years before her father had taken her to the Andes.

A home she had believed no one else could have known about. Evidently, they had known though. She shifted painfully in the thickly cushioned chair they had dumped her in, lifted her hand to her head and, as she brought her fingers down, stared at the blood that seeped at her temple.

That was why she felt so dizzy and sick to her stomach.

"Get her some water, Coyote," Gena ordered the Breed, using the degrading version of his species name to address him.

Marx didn't seem to mind. He moved to the kitchen and returned moments later with a bottle of cold water.

He pushed it into her hands then moved back to the leather couch where Gena sat, his brown eyes stone hard, emotionless. They weren't cold. Cold denoted hidden emotions. There was just simply no emotion there.

Lightning flashed in the forested night behind her, the jagged bolts of light illuminating Gena and Marx's faces. There was no mercy in their expressions, nothing but determination and chilling death.

Damn. Storme guessed she should have wondered before now why Gena had managed to keep from being killed all these years by the Coyotes that chased her. Everyone else that had tried to befriend Storme had suffered for it, if not given their lives for it. Yet Gena had always managed to remain unscathed.

Because she was a part of them. A part of the Council, the scientists and the monsters chasing after the information Storme's father had managed to steal.

Damn, maybe she should have just given Styx the ring to begin with rather than waiting.

Storme sipped at the water, desperate to delay the inevitable even as she found herself praying silently that Styx had survived.

The memory of him lying in the dirt, unconscious, all that fierce challenge that was so much a part of him silenced, sent terror racing through her.

If they could defeat Styx, then what chance did she have against them?

"You ruined a hell of a plan," Gena drawled as a smirk, similar to Marx's, twisted her thin lips. "Hell, we had no idea you were there. When you disappeared, I simply assumed someone had finally managed to kill you."

So cold and matter-of-fact, as though Storme's life, or her death, meant nothing.

"And what plan was that?" Her throat hurt from the smoke and debris she had breathed in during the explosions.

"The plan to kidnap the Wolf Breed princess, Cassandra Sinclair, and the Feline heir, David Lyons. If we could have snagged a nice little alpha mate, or killed one of the alpha leaders, that would have been an added bonus." Gena smiled as she spoke, crossing one leg over the opposite knee and smoothing a hand down a leather-clad leg as she continued. "Instead, the Sinclairs escaped in a waiting heli-jet and some black-clad bastards melted out of the night and snagged the alpha mates and their little brats right out of our gasp."

Storme almost closed her eyes in thankfulness. They were okay. Hope was still with Wolfe, Merinus Lyons was still with her handsome Lion Breed husband, Callan.

"How did you manage it?" She shook her head in confusion. "There had to have been more involved."

"Of course there was," Gena snorted. "Sanctuary isn't the only Breed stronghold with spies. The spies we have in Haven are just better at what they do. That simple."

Gena had a problem with ego. Storme was surprised she had forgotten about that.

Spiked dark blond hair looked more disheveled than normal, and soot marred her face. She hadn't had as easy a time getting out of Haven as she would pretend.

"Your boyfriend was much easier to kill though," Gena said and smiled maliciously. "Amazing how effective a bullet can be when faced with a Breed. It takes all the fight right out of the little mutants."

No. He wasn't dead. She fought back the agony streaking through her. She hadn't seen blood. She was positive he had been breathing, just shallowly. He wasn't dead. He wouldn't allow something this evil and malicious to kill him.

"They're here," she whispered, her index finger rubbing at the sapphire stone that held exactly what everyone wanted from her. "You can't escape them that easily, Gena. They're out there, I promise you that."

Even Styx. He had wanted one thing, and he had done what he believed would ensure her cooperation. He had taken her to his bed, given her his warmth, a sense of security in his arms, and at the same time demanded she give over secrets she was terrified to allow anyone to have. Secrets she found herself wanting to give him.

It didn't matter why he had taken her to his bed. It didn't matter what would happen once she gave him the data chip. He would have it. He had given her what no one else had ever attempted to allow her. Security. Warmth. A sense of caring when the darkness of the nightmares chiseled at her confidence.

"It really doesn't matter if they are." Gena shrugged. "Before I leave, they'll believe you simply handed the information over and that you betrayed him as easily as Marx did." She shot Marx a chilling smile over her shoulder. One he returned before lowering his hand to her shoulder and caressing it, with gentleness, before he leaned down and kissed her lips as though he . . . loved her?

"Gross," Storme muttered. "How can you kiss that mouth? He eats people's blood, Gena."

Her smile was filled with relish as she stared back at Storme. "And I share it with him whenever I get the chance."

"I think I need to hurl." She swallowed tightly as she caught the glitter of anger in the other woman's eyes.

Gena was always calm, no matter the situation, and in the past six years, there had been plenty of situations. Tattooed, pierced, easygoing but as tough as nails, the blonde biker rarely seemed ruffled. Until Storme insulted the killer Breed behind her.

"At least I'm honest in my enjoyment of him," Gena drawled. "Tell me, Storme, did you enjoy fucking your Wolf near as much?" She leaned forward, her elbows propped on her knees as her nose wrinkled in a grimace. "Styx Mackenzie is a dirty little dog that pretends to be better than what he is. He was forced to eat as a pup just as the rest of them were."

Storme arched her brow mockingly, knowingly. She knew better. Styx Mackenzie hadn't been trained as the other Breeds had been. From birth he had been personally reared by the man who considered himself Styx's grandfather.

Evidently, Gena didn't know nearly as much about the individual Breeds as she thought she did.

"Let's stop wasting time now." Gena sat back and lifted the weapon lying at her side.

The light but powerful laser-powered handgun was pointed directly at Storme's chest. "The data chip, if you please. This is the only place he could have stashed the damned thing and we're tired of searching for it. Retrieve it, Storme, before I have to kill you."

"It's been ten years," Storme mused quietly. "You of all people should know I don't have what the Council wants."

She had fought this battle for so long. For too long.

God why hadn't she just given in to Styx and Jonas while she had been at Haven. There would have been no need for this then, no need for Gena and Marx to believe that kidnapping her would get them what they wanted.

"You didn't give it to the Breeds." Gena frowned at the thought. "Some of those Breeds gossip to one another like old women. If you had given Jonas Wyatt what he wanted, then Marx would have heard about it."

"Would he have?" Storme glanced at the Coyote as he glared back at her. "Why should they? Jonas Wyatt wouldn't have given that information to anyone any more than he would have given out the location of Brandenmore's grave site."

The pure blood societies believed Brandenmore was dead. It was something Storme knew wasn't the truth. She had seen the truth when Jonas stared at her as she threw the accusation in his face that he was keeping Brandenmore alive.

"Where is it?" Marx nearly came over the back of the couch, his eyes glittering now with bloodthirsty excitement.

"She doesn't know where it's at, moron," Gena drawled in amusement as Storme stared back at her. "Wyatt would have never trusted her with that information."

"I didn't say I knew where it was." Storme shrugged. "I said he wouldn't have gossiped about the chip any more than they were gossiping about Brandenmore. It's that simple."

Gena laughed. A harsh sound that grated against Storme's ears.

"Such a little liar," she exclaimed. "I know you better than that, Storme. You don't trust Styx, therefore you don't trust Wyatt."

"He mated her, Gena."

That comment caused Gena to pause as she stared back at Storme.

"You told me you couldn't smell the mating scent." She turned and stared back at Marx as though in confusion.

"I didn't, until this evening." The Coyote shrugged. "It's come on slowly. I would say if he wasn't dead, then the next time he saw her it would have been full-blown heat."

"Interesting." Gena turned to stare back at her. "It took long enough."

Storme kept her expression smooth, praying they didn't see or sense her confusion.

"So has the big boy knotted you yet?" Gena questioned her as she stared back at her curiously. "I hear he's hung rather well. One of those big ole canine knots up inside you can't feel pleasant."

"Jealous?" Storme asked archly, correctly interpreting Gena's lascivious interest.

They obviously believed the tabloid stories that printed that trash, she thought. Stories of some hormonal, genetic virus, an animal mating reaction and uncontrollable sexual urges.

The hateful glare the other woman shot her warned Storme that Gena would exact a bit of vengeance before actually killing her.

"I'm tired of wasting my time is what I am," she announced, her voice cold once again. "You have about sixty seconds, Storme, then I start hurting you. Rather badly."

She had been hurt before, Storme assured herself. She carried scars that she hadn't carried when she was fourteen. The scars of attacks by Council Coyotes and soldiers who had been sent to force the information from her.

Gena crossed a slender leg over the opposite knee, crossed her arms over her breasts and stared back at her with a cool expression.

"Then I guess you better get started," Storme stated as she steeled herself for whatever was coming.

Her brother and her father had given their lives for this information, Styx had possibly given his life in his attempt to save her and the other women caught in the attack.

She had promised herself that if she was ever caught, she would be as strong as her father had been.

"She thinks she's so brave," Marx growled then. "Protecting the information Daddy trusted her with. I wonder how she feels knowing Daddy gave her up all those years ago. That he told us exactly who had hidden the chip for him."

They were lying and she knew it. Her father knew where it was hidden, and how he had hidden it. He had died to keep it secret.

"It wouldn't take Einstein to figure out he entrusted

me with it." She shrugged easily. "I wasn't there, the chip wasn't there, and one and one equals two. Big deal."

Marx laughed. "And Daddy died begging us for his life and swearing to make you give it up to us. Don't bother lying, sweetie, we know you hid it. Just tell us where it's hid."

Her gaze flicked to Gena, catching the other woman staring suspiciously out the picture window behind Storme's chair.

"They're out there, aren't they?" she asked the other woman softly. "Styx isn't dead, Gena. I'm his mate. He'll never let me go."

She would have laughed at her own statement if they hadn't seem so damned serious about it.

It was beginning to make her wonder. Hell, it might be scaring the hell out of her. Because she knew she wasn't his mate.

Gena's gaze flicked to the windows again.

"Ghost Team," Marx whispered. "They were the ones that came out at us when we tried to grab the felina and her brats."

"They've not found us." False bravado filled Gena's voice now. "We may not have gotten the prized princess or their brats, but we got this little whore. Once we get that chip . . ."

Storme shook her head. "Styx has that chip, Gena."

"You're a lying little tramp!" Gena came to her feet in a burst of fury, came across the room and slapped Storme full across the face with all the fury of an enraged demon. "I want that fucking chip!" she screamed.

Storme could hear her ears ringing from the blow as the side of her face burned with a fiery numbness and the taste of blood filled her mouth where her lips had split against her teeth.

Storme blinked against the dizziness that filled her head and fought to hold on to her consciousness.

Swallowing tightly, she focused on Gena as she paced back to Marx, reached up, grabbed a handful of short hair and jerked his head down for a deep, tongue-tangling kiss.

Hell, maybe Storme would get lucky and they'd entertain

themselves long enough for her to figure out a way to escape this time.

This was becoming ridiculous. In ten years she had never been captured until Styx had managed it. He had jinxed her or something, she decided. In ten years, she had never been so damned unlucky, and she had always been smarter than to allow herself to be caught the first time.

She had learned how to hide. She had changed her name several times, her hair. She had worn colored contact lenses and padded her clothing with shape-altering prosthetics. And still, sooner or later, she was always found, but she was never caught.

Through the years, there had been one constant though. No matter who found her, no matter the trouble she was in or how hot the situation, Gena had always managed to pull her ass out of the fire with a smile and a friendly warning to keep her head down.

At least, that was how Gena had made it appear. There had been times Storme couldn't figure out exactly how Gena pulled off some of the things she had pulled off to get Storme out of a tight situation, but now she knew. Because she had been slowly reeling Storme in, gaining her trust, believing Storme would betray her father and tell her best and only friend where the data chip had been hid.

Storme now thanked God that over the years she had never followed through with the urge to confide in the other woman.

"Storme, I will hurt you." Gena turned back to her, raging again. "Trust me, once Marx starts playing with you, you'll be begging me to let you tell me the location of that chip."

Gena's hazel green eyes narrowed, spat in fury and glittered with an almost insane rage. How in the hell had she managed to hide this side of herself from Storme for so long?

Oh yeah, right, they only saw each other a few days at a time, perhaps once a month. Gena had pretended to help her all these years, which likely made controlling it easier.

Storme forced herself to stand, aware of Gena and Marx watching her suspiciously. Pacing back to the glass doors, she stared into the night, watching, waiting.

"The past six years have been nothing but a lie." She turned back to the other woman quickly, but rather than catching any hint of guilt in Gena's expression, she found only mocking amusement mixed with the anger.

"You were eighteen when I found you outside that bar in Dallas," Gena sneered back at her. "Starving, dirty and stinking. Tell me, Storme, did you really think I helped you out of the kindness of my heart?"

There had been those who had tried to help her out of the kindness of their heart, and they had paid for it. Which left Storme staring into the face of the one person she had actually trusted until Styx.

How could she have been so wrong? And did it really matter now?

"It doesn't matter." Storme forced the words past her lips as she rubbed at her arms, feeling lost and alone. Styx wasn't out there, he wasn't going to rescue her or he would have already done so.

How was she going to face life without Styx now? Without the chance of feeling the warmth of his arms.

Rubbing at her arms, she felt the ache centered in the pit of her stomach, and could have sworn she felt the subtle taste of cinnamon in her mouth.

Why had it taken her so long to realize so much? "I trusted you," she whispered to the other woman as she stared into the dark once again and fought the overwhelming grief.

She had tried to assure herself he was okay. The few moments of consciousness before she'd fully awakened, she'd kept expecting that when she finally managed to escape the heavy darkness surrounding her, then Styx would be there.

But he wasn't here.

Gena and Marx had managed to destroy the beauty of the courtyard, as well as the security of Haven. Just as

Gena had managed to destroy any security Storme had thought to find in the past years.

Gena's low rasp of laughter raked over her nerve endings.

"You trust too much in human compassion," the other woman informed her censoriously. "There is no such thing as that, just as there is no such thing as Breed mercy. I would have thought you had learned that lesson years ago, Storme. I kept expecting you to get a clue, and you never did."

Storme flinched at the sarcasm in Gena's voice while quickly considering her options, and the best route for escape.

"And the reason the Breeds and Council soldiers and Coyotes kept finding me was because of you." She should have realized that years ago. All the signs had been there, but as Gena had said, she just hadn't gotten a clue.

"Not hardly, sweetheart," Gena grunted. "The last thing I needed was a team of furry Breeds on your ass when the Council grew tired of trying to reason with you. I work for the Genetics Council, not those fucking upstarts that think they deserve some sort of respect." She sneered. "No, Storme, I'm no Breed lover. What I am, is your worst fucking nightmare if you don't tell me where you hid the information your father stole from those labs ten years ago." Her voice slowly rose until she was screaming and Storme turned to face her.

The business end of that damned laser-powered handgun stared back at her as Gena's face twisted with renewed fury and Marx glared at her as though she had actually cut his dick off rather than just wishing she could.

She was so tired. She was tired of running, tired of being hungry, alone, and hurting. And she couldn't forget the few short weeks that she had been safe, warm. When Styx had kissed her, held her. When she had felt as though the next day would bring more than just additional danger.

She stared at the weapon and knew the end of the road was here. She had run as far as she could run, and at the end of the road she found herself exactly where she had begun at the tender, too innocent age of fourteen.

Alone.

"Look, don't make me have Marx hold you down and rape you, Storme. Styx mated you. You're aware by now that another male's touch is going to be agonizing." She glanced to where Storme was still rubbing at her arms. "It still hurts, even now, hours after he hauled you out of Haven. Imagine how it's going to hurt when he fucks you until you're screaming."

God, she would love to ask Gena what the fuck she was talking about. One thing was for sure, something was wrong with her. Just beneath her skin was a tingle of pain, as though she should be bruised. And that didn't go along with the fact that there were no bruises on her arms, only her face and possibly her ribs.

Storme stared back at the former friend and the weapon she pointed, as she fought to find a way out of this particular mess. She had never entertained the nightmare that Gena could possibly turn on her.

She had been suspicious of everyone else in her life, but never Gena. Gena had found her when she was hurt, hungry, dirty and at the end of a mental rope.

She had been running for four years the night Gena had walked behind that bar and found her cowering in fear. Storme had been panicked, terrified and grappling with her conscience as she fought the need to disobey her father then as well.

If she turned over the information her father had stolen, to either Breed or Council, then the danger would just go away. How many times had the Breeds sworn they would protect her, compensate her, provide any payment she asked in return for the data chip?

"Do what you have to, Gena." She blinked back the tears that threatened to fill her eyes. "I gave Styx that chip. By now, Jonas Wyatt has it. That's why the Breeds haven't come for me, Gena. That's why they don't care if I live or die now."

"Tell me that fucking bitch is lying," Gena turned to scream at Marx.

He was watching Storme carefully, breathing in deep and slow as his brown eyes glittered back at her in anger.

She could only pray she'd learned to lie without that particular response.

"I can't be sure," he growled. "She stinks of fear, pain and Styx. Mating changes the scent too much at first to be able to detect something as subtle as a lie."

If she managed to get her hands on Styx, and she prayed she did, then she was so going to make him hurt for the confusion she was feeling at the moment.

The more they mentioned that damned mating heat, the more it made the tabloid stories sound true rather than the product of a reporter's fanciful imagination.

And all that aside, as she watched Gena's face, she slowly sat back down in the chair and allowed her fingers to slide between the seat cushion and the arm, where she had hidden only one of the many weapons in the house during her last visit.

This was her refuge. The only place she had been able to escape for a few days of peace. She'd used it rarely, but she'd kept the house prepared, just in case.

"Then I say she's lying." Gena decided with a cold, hard smile. "And I've decided she needs to be convinced to tell us the truth."

Storme shook her head slowly. "Don't do this, Gena. It's not going to get you what you want."

Gena's lips curled in furious mockery. "Six years I've had to shadow your skinny ass and pull it out of the fires you were too stupid to keep from walking into." Gena shook her head in disgust. "You won't kill a Breed, even when they're running you to ground like a hound would a hare. Still, you just tuck your little tail and run like the frightened little rabbit you've always been. Well, bitch, your running days are over. I'm so going to enjoy listening to you scream as he rapes your skinny ass."

Storme's fingers curled over the butt of the weapon tucked at the side of the chair cushion. She didn't have much of a chance. It was going to be damned close. And bullets weren't always a good bet against a laser-powered weapon.

"You're not going to beg me to believe you?" Gena tilted her head, the short spikes of her dark blond hair throwing an odd shadow across the room as she advanced on Storme.

Just a little closer, Storme thought. She hadn't anticipated that Gena would be the one to come closer to her. She'd expected Marx. But this was even better.

"Get up, Breed tramp," Gena ordered as she extended the weapon and motioned furiously. "It's time to find out how a Coyote fucks. While I watch." She came closer. "And he follows orders so well. He'll fuck you just like I tell him to."

An inch closer. Gena laughed and pushed the barrel of the weapon into Storme's shoulder.

Storme moved.

Her hand lashed out, gripped Gena's wrist and twisted. The laser-powered weapon discharged harmlessly into the wall as Storme threw all her weight into the surprise move, twisted and slammed the other woman into the wall as she jumped to the back of the chair, covered her face with her arms and launched herself through the window.

Hitting the ground, Storme barely managed to smother a cry as she felt a sharp, raking fire along her side, where her shirt had shifted high and revealed vulnerable flesh to the glass raining to the ground ahead of her.

She would check it later, she promised herself as she struggled to her feet and began praying. It wasn't the first wound she had taken, and it would likely not be the last. If she survived, that is.

She could hear the discharge of laser fire even now, as she raced into the forest surrounding the cabin. Raised voices and automatic rifle fire began to echo in the distance as she ran as though the hounds of hell were snapping at her heels.

The sounds of laser fire and bullets combined were echoing behind her as she raced through the night and the thunderstorm that had threatened opened up in the heavens above.

Rain poured to the ground, making the ground slippery, wet. The sounds behind her indicated that there were others besides Gena there. Others who were possibly delaying Gena and Marx from following her.

Breeds. Breeds had been hiding in the night, but it hadn't been Styx. If Styx had been there he would have saved her. He would have been there in the cabin. He wouldn't have waited.

Her breathing hitched on a sob as she stumbled, went to her knees and fought to hold back the tears and the pain welling inside her.

He would have been here, if he could have been. He wouldn't have made her run through the night as she fought for her life.

"You whore!" Gena's enraged scream echoed in the darkness as weapon fire broke, then began the rat-a-tat-tat once again.

It was like hearing hell. Like being in the middle of a war that she had no idea how to fight.

Her fingers curled around the butt of the weapon she had managed hold on to. Forcing herself back to her feet, she kept running. She had been running for ten years, it was the only thing she knew. Maybe, if she kept running, she would forget. She would forget that for a while she had been warm and safe. That for a while she had known something she had never known before.

She didn't have much of a head start. Hell, she probably didn't have a head start at all considering how fast a Breed Coyote could run. If Marx was behind her, then she would be lucky if whoever had delayed them gave her a few minutes at best.

But if she were lucky, very very lucky, she might be able to flag down a car on the busy road and get a ride to the nearest town. It would be easier to lose Marx and Gena in town. It was harder for a Breed to track individual scent when faced with so many scents, she knew that. It was one of the reasons Council members, former trainers under warrant by the Breeds, and soldiers that had been a part of brutalizing Breeds had moved to such locations as New York City, Los Angeles, Dallas.

All she had to do was reach the main road.

Luck. If luck were on her side, then the Breeds and the Coyote Gena had brought with her would still be fighting it out at the cabin, neither side any wiser to the fact that she was once again on the run.

Styx wasn't with the Breeds. He couldn't be. She knew he wasn't. He wouldn't have left her like that, alone and frightened.

If she could get a ride into town and find a hole to hide in for just a few hours, then maybe she could figure out where to go next, what to do next and how to get the ring to Jonas Wyatt safely.

One thing was for certain, the information her father had left in her care was going to get her killed if she didn't do something. Just as it may have gotten Styx killed.

She had to give it to Jonas, she couldn't allow the Council to take it from her. That left her stuck between a rock and a hard place, with no room to turn in, and she was so tired of running.

As she raced up the steep incline before her, the soil beneath her feet gave, throwing her off balance for precious seconds. Grabbing a slender branch on a nearby bush, she couldn't stop the cry that passed her lips when thorns dug into her flesh.

Instinct and pain had her jerking back, completing a disastrous arc that sent her spinning on the wet dirt and tumbling down the slope.

Her body hit hard, her face slamming into the ground as she hit the bottom and dug her nails into the dirt, fighting to push herself to her feet.

One more try.

Breathing hard, weakness slamming through her, Storme stumbled again as she struggled to drag herself up the hill to the road above. She could see the lights of the passing vehicles, smell the asphalt and the heat of the tires racing over the road.

It wasn't that far, she told herself desperately.

She could make it.

Just a few more feet. She was just a few more feet to safety.

Digging her fingers into the wet earth, she clawed her way up the slope, stumbled onto the shoulder and swayed as lights pierced her vision, blinding her for precious seconds as the sound of squealing tires streaked through her senses.

A vehicle, dark and large, slammed to a stop in front of her. A van of some kind. Storme swayed dizzily as the side door slid back with a thud and she found herself hauled into the darkened interior.

Dizzy, exhausted, there was no way she could fight the too strong grip, or the male bodies that shifted around her, blocking the exit before the door slid closed with a bang and the vehicle accelerated quickly from its position.

All she knew was the fact that she was fucked. So well and truly dead that she might as well go ahead and say her final words to her maker, because sure as hell, she was getting ready to meet him real damned soon.

Only Council soldiers or Breeds could have staged this. And she knew the Breeds were busy protecting their own now.

She wasn't one of their own, therefore she wasn't protected.

Styx hadn't come for her.

The flight, the dizziness, the terror and the sheer heartbreak that suddenly suffused her raced over her senses then. She felt the darkness, felt the blessed oblivion, and sank willingly, gratefully within it.

◆　◆　◆

Mating heat.

Styx held his mate against his chest, feral fury pouring through him as the scent of the other Breeds became offensive to his senses.

The animal howling inside him demanded that he get his mate to safety, that he check the wounds on her body, that he do something to ease the heartrending agony he had felt inside her before she passed out in his arms.

The rage that had burned inside him when he had regained consciousness at Haven, only to learn his mate had been taken, was something Styx never wanted to feel again. He never wanted to feel that bloody primal fury overtake him, control him.

The Wolf had been acting on instinct alone. Nothing had mattered to him, nothing had existed in his world but finding his mate.

The glands beneath his tongue had instantly pumped full of the mating hormone. His mind had filled with the need for her, the possessiveness and overriding protectiveness that had obliterated any other thought or instinct in his mind.

When he had learned Ghost Team had allowed Marx Whitman and Gena Waters to escape with his mate, he had nearly gone mad.

God help those bastard Breeds if he ever learned who they were. God knew he would kill them himself. It was a damned good thing they were rumored to be able to control their scent markers, because if he had known or ever recognized their scent, he would have been unable to resist the urge to kill.

Staring down at his mate, he could feel the mating hormone spilling to his mouth. His cock was so damned hard he was certain he could pound railway spikes with it. His flesh was sensitive to her warmth, soaking it up and spilling more back to him as every cell in his body seemed to reach for her.

"We have company coming in behind us," Mordecai called out as the van began to speed up.

"McCrae, contact Brogan and give him our ETA to the heli-jet," Styx ordered quickly, instinct moving to give the appropriate responses required to get his mate to safety. "I want Haven appraised of our position and situation and a team sent out immediately to capture Gena Waters and her Coyote bastard."

Marx Whitman was a dead Coyote.

"Alpha Delgado has already sent a team out," Mordecai responded as he took a curve with enough force to leave the tires screaming as they fought to keep contact with the road. "Our ETA is one minute."

"And our company is getting closer," Navarro spoke from the passenger seat as he armed a laser rifle. "Delgado's team might not have to worry about collecting them."

There was murder in Navarro's tone now. His gaze glittered with savage death, and as it flickered to Storme's unconscious form, compassion seemed to soften it.

"Get ready to roll," Mordecai announced as the van sped toward the lights of the heli-jet as it waited in the large clearing just off the road. "I'm coming in close. Jump and run."

The doors to the van were thrown open as the vehicle slid to a rocking stop within six feet of the opened doors of the black heli-jet, which hummed with power.

Styx was out of the vehicle at a dead run, jumping into the craft as the others came in behind him, the van left to idle and block the motorcycle bearing down on them.

Before Marx and Gena could reach them, the craft lifted off, the laser fire aimed at it striking harmlessly into thin air as powerful jets engaged and they were streaking across the sky.

"She's bleeding," Navarro commented as Styx laid his head back along the long seat at the back of the jet.

"A wound at her hip," Styx replied. "It had just healed. I'm going to have to discuss with her this penchant for jumping from windows, it appears."

As they had sped to the cabin, reports had come in by the second from the one member of Ghost Team who had followed Marx and Gena after they kidnapped Storme.

The Breed had stayed on their asses, finally radioing their location in just as Styx had felt as though he were going mad waiting.

"Marx had help," Navarro muttered. "We've pulled in a human and two Coyotes. Del Rey took care of the Coyotes himself. They're being disposed of as we speak."

Styx closed his eyes, grief threatening to swamp him.

Breed Law was exacting. It was a contract every Breed signed before being allowed into Sanctuary or Haven. A contract humans signed, though their punishments were far more lenient than Breeds'.

Betraying Haven or Sanctuary was fatal. Any Breed willingly accepting the role of traitor didn't get to live to regret it. No pleas were heard. No mercy was given. They were killed.

"Who was it?" he asked numbly, his arms tightening around his mate.

"Two of the Coyotes Del Rey rescued from Russia. The coya is taking it hard, Styx," Navarro sighed. "She feels responsible for what happened to Storme because they were Coyotes she helped to rescue."

Styx shook his head. He could never blame the tiny mate of the Coyote alpha whose soft heart had led her to aid in the rescue of the Coyotes her father had overseen in Russia.

"Was it one of the women?" He prayed it wasn't. If Del Rey had been forced to kill one of the fragile Coyote females of his pack, then he would never forgive himself.

Navarro shook his head. "Jacob reports it was two males. Greg and Fargo. The moment they admitted to it, Ashley killed them both."

"God." Styx almost shuddered. Ashley was almost the baby of the Coyote pack. Temperamental, so girly it made a man's back teeth ache, and so fierce in combat it made his balls shrivel. The thought of her killing anyone, especially a pack mate, never failed to shock him.

"Why didn't Del Rey take care of it?" Styx questioned harshly.

"Ashley didn't take it to Del Rey," Navarro said. "She was with the team sent to collect the two men for questioning."

"ETA to Haven is two minutes," Mordecai reported as his gaze constantly scanned the dark sky around them. "Your cabin is still standing and unaffected by the explosions. Security has a net around the entire area and the alphas and their mates are currently residing in the secured suites in security control." Security control was the heavily reinforced maze of bunkers beneath Wolf Mountain.

Styx lowered his head, drawing in the scent of his mate as he thanked God that the other women were safe and unharmed.

"They were after the children and mates," Navarro growled. "Marx hadn't been aware Storme was there until the party. Gena was in on the attack from the beginning."

Styx stroked his hand down her back, feeling the fragility of her small body, terror still racing through him at the thought of how easily she could have been taken from him.

That last blast had sent debris raining around them. He'd tried to shelter Storme from the worst of it, but a heavy piece of timber had struck his back and neck, knocking him out cold.

He'd left his mate undefended.

How the hell was he supposed to forgive himself for that? For the fact that he hadn't been there when Storme needed him, when the danger to her had been at its height.

"It won't happen again, Styx," Navarro assured him. "Ghost Team was unaware of her status. She was considered a captive, not a mate."

Therefore the priority placed on her life had been lower than that of the mated females and children that were rushed to safety. Because he had allowed her to hide from the packs rather than pulling her into the integrated society being established within Haven.

"No, it won't happen again," he agreed, his voice hardening as the heli-jet landed. "Never again, Navarro. I will see to it personally."

The heavy doors slid open at the wide stone walk that led to the front doors.

Cradling Storme against his chest, he moved from the heli-jet as Navarro ran ahead of him to open the doors to the house.

Around them, trees and cabins lay in ruins. The beauty and unique design of the main community had been wounded. It would be built back, but they would never forget that once again one of their own had betrayed them.

Stepping into the house, he was aware of Navarro closing the door behind him, and for the first time since moving into the spacious cabin Styx locked the door before carrying his precious burden to the bedroom.

As he neared the bedroom door, he almost came to a hard stop at the scent that filtered from the bedroom.

"Styx?" Cassie was waiting in the room, curled in one of the large easy chairs that sat along the side of the room.

"Go home, Cassie." He couldn't deal with anyone but his mate right now. With anything but assuring himself that she was simply exhausted, her body fighting off the effects of the sedative he could sense in her system.

Cassie rose slowly to her feet as Styx laid Storme in their bed and smoothed back the long strands of black hair from her pale, dirt-smeared face.

"Listen to me, Styx." Cassie moved behind him, her voice quiet, saddened. "She believes you're dead. That was why she escaped as she did in unconsciousness. She couldn't face any more. She's reached the end of a very long road."

Cassie sat on the edge of the bed, her gaze compassionate as it rested on Storme.

"Cassie, whatever the reason, she'll awaken," he assured her. "I'll ensure it. Now you need to return to the bunker. I'm certain your parents are looking for you."

"You still talk to me as though I'm a child," she said and sighed. "No one understands Breed Law as well as I, nor can anyone else hear the secrets I hear, yet you continue to speak to me and to act as though I'm still nine."

"Or refusing to do as I ask so I can have a moment alone with my mate," he growled in exasperation.

"Perhaps one of these days someone will find it in them to treat me as an adult," she snorted before rising from the bed. "I just thought I should tell you that it will be a girl."

Styx froze before lifting his head slowly and staring back at her in shock. "What did you say?"

"Figure it out." She glared back at him.

He straightened, tensing. "She's going to become pregnant?"

Cassie rolled her eyes. "She's already pregnant, big boy. You and your little mate are about to become yet another scientific wonder. Contact your grandfather, perhaps he can figure out why. And don't worry about mating heat, or the hormones. It's only going to make her more unique."

She turned then and stalked from the bedroom with an air of offended feminine outrage, and he only barely noticed.

His eyes were on his mate. His entire being was concentrated on his mate as he tried to draw in the scent of new life.

And there it was. Subtle, so very new, no more than days.

His hand lifted his fingers to spread over her stomach as he felt his heart clench with such emotion that he truly wasn't certain what he was supposed to do with it.

As he stared down at where his darker palm lay over her pale flesh, he felt the glands beneath his tongue throb once again and the taste of the mating hormone filled his mouth.

The need to share it was driving him damned crazy.

He wanted to bind her to him, possess her in ways that she would never be free of. He wanted to possess her heart, her soul, the very essence of her feminine spirit.

"Ah, lass, how much more of a miracle could ye be to me?" he whispered as his head lowered, his lips touching hers, though he was careful to hold back the hormone that would strike a quick flame to the arousal that simmered between them whenever they were together.

"Wake up, Sugar," he whispered. "Come tae me, Storme. How am I supposed to exist without you?"

He couldn't exist without her. There was no life, no sense of accomplishment, joy, or freedom if she wasn't by his side.

When she lay unmoving, a sigh slipped past his lips. He would allow her to sleep a bit longer. But until then, he could at least make certain she was clean. Marx and Gena had dragged her hundreds of miles from Haven, to the old, abandoned cabin Storme's parents had once lived in.

In the huge garden tub that sat in his own bathroom Styx ran a half a tub of steaming water before stripping himself and then his mate and carrying her to the bathroom.

He eased into the heated water as he held her against his chest, fighting to hold her gently, to ensure that so much as a single bruise wasn't added to those that already marred her tender flesh.

Using a soft cloth he cleaned her gently, his hands stroking over her, his heat and the water's warming her chilled body. She'd been soaked to the skin from the rain and mud when they'd pulled her into the van.

Hell, they'd nearly run her over as they raced to the cabin behind the single member of Ghost Team who had set out after Marx and Gena despite orders to stay with the rest of the team and protect the alpha wives.

The team member had Styx's undying gratitude. The others had left Storme to her fate because she didn't carry the mating scent, because she hadn't been claimed by a Breed. All but the one who had followed against orders and relayed her location once he caught up with the Coyote and his bitch handler.

After washing and conditioning the long strands of her black hair, Styx emptied the tub as he used the handheld shower to rain the warming caress of the water over her body and keep the chill from her.

As the last lingering grains of dirt washed down the drain, he rinsed them both again before wrapping a large towel around her and carrying her back to the bed.

He laid her on the dry side and hurriedly stripped the blankets that were damp and marred with mud from earlier. Clean, soft sheets and a heavy comforter went on the bed before he finished drying her hair, combed it gently then tucked her beneath the blankets and crawled in with her.

He was so damned hard he could barely stand to breathe with the ache in his balls. The need to kiss her, to share the mating hormone with her, was so overwhelming he found himself once again brushing his lips against hers.

She moved beneath him, causing him to still, to gaze down at her in desperate hope as he watched her lashes flutter open.

At first, fear and desperation flashed in the emerald

depths, before confusion, then complete joy brightened the beautiful green of her eyes.

"Styx?" She whispered his name, her hand lifting, fingers trembling as she touched his face.

"Aye, lass, I'm no so easy to get rid of." He tried to grin and couldn't.

He was damned if amusement would rise inside him when he had come so close to losing her.

"I thought you were gone," she whispered, her lips trembling as tears filled her eyes. "I didn't get to tell you I loved you. That you changed me." A sob caught in her voice as he felt his own eyes moisten at the emotion he heard there, glimpsed in her gaze.

"Ah, lass, you let those bastards drag you off before I could tell you the same," he growled as his fingers lifted to touch the soft line of her lips. "I lost what was left of my senses when I realized you were gone."

Her lips quirked. "There's not much there to lose, Styx."

"Aye," he agreed. "And soon, there will be even less. Come, lass, kiss me. Give me your heart so I know tomorrow at least has hope."

Hope that even if the danger surrounding them didn't go away, then at the very least there would be happiness, joy.

Once again his fingers caressed her stomach as his lips lowered to hers and the cinnamon- and chocolate-infused mating hormone filled both their senses.

She moaned beneath him, her tongue licking at his, stroking it, before her wee lips suckled at it and she arched against him as though demanding more.

She was demanding.

Storme felt the heat that filled her mouth, the spiciness of his kiss sinking into her and the incredible pleasure that began to build from it.

The hormone-laced mating kiss. The tabloids and gossip rags printed stories and articles relating to the suspected phenomenon. Most people didn't believe it. Certain pure blood fanatics swore it was true. There had been rumors among Council soldiers, and Storme vaguely remembered her father and brother discussing something similar.

Personally, Storme had always scoffed at the notion. Now she knew it was true.

As she arched, her body heated, her pussy creaming until she swore she felt the dampness against her thighs.

A desperate moan left her lips as he abandoned the kiss, his lips stroking along her jaw, to the arched column of her neck and then to the hard, tight peaks of her nipples.

Covering a hard bud with his lips and sucking it in, his hands stroked over her arms. His calloused fingertips, slightly rough, traced down her arm, across her hip, along her thighs. His hands were never still, his fingers never caressing her the same way twice, but each stroke fired nerve endings and created a sensitivity to pleasure so intense it took only minutes before she was crying out from the extremity of it.

Her pussy clenched, her juices gathered like thick syrup along the bare flesh of her pussy lips and sensitized her clit to the point that it was pounding with sensation.

Even the air against her flesh was a caress, fired and intensified by the small growls and groans that sounded as if they'd been forced from Styx's chest.

His cock lay against the inside of her leg, thick and so hard it felt like hot iron against her flesh.

As his lips loved over her breasts, suckling first one, then the other of the tight, sensitive nipples, Storme fought the need to grab his head and push him to the sensitive flesh of her thighs.

She needed his kiss there. Needed the stroke of his tongue against her clit, those hungry growls vibrating against it.

Her hips arched, strangled cries tearing from her throat as those heated kisses began to trail down her torso, over her stomach.

Stopping at the flat plane of her midriff, he paid particular attention to her lower stomach, his tongue stroking, his fingers caressing before he moved lower.

Lower.

"Oh God. Styx!"

His tongue swiped through the drenched folds of bare flesh, so hot and wicked she swore she nearly came from the first lick.

But her lover was more diabolical than that.

The Breed known to fulfill every woman's greatest sexual fantasies whispered against the heated, swollen flesh. "Mine!"

His teeth nipped at the tender folds, sending a rush of excited sensation racing along the nerve endings, straight to the sensitive bud of her clit.

Her juices spilled, only to be caught by his sensual, hungry tongue. Her pussy clenched violently as he parted the inner lips, his tongue flicking against the entrance before thrusting inside with a fierce, hard stab.

Her hips came off the bed.

Hard male hands gripped her thighs, holding her in place as he began to fuck her with his tongue, driving her to the brink of release before pulling back then pushing her to the edge once again.

She wanted to scream in need. She would have, but he kept stealing her breath with the pleasure.

She wanted to demand more, demand her orgasm and whatever came with this new, blazing sensation, but she couldn't keep her senses intact enough to force the words to her lips.

Chocolate and cinnamon filled her senses as she pressed against his shoulders with her hands, pressing him back, pushing at him until he lay back for her, his large body a banquet of tastes and sensation for her greedy senses.

Her palms stroked along his chest and his abdomen, her lips moved over his, her tongue licking at his, dipping into the hormone-infused well of pleasure as she tried to straddle his hard body.

She meant to straddle him.

She wanted to. She wanted to ride him until nothing mattered, until all she felt, tasted or knew was the touch of him.

But Styx obviously had other plans.

Before she could press the aching flesh of her pussy against the engorged crest of his cock, he moved.

A growl rumbled in his chest as he lifted her, turned her, pressed her to her knees then came behind her with a dominance that completely rocked her senses.

His teeth nipped at the tender flesh of her shoulder as the weight of his chest leaned against her, pressing her shoulders to the bed.

"Ah lass," he growled at her ear as she felt his cock pressing against the slick, wet folds of her pussy. "More foreplay next time, I swear it to you."

More foreplay? Any more and she might have expired permanently from the excitement.

She might yet.

Storme stilled as she felt the press of the engorged crest at the entrance of her sex. Pausing, the head tucked against the entrance, she felt that first, rumored spurt of pre-cum from his cock.

Lubricating, heated, the suspected hormone-laced fluid rushed inside her, coating tender flesh and sensitive nerve endings.

As tension tightened through her body, still she felt the marginal relaxation of her pussy. The next heated spurt sent sparks of sensation racing through her and eased the tight muscles further as he began to press inside her.

Breathing in roughly, she focused on the pure fiery pleasure of the flesh parting, burning, stretching around him as he worked his own hard flesh inside her with short, tight thrusts.

Each measured penetration sent a blaze of sensation rushing to her clit. It throbbed and ached, swelling until it seemed ready to burst as she threw her head back, tilted it, and felt his lips along the sensitive column of her neck.

She'd seen the mark Hope, Faith and Charity carried there. The mating mark it was called. All wives of Breeds or wives who were Breeds themselves carried that mark.

As the pleasure tore through her system, lighting a

wildfire of sensation along each nerve ending, Storme ached for the mark. She ached for each touch, every level of possession, and hungered for his kiss.

Fighting to breathe, she strained to take the heavy width of flesh penetrating her as he forged deeper inside the slick recesses of her pussy.

Tender nerve endings were revealed as blazing need was stoked and built to a level of intensity that she wondered if she could survive.

Holding on to her hip with one hand, the other pressed to the bed beside her, Storme felt that last, imperative thrust that buried him to the hilt inside her.

"Oh God!" She arched her back with ecstatic pleasure. She'd never been so close to coming without actually reaching orgasm.

"Ah hell, Sugar. How tight you are." Hoarse and growling, his voice rumbled at her ear. "It feels as though my dick is lodged in a vise. A perfect, hot, slick wee vise that does nothin' but pleasure it."

Pleasure surrounded her. She trembled, shuddered in the grip of it as she fought to hold on to to something, anything, that would allow her to maintain just enough of her senses to memorize each touch, each sound, each stroke.

She thought she'd known the most pleasure she could feel. That it couldn't get better, that it couldn't become more intense, until he began moving.

The feel of his cock tunneling inside her, stroking the tight, brutally sensitive flesh, stole that last measure of sanity she had been desperate to hold on to.

Instinct became all that kept her breathing. It kept her crying out his name as she begged for release, as the pleasure stroked through the overly sensitive channel that fought to grip and hold him in place.

Digging her nails into the blankets, Storme thrust back against him, taking him deeper, harder as he groaned behind her.

It was exquisite.

"So good," she moaned, dazed, near senseless from the

pleasure that built to a burning, desperate peak. "Oh God, Styx. Harder. It's so good."

It was pure ecstasy, undiluted and raging through her system, burning through her mind.

The heavy thrusts were destroying her, pushing her higher and tightening through her body until she felt her orgasm beginning to blaze through her.

She tried to scream. Her body tightened until she wondered if it would break. Behind her, Styx thrust again and again, then with a deep, hard growl in her ear, she felt the first pulse of his release, the hard, burning swell of his cock in the sensitive mass of muscles gripping the erection.

Her eyes widened as a wailing cry of rapture tore from her throat. The knot extended, stretching her tighter, locking him deeper inside her as she felt his semen spurting against the entrance of her womb.

Ecstasy enveloped her. She came and came, each shuddering rush of pleasure a burning firestorm of sensation as she shook beneath him, her shoulders collapsing to the bed as her hips pressed tighter into his and another surge of release swept through her, like a tidal wave of sensation, and she felt his teeth rake, then lock into the sensitive flesh of her neck.

It seemed never ending. Each pulse of the knot locked inside her sent another wave of agonizing pleasure rushing across her senses. Each spurt of semen, each hard jerk of his hips was catastrophic.

She could do nothing but tremble in his grasp, give herself to each sensation and marvel at what she had found in her Breed's embrace.

This was perfection, she thought. Or as close as she was going to get.

As he collapsed against her, his hard body sheltering her, Storme finally understood why she had always been so torn where the Breeds were concerned.

Not simply because her hatred had been based on the actions of only one. Not just because of her fears. She had been torn because she belonged to one. Because a part of her had always known the injustices they suffered were just as much her fault as they were her father's, her brother's, or the fault of any Council member who allowed it to happen.

The Breeds were animals, creatures or creations. They were as deserving of life, freedom and love as any other living being on Earth.

This man though, he was hers.

⋆ E P Í L O G U E ⋆

Ashley True and her Enforcer partner, Sharone, flanked their coya, Anya Delgado, as she stood at the front door of Styx's home. Their alpha, Del Rey, his second in command Brim Stone, the Wolf Breed alpha Wolfe, and Hope Gunnar stood respectfully behind Ashley.

Styx stepped to the side and allowed them to enter, his gaze taking in the ravaged pale features of the coya and the steely, hard-eyed purpose in the female Coyotes that served as her personal bodyguards whenever her mate wasn't at her side.

Storme stood inside the living room, dressed, still scratched, her green eyes solemn as Anya stepped before her.

"We haven't met." Anya's voice was husky and tear-roughened. "I'm Alpha Delgado's mate and coya of the Coyote Breeds, Anya Delgado."

"Coya Delgado." Storme inclined her head in respect, but as normal with a newly mated lover, she didn't attempt to touch the other woman, and the coya knew well not to attempt to touch Storme.

The first weeks during the initial mating heat were

exacting on a woman. Her body didn't want to tolerate even the touch of the Breed doctor, or suffer the tests required to allow the scientist to create a hormonal therapy that would ease the symptoms of her mating.

"Ms. Montague," the coya's voice roughened again as she clasped her hands in front of her and a tear eased from an eye, "please accept my most sincere apology . . ."

"Coya, please don't." Storme shook her head as she spoke gently. "What happened wasn't your fault, your alpha's or Alpha Gunnar's. Marx, Greg and Fargo made their own choices. I would never hold you or anyone else in Haven responsible for that."

For a moment, Ashley and Sharone's stony masks slipped and Styx glimpsed pure relief in their expressions. Del Rey had called earlier and expressed his own regret at the actions of the Coyotes of his pack. He'd told Styx the grief Anya was suffering that Styx's mate had been attacked and kidnapped. She had been inconsolable with sorrow and terrified Styx would hold the Coyote packs accountable for the actions of a few.

"If there's anything the Coyote packs can do . . ." Anya's voice hitched. "I hope all in Haven know that the Coyote packs are as loyal and dedicated to the survival of Haven as the Wolves who began it have always been." She looked around the room, her eyes still tear-filled. "Should we be needed in any capacity, we're always there."

Styx saw it then. The narrowing of Storme's eyes. A flash of thought, and he wondered what his new mate was now up to.

"Styx is demanding a joining ceremony." Storme grinned as though amused, but her voice reflected the joy he glimpsed in her eyes. "I would appreciate it if you would join the lupina and felina in standing beside me as I accept my mate. And I hope you'll give my personal invitation to your packs to join the ceremony as well as the celebration afterwards."

It was a first. Normally, the only Coyote Breeds that arrived at the evening dinners or celebrations were those intrepid few that didn't care about crashing a private party, or those personally invited by a Wolf Breed.

Wolfe and Hope left it up to the individual members of the Wolf packs to invite the Coyotes. They were the ones that had to accept them, he had always said.

"I would love to stand for you during your ceremony." Surprise and pleasure reflected in the coya's gentle expression then, as approval lit her bodyguards' eyes.

Ashley and Sharone could be bitter enemies if they had a mind to be. Had their coya been insulted, or felt blamed for the attack, then Storme would have gained their undying resentment.

Instead, she had now made friends, most likely for life. Ashley would of course insist on doing Storme's nails and makeup. She'd be kidnapping Styx's mate for shopping trips and likely slipping her out of Haven as they slipped the coya out for a girls' night in a backstreet bar, where the owner always called and warned Delgado so he could send bodyguards to ensure their safety.

The bodyguards never interfered in the fun, or the drink consumed by the girls. More often than not they did act as designated drivers though.

Styx almost grinned at the thought.

Storme turned to her mate, caught his smile, and a thrill of excitement lanced through her.

He'd told no one about their child yet, only her. She was still put out that he'd known before she had.

But he was filled with joy, and that joy was contagious. It filled her heart, and it filled her life.

He was her chocolate lover, and he called her his most perfect storm because she'd swept in and completely cleansed his life.

Life would never be perfect, but as he moved to her, his arm going around her waist, and Hope and Anya began questioning her about the ceremony, Storme knew it would be better than she had ever imagined life could be.

She was secure, warm, and she was loved in the same

depth that she loved. Her Scots warrior would always see to her safety, her heart and her joy.

And what more could a woman ask for?

"Storme, Jonas has asked me to extend his personal apologies as well as his gratitude for the data chip you provided. The information found there is proving highly important." Wolfe stepped forward, his expression, his voice, somber. "I don't have full details as of yet, but he's promised to return within the week to appraise our doctors of the information. According to him, your father and brother were not just true geniuses, but also true friends where the Breeds were concerned."

"And Navarro extends his apologies as well," Hope stated sadly. "During the rescues he was severly wounded. It was Navarro who was entrusted by your father to come to you and convince you to turn the information over to the Breeds. He spent years healing, and he still carries the scars, as well as other disabilities of those wounds."

Storme breathed out roughly as Styx pulled her to him, his body sheltering her as she came to grips both physically as well as emotionally to the changes within her life now.

"Navarro would have had a hard time gaining trust then," she stated. "It wasn't his fault, Alpha Gunnar. The years I've spent running were something that would have happened regardless of trust."

She'd needed to hold on to that last part of her family. The data chip, the trust her father had given her to protect it, and the fear of losing that last link to her beloved father and brother, had kept alive a hatred that may not have been born otherwise.

"We all have reasons for the battles we have to fight, Storme," Hope stated softly. "And we all work together to help one another. Welcome to Haven."

"Welcome home," Styx whispered at her ear, and immediately heat flared inside her, comforting, warm, belonging. She could feel that "something" settle inside her. The way her heart eased, the tension flowing from her, and a sense of hope, a sense of the future brightening inside her.

"I'm sorry." She stared back at Hope, true regret welling inside her now. "I never understood."

She hadn't understood the love, the dedication or the battle she fought for the survival of her mate as well as the Breeds. She understood now, and she hoped it was a battle Hope would now share with her.

Hope's smile was gentle, her gaze filled with acceptance. "A new start, Storme. We have a new beginning. We'll build from there."

A new beginning.

Storme stared back at her lover. Her mate. The man who had wiped away the fear, the misunderstandings. The man that loved her.

His hand lifted, the backs of his fingers smoothing her cheek. "My perfect storm," he whispered.

And he was her Styx. Her heart.

She grinned back at him and whispered, "I have chocolate . . ."

Penguin Group (USA) Inc.
is proud to present

GREAT READS—GUARANTEED

We are so confident you will love
this book that we are offering a
100% money-back guarantee!

If you are not 100% satisfied with
this publication, Penguin Group (USA) Inc.
will refund your money!
Simply return the book before
December 5, 2010 for a full refund.

From #1 *New York Times* Bestselling Author

LORA LEIGH

and National Bestselling Author

JACI BURTON

NAUTI AND WILD

Two all-new novellas of the games men and women play between chrome and hot leather.

Lora Leigh revisits her sultry Southern landscape with a story of a good girl gone bad. But she's not the only one going down that road . . .

Jaci Burton writes the story of a hot biker hired to keep an eye on the reckless daughter of a Nevada senator. She's hooked up with a rival biker gang— a dangerous move that makes the wild beauty more vulnerable than she imagined . . .

penguin.com

M698T0510